# HIGH PRAISE FOR RAY GARTON!

"*Live Girls* is gripping, original, and sly. I finished it in one bite."

—Dean Koontz

"The most nightmarish vampire story I have ever read."
—Ramsey Campbell on *Live Girls*

"It's scary, it's involving, and it's also mature and thoughtful."

—Stephen King on *Dark Channel*

"Garton never fails to go for the throat!"
—Richard Laymon, author of *Dark Mountain*

"Garton has a flair for taking veteran horror themes and twisting them to evocative or entertaining effect."
—*Publishers Weekly*

"Ray Garton has consistently created some of the best horror ever set to print."

—*Cemetery Dance*

"Ray Garton writes horror fiction at its most frightening best."

—*Midwest Book Review*

"Garton is, simply put, one of the masters."
—James Moore, author of *Blood Red*

"A real  *Slab* magazine

## PRAISE FOR *RAVENOUS*!

"Hurley is a sheriff to root for, and Garton's well-paced horror novel reworks the werewolf myth to great effect."
—*Publishers Weekly*

"*Ravenous* is Ray Garton's most disturbing, affecting, and ferocious novel since *Crucifax Autumn*—which is to say, he's going to cost you a lot of sleep with this one. There are images and sequences in this book that only a frontal lobotomy will make you forget."
—Gary A. Braunbeck, Bram Stoker award–winning author of *Coffin County*

"Witty, warped, and steeped in blood, this novel of hungry horror tumbles toward a delicious finale that will only leave you wanting to read more and more of Garton's ferocious fiction."
—Douglas E. Winter, author of *Run*

"Garton doesn't shirk in his writing, which makes him one of the top horror writers working today."
—Down in the Cellar

"*Ravenous* grabs you by the throat in chapter one and never lets go. Ray Garton, master frightener, is at his best in this one. Read it alone at your peril."
—Gary Brandner, author of *The Howling*

"Ray Garton is one of the true kings of old-school horror. *Ravenous* is fierce, fearsome, blood-soaked fare, a werewolf novel that's bound to snap its jaws together on your throat."
—Tom Piccirilli, author of *The Midnight Road*

"Expect nothing more than thrills and chills...Fans of wild horror will want to make it Number One on their to-read list...with a (silver) bullet."
—*Bookgasm*

## SO MUCH BLOOD

Abe went through the empty kitchen, down a hall to the living room. There was no sign of life. His dread was joined by a cramping feeling of urgency. As he started up the stairs, he found himself clutching his cell phone in a fist and relaxed his grip before it broke. He tensed when he caught a whiff of a familiar odor. Just before reaching the landing, he called out Seth's name again. No response.

The smell of blood filled Abe's nostrils.

At the top of the stairs, he looked down the hall and saw something on the floor, something smeared and splattered on the walls—red, a great deal of red. Along with the blood were four long trenches that had been cut through the pale creamy wallpaper and into the plaster. The cuts in the wall formed a curved, downward-sweeping arc.

Frowning, Abe squinted slightly, trying to make out the thing on the floor—it looked like a pile of objects coated in red. Blood, of course—he recognized blood when he saw it and smelled it. But there was…*so much*….

# RAY GARTON

# BESTIAL

LEISURE BOOKS  NEW YORK CITY

A LEISURE BOOK®

April 2009

Published by

Dorchester Publishing Co., Inc.
200 Madison Avenue
New York, NY 10016

ISBN 10: 0-8439-6185-6
ISBN 13: 978-0-8439-6185-0

The name "Leisure Books" and the stylized "L" with design are trademarks of Dorchester Publishing Co., Inc.

Printed in the United States of America.

10 9 8 7 6 5 4 3 2

Visit us on the web at www.dorchesterpub.com.

*This book is for my other family:*
*Brian Hodges,*
*my brother since sixth grade,*
*my boarding school roommate,*
*and one of my oldest and dearest friends;*
*his wonderful wife Tanya,*
*and their beautiful, talented children,*
*Cassandra, Hillary, and Alex.*
*I love you guys.*

*And, as always,*
*for Dawn,*
*who has been my life*
*for 21 years.*

## ACKNOWLEDGMENTS

My deepest gratitude for the help, encouragement, and friendship of the following people: my wife Dawn; Scott Sandin, the greatest editor I've had in 26 years of writing professionally, and my best friend; Derek Sandin, whose input was invaluable; Brian Hodges, who's always ready to read what I'm working on; Steven Spruill, my brother from another mother; Karen Leonard, who read it as I wrote it; my agent Richard Curtis, whose sage advice and enthusiastic support keeps me going; Dr. Evan K. Reasor, Bill Lindblad, Jen Orosel, Lisa Kessler, Liz Rowell, Michael Aquino, Jamey Sturm, Jane Naccarato, Joe Parks, and the great people at the Red Light District message board.

# BESTIAL

BESTIAL

# PROLOGUE

*Big Rock, California—four months ago . . .*

The unusually warm spring night was still except for a gentle breeze, and the sprawling house was mostly dark, with a glow in only one open upstairs window. From inside, the piercing cry of a baby cut through the calm, stopped only to gasp for breath, then continued to wail. Crickets sang all around, and the whispering breeze was accompanied by the ocean surf as it huffed and pounded against the rocks of the nearby shore. And something else—a hushed, sibilant sound rose and fell slightly in the night's warm darkness. It was the secret sound of tense, anticipatory whispering in the dark all around the outside of the house. A black sky covered it all, clear and sparkling with stars, touched by the glowing, bluish white curl of a crescent moon. The baby's cry, which had been sounding for some time, continued to come from inside the house, muffled but distinct.

The house had belonged to a man named Marvin Cooper, the owner of a chain of used-car dealerships that had begun there in town thirty-three years ago and had spread throughout California. Marvin had no use for the house now. A few months ago, what was left of his bloody and ravaged remains had been found in Hallwell Park near the big rock after which the town had been named. Marvin's home had been taken over by others since his death.

In the upstairs bedroom beyond that single glowing open window, three people were gathered around a king-size platform bed beneath a bright overhead light. A fourth person lay on the bed, a young woman named Cynthia Newell.

A blanket covered Cynthia's upper torso, rising up over the enormous bulge of her pregnant belly. White towels were spread out beneath the lower half of her body. Reflections of light shimmered on the perspiring flesh of her face and neck and uncovered arms as she desperately inhaled, then exhaled explosively, puffing her cheeks as she blew again and again. Tendons stood out on her neck like taut wires. Ropes of sweat-matted hair clung to the sides of her face. Her bare, shiny legs were spread wide, knees up, feet on the bottom edge of the mattress. A short, plump woman sat on a stool at the foot of the bed and leaned forward between Cynthia's legs. A taller, younger woman sat on the bed beside Cynthia, dabbing her pained face with a wet cloth, murmuring to her comfortingly, instructing her quietly. A tall, slender, bald man stood at a bottom corner of the bed, his hands joined behind his back, and watched silently.

The baby that had been screaming for awhile, at least a month old, lay beside Cynthia, naked and uncovered, untended. Its tiny arms and legs jerked and kicked spastically, its eyes nothing more than tightly clenched slits in its round, pink face, its mouth a gaping, wailing hole.

Through the open window, the crickets were a distant background chirping sound, and buried somewhere beneath that at an almost subliminal level came the other, more secret sound of whispering.

Cynthia cried out in pain, her voice a ragged, choked

shriek. Her sweaty arms, trembling with tension, reached out at each side, and her fists closed on the bedsheets.

At twenty-two, Cynthia was single, but already had a number of relationships behind her, all of them bad. Her taste in men had been about as reliable as her ability to hold a job. She had just begun a new waitressing job at the time of her rape, but that job, like her last boyfriend, had been only the most recent in a long line. The rape had occurred in the parking lot behind the twenty-four-hour restaurant where she worked the graveyard shift. She'd just arrived, had parked her car, and was making her way to the restaurant's rear entrance when her attacker rushed out of the darkness and slammed into her, knocking her into a dizzy stupor. He'd dragged her behind two garbage Dumpsters, where she'd lost consciousness. She'd awakened there later, beaten and bleeding, with the rapist's gamey smell clinging to her nostrils. Crying as she tried to get back on her feet, she'd been discovered by a startled young busboy.

The next few days remained a blur, but she'd done her best to pull herself together and go back to her life. She'd walked through the following week numb, stunned. She'd told no one of the rape, only that she'd been attacked and beaten, and she'd tried to keep even that information as quiet as possible. Until chilling suspicions began to sicken her only days after the rape. She'd begun feeling nauseated in the morning, had vomited a couple of times. It seemed awfully soon for such signs, but there they were. A home pregnancy test had made real her biggest fear.

The rapid pregnancy had not been the only frightening development in her life. She'd felt a hunger she could not quite satisfy, and she'd had nightmares in which she'd fed that hunger with human flesh. She'd thought they were nightmares, anyway—at first. Until she'd awakened one morning to find blood on her sheets, blood that had not come from her body.

In the examination room of her doctor's office, she'd broken down and told him the whole story. She could not understand why these things were happening so *fast*. In only the second week after the rape, she'd begun to gain weight, and a slight swelling had begun in her abdomen. That had been made only worse by the ravenous hunger, the awful nightmares, and the blood in her bed. Dr. Morgan had listened quietly, and when she was done, he'd remained silent for some time, frowning thoughtfully. Then he'd smiled at her and reacted compassionately, saying he wanted to introduce her to some people he thought might be able to help her. She'd thought he was referring to counselors, perhaps some kind of support group. But no.

He had introduced her to the two women now in the room with her—dark, matronly, middle-aged Carmen at the foot of the bed, and Beth, the beautiful, blonde woman in her late twenties who sat beside her—and they had introduced her to Jeremiah, the tall, gaunt man who now stood watching her. Jeremiah had taken her then, away from her apartment and her friends and her life, and nothing had been the same since then—not even Cynthia. The pregnancy had progressed with frightening speed. The shocking changes that had occurred in her since the rape had been terrifying—the hunger and nightmares, at first, then the horrible and painful physical changes that had taken place one frightening night. And worst of all, that same night, the feeding through which Carmen and Beth had guided her, the first she'd been aware of, but not really the first at all. It had been a bum, some middle-aged man spending the night on the beach alone, trying to warm himself by a small fire. When he saw her, he'd tried to scream, but he'd been dead before he could make a sound.

At the same time, though, as nightmarish as those things had been, they also had been exhilarating. They had sickened her, and yet invigorated her. The pregnancy itself had seemed surreal. In the final week, Jeremiah had introduced her to the man who now waited downstairs, a man with an eye patch who had about him a certain . . . something. A strength, a presence, an invisible, compelling force. The sheriff. She had known almost instantly that he was in charge of everything, of all of them . . . of her.

"*Push*, Cynthia!" Carmen said.

The pain was inconceivable. It engulfed her. Along with it came the startling sensations with which she'd become familiar in the last three months—the feelings of movement inside her, of her bones snapping and repositioning, of her tissue tearing, growing, stretching.

The baby on the bed beside her continued to scream. Cynthia had asked earlier why it was there, whose baby it was, why it wasn't being cared for and held and made to stop that god-awful screaming. They would not answer her and behaved as if the baby weren't there at all.

"Push, Cynthia, *now!*" Carmen said, her voice loud and stern.

Cynthia's body bulged uncontrollably in places, made thick, wet, popping sounds as her face elongated and her teeth narrowed, lengthened, and sharpened. A moment later, she melted back to her original form, only to go through the change again, then change back.

As impossible as it seemed, the pain grew even worse, and Cynthia felt as if her insides were being violently pulled out of her. Everything—the light, the room, the world—blinked, and for a moment, Cynthia felt as if she did not exist.

Jeremiah stood at the corner of the bed and watched, back straight, shoulders even, hands behind him. The overhead light was reflected in a puddle of white on the smooth, bare scalp of his narrow, oval head. He wore a black, long-sleeved turtleneck shirt, gray slacks, shiny black shoes. He was unmoved by Cynthia's screams, which thickened into a different sound, a throatier shriek that soon leveled back out into a human scream, until it changed again, back and forth. His dark eyes, looking bored and uninterested beneath narrow, arched eyebrows, stayed on the spot between Cynthia's legs where Carmen's hands waited. He watched as the head appeared, as the baby finally came into the world in a rush of blood and fluids, as Cynthia's screams altered again and again in her pain. His right eyebrow rose as Carmen took the newborn into her hands. It squirmed, glistening with viscous blood, still attached to its mother by a gnarled umbilical.

Beth hurried to Carmen's side and produced a sharp knife. The cord was cut, and a moment later the thin, mewling cry of the infant mingled with the wailing sound of the other crying baby on the bed. Carmen placed the newborn on the white towel to the side of Cynthia's spread legs.

"My baby!" Cynthia cried, her voice thick and trembling, words slurring together. "Whuh-where's my b-baby?"

Cynthia was ignored.

Carmen stood and went to the older bawling, pink baby on the bed beside Cynthia, picked it up, and placed it near the glistening, wet newborn.

Jeremiah's eyes narrowed slightly as he watched the bloody newborn. Nothing in his face revealed the anticipation and suspense he felt inside his narrow chest as he waited.

The newborn's cries grew louder, richer. Its tiny arms and legs twitched and kicked.

"My b-baby . . . Guh-give me my baby!" Cynthia said sluggishly.

Carmen and Beth stood together, looking at the newborn.

Jeremiah watched, waited.

The other naked baby—clean and plump and pink—rolled slightly back and forth as it continued to cry, gulp for air, and cry some more.

The newborn's small, blood-streaked body and limbs bulged here and there—gently at first, then with greater force. The puckered little face shifted, then suddenly jutted forward away from the skull. The clenched eyes opened to reveal silver.

One corner of Jeremiah's thin-lipped razor slice of a mouth twitched upward, but that was the only outer expression of his inner excitement.

The newborn's arms and legs lengthened a bit, the tiny hands and feet changed. It became quiet as the nostrils flared at the end of its snout. The silver eyes began to roll in the direction of the other infant. In a quick, unexpected motion, the newborn rolled onto its stomach.

Beth gasped and her right hand shot up to touch fingertips to her chin.

The silver eyes found the pink, bawling baby. The newborn silently pulled itself forward until it was at the crying infant's side. It sniffed the baby, curled its tongue out briefly, and touched the tip to the baby's pink flesh.

The crying infant remained oblivious, eyes still shut, mouth still gaping.

The newborn held perfectly still for several seconds, then made a small, deep sound. It pounced in a blurry flash of fangs. Blood spurted.

A quiet gasp rose from the two women.

One half of Jeremiah's mouth turned up.

The baby's crying ended in an abrupt cough, and with a rush of wet, tearing sounds, the newborn began to eat.

Downstairs, the house was dark. The only light in the sunken living room came from the fireplace, where a healthy fire crackled and roared. The man with the eye patch sat leaning forward in a club chair directly before the fire, elbows on the armrests, head inclined as he stared into the flames. The fire's orange light poured over his face like rain dribbling down a windowpane. The black patch covered his left eye, but his right, a clear blue, glimmered with the glow of the flames as it stared intensely. The man's chin worked slowly, thoughtfully, back and forth. He wore a khaki sheriff's uniform with a silver badge over the left breast pocket, a heavy leather belt around his waist that held, among other things, a holstered gun.

A sound of movement startled him and he turned sharply to look over his right shoulder.

"Jeremiah," he said. He stood and faced the older, taller man, took in a deep breath, and released it in a long sigh. "Well?"

Jeremiah leaned forward and said something very quietly into his right ear.

The man smiled as Jeremiah pulled away. They held each other's gaze for a long moment, then the man turned and left Jeremiah behind as he hurried out of the room.

In the foyer, the man swept a flashlight off a small desk with his left hand and opened the front door with his right. As he pushed the security door open and stepped out onto the covered wooden porch, he thumbed the flashlight's button and a beam of light stabbed the darkness. He crossed the porch and stood at the top of the steps a moment, peering into the darkness of the yard with his good eye.

In the background, the ocean breathed its nighttime breaths and the crickets chirruped.

The eager susurrations that had been ongoing in the darkness around the house abruptly fell silent.

The man moved down a step. The flashlight beam rose and passed back and forth over the yard. It oozed over the dark, shadowy figures gathered there. They stood close together, covering the grass, spreading out to spill past the sprawling yard and over the driveway to the fence, and farther out to the narrow road that passed between the house and the beach beyond. The light glowed eerily in the many pairs of reflective silver eyes that turned with anticipation to the man on the porch steps, waiting.

The moment hung heavily in the air like a thick, damp, tropical heat as the man's single eye passed over the lake of eyes before him.

He tipped his head back slightly and shouted, "It's a girl!"

The chirping of the crickets stopped. Even the sea seemed to pause.

The weighty heat of the moment remained in the silence that followed, until the man spoke again.

"And it's *thriving*!"

In the near distance, another ocean wave rushed in against the beach.

A new sound rose from the dark, still crowd, but only for a moment—a brief sound of inhalation, the drawing in of a single breath by many.

In the dark, the heads of the crowd bent backward, faces turned to the glittering night sky, and together they filled the night with a loud, reverberating sound.

A rich, triumphant, lupine howl.

*Big Rock, California—Lemon Tree Mobile Home Park— three months ago . . .*

Penny Anderson and Byron Clifton walked together down the road that ran through the center of the Lemon Tree Mobile Home Park. It was a cool night in early summer, with the sound of televisions playing throughout the trailer park. Penny's dark blue flip-flops slapped against her heels with each step. She held a folded blanket tucked beneath her left arm. Byron was seventeen, a year older than Penny, but with his childlike mind, he giggled at nothing in particular and sometimes walked circles around Penny as they moved through the faint glow from the windows of mobile homes on either side of them. His black skin made him difficult to see in the night, while her thick, pale arms and moonlike, double-chinned face practically glowed. They were on their way to their secret hiding place, known only to them, in the patch of woods beyond the back edge of the trailer park.

Penny's mother Gretchen had gone out with one of her tricks—a new guy this time, bald and flabby, with a bushy mustache—giving Penny yet another summer night to kill by herself. She'd already gone through a package of Chips Ahoy! chocolate-chip cookies and half of the upside-down pineapple cake Aunt Tess had brought them on Sunday, all while watching reruns of sitcoms on TV. She couldn't eat that way while Gretchen was around, not without getting yelled at and sometimes slapped.

"How can you look at yourself in the mirror and keep eating like that?" Gretchen often shouted. "You're *way* over two hundred pounds and you look like a fuckin' *whale*! I don't even like you being here when guys come over, because you disgust them and turn them *off*, and then they don't wanna *fuck*!"

Sometimes she watched Gretchen with her tricks. Penny was always to call her by name, never "Mom," because the word *Mom* wasn't exactly a turn-on to her clientele. Gretchen made no effort to keep her business private and even had sex with her men on the living-room couch sometimes. Penny watched and masturbated. Sometimes she masturbated when there was nothing to watch. She thought of little besides food and sex, sex and food. The trailer smelled of sex all the time, and Gretchen always kept pornography around because some of her men liked to look at it. Penny often perused the magazines or watched the DVDs when Gretchen wasn't around.

School was Penny's idea of hell. She was tortured endlessly by her classmates, and even the teachers sometimes chimed in with cruel remarks or derisive laughter. She lived for weekends, and especially for the summer break, which was about to start. Then, she didn't have to be anywhere or do anything. When she wasn't eating or masturbating, she spent time with Byron, her only friend, who lived just a few trailers down with his parents. Byron's parents were always screaming at each other, and sometimes his dad beat up on his mom, so Byron always welcomed a chance to get away from them with Penny.

Recently, Penny had started experimenting with Byron. He was retarded, like a little boy, so it didn't matter to him that she was so fat and had pimples all over her face. And yet, as childlike as he was, he was seventeen, after all, and as horny as she. He often sported an erection, so he welcomed Penny's advances. A couple of weeks ago, she'd taken him to their hiding place and they'd spent some time kissing. Byron had gotten so excited that he'd begun humping Penny's leg as they kissed. When she stopped and refused to kiss any more, Byron had frantically opened his pants and jerked off, grinning and grunting the word *good* over and over. Penny had found it exciting to watch—he was hung better than most of Gretchen's tricks, but then Gretchen always said black guys had bigger dicks than anybody else. The next time, Penny had jerked him off, and the time after that, she'd given oral sex a try on Byron while masturbating herself. Then she'd let him fondle her fleshy breasts, which were only slightly larger than the rolls of fat beneath them. She'd let him touch her later and had taught him to call the hairy mound between her massive thighs her "coochy," which had made him laugh. This time, she had other plans.

They passed the last two trailers and moved into the wooded area behind the park.

"You gawn lemme play wit' yer coochy?" Byron said with a guffaw as they passed through the wall of bushes and into the small clearing that was their hideout. It was surrounded by trees and bushes and a couple of large rocks.

"Something better than that this time, Byron," Penny said with a smile. She spread out the blanket on the ground. As Byron sat down cross-legged on the blanket, Penny took off her black tank top and hiked up her purple skirt. She wore no underwear. "You wanna stick your wiener in my coochy, Byron?" she said.

Byron guffawed. "'Zit gawn feel good?"

"Oh, yeah. It'll feel real good. For both of us."

More laughing as he slapped his big hands against his thighs. "Yeah, sure, yeah."

A faint breeze whispered through the tops of the trees around them, and they could still hear the faint sound of television sets playing in trailers in the park.

"Take your pants off," Penny said. Byron stood and dropped his pants as she stretched out and spread her legs. "Now you lay down between my legs, Byron."

" 'Tween yer legs?" He thought about that a moment, giggled, then got down on top of her.

Penny reached over her fat middle and grabbed his cock, which was already erect—it seemed to be most of the time—and put it in her. An explosion of breath came from her lungs. She whispered, "Okay, Byron, in and out. In and out. Fuck me."

"Fuck you?" He laughed. "Momma says that's a dirty word an' I shouldn't never say—"

"Just *do it*."

As Byron moved, Penny struggled to reach down between his belly and her rolls of fat to rub her clitoris. Byron moaned as Penny bit her lower lip and clenched her eyes shut, losing herself in the sensation of his thrusts. She lifted her big legs into the air, spread them as far as she could. Byron began chanting, "Good . . . good," with each thrust, but Penny barely heard him. She was lost in the new feelings she was experiencing. She climbed toward her orgasm, felt it build, ready to explode into a bright flash of inner white light.

Byron grunted, then cried out.

A moment later, Penny realized he'd pulled out and was no longer on top of her. She opened her eyes and saw nothing but darkness at first. Then there was movement above her, and weight pressed down on her again. Byron—at least, she *thought* it was Byron at first—slid back into her, and she clenched her eyes shut again. But now he began to pound her much harder. Hands roughly clutched the backs of her knees and pushed her legs back hard, so far that it made her hips hurt. A sharp, foul smell filled Penny's nostrils as an unfamiliar voice growled above her. She opened her eyes again.

The face that hovered above her was not Byron's. It was white and darkly bearded and the eyes—

A ragged gasp tore from Penny's throat.

The eyes above her were a sparkling silver.

"Byron?" she croaked. *"Byron?"*

The man on top of her pounded harder. Spittle dribbled from his open mouth as he growled again and again. His hands gripped the backs of her knees so hard that she thought he was going to break the skin.

The darkness was distorting the face of the man who was fucking her—that had to be it, she decided, because she could not be seeing what she *thought* she was seeing.

*Closer, closer,* she thought. *Almost, so close . . .*

His face was changing shape. Strange sounds came from him—popping and crunching—as his nose seemed to grow longer. The entire bottom half of his face jutted out from his skull in a sudden, trembling thrust, and he opened his mouth—now a snout—as his teeth became long and sharp.

*No, no, this isn't happening, but . . . closer, closer . . . oh God it's a nightmare I'm having a nightmare . . . closer, closer . . .*

As she came in a bright flash of pure white inside her head, the large, heavy figure on top of her slammed into her with increased force, swelled inside her, and released a sound that was a mixture of impassioned cry and roaring howl.

She gasped for breath, her fatty flesh quivering as she attempted to crawl backward on the blanket, away from the hulking man above her. He pulled away from her, got up on his knees, and pulled his right arm back. He swung his fist down hard and it connected with Penny's left temple.

There was another bright flash of white, but this one was not at all orgasmic.

When she opened her eyes, the dark shape above her was gone and her ears rang with a deafening silence. Even the murmur of televisions playing in the trailer park had stopped. Moonlight shone through the tops of the trees above her and gave everything a faint bluish tinge.

"Byron?" she said, her throat dry, voice hoarse. She propped herself up on her elbows, then slowly climbed to her feet and straightened her bunched-up skirt. She found her tank top on the blanket and pulled it on, then looked around for Byron. She called his name again, but got no response. She quickly folded up the blanket and tucked it under her arm. "Byron, are you still here?"

She wondered who the man had been, the one who had replaced Byron between her legs. For the first time since it happened, she felt a wave of fear, of . . . *creepiness*. Some stranger, a man who was not her friend Byron, had fucked her. She'd always been queasy about her mother's lifestyle—having sex with virtual strangers, trading sex for money and/or drugs, bringing them home and fucking them and sending them on their way without ever knowing anything about them, even their real names. And now, *she* had done something like that—but it had not been by choice. Had it?

*Have I been raped?* Penny wondered.

She walked toward the edge of the little clearing that had become her and Byron's secret place—

—and her foot caught on something, throwing her forward. The ground swung up and slammed into her with a thud, knocking an explosive grunt from her lungs. Penny clumsily and heavily climbed to her feet, picked up the blanket, and turned around. She looked down to find that she'd tripped over Byron's legs, his pants down around his ankles. Her eyes followed his legs up to his bare ass, and then . . .

From the waist up, Byron disappeared in a black mass of glistening lumps and jagged bones.

Penny gasped. It wasn't until then that she caught a whiff of the thick, coppery scent in the air. She stumbled backward away from the torn body, hugging the blanket to her chest. A storm of emotions raced through her—fear, sadness, guilt. She looked down at her feet in their flip-flops. Had she stepped in blood?

A possible scenario played out in her mind: she tracked blood back to the trailer; the cops followed her steps; and Gretchen found out about what she'd been doing with Byron, that she was guilty of luring Byron out to the hiding place to be killed by this stranger from nowhere. Penny could not let that happen. Moving numbly and without much thought, she took off her flip-flops and wrapped them in her blanket. She walked a good distance around Byron's body, left the hiding place, and hurried back to the trailer.

In her tiny, cramped bedroom, she opened the blanket and looked at her flip-flops. The bottoms were dark with blood. She wrapped them in the blanket again, stuffed the blanket into a plastic trash bag, and looked at the clock on the DVD player. It was just past eleven. Gretchen probably wouldn't be home for another couple of hours. Penny left the trailer, walked toward the front of the park, and took a sharp turn to the right between two trailers. She took a shortcut—a narrow path through the woods that led to a nearby 7-Eleven. There was a large Dumpster behind the convenience store. Penny opened the Dumpster and stuffed her bag deep into the garbage. Her forearm was sticky and smelly when she pulled it out.

She went back to the trailer, took a long, hot shower, then put on a T-shirt and sweatpants. She sat in front of the TV with a bag of Lay's Wavy chips and a jar of ranch-style dip. She watched TV and ate and tried to push everything that had happened that night far from her mind—including the image of Byron's ripped and mangled body spread over the ground in their secret hiding place.

# CHAPTER ONE

*Driving Back to the Seventies*

The silver Mercedes coupé put Carmel behind it on California's Highway 1 and sped south. To the right, the meringue breakers of the gray-blue Pacific repeatedly surged against the rocky cliffs and flat expanses of wet, shiny sand, stirring a thin, silvery mist. It was a bright, sparklingly clear Friday in July, and the morning neared its end.

In the passenger seat, Karen Moffett smoked a Winston and occasionally flicked ashes out of the three-inch opening in the window. She had been annoyed with car manufacturers ever since they'd stopped installing ashtrays in cars. She took a drag and exhaled smoke as she waited for the driver to respond to the explanation she'd just given.

"So let me get this straight," Gavin Keoph said as he drove. "Essentially, we're, uh . . . traveling back in time to the seventies. Is that it?"

"I haven't been to this place myself, but yeah, that's pretty much the case."

Gavin eyed the cigarette between the first two fingers of her right hand.

"From what I've learned," she went on, "the Esalen

Institute has perfectly preserved the philosophies and pop psychology of the seventies in a hermetically sealed environment. Sort of like stepping back in time to Marin County, circa 1973."

Karen noticed that his eyes glanced at the road but spent most of their time on her cigarette.

"Can I have a drag off that?" he said.

"Didn't you bring your own?"

"I'm trying to quit."

She laughed as she handed him the half-smoked cigarette. Gavin pulled on the cigarette, and his eyes closed briefly with pleasure as he inhaled while Karen watched. As he exhaled the smoke slowly with a sigh, his eyes opened only halfway to watch the road, and his body slumped in the seat, suddenly relaxed, soothed.

"Careful," Karen said. "You enjoy that any more and you're going to need a cigarette *afterwards*, if you know what I mean."

Gavin chuckled as he handed the cigarette back to her.

"How long has it been since your last smoke?" she said.

"Oh . . ." He looked at his watch. "About nine hours."

"They have pills for that now, you know."

"I don't believe in pills."

"You may not believe in them, Keoph, but they *do* exist." At Karen's feet was an Aquafina bottle with some dead cigarette butts floating in a few inches of water. She took another drag, then picked up the bottle, removed the cap, and dropped the remainder of the cigarette into it. She replaced the cap and put the bottle back down by her feet.

"We've known each other for a couple years now, and you're still calling me Keoph," he said, smiling. "I hate that."

"You do? Why haven't you ever said so?"

"I have. At least twice."

"You have? Oh. Well, what do I call you?"

"How about my first name? Gavin."

"All right, Gavin it is. Sometimes I get distracted and don't hear things. Sorry I didn't hear you."

"So, what is Martin Burgess doing at the Esalen Institute?"

Karen laughed. "You've known him awhile now, and you have to ask?"

"You know him better than I do. You've spent more time with him because he's got a house down in Los Angeles. Which is why I suppose he always calls you with assignments, and never me."

"Yes, but you know his . . . *leanings*, so to speak. Esalen is right up his alley. He's attending a weeklong seminar on remote viewing."

"Remote viewing?"

"It's a form of ESP. Allegedly, those with an aptitude for it can develop it with time and practice, hone it. Like . . . I don't know . . . crocheting, or playing the accordion. It's the ability to gather information about a person or place or event that's outside the physical perception of the viewer. For example, using remote viewing, you might track the movements of a person who's on the other side of the country."

Gavin frowned. "With my mind?"

She nodded. "The CIA has done all kinds of research into it in the past, and for all we know, they may have used it. They *still* may be using it."

"What's Burgess want with it?"

"He writes horror novels. It's grist for his mill."

"So, he's at Esalen for the whole weekend?"

"At least. It's a resort-style conference center where people gather to meditate, discuss alternative science, the soul, philosophy and odd religious stuff, nutrition, whatever."

He grunted. "Sounds like a circle jerk for people with too much money and time on their hands."

"We think alike, Mr. Keoph. At least it'll be pretty. Big Sur is gorgeous."

Gavin turned his head to the right and looked out at the richly colored coast. "Everything is gorgeous around here. If Burgess is busy with this weird seminar, what does he want with us?"

"The usual. He has something for us to do. You know him. It couldn't wait."

"What's with the ring size?"

Burgess had asked for their ring sizes. Left hand, wedding finger.

"I don't know," Karen said. "All I know is that he has someone there he wants us to meet, and then he's going to give us another assignment."

They were silent for awhile as Gavin drove. Finally, he frowned and turned to Karen. "They discuss 'alternative science'? What is *alternative* science, anyway? I mean, there's . . . empiricism, right? What other kind of science— I mean, *real* science—is there?"

Karen shrugged. "I'm okay, you're okay? If it feels good, do it? That sort of thing."

Gavin's eyebrows rose and he nodded. "Ah, okay. Get in touch with your inner child. Make love, not war."

"Today is the first day of the rest of your life."

"Sit on it, Potsie."

Karen laughed.

Gavin shook his head slowly and said, "We are working for a loon."

"Ah, yes, but he's a loon who pays *very* well."

Martin Burgess, the loon to whom they referred, was a writer of gruesome horror novels that routinely made the bestseller lists and were typically made into bad movies that yielded bigger box office receipts than they deserved. His work, combined with his quirky, witty personality, made him a frequent guest on talk shows.

"Did you see him on Letterman last week?" Gavin asked.

"Burgess? Sure. He and Letterman are good together."

Gavin chuckled. "Letterman always acts like he's a little afraid of him. It's funny."

"Anyone who's read his books has got to be a little nervous about him at first. I mean, he writes some pretty . . . well, strange stuff. That last book, the one about the alien women with fanged vaginas—What kind of person thinks that stuff up?"

"Oh, I don't know. Any man who's dated for any length of time?"

"Chauvinist pig."

"Ah, more seventies jargon."

She laughed. "Burgess is harmless. He's just got a wild imagination."

"Oh, yeah, he's a nice guy. I actually like him. He's just . . . I don't know."

"A loon."

"Yeah."

The two of them had met two years earlier when Martin Burgess, whom they'd heard of but hadn't known at the time, summoned them to the Beverly Hills Hotel. Karen was co-owner of Moffett and Brand Private Investigators in Los Angeles, and Gavin owned Burning Lizard Security and Investigations in San Francisco. Burgess had conducted a lengthy search for private investigators who he felt were well-suited to his needs, and they were the best he'd found. He'd made them an offer. They were to farm out their current clients to other investigators in their employ and place their firms temporarily in the care of others while they devoted their full time to an investigation for Burgess, for which he would pay them handsomely. *Very* handsomely. Once they'd learned the details of the investigation, though, they saw the large paycheck in a different light. The whole thing—the investigation, the money—had struck them both, at first, as the whim of a rich, happy lunatic.

In the course of that investigation, a number of people had been killed—some for the *second* time—and Karen and Gavin had come close to joining them. Karen's fate had been especially dark, and it had taken her awhile to get past it. She'd put up a good front at first, but inside, a part of her had died. She had been kidnapped, tortured, beaten, and brutally raped. Mrs. Dupassie, a petite old chocolate-colored woman who swore like a sailor, had helped them in their investigation, and she'd given Karen a lot of support afterward. Mrs. Dupassie had put her in touch with a psychiatrist, whom she still saw—Dr. Roderick Kincaid. These days, she saw him once or twice a month, but at first, she'd been in his home office four or five times a week. He had been very understanding, far more understanding than any typical psychiatrist would have been. He was not typical at all . . . just as Mrs. Dupassie was not typical. . . .

Along with endangering their lives, it had changed the way they looked at the world. It had changed them. Both were well educated, and before that investigation, they had been in solid mental health. As Karen sometimes put it, "I drop something now and then, but I have most of my shit together." But after that first investigation for Burgess, their beliefs, their outlooks, and their sanity had been shaken. Especially Karen's. Afterward, she had not slept as well. She still didn't. Gavin had been surprised to discover that he had a new fear of the dark. After conquering their initial fears of encountering anything as deadly or horrific as the things they'd faced in that first job, they'd worked on two more cases for Burgess. Neither investigation had turned out to be much of anything, which had been a tremendous relief to both Karen and Gavin.

It had been a difficult decision to go back to work for Burgess. Karen could not get the memories of her torture and rape at the hands of those . . . *creatures* . . . out of her mind, and she knew she never would. The risk of going through something like that again seemed great at first. But she began to realize that the chances of that were small. On top of that, Burgess had sweetened the pot with a bigger fee, and she'd been unable to turn it down. "It was a fluke," Gavin had told her, and she knew he was probably right.

But they still didn't talk about that first case. They'd tried a couple of times, but she had been unable to discuss it without stammering, without trembling and being unable to meet Gavin's eyes. The experience had had a great impact on them both, but it had scarred Karen. Daylight wasn't so bad. But the nights were still tough at times, even after the passage of time. She'd come from a stoic family of people who kept their emotions locked up tight, so she seldom showed to anyone the damage that had been done. But it was there.

More than anything, the things they had discovered and faced during that investigation for Burgess had damaged the firm hold they each had on reality. After looking into the predatory eyes of creatures that were not supposed to exist, Karen and Gavin had come to wonder what *else* might be out there in the world . . . what other boogeymen they'd previously dismissed as fantasy were lurking in the shadows of hard, cold reality.

"That first time Burgess called," Gavin said, "I was genuinely baffled. He wouldn't tell me anything on the phone, wouldn't say why he specifically wanted to see me. I offered to send someone from my firm, but he refused."

"Yeah, same here. After he called, I dug up all the information I could find on him just out of curiosity."

Gavin chuckled. "So did I."

"That first time we met in the hotel, I figured it had something to do with his wife, Denise. With her being so much younger, I figured he didn't trust her. I thought maybe he wanted us to follow her around, see if she was cheating, or something." After a pause, Karen said, "She finally left him, you know."

"Well, I'm not surprised, after—"

The air between them became thick. They both stared straight ahead at the road, silent, a little stiff.

Before they'd met him, Burgess had left Sheila, his wife of nearly twenty years, to marry Denise Sykes, one of his twenty-something writing students. During their initial investigation for Burgess, Denise, like Karen, had been raped and badly beaten due to her husband's bungling. Also like Karen, she hadn't been the same after that. But Denise had been much less able to handle the experience and had spent a little time in a mental hospital in Connecticut that specialized in the discreet treatment of celebrities.

Karen clenched her teeth as she stared out at the highway. A single word rose up in her mind.

*Vampires.*

They had been monsters. Not *all* of them—some fought their nature and refused to prey on people for the blood they needed. Mrs. Dupassie was such a vampire, as were a few of the others they'd worked with on the investigation. Such was the case with Dr. Kincaid. The fact that he was one of them had allowed Karen to be totally honest with him about her experience and feelings. How would she have told a normal psychiatrist that she had been beaten and raped by vampires who had bitten her and sucked her blood?

Gooseflesh crawled across her shoulders and down her back, and she gave a small start.

Gavin caught the movement in the corner of his eye and turned to her. "You okay?" he asked.

She lit another cigarette and nodded.

After a moment, Gavin said, "It's a little after noon and I'm getting hungry. Didn't eat much breakfast. You want to stop somewhere and get some lunch?"

Keeping her eyes front, Karen said, "Yeah, okay." She

puffed on the cigarette. "Does the radio work in this crate? How about some music?"

"Sure." He reached down and turned on the radio. "That button is the tuner. Have a party." As Karen reached down to find a radio station, Gavin noticed the tremble in her hand. He didn't have to ask why. He knew.

Three songs played on the radio before Karen finally spoke again. "If this is . . . Um, I mean, if Burgess wants us to do something that's, uh . . . well, *dangerous* . . . I'm just wondering—"

"Don't worry, Karen," Gavin said quietly. "It won't happen again. I told you once before—it was a fluke. That's all. Just a fluke."

They said little for the rest of the drive.

# CHAPTER TWO

*At the Esalen Institute*

Martin Burgess burst into the room with a big smile and heartily shook their hands. "Good to see you again," he said.

He reminded Karen of a big, mischievous high school kid who always looked as if he were on his way to a kegger in a hurry. He'd changed little since their first meeting—a couple of years older (he would turn fifty soon), a little heavier, maybe, his scalp a bit more visible on top where he was losing his dark hair, which was always mussed. He wore jeans and a black T-shirt that read, 667—NEIGHBOR OF THE BEAST. Burgess's collection of slogan-bearing T-shirts and sweatshirts was legendary, and constantly grew larger as his many fans sent him more. He'd once taken Karen on a tour of his Los Angeles home and had shown her the large room that he used as a closet in which to store all of them.

Burgess was accompanied by a curvaceous brunette woman in her twenties. A brown leather satchel hung from her shoulder.

"Gavin, you're looking good," Burgess said. "Karen, lovely as ever. Have a nice trip?"

"The flight into San Francisco was uneventful," she said. "Which is the best kind of flight to have."

"This is my new personal assistant, Brandy," he said, placing a hand against her back.

*Personal assistant, huh?* Karen thought with a smirk.

"And I'd like you to meet—" Burgess glanced over his shoulder and found that no one stood behind him. "Where'd he go?"

"I thought he was right behind us," Brandy said.

"Could you go find him?"

"Sure." Brandy went back out the door.

They stood in a plain, large room with unadorned white walls and a teal carpet, a fireplace. Several cushioned chairs were arranged casually, and an easel holding a blank white-board stood in a corner. Windows provided a view of a sloping lawn and the shimmering blue Pacific in the distance.

The Esalen Institute was an informal collection of buildings scattered over a lush, green, hilly landscape by the sea. When they arrived, a pleasant woman in her sixties had led them to this house, where they'd waited for Burgess for a few minutes.

"They call this the Big House," Burgess said. "Sounds like a place where they send people as a punishment, but they hold meetings and other gatherings here."

Brandy quickly returned with a short, stubby, nervous man in tow. Karen estimated he was in his early thirties. He wore an ill-fitting, short-sleeved blue shirt only partially tucked into his gray slacks, which weren't quite long enough to cover his white socks. One of his sneakers was untied. He wore thick, metal-framed glasses that slightly magnified his eyes. His sandy hair was cut short and parted rigidly on the left. Carrying a scuffed black briefcase, he stumbled into the room behind Brandy and came to an abrupt halt when his eyes fell on Karen. His mouth opened a moment, then snapped shut. He quickly pushed his glasses up on his nose with a finger as he nervously averted his eyes, then cleared his throat.

"I'd like you to meet Harvey Altman," Burgess said. "Harvey, these are the investigators I told you about— Karen Moffett from Los Angeles, Gavin Keoph from San Francisco." He turned to them again. "Would you like anything? Something to drink or eat?"

"We stopped for lunch on the road," Gavin said. "I'm fine. Karen?"

"Nothing for me."

"Then let's get comfortable," Burgess said. "Have a seat." He pulled five of the chairs into a circle and they each took a seat. Harvey put his briefcase on the floor beside his chair, and Brandy did the same with her bulging satchel. Burgess checked his watch. "We have plenty of time before your jet is ready to take off, so we don't have to rush."

"Our jet?" Gavin said.

"I'll explain in a minute." He reached over and put a hand on Harvey's shoulder. "I've known Harvey for about six years now. He's brilliant, a hard worker. He's done a lot of research for me, and he keeps me up-to-date on events in the, uh . . . well, you two know the kind of things I'm interested in. Harvey has his finger on the pulse of the paranormal community. He's a computer wiz, and when it comes to researching a subject, he's like a bloodhound, he can find anything and everything. He's only one of the network of sources who help me out in my work and in my own personal interests, but he's the best. He's honest and trustworthy, and I want you to take what he has to say very seriously. Harvey is incredibly devoted to his work, so he doesn't get out much, and he's uncomfortable in groups of strangers, so bear with him." Burgess turned to the younger man. "Okay, Harvey. You're among friends. Don't be embarrassed. Fill them in on this whole thing."

"Uh, okay, well . . ." Harvey pushed his glasses up on his nose again. As he spoke, his nervous eyes flitted only now and then to Karen and Gavin. "My, uh . . . associates and I have been tracking a man named Daniel Fargo for a few years now. We stumbled onto something called the FRC—the Fargo Research Center—which had been set up more than a decade before. Completely funded by Daniel Fargo. He was an English professor at Harvard, married to the heiress of a glue fortune. His wife and pregnant daughter and her husband were murdered on Thanksgiving Day in 1992 when a group of intruders burst into their home and brutally attacked them. Fargo was badly beaten and almost died, spent a lot of time in the hospital. After recovering, he disappeared. Just seemed to vanish. He used his wife's fortune to fund this research center, but the field of research was very hard to determine. The whole thing was shrouded in secrecy. But we kept digging. It seems that the FRC focuses all its time and money on one thing only—a virus. Lupus venerus. *Venerus* meaning that it's, um . . ." He cleared his throat abruptly as his embarrassed eyes glanced at Karen. "Meaning it's, uh, sexually transmitted. *Lupus* meaning, um . . . well, *wolf*."

Karen glanced at Gavin to find that he was glancing at her. The look they exchanged was familiar—they seemed to exchange it at least once whenever they were being briefed by Burgess. They said nothing and returned their attention to Harvey.

"There is no other research available on this virus," he said. "No literature exists on it, no papers, no articles. It doesn't even seem to exist—except in Fargo's lab. As far as we can tell, lupus venerus is known only to those who work at FRC, who are required to sign legally binding nondisclosure forms. And to Daniel Fargo himself. A little more digging revealed the fact that Fargo has been funding the manufacture of silver bullets. He has a little place in rural Massachusetts that—"

"Excuse me," Gavin said. "*Silver* bullets?"

"That's right. Silver bullets."

Karen said, "Silver bullets and a sexually transmitted wolf virus."

Harvey looked at Karen for a moment, seemed to force himself to hold her gaze, then quickly looked away, blushing. "Yes, that's right. I—I know how it sounds, but, um . . . well, it took some time, but we finally tracked down Fargo himself. He was on the move, heading west and apparently making an effort to cover his tracks and not be noticed." He reached down and picked up the briefcase beside his chair, put it on his lap, and opened it. He removed a grainy, slightly blurred photograph and handed it to Burgess, who passed it to Karen and Gavin, who looked at it together. "That's the best picture we have of him."

A man in a dark coat stood on a street corner with his hat in one hand, the other hand moving back through his hair. His face was terribly distorted by what appeared to be long scars.

"Did that happen to him when he and his family were attacked?" Gavin said.

Harvey nodded. "We believe so, yes."

"Were they caught? The people who did it?"

"No. But we think that's what he was doing," Harvey said. "Tracking them down."

"Has he found them?" Gavin said, handing the picture back to Harvey.

"We're, um, not sure. But we suspect he found . . . *something*. Or, uh, something . . . found him." He put the photograph back in the briefcase. "His trail ends in Big Rock, a little town up the coast from here, near Eureka. He got there seven months ago. A little while after that, it seems he . . . well, he just disappeared. Again. We've been unable to pick up his trail ever since. It ends there in Big Rock. Permanently, we think."

Karen felt a knot tightening in her stomach, felt the muscles across the top of her back begin to tense. She took a slow, deep breath, let it out slowly, then turned to Burgess. "You want us to find this guy?"

He shook his head. "No. We don't think there's anything to find. Go on, Harvey."

Harvey pushed the glasses up, cleared his throat again. "Something, um, strange is going on in Big Rock." He took a folder from the briefcase and passed it down to Karen and Gavin. "That's a file of autopsy reports and newspaper articles and some other documents."

Gavin opened the folder and handed some of the papers to Karen, who frowned as she looked them over quickly. The knot grew tighter, her muscles became more tense, and her mouth began to dry. She licked her lips and turned to Harvey. "What's the 'something strange' that's going on in Big Rock?"

"Animal attacks," Harvey said. "At least, that's what they're being called. A lot of people have been killed. Pretty, uh, brutally. Killed and in many cases partly, um . . . eaten."

*"Eaten?"* Gavin said.

Harvey nodded.

Karen saw that Burgess was watching them as they absorbed what Harvey had said and looked over the contents of the file. The right corner of his mouth curled ever so slightly upward. It made her a little angry. In light of everything that had happened during their first investigation for him, how could he find amusement in this? A hot rush of anger moved through her, but she held it down, absorbed it, kept it inside.

Finally, Burgess spoke. "I'm sure you've already made the connection. Fargo . . . lupus venerus . . . silver bullets . . . animal atta—"

"Werewolves?" Karen said.

Burgess grinned, widened his eyes, and spread his arms like a game-show host. "You win the dinette set and the trip to Fiji!"

Gavin said, "You're saying there are werewolves in this town . . . what's it called again?"

"Big Rock," Burgess said. "Population eleven thousand and forty-one. Well, less than that now, thanks to a number of *animal attacks*." He spoke the last two words emphatically and made invisible quotation marks in the air with the first two fingers of each hand. "I've never been there, although I've spent some time in the area. By all accounts, a nice little town . . . where people are being killed and eaten, and where a man hunting werewolves vanished into thin air."

Karen's mind flashed with vivid memories of what had happened during that first investigation two years earlier. "Do we know anything about Fargo's disappearance?" she said, trying but failing to keep the slightest tremble out of her voice.

"Not yet," Burgess said. "He was staying at the—Where did you say he was staying, Harvey?"

Harvey cleared his throat. "The Beachcomber Motor Lodge."

"That's right," Burgess said, nodding. He smiled at Karen and Gavin. "That's where you'll be staying."

Gavin's eyebrows rose slowly. "Oh?"

Karen felt a chill that seemed to run through her very bones.

"Fargo was staying in one of the outside rooms," Harvey said. "Not in the motel's main building. And then, um . . . he wasn't. All of a sudden."

"So, he just disappeared," Gavin said. "Didn't anyone go look for him? Any employees, business associates?"

"Yes, I was getting to that." Harvey held the open briefcase steady on his lap as he shifted in his chair and adjusted his glasses. "It seems a man from the FRC went to Big Rock to find him. A man named"—he consulted a sheet of paper from his briefcase—"Aaron Cramer." He lifted his magnified eyes from the paper and looked at

Gavin. "He hasn't been seen or heard from since. By anyone."

"Have you talked to anyone at the lab?" Karen said.

"Dr. Georgia Hopper," Burgess said. "She's the head brain there. She wasn't too keen on discussing any of this, but once she learned what we knew, she opened up a little. She wasn't able to tell my people much that we didn't already know, but when asked about Cramer, she said they were uncertain about his fate. His life had been a bit of a mess when he went in search of Fargo. His wife was divorcing him, and he owed a lot of money to the kind of people who don't necessarily observe the law when getting their money back, if you know what I mean. That was why his wife was divorcing him. He had a gambling problem, it seems. Dr. Hopper says that when Cramer disappeared, they informed the police, and once they learned of Cramer's situation, they figured he'd taken the opportunity to make himself scarce. They went to Big Rock, looked around, asked some questions, but found no evidence of foul play. They concluded that Mr. Cramer's disappearance was most likely self-imposed." He turned to Harvey. "Go ahead, Harv. Sorry to interrupt."

Harvey shuffled around in the briefcase for another sheet of paper. "Big Rock is in Pine County, the smallest county in California. The county seat. Until eighteen months ago, the sheriff was a man named Arlin Hurley. Then he was killed. Apparently in a meth-lab explosion in a deserted house being used by drug dealers. He was replaced by an interim sheriff until a new election could be held, a man named, uh, Irving Taggart. But that was seven months ago. No election has been held, and Taggart still holds the office."

"Was Taggart a deputy?" Gavin said.

"That's the thing. There's no record of Taggart in the department. We don't know who he is or where he came from."

Burgess leaned forward, put his elbows on his knees, joined his hands before him, and smiled. "Suspicious, ain't it?"

"What are you suggesting?" Karen said.

"Only that it's suspicious," Burgess said. "That something odd is going on in Big Rock."

"And you want us to look into it," Karen said.

"Harvey, give them everything you have," Burgess said.

Harvey stood, put the briefcase on the chair, removed a few manila folders from it, and handed them to Karen. He fidgeted as he stood before her and Gavin, straightened his glasses. "That's everything we've been able to gather. I'm, uh, sorry it's not more, but there's not a whole lot available. We did the best we could."

"Later today," Burgess said, "you two will be going to the Monterey Peninsula Airport, where a jet will spirit you away to Eureka."

"You have a jet?" Gavin said.

"Oh, it's not mine. It's just a little thing, nothing fancy. A friend of mine who's a lot richer than I is giving me the use of it for a little while. There will be a car waiting for you at the airport in Eureka, and you'll drive to Big Rock, where a room will be waiting for you at the Beachcomber Motor Lodge in the name of Mr. and Mrs. Gavin Keoph."

Karen exchanged another glance with Gavin.

"Yes, you'll be posing as a newlywed couple interested in possibly moving to Big Rock," Burgess said. "That will give you a good reason to look around and ask questions. Don't you think? I've had rings made up for you, which is why I wanted your ring sizes. The rings will be delivered here a little later. At least, I hope it's only a little later—it was kind of a last-minute order. Any questions?"

Karen began to fidget. She quickly went over the last few minutes in her mind, everything that Burgess and Harvey had said. She felt a crawling sensation on her skull, as if her scalp were shrinking. People being killed and eaten. People disappearing. Frightening memories from that first nightmarish investigation—

*Vampires* . . .

—flashed in her mind. A tremor passed through her, and to hide it from the others, she stood suddenly and began to pace.

Gavin frowned. "Karen?"

"Could we speak to you alone for a moment?" Karen said to Burgess, her voice quiet and quavering.

Eyebrows high with mild surprise, Burgess said, "Sure. Brandy, Harvey, could you step out for a moment?"

Harvey closed his briefcase as Brandy stood and hefted the strap of her satchel over her shoulder. They went out the door, and Brandy pulled it closed behind her.

Burgess stood and faced Karen, frowning. "Is something wrong?"

Karen paced a short distance, back and forth, moving quickly, her fists clenched at her sides.

Gavin stood. "Karen, what is it?"

Finally, she stopped, and turned to face Burgess. "The last two snipe hunts you sent us on were pretty harmless— the haunted house that turned out to be a hoax, the little boy whose demon possession turned out to be a brain tumor. That's fine, I can handle that stuff. But *this*." She started pacing again. "I don't have to remind you what happened a couple of years ago. In Los Angeles. People died. We were almost killed. So was your wife. Like your wife, I was beaten and ruh . . . raped. Tortured. Now you want us to get involved in this . . . this *whatever* it is? Where people are being mauled? *Eaten?* Unless there's something you haven't told us yet, that doesn't sound very harmless. Not harmless at *all*."

"Karen," Burgess said as he stepped forward, reached out, and touched her arm. When she stopped pacing and faced him again, he placed a hand on each of her shoulders. "Karen, what happened that first time—I've told you how I felt about . . . what that *did* to me. It's not something I take lightly. I'm not going to let anything like that happen again. I promise. I *swear*. I'm not sending you into this blindly. Whatever it is that's happening in Big Rock, you will be prepared for it." He dropped his hands to his side, then turned to include Gavin. "You'll be sufficiently armed, I assure you. That's why I've borrowed my friend's jet. You can't very well take a commercial flight when you're as armed as you'll be. You'll have everything you need to protect yourselves, including silver bullets. Just in case. And this time, I'm prepared for the worst. If things get too sticky—if they even *look* like they're getting sticky—I've got reinforcements to send in. They'll join you if necessary." He looked back and forth between them for a moment.

Karen still felt tense, still had a knot in her gut. She couldn't shake the bad feeling she had about going to Big Rock. Burgess seemed to sense this and smiled warmly at her.

"Don't worry," he said. "Everything's going to be fine."

"I don't . . . I don't know," she said.

"The weapons and reinforcements aren't all," Burgess said. "I'll make this even more worth your while than usual with a 50 percent increase in your normal pay."

Gavin blinked with surprise. He gave her a look that said, *That's a lot of money.*

Karen sighed, thought about it a moment. "On one condition."

"Anything," Burgess said.

She said, "If we get there and this doesn't feel right . . . if I think it's dangerous, or if, for any reason, I feel uncomfortable with it, we back out."

Burgess considered that. "In that case, you would forfeit your pay, of course."

"Of course," Karen said with a nod. "Just so you know. I'm not walking into another deadly clusterfuck like the one in Los Angeles."

"No clusterfucks, I promise." Burgess smiled at them. "Well. Do we have a deal?"

Karen and Gavin held a long, silent look, then she said to Burgess, "All right. We have a deal."

# CHAPTER THREE

*Emergency Room*

Dr. Abel Dinescu took a moment to tear open the wrapper of a granola bar. His unexpected double shift in the Sisters of Mercy emergency room had kept him from eating since lunch, and it was well past dinnertime. He'd just treated a sixty-eight-year-old man with breathing problems who had seemed surprised by Abe's suggestion that perhaps his four-pack-a-day habit had something to do with it. As he chewed a bite of granola, he realized the ER was empty. Maybe he could sneak off to the cafeteria for a quick hot meal.

He should have been home three hours ago, but his relief, Dr. Seth Fulton, had not shown up. He hadn't called to say he wasn't coming in, which was unusual for Seth, a stickler for protocol and typically considerate of others, not the type to blow off a night's work and not tell anyone. He was vaguely worried about Seth, wondering what had become of him.

Abe stopped a passing nurse. "Irene, has anyone heard from Seth?"

"Not a word. Maggie's called his house, his cell phone—nothing."

He frowned, and when he spoke, his words were touched by the slightest lingering ghost of his Romanian

accent. "You haven't heard anything, have you? I mean . . .
Well, you and Seth—"

Irene was a petite woman in her early thirties and wore
scrubs like all the nurses—hers were a powder blue. She
smiled and said, "We only went out on one date, Dr. Dinescu. Nothing more. I'm afraid I'm not one of Dr. Fulton's many conquests, so I have no idea where he might
be. We're trying to track down Dr. Rodriguez and bring
him in to relieve you."

Abe smiled and nodded. "Okay, thanks." As Irene walked
away, he wrapped the granola bar up and stuffed it into the
pocket of his white coat, then went to find Maggie, the ER
charge nurse. They almost collided in the doorway that led
to the office.

"Maggie, I'm going down to the cafeteria for—"

"I don't think so, Dr. Dinescu," she said. "We've got
incoming." She was a short, slender woman in her forties
who always moved rapidly and spoke in clipped, staccato
rhythms, as if constantly in a hurry. Her eyes were bright
behind her large glasses. She held a clipboard. "The call
just came in. Motorcyclists."

Abe sighed, took the granola bar back out of his pocket.

"Seems a moving van blew a tire, lost control, swerved
into the other lane, and plowed into four motorcycles.
The driver of the van wasn't wearing a seat belt and went
through the windshield when he hit a tree."

"What've we got?" he said, then took another bite of
the bar.

Maggie looked at the clipboard. "Two of the bikers
weren't too severely injured, mostly minor stuff. The other
two are in bad shape. Severe abrasions, lacerations, blood
loss. Possible ruptured spleen and other internals. One of
them lost consciousness for awhile, then regained consciousness, but is disoriented and incoherent. The other
is experiencing respiratory distress, numbness in the right
arm, compound fracture of the femur, and has . . ."

Abe listened to Maggie read off the list of injuries as he ate his granola bar. He wished he were at home. Claire had fixed Chicken Parmesan, one of his favorites. She was a schoolteacher, off for the summer. She loved to cook, and she was good at it, a collector of recipes, a regular viewer of the Food Network, always trying out new dishes or improving old favorites. If he were home now, he'd be in front of the TV with Claire and Illy, his belly full and warm, sipping some wine, maybe watching an old movie, letting the day flow out of him.

A year before they'd left San Bernardino, Claire's first pregnancy had ended in a miscarriage. They'd waited longer than most to have a child, wanting to make sure their financial security and home situation were firm. By the time Claire became pregnant, they'd already begun to grow tired of San Bernardino. It was an ugly city in a hot desert. They'd spoken often of living near the ocean in a small town, someplace quiet and clean. During a vacation, they'd taken a long coastal road trip and had fallen in love with the northern California coast. After the miscarriage, Claire had become depressed. She'd admitted to Abe that their surroundings did not help at all. They'd reached a quick decision. Abe immediately went to work making the arrangements. Since moving to Big Rock, Claire's spirits had climbed. The area was very therapeutic. Abe vastly preferred his job at Sisters of Mercy—it was smaller, quieter, and less stressful.

He finished the granola bar, tossed the wrapper into a nearby waste can, and brushed off his hands. He opened his mouth to speak but stopped when Winona, the receptionist who worked the front window, stepped up to them.

"I reached Dr. Rodriguez and he's on his way in." She turned and headed back to her station.

"Good," Abe said with some relief. To Maggie, he said, "Okay, let's get ready for them." When he turned to go back into the treatment area, he found there was no time to prepare. The EMTs rushed in pushing the gurneys ahead of them. Suddenly there was blood everywhere—on the EMTs, spattering onto the pale tile floor—and someone cried out in agonizing pain. As he headed toward the mess, Abe heard another voice speak behind him.

"Just got a call from a mother on the way in with her son. He was mauled by an unidentified animal."

Abe stumbled slightly as he looked back at Winona, thinking, *Another animal attack? What the hell is* out *there?*

He faced front and walked toward all that wet, spattering red.

Grandma whimpered in the passenger seat as Bob Berens drove up the hill to the hospital. Long accustomed to her whimpering, he barely heard it. He focused his attention on the talk station that was playing on the radio—KGO from San Francisco—but as usual, he was unable to tune Grandma out entirely. His window was down, and the warm evening air hit his face as he chewed a stick of Juicy Fruit.

"If only I could afford to go to the sanitarium," Grandma said. "I'd feel so much better there. They'd treat me well, take care of me."

"It hasn't been called the sanitarium for a long, long time, Grandma," Bob said. "It's Sisters of Mercy Hospital."

"It's *still* the sanitarium," she said testily. "Sister White was treated there. She died there."

Bob expelled a burst of breath from his nose. "Guess they didn't treat her too well, huh?"

Grandma scowled at him. "She was *eighty-seven*. It was her *time*. That was a long life back then. People didn't often live to be eighty-seven in 1915. But she was God's chosen messenger. The Lesser Light. So she lived a long life because she lived for God. Led an unblemished life. Ate healthfully. Did God's work."

Bob tried to narrow in on the talk show again. Grandma

went on and on about Sister White as he drove. It didn't matter that he wasn't listening to her—she didn't care. As she did so often and always had, she quoted Sister White's writings, rambled on about the problems the Seventh-day Adventist prophetess had overcome—being hit in the head with a rock at age nine, comatose for two weeks, disfigured by the injury—and yet she'd gone on to write so many divinely inspired books, to receive so many prophetic visions directly from God, and to lead the Remnant Church to his light. That was one of Grandma's favorite stories about Sister White, the injury early in her life that the church claimed had twisted her features and plagued her health for all her years. Many people claimed that the injury had brought about in Sister White a condition called temporal lobe epilepsy, a symptom of which is often ecstatic religious "visions" and delusions of grandeur, but Adventists didn't like that theory one little bit.

Mom and Grandma had a few pictures of Sister White hanging on the walls of the house. The pictures had been there Bob's whole life, a permanent part of his environment. He'd decided that getting hit in the head with that rock had not disfigured her at all. She'd simply been a very ugly woman, and probably had been an equally ugly little girl. Blaming it on the rock sounded better, of course. It was good marketing.

As a boy, the grainy black-and-white pictures of Sister White had haunted his dreams—her stern, homely face glaring at him from the past, those fat lips pressed together hard in a straight line, sharp eyes accusing him, condemning him. The Lesser Light (as they called her), the cofounder of the Seventh-day Adventist church and prophetess of God, the final and infallible interpreter of scripture and arbiter of doctrine for the church, seemed to glare across the decades into Bob Berens's eyes to let him know how wicked he was, how iniquitous and base . . . how doomed.

Of course, she still haunted his dreams, even though he was now thirty-eight. Sometimes she even haunted his waking thoughts. The stern face, condemning eyes, all those hundreds of thousands of words she'd written, which seemed to exist only to tell him how sinful he'd been his entire life. Sometimes he imagined a great mountain of all her red hardcover books piled on top of him, crushing and smothering him.

Grandma's ramblings were not the result of senility. At eighty-eight, she was sharper than Bob's mother, and probably healthier than he, although she enjoyed whining about her myriad ailments. When she was hit with one of her "spells," she insisted he take her to the emergency room. Doctors familiar with her—and there were several in Big Rock, including those in the ER—always sighed when they saw Marion Berens coming. They knew not only that they would have to tell her, once again, that there was nothing physically wrong with her, but that they would be subjected to her sermonizing and proselytizing, that she would invariably dig some Adventist literature from her purse and insist they take it home and read it. *And when you read it*, she would say, *think about your sins, and about eternity.* Bob felt sorry for Grandma's doctors. His mother's, too, for that matter—Mom had a lot in common with her mother-in-law, although she'd rather have died than admit it.

When the road forked, Bob veered to the left and into the emergency-room parking lot. He got out, went around to the passenger side, opened the door, and helped Grandma out of the car. He held her elbow as she walked slowly and haltingly to the ER entrance. At home, she walked with the speed and steadiness of a woman decades her junior, but now she shuffled along like an old cripple. Bob knew better than to offer to get a wheelchair for her. She preferred to be seen making a tremendous effort to get into the hospital. It made her look more frail and sick, and more courageous, than being wheeled easily through the door in a chair.

When they entered the emergency room, Bob heard muffled shouting and what sounded like frantic activity coming from somewhere. He took Grandma to the front window. The woman on the other side looked harried and distracted. Her name was Winona, and she was a willowy, youthful woman in her fifties who had checked Grandma in on some of their previous trips to the emergency room.

"Hello again," Winona said. "Can I help you?"

Bob slid a chair to Grandma and she slowly lowered her slender frame into it. "Yes," Grandma said, "I need help. I'm feeling . . . well . . . my nerves . . . I'm short of breath and very weak and shaky, and I have a rapid heart-beat, and I . . ."

As Grandma listed off her symptoms, Bob looked beyond Winona and through the half-open door behind her. All the shouting and activity was coming from beyond that door. Bob caught glimpses of quick movement through the opening. Even worse, he saw red splashes of blood on the floor and heard a cry of pain so agonizing that it made him wince. Someone back there was seriously hurt, and it was keeping everyone very busy.

Bob bent toward the window and placed his hands on the counter as he interrupted Grandma. "Excuse me, but you seem to have your hands full back there."

"Yes, we do," Winona said. "We're pretty swamped at the moment."

Bob glanced again at the blood beyond the open door. "They'll probably be busy for awhile, won't they?"

"Oh, yes." She turned to Grandma. "I'm afraid you'll have to wait some time before anyone can see you."

Frowning, Grandma leaned forward slightly and peered through the open door, as if skeptical that something back there could be more pressing than her own needs.

"Grandma, do you want to wait?" Bob said. "It's going to be awhile."

She sat up straight in the chair a moment, thinking. Finally, she slowly stood. "I don't have time to wait at my age. I could go any second. Let's go home, Bobby."

Bob sighed and smiled at Winona. "Thank you," he said as he led Grandma back out. At the emergency-room door, he tossed his gum into a nearby garbage can.

Behind the wheel again, Bob started the car, backed out, and left the hospital to return home. Home to the house where he lived with his mother and grandmother; home to the Victorian-era pictures of stern, condemning Ellen G. White on the walls; home to the bedroom in which he'd played and slept as a little boy, in which he'd masturbated with frantic adolescent energy . . . and in which he still masturbated as a single, middle-aged man with no social life, no love life, no life at all apart from his mother and grandmother and the religion that dominated them.

His younger sister, Rochelle, had left the house years ago to pursue a life of her own—she was married and had an eleven-year-old son. She took every opportunity to point out to Bob how dysfunctional he was, still living at home at his age, contributing little with his part-time job keeping the church clean and helping out Pastor Edson now and then. Rochelle seemed to enjoy pointing that out almost as much as Mom and Grandma did.

Bob wished more than anything that he were not going back to that house, that he were going anywhere but there. But he had nowhere else to go.

All that remained of the most recent patients in the ER was the blood on the floor that had not yet been cleaned up by someone from housekeeping. Adrenaline still pumped through Abe as he tried to come down from the pressure of treating the two severely injured bikers, one of whom hadn't made it, as well as the driver of the moving van, who had gone straight into surgery, and the little nine-year-old boy who had been viciously mauled by an unidentified animal in his backyard just after sunset. He went to the refrigerator in the small, cluttered lounge area in back and got a bottle of water, removed the cap, and drank. Dr. Rodriguez had arrived and was ready to relieve him.

*Another animal attack*, Abe thought again. He'd been at Sisters of Mercy a little more than three months, and the boy he'd just treated was the third animal-attack victim he had seen. That did not include those he had not treated himself, or those that had taken place before he began working at Sisters of Mercy. There had been an inordinate number of animal attacks in the Big Rock area for the last several months, as far as he could make out. He'd heard about them from nurses and other doctors, and there even was a little talk about them around town. No one seemed to know what kind of animal was doing the attacking or if there was more than one such animal, and oddly, no one seemed to care much. The attacks did not happen often enough to raise any real alarm, but at the same time, they seemed frequent enough to Abe to be a concern.

Abe's thoughts were interrupted by a hand on his shoulder.

"You look like five miles of bumpy road."

He turned to Dr. Hugo Rodriguez and smiled wearily. "Rough evening," he said. "Four motorcyclists hit by a moving van, two not so bad, two a real mess, and one died. While we were working on them, a woman brought her little boy in after he was mauled by some kind of animal."

"We have leash laws in this county, dammit," Hugo said as he went to the coffeemaker and poured some coffee into a white mug. "It's about time people started following them." He was in his midthirties, around Abe's age; of medium height; a bit soft and fleshy, with a paunch, light brown skin, and a full head of black hair that usually looked uncombed.

"I'm not so sure this was a dog," Abe said as he removed his white coat and hung it in the locker. "The boy kept saying it was . . . well, *big*."

"So maybe it was a *big* dog." Hugo put some sweetener into his coffee.

"No. He said it was upright."

Hugo kept his back to Abe and said nothing a moment as he stirred his coffee. Finally, he turned slowly as he took a sip. "That's a pretty strange dog, Abe."

"Yeah, that's what I mean. It couldn't be a dog, if it was upright."

"What kind of animal around here walks upright?" He smirked. "Have we got chimps on the loose, or something?"

"Chimps don't growl. At least, I don't think they growl the way the boy said *this* animal growled. I was thinking a bear, maybe."

"Haven't been any bear sightings around here in a long time that I'm aware of. Not since I've been here, and that's seven years." He winked joshingly. "Maybe it was Bigfoot. Where did it happen?"

"In the backyard of a house over on Sutter, in the Cooper Heights neighborhood. The boy had forgotten to feed his dog, so he went out after dark to do it. The yard is fenced, with a patch of woods backed up against it, but there's a narrow segment of the back fence that's broken down near the doghouse. The boy was feeding his dog when something—this animal, whatever it was—reached through the opening in the fence and tried to pull him through it."

Hugo tilted his head back slightly and frowned. "So he didn't actually *see* the animal."

"Oh, he saw it. The mother said there's a light that

shines over the yard from the back of the house, so visibility wasn't bad. And this thing pulled him through that gap in the fence. By the legs. The dog saved him. The boy said the thing's arms were hairy, the hands clawed, but it was standing up. It tore up his—"

"Arms? *Hands?*"

Abe shrugged. "That's how the boy put it. It tore up his legs pretty bad, ripped his pants to shreds. Lost a good deal of blood."

"So maybe it wasn't an animal," Hugo said. "Maybe some guy in a, uh . . . I don't know, a gorilla suit?" He smirked again.

"He said it smelled like an animal. It stank." Abe took another drink and put the cap back on the bottle of water. "You notice a lot of animal attacks around here, Hugo? In Big Rock?"

Hugo shrugged. "Dog attacks, mostly. Like I said, people don't follow the leash laws. Read a letter to the editor about it just the other day in the paper, people complaining about it. It's a problem. What became of Seth tonight? Why isn't he here?"

"Nobody knows. He didn't call, nobody can reach him. Just disappeared tonight."

Hugo chuckled as he put his stethoscope around his neck. "That Seth. Probably found a woman he couldn't resist. That guy gets more pussy than a toilet seat. He'd blow off anything for some tail. He'll miss his own funeral getting laid."

But Abe wasn't so sure. He'd been worried about Seth all evening, wondering where he was that he couldn't call in to say he wasn't coming. He carried a cell phone that was always on—wouldn't want to miss a booty call from some nurse he knew, or a cute young lab tech. But he simply didn't strike Abe as the type to miss work for a little nookie. He got all of that he wanted on his free time.

"I think I'm going to stop by his house on the way

home, see if I can catch him there," Abe said. He said good night to Hugo and left the room. On his way out, he passed a phlebotomist named Susan Pike, who had recently dated Seth for a stretch.

"Susan, got a minute?"

She turned to him and smiled, a pretty twenty-something with short brown hair and a pixie face. "Hi, Dr. Dinescu."

"Tell me, have you been in touch with Seth lately?" he asked.

"Not in the last week or so. I mean, I've seen him around, but we haven't gotten together in awhile. Why?"

"He seems to have disappeared. He didn't show up for work tonight, and no one can reach him. Any idea where he might be?"

Her smooth forehead wrinkled a little. "That's not like him."

"No, it's not. I thought maybe he'd mentioned something to you about going out of town. Maybe he forgot to tell anyone here in the ER."

"No, he hasn't said anything. I can't imagine him going on a trip without making arrangements first."

He shook his head. "No, I can't, either. Well, thanks, Susan."

Abe left the hospital and walked into the warm, clear summer night. He drove his SUV down the hill and across town, then up another hill to Sunset Terrace, where Seth lived. He went slowly up the long drive to the house that huddled in the shade of a dense cover of trees and eased to a stop.

Seth's hog was parked at the edge of the front yard, but the garage door was closed so Abe couldn't see whether or not his old, but pristine, cherry red Mustang was there. It would be very unusual for Seth to leave his Harley out of the garage if he went somewhere. He killed the engine and got out, closed the door. He looked around as he went up the front walk. A warm breeze sighed through the trees, and a dog barked in the distance. The porch light was not on and the front windows were dark. He felt a tension in his gut, like the clutching tightness that came just before the pain of a cramp.

He stepped up on the covered porch, went to the door, and pushed the bell. He heard its muted ring inside the house, then listened for movement, for footsteps heading toward the door. He heard nothing, even after several seconds had passed.

"Seth?" he called, then knocked hard on the door. It hadn't been completely closed and swung open a few inches from the force of his knock.

Abe stopped breathing. The silence of the house was like a sonic boom in his ears.

"Seth?" he called again, and his voice was deafening.

There was no response, no sound but the gentle blowing of the trees.

He reached inside the door to the right and found the light switch, flipped it up. The foyer light came on. A heavy sense of dread settled over him as he stepped inside. Abe reached into his pocket and removed his cell phone, ready to call 911.

He went through the empty kitchen, down a hall to the living room. There was no sign of life. His dread was joined by a cramping feeling of urgency. As he started up the stairs, he found himself clutching his cell phone in a fist and relaxed his grip before it broke. In spite of his sense of urgency, he moved slowly up the stairs, held back by the weight of his dread. He tensed when he caught a whiff of a familiar odor. It was the same odor that had tinged the air in the emergency room that night, but then it had been fresh. The odor in Seth's house was stale, which made it worse. Just before reaching the landing, he called out Seth's name again. No response.

The smell of blood filled Abe's nostrils.

At the top of the stairs, he looked down the hall and saw something on the floor, something smeared and splattered on the walls—red, a great deal of red. A frame that held several family photographs had fallen from the wall to the floor. The red was splashed and splattered on the walls. Along with the blood were four long trenches that had been cut through the pale, creamy wallpaper and into the plaster. The cuts in the wall formed a curved, downward-sweeping arc.

Frowning, Abe squinted slightly, trying to make out the thing on the floor. It looked like a pile of objects coated in red. Blood, of course—he recognized blood when he saw it and smelled it. But there was . . . *so much*.

"Seth," he said in a quiet, hoarse voice as he slowly advanced toward the remains. He did not call the name out this time—he knew no response would come—but said it with a note of sadness. His mouth was dry and his heart kicked hard against his ribs.

It was, indeed, Seth Fulton. Abe recognized the man's face—the half of it that remained on the severed head, anyway.

As a low groan escaped his chest, he opened the cell phone, turned it on, and punched in the three numbers.

# CHAPTER FOUR

*Ending the Day*

"You're in 309, here in the main building," the woman at the motel's front desk said. She was in her fifties, shapeless in her black jersey and stretch pants, dark roots showing in her unruly bleached hair. Her cigarette-harsh voice sounded bored. "The elevator's behind you. Take it to the third floor, turn right out of the elevator, and the room'll be on your left a few doors down." She handed him the key. "Welcome to the Beachcomber Motor Lodge. Enjoy your stay."

Karen and Gavin carried their bags through the small lobby, with its potted plants, shelves of maps and brochures, and posters advertising local restaurants. In the cramped elevator, Karen turned to Gavin. He looked as tired as she felt. There had been a long delay with the wedding rings Burgess had ordered for them, and they'd left Esalen later than planned. They'd read on the flight—Burgess had provided them with several reference books that covered werewolf mythology and answered any questions they might have about lycanthropy. Although Karen had offered to take the wheel of the black Cadillac Escalade Burgess had provided them, Gavin had insisted on driving the rest of the way from Eureka to Big Rock.

"You as tired as I am?" Gavin said as the elevator slowly rose.

"At the moment, my body is taking a nap," Karen said. "When this elevator stops, I don't know if I'll be able to move."

When the doors slid open, they left the elevator and went down the hall, and Gavin unlocked their room, reached in, and flipped on the light. Karen stepped inside and looked around.

It was what she'd expected from the Beachcomber Motor Lodge—an ugly, wheat-colored carpet, cream walls, a king-size bed and two nightstands, an assembly-line painting of a fishing village on the wall, a table, two chairs, a dresser with a TV on it and a mirror over it, and a small alcove with a sink and mirror connecting to the bathroom, which had a shower and no tub.

"I know we both need some sleep," Gavin said, "but I'm going down to the SUV to get the rest of the bags first. I don't want to leave those weapons in there any longer than necessary, and we should look them over. Burgess's rundown was pretty quick and perfunctory. I'd like to see what we've got."

She sat down on the edge of the bed with a sigh, then said, "What we've got is enough weaponry to storm a terrorist cell. I don't know whether to be glad he's got us covered or scared shitless that he thinks we might *need* all that firepower."

"I'd suggest a little of both. Be right back."

After Gavin left the room, Karen flopped back on the bed with her arms spread at her sides. As she fingered the unfamiliar wedding ring on her finger, she wondered about the sleeping arrangements during their stay at the motel. They didn't have much choice—there was nowhere to sleep but the bed, so it looked like they were going to be sharing it. It wasn't a problem, she didn't mind sleeping

with him. In fact, she wouldn't mind doing more than
*sleeping* with him, except that they worked together and . . .
something else.

Gavin was a nice guy. Intelligent, funny, compassion-
ate. He wasn't exactly ugly, either. She found the strong
features of his chiseled, somewhat angular face very appealing, was drawn to his thick black hair with its strands
of silver glinting in the light, and had already given
thought to kissing the full lips of his slightly uneven
mouth. He was tall and fit, quite attractive. But whenever
relationships or dating or marriage came up in their conversations, a weariness seemed to fall over him as if the
subject made him tired, and a little sad. He'd been married twice. The first time was an early, ill-advised marriage in his romantic and impetuous youth that had lasted
not quite three years. The second was more mature and
had lasted twelve years, until he learned that he was the
only one in his circle of friends and family who did not
know that his wife, Jan, whom he so dearly and blindly
loved, had been spreading her legs for nearly everything
with a functioning penis for most of their marriage. As
far as Karen could tell, he had not dated since his divorce
and had no interest in doing so. That, combined with her
self-imposed rule against getting involved with cowork-
ers, had kept her from acting on any interest she might
have in Gavin Keoph beyond their professional relationship.

She closed her eyes and found herself drifting off into
a pleasant sleep, until the door opened again and Gavin
came in with two black suitcases. Karen got to her feet
and yawned, stretching her arms over her head as Gavin
put the suitcases on the bed and opened them.

One contained two sinister-looking black Uzis and a
lot of ammunition, and the second contained more ammunition. Burgess had even unexpectedly provided them

with plenty of ammunition for their own sidearms—Karen's Taurus 9-millimeter compact and Gavin's .40-caliber Glock—with a note that read, "Just so you'll know I have your safety and best interests in mind. Use them in good health." All the ammunition, for the Uzis as well as their sidearms, was made of silver.

"Well, at least he's taking care of us," Karen said.

"Seems that way," Gavin muttered, inspecting one of the Uzis. "But I'm not so sure he's thought ahead. There's a lot of ammo here, but Uzis eat bullets at the speed of sound, and . . ."

When he didn't continue, Karen said, "And what?"

He shrugged. "Nothing. I'm too tired to be thinking of worst-case scenarios right now." He put the Uzi back in the suitcase, then turned to the second case and removed the boxes of ammunition for their sidearms. "Let's keep these with us," he said, putting them on the dresser. "Never know when we'll need them." He closed and snapped both cases and slid them under the bed.

She yawned again. "I'm ready to turn in. Are you going to mind sharing a bed with me, Gavin?"

Smiling, he turned to her. "Why, Karen. I thought you'd never ask."

Karen's right eyebrow rose and she lowered her eyelids slightly.

"I'm joking," he said, his smile melting away.

"Hey. Don't look so offended," she said, trying to hide another yawn. "Under different circumstances . . . I mean, absent a working relationship . . ."

He smirked. "I'm going to take a quick shower. We should get up early and take a look around this burg." He took a few things from his suitcase, went into the bathroom, and closed the door.

Karen opened her case, changed into a pair of shorts and a tank top, hung her clothes in the closet, and got into bed. She was asleep before Gavin turned off the shower.

He stood under the hot stream of water and thought about getting into bed with Karen. He was an adult; he could handle it without a problem. At the same time, though, it had been a long while since he'd been with a woman, since he'd had a warm body beside him under the covers. It had happened only once since his marriage ended, and it had not gone well at all. In spite of the divorce, he'd been unable to shake the feeling that he was being unfaithful to his wife. And once he got beyond that, the possibility that a relationship might develop with the woman he was with— a pretty and eager, if inebriated, brunette named Ruth, whom he'd met in a bar—frightened him, because after Jan's massive betrayal, he wasn't sure if he was capable of trusting anyone again. It had not been an enjoyable experience, and aside from patronizing the occasional prostitute, he hadn't tried again since.

He found Karen attractive—sometimes distractingly so. He remembered seeing her for the first time as they'd waited for the elevator in the Beverly Hills Hotel, both unaware that they'd been summoned to Martin Burgess's room for an interview. As he looked at her standing there, so confident and beautiful, his first thought had been, *Damn, if only I were still single.* Then he'd remembered that he *was* single—the divorce had gone through—and he'd found that fact so depressing that he'd been unable to speak to the lovely woman beside him. He and Karen had worked together a couple of times since then, and they'd stayed in casual touch between jobs. He often wondered if she'd ever noticed him eyeing her when she wasn't looking, admiring that intelligent, striking face, that long, shapely body.

Gavin had been torn up by what had happened to Karen during their first job together. He'd been stunned by how quickly she'd snapped back from it—or had seemed to, at least. He had no doubt the vicious experience had left deep emotional wounds, and that was one of the reasons he'd been so reluctant to act on his attraction to her. He had no way of knowing how damaged she'd really been, other than what she'd told him, and one of the first things he'd learned about Karen Moffett was that she put up a strong, confident front. He knew that however well she claimed to be holding up after the horrible things that had been done to her, it was not necessarily the whole truth. And now she was willing to walk into another of Burgess's bizarre assignments—one in which people had already died—in spite of what had happened before. She had tremendous strength, no doubt about that. He suspected she was stronger than he. His experience with the vampires had not been nearly as horrific as Karen's, but it had been enough to traumatize him . . . and enough to stir some serious butterflies in his stomach over the possibility of encountering werewolves on *this* job, although he'd never admit it.

He scrubbed up a lather, washed his hair, rinsed clean, and turned off the shower. Steam billowed in the room like a fog. After drying and putting on a T-shirt and shorts, he left the bathroom and found Karen breathing softly in sleep. He took his alarm clock from his suitcase, set it, and got into bed. She stirred a little, but did not wake. He propped himself up on an elbow and enjoyed for a long moment the luxury of being able to watch her without the chance of being caught. Then he rolled over, turned out the light, and went to sleep.

From the partially open bathroom door came the glow of the light Gavin had left on in there. He could not sleep in total darkness. Not anymore.

Abe felt the tension leave his body as he sipped his vodka and tonic. Claire had nuked the Chicken Parmesan dinner, which she'd cooked for him hours ago, and he'd eaten it

after his first cocktail. Normally, he had only one drink after work, every now and then two. He was on his third,
and he suspected it would be his last . . . unless he found he
needed a fourth.

The emergency room at Sisters of Mercy typically was
not very busy. Even when a bad case came in, it was just
one. That night had been the most stressful and bloody
experience he'd had since starting work at the hospital.
But finding Seth's gory remains had been far worse than
anything that had happened at work. As he called 911 on
the landing of the stairs in Seth's house, Abe's tired bones
had ached even more with the anticipation of what he'd
thought would be a lengthy and tedious encounter with
law enforcement. But he'd been surprised when that had
not happened.

Now he was slumped on the couch in sweatpants and a
T-shirt, legs splayed, staring dull eyed at a documentary
on the television about meerkats, the volume low. The
only light came from the television screen and the archway that led to the dining room and hallway. He had his
left arm around Claire, and she leaned her head against
his shoulder as they talked quietly.

"Illy and I went to the mall today," she said. "I found a
new cover for the porch light. Did you notice it when you
came in tonight?"

"I'm sorry, honey," he said. "About the only things I
noticed tonight were how delicious dinner was and how
nice your ass looked in those new jeans."

She laughed breathily through her nose.

"You got the porch light cover on okay?" he said.

"Of course, no problem at all."

"You're so handy. You don't need me around here."

"My ass needs you."

He smiled, sipped his drink. "Did Illy get a smoothie at
the mall?"

"Every time. She's crazy about those strawberry smoothies, just sucks 'em right down. I'm going to have to start making them for her here."

Illy was Abe's maternal grandmother, Ileana Kobori, who had brought him to America from Romania when he was a boy. At eighty-five, she was still quite healthy and sharp, and fiercely independent. She lived in the guesthouse behind their home and had gone to bed before Abe arrived.

Abe and Claire said nothing for a few minutes and watched the meerkats. He stroked her upper arm and she cuddled her head against him, placed a hand on his thigh.

"Are you sure you're all right?" she said, almost whispering.

He sighed. "I'm okay. Wish I could say the same for Seth."

After calling 911, Abe had walked out of Seth's house numbly, unable to feel his legs, and had stood trembling on the porch for awhile. It was a warm, still summer night filled with chirping crickets and the sounds of cranky frogs. Abe had crossed the yard, got into his Navigator, and waited until he saw the lights of the sheriff's-department cruiser coming up the drive. He'd gotten out and squinted when the cruiser's searchlight came on in an explosion of white. The cruiser stopped, the door opened, and a single deputy got out and slowly made his way toward Abe. He identified himself as Deputy Maurice Eckhart, a pear-shaped fellow whose khaki uniform apparently had not been let out in a while, with little crow's-feet springing out on each side of the shirt's buttons as they strained against his belly. The lower half of his jowly face worked back and forth on some chewing gum. He moved in that slow, unhurried, unworried manner all cops seemed to have, especially in small towns. Abe approached him, introduced himself, and explained the situation, while the deputy scribbled occasionally in a little notebook in the glow of the searchlight.

"You didn't call an ambulance?" Deputy Eckhart said. He spoke slowly.

"There's nothing an ambulance can do. He's dead. I mean he's . . . Well, it looks like he's been . . . I don't know, torn apart. Dismantled."

Deputy Eckhart looked up from his notebook and squinted one eye as he chewed his gum. "Dismantled, you say? What's that mean?"

"It means . . . Well, I saw him on the floor in his upstairs hall, and he was . . . there was just a little pile of what was left of him. He'd been taken apart, dismembered from what I could tell, but there weren't . . . It looked as if he wasn't all there."

"Parts of him missing?"

"I couldn't tell you what parts, I didn't look long enough or closely enough."

"You think this was done to him intentionally?"

Abe frowned and cocked his head to the side, thinking, *No, he tore* himself *apart, you dolt.*

Before he could respond to the deputy's idiotic question, two more cruisers arrived. Two deputies got out of one, and a tall, lean man in a khaki uniform and cowboy hat got out of the other. The man in the hat had a black patch over his left eye. He took the lead and walked right up to Abe, offering his hand.

"Sheriff Irving Taggart," he said.

Abe introduced himself as they shook.

The sheriff looked him up and down slowly. He had an air of supreme confidence about him, an invisible strength, a strong vibe of being . . . in charge. Indefinable and undeniable.

"What happened here?" Taggart planted his hands on his hips and listened as Abe repeated the story he'd told Deputy Eckhart. The sheriff nodded gravely as Abe spoke, then asked, "Did you see anyone else here? Inside or outside the house? Hear anything at all?"

"No. In fact, it was dead silent when I got here. Not a sign of life anywhere."

Taggart frowned and nodded some more. "All right Dr. Din . . . Din . . . I'm sorry, what was your name again?"

"Dinescu. Abel Dinescu."

Taggart turned to Eckhart and said, "Did you get that?"

"Yep."

"Okay, good. Thank you, Dr. Dinescu, for calling us, and for coming outside and not wandering around the scene. I appreciate it." He turned to Eckhart. "You get his contact information?"

"Yep."

"Good. We'll be in touch with you if necessary, Doctor. Thanks for your help."

"That's . . . all?" Abe said.

Taggart nodded. "Yes, that's all."

"You're sure?" Abe said. "I mean, don't you want to—"

"No, that's all, Doctor. Really. You can go. Thank you." He nodded, then turned and walked toward the house, followed by the deputies.

Abe had driven home, where he'd called the hospital to tell them about Seth. It had been a relief to sit down to a hot meal. He'd told Claire about Seth slowly over dinner.

As Abe took another swallow of his drink, slumped on the couch beside Claire, he heard the glass door in the dining room slide open, then closed, heard Illy's slightly shuffling steps. She came into the living room and sat down in the club chair near the couch.

"Can't sleep, Illy?" Abe said.

She shrugged. "Not sleeping so well these nights." She was a short, thick woman with a round, sweet face that usually wore a smile. Tonight, her brow was creased in a frown. She wore a pink robe and fuzzy white slippers. Her iron gray hair, tied in back, ran down her spine in a long, thick rope. Her accent was still strong, all these years later.

"Can I get you something, Illy?" Claire said. "You want some tea, or cocoa?"

"Meh," she said with a little wave. "Thank you, but no." She turned to Abe. "Why you come home so late, Abel? They working you too hard at that hospital?"

He smiled. "No, my relief didn't show up and I had to cover part of another shift. It was very busy. We had a rush tonight."

"A rush? Why so many people sick all at once?"

"There was a bad traffic accident. And then a little boy was hurt. Another animal attack."

Illy's head turned slowly to the television as her frown deepened. She reached up and tugged on her ear, scratched the side of her face, then dropped her hand to her lap. After a long moment, she turned that dark frown to Abe again, tipped her head forward slightly, and said, "Animal attack? A little boy? You mean . . . *another* animal attack?"

"I'm afraid so."

"What animal?"

"I have no idea, Illy. I have to admit, I'm beginning to wonder about these attacks. It just seems strange that they happen as often as they do and no one seems to be able to identify the animal, and . . . Well, it's almost as if no one cares."

Illy's eyes stared into the center of the living room at something distant and invisible. "No one cares," she muttered.

"Come to think of it," Claire said, still leaning against Abe, "I haven't seen anything about it on the local news." She frowned absently at the TV. "Surely animal control is on it."

"You'd think," Abe said.

As he watched the last few minutes of the meerkat documentary, Abe began to notice that Illy was fidgeting in the chair. He watched her lips moving; she was whispering to herself with a look of agitation, lost in thought.

She talked to herself frequently. It wasn't a sign of senility—she'd been doing it for Abe's entire life, and no doubt longer.

"You okay, Illy?" he said.

Her mutterings grew louder and he realized she was speaking Romanian, which she often did when talking to herself. She pushed herself out of the chair and stood.

"I go back to bed," she said. She headed out of the room and continued muttering.

"Good night, Illy," Abe said, and Claire did the same.

The old woman lifted a hand and gave them a wave on her way out. Abe picked up a single word from her mumblings: *moroi*.

When Illy had brought Abe to America as a boy, she'd brought the many superstitions of her home country along with them. The *moroi* were among those superstitions—evil spirits of the dead that oozed up out of their graves in the night, took the shape of animals, and terrorized anyone they encountered, spreading fear and death and chaos. The word made him smile a little with memories of how Illy had frightened him as a little boy with her tales of the *moroi*. Along with her superstitions, Illy had brought to America many of the weapons she used to battle those superstitions. The guest cottage was scattered with religious icons and talismans designed to repel demons and evil spirits. On the wall over her bed hung a beautiful old ornamental dagger that had been passed down to her from her great-grandfather. It had an eight-inch blade of blued steel heavily inlaid with beautiful silver filigree. The handle was a finely-carved crucifix with an emaciated, corpselike Christ whose mouth yawned open in misery. Illy regularly took the dagger off the wall and cleaned it and cared for it, which is why it did not look nearly as old as it was. She claimed it once had belonged to and had been blessed by a bishop who had used it to dispatch the undead creatures of the night that had terrorized his people.

Abe turned to Claire and found that she was looking at the archway through which Illy had passed, frowning.

"Something wrong?" he said.

She looked at him. "Has Illy seemed to you more . . . I don't know, more worried than usual?"

"Worried? About what?"

"I don't know. Something seems to be bothering her. I asked her about it yesterday, and *that* seemed to bother her."

"What did she say?"

"Nothing. She avoided the question."

"Hm. Maybe I should talk to her." He finished off his vodka tonic, crunched a piece of ice between his teeth. He closed his eyes and leaned his head back.

"You should get some sleep," Claire said.

"Exactly what I was thinking." He squeezed her to him, kissed her, then stood and said, "I'm going to bed."

# CHAPTER FIVE

*Preparation H Day*

At midnight on that Friday night, Bob Berens sat at his computer wearing only a T-shirt, masturbating slowly as he watched a buxom brunette woman perform oral sex on a petite, skinny blonde. Bob spent a lot of time masturbating at his computer. Other people had friends and lovers, attended parties, went to the movies, went out dancing or drinking, had things to look forward to and fill their leisure time. But Bob, when he was not caring for his mother and grandmother (which was most of the time), typically sat at the computer and masturbated.

Seventh-day Adventists observed the seventh-day Sabbath, and Friday was known as Preparation Day. Sabbath began at sundown Friday, so the day was spent preparing for its arrival by cleaning the house and doing extra chores to make sure no work would have to be done on the Sabbath. From sundown Friday to sundown Saturday, there was to be no TV watching, no buying or selling or conducting business of any kind, no listening to secular music or reading secular material. However, there always was a great deal of napping, jokingly referred to as "lay activities." Bob had attended Adventist private schools from first grade into college, and back in his school days, he and his friends had referred to Preparation Day as Preparation H Day. It embarrassed him that the joke still made him chuckle all these years later.

The video he was watching on the monitor ended and he scrolled through the Web site's selection, found another that appealed to him, and clicked on it. A redhead and an Asian girl this time.

The day had been tense, as Fridays always were in his house. It had been Bob's experience that Friday brought a certain tension to many Adventist homes. His oldest friend Royce Garver agreed, and back in their boyhood had labeled it "the Friday willies." When Bob's dad was alive, his parents used to shout and fight more often on Fridays. Actually, it was his mother who did all the shouting—Dad always clammed up and did not react, beyond an occasional nod. She would loudly berate him and Bob as she rushed about the house anxiously getting ready for the Sabbath, as if they expected Jesus to drop by for a visit—or maybe Sister White. Bob sometimes imagined the dusty, long-rotted corpse of Ellen G. White standing at the front door with the gray tatters of a decayed old conservative, nineteenth-century dress hanging from her like the skin that was no longer there, her ugly face far uglier than ever, smelling of the mustiness of the grave and the moist, funky odor of earthworms, grinning, maybe with her lower jaw missing, rotten tongue waggling in what was left of her mouth, words garbled and hoarse as she tried to say, *Happy Sabbath!*

As a boy visiting friends, he'd noticed their parents barking at each other more on Fridays, too. Royce had said his had done the same. The Adventists Bob had known had smiled so much when they were around non-Adventists, always setting a shining example for their church, sparkling clean and appearing so healthy and happy. But Bob had found that when they were at home with each other, they were very different. The thickness of the tension varied from house to house, but it was always there.

"It's because they have to be perfect all the time," Royce had said once. "According to Ellen, we achieve salvation through our behavior. It wasn't given to us by Christ's crucifixion; that wasn't enough. We have to *earn* it with what we do and say and eat, and what we think and wear and read and watch and listen to. So the Adventists have to be perfect all the time, even though they're imperfect humans. Who can be happy living like *that*? I mean, the Adventists don't even—" Then, as he usually did at some point while ranting about Adventists, he closed his eyes, raised his hands with palms out, and said, "Ah—ah—ah. Don't get me started."

Royce had been raised an Adventist, but had grown to despise the religion. A talented artist since grammar school, he had gone pro years ago and had done quite well for himself. A longtime fan of horror movies and fiction, he'd developed a strong reputation as a creator of eye-catching covers for horror novels. He'd won awards, and his work was in demand. Members of his strict Adventist family had always disapproved of his tastes, but had clenched their teeth and tolerated him. When he became a professional, however, they'd disowned him, cementing his dislike of the church and making him bitter.

Bob and Royce spoke on the phone a few times a week, had lunch now and then. Royce tried repeatedly to convince Bob he was living under a cloud of fear put there by his Adventist upbringing, that it was destroying his life, and that he'd better get out from under it and away from the cult—Royce always referred to it as a cult, never a church—fast before he had no life left to live. A part of Bob knew he was right, had no doubt about it. But another part, the guilty, afraid part of him that never withered or fell completely silent, always whispered, *But what if they're* right *about everything?*

Bob sighed and flopped back in his squeaky chair, distracted from masturbation by his thoughts. He was so horny, he was driven to do it, *had* to do it—he was *always* horny, it seemed—but he couldn't turn off his brain. He was distracted by guilt, his old friend and constant companion.

A more pleasant distraction lured his attention away from the naked women on the screen: Vanessa Peterman. Beautiful Vanessa, with her thick, long auburn hair . . . breasts generous and round enough to draw open stares even in church . . . the way she sometimes held her mouth, lips pressed upward slightly, just a bit pursed, the spot of skin beneath her lower lip sucked in a little, thoughtful, but as if her thoughts were naughty . . .

Bob's day had begun with a breakfast of Scramblers (instead of eggs) and Veggie Bacon Strips (instead of bacon). Most Adventists didn't eat any meat at all, but all Adventists refrained from any "unclean" flesh like pork or seafood. They were very proud of their "health message," which began in 1863 in Otsego, Michigan, when God showed Sister White a forty-five-minute vision that contained, according to church lore, extremely advanced principles of health and medicine, including the direction to avoid meat, cheese, and spicy foods. It had always made sense to Bob. Within his lifetime, it had been discovered that red meat was harmful to the body and shortened the lifespan. Of course, Royce felt differently. After being cut off by his family, Royce had spent years researching the history of Sister White and the Seventh-day Adventist church, and was always bringing up what he'd learned, throwing it at Bob. He took delight in pointing out the fact that the church taught that it was the only true church and that all the "Sunday-keepers" in mainstream Christianity were just blindly following the Catholic church and its Pope (which Adventism identified as the Beast of Revelation) to their doom. He often referred to Sister White as a drunk or a lush, because she had admitted in her writing an addiction to vinegar, which back then was very alcoholic. He enjoyed bringing up the fact that while she was telling her followers to eat no unclean meats, she herself had a large appetite for oysters. And when the subject of the Adventist health message came up, Royce always said the same thing.

"That vision in Otsego?" he'd said one day at the diner where they ate. Bob had ordered a veggie burger, and that had set Royce off. "You know what God showed her? You know what that great divine revelation about health was? That eating animal flesh stirs the animal *passions* in people and makes them masturbate."

Bob had laughed. "Stop it."

"I'm *serious*. She wrote a pamphlet about it called 'An Appeal to Mothers: The Great Cause of the Physical, Mental, and Moral Ruin of Many of the Children of Our Time,' her first contribution to the great Adventist health message given to her by God. The evils of *solitary vice*, which she claimed caused kidney, liver, and lung disease, cancer, headaches, nervous disorders, memory loss, and of course *death*. And she said *God* told her this *personally*. I've got a copy—I'll show it to you. Of course, these were common beliefs about masturbation in her time and she was just ripping off writers who'd made those claims, just like she ripped off writers for all her *other* books, and even the visions God supposedly gave her. Adventists think they're vegetarian because it's healthy and God wants them to be. These days, most don't know that Ellen said God told her that meat *eating* leads to meat *beating*. And they're *still* hung up on masturbation—which is why you're so afraid you're gonna burn for whackin' your willie. I mean, for crying out loud, if that's so—" Eyes closed, hands up, palms out. "Ah—ah—ah. Don't get me started."

Bob sighed again as he stared at the naked women on his computer monitor. He hated to admit it, but Royce was right. Masturbation was the only sex he had—and it was the source of guilt and fear that ate at his guts like a burning, bleeding ulcer.

"You need to cut back that brush in the backyard," Mom had said over breakfast that morning. "And then fix the lawn mower and cut the lawn before it gets taller than the house. Grandma and I need to go to the store today, so you'll have to drive us."

As she spoke, her voice loud and shrill, Bob kept his head down over his breakfast as he slowly ate. On the radio, the local Christian station played a song about bathing in Christ's blood. Bob was disturbed by the wet mental image it conjured.

Mom said, "You'll have to go pick up my prescription at the pharmacy because I need to take my pills before we go to town, and make sure you gas up the car. If you're too lazy to go out and get a *job* like most men your age, you can at least make yourself useful around here."

Bob heard that a lot from Mom. Every time she said it, a quiet, distant voice somewhere far in the back of his head muttered, *It's not that I'm lazy . . . It's that I don't have the* time *to go out and get a job, Mom. You won't let* me.

"And you need to give me a bath before the Sabbath," she added.

The bath. He didn't think about it anymore. He'd learned how to shut his mind down while he washed her. She'd had a bad back problem for decades that gave her a lot of pain, and as it worsened with time, it made her so unsteady on her feet that she had to walk with a cane. Their bathroom had a bathtub with a showerhead and a curtain. She found it difficult to step up over the tub's edge, impossible to sit down and get up in it, and was unable to move freely enough to properly wash herself. Bob had offered to install safety rails and a gate in the side of the tub that would make it easier for her to get in and out, but she always claimed it was too expensive and refused.

So a few times a week—for years now, though Bob had lost track of how many—he would go into the bathroom with her, start the shower as she undressed, and help her into the tub. He would wet a washcloth, soap it up, and bathe her as she stood naked before him. He would invariably scrub her too fast—"Slow down, this isn't a race," she would say—and have to slow his movements as he ran the sudsy cloth over her loose, pale flesh . . . over the flat, sagging flaps of her breasts . . . over her drooping buttocks and up and down her legs . . . up one inner thigh, then in her groin . . . over the patch of silvering hair— "Make sure you get that good and clean," she sometimes would say—and between the vertical folds of flesh beneath the sagging scoop of her belly. She was the only naked woman he had ever seen in person, the only female body he had touched so intimately.

During one blue-skied teenage summer, there had been a girl a couple of years younger than he, a stubby, homely girl named Gladys, who had sucked him off and allowed him to explore between her legs with his hand, and finally to hike up her skirt and clumsily fuck her behind some bushes at the back of an empty lot in the neighborhood. Gladys hadn't made a sound the entire time, except to breathe through her nose, which was noisy with allergies. Afterward, he'd lost sleep for weeks worrying that she would get pregnant. That had happened once with Gladys, then never again for Bob. The only naked women he saw after that were those involved in the porn industry . . . until he'd begun bathing his mother.

He stayed up until the darkest hours of the morning watching porn online—beautiful young women with smooth, taut skin and pert breasts, slender, shapely legs, and tight asses. Then he stood in the bathroom and slowly moved his hand over his mother's aging naked body with jiggling flesh that hung low. It was depressing, so he tried not to think about it, diverted his mind as he washed her, even closed his eyes occasionally. But it was a body, the only one with which he was intimate, and sometimes . . . sometimes . . .

*No*, he would tell himself, *it's just coincidental, that's all, it's not related, it's not really happening, not for that reason, no, my mother isn't doing that, my mother is* NOT MAKING ME HARD!

He'd spent much of his Preparation H Day clearing brush in the backyard and mowing the front lawn. While passing the mower up and down the lawn, he spent half his time facing across the street, toward the Stewart house. Donny Stewart sat in the front window, as usual: thick and fleshy and pale, slumped in his chair beside the lamp, shoulders sagging, arms draped loosely in his lap, head drooped to one side, mouth hanging open, staring, unmoving. He was almost always there, staring out the window, kept alive by his respirator. Even at night, he sat in the golden glow of the tall lamp beside and slightly behind him, half of his face and body in shadow.

During a couple of passes over the lawn, Bob saw Donny's mother Debra beside him, bent forward, saying something to him, one hand on the top of his head, the other wiping his mouth with a cloth. Donny was nine years younger than Bob and had been in his current condition all his life. He had sustained a high spinal cord injury while being removed from the birth canal, a mistake that had cost the doctor's and hospital's insurance companies a lot of money. The Stewarts had put the money away back then and used it to care for Donny—and he required constant care. The money would ensure that he would be provided for even after his parents were gone. That chair and that window made up the small world from which he watched the larger world, unable to move or speak, communicating only by blinking his eyes as drool glistened on his slack jaw.

*At least he has an excuse*, Bob thought as he pushed the mower. *I'm almost a decade older than Donny, and here I am, in the same place he is—still here, at home, with Mom and Grandma.*

His hands clenched on the handle of the mower, his skin sweaty against the chrome, knuckles milky white. He clenched his teeth until they made crunching sounds inside his head.

And there sat Donny, still as a corpse, in the window. He seemed to be looking directly at Bob, mocking him behind the slack, dead expression he wore, laughing inside at Bob for being even more pathetic than he.

Bob spent the rest of the day driving around, taking Mom and Grandma to town, listening to the religious preaching and music that Mom *always* had to have playing on the radio, and then bathing her. Yet again.

Now he tried to relax and get off at the computer as he watched two beautiful young women writhe and lick and suck each other. But he could feel the hot, fetid breath of guilt on his neck—

*solitaryvice selfabuse chokingthechicken while Jesus watches*

—even as thoughts of the beautiful Vanessa Peterman's long, tall body and beautiful face rose up in his mind—

*with flashes of Mommy's puckered breasts and flabby graying folds*

—and his back stiffened, and his head began to hurt, and suddenly his chest filled with an ache and he felt as if he were about to burst into tears, sob like a baby. He took a deep breath, swallowed hard, made the feeling pass. His erection wilted in his hand.

*Maybe I should just go to bed*, he thought. *Gotta get up for church tomorrow.*

Church . . . which meant he would see Vanessa again.

With a heavy sigh, he pushed his chair away from the table, shut the computer down, and got ready for bed.

# CHAPTER SIX

*Saturday Morning*

Karen and Gavin had a big breakfast in the Seascape Diner near the motel. As he paid the bill at the register in front, Gavin spoke with the hostess.

"We've never been here before and we'd like to see the sights," he said. "Do you recommend anything in particular?"

She was a chubby young woman, blonde hair in a bun, and she gave him a perky, dimpled smile. "Weekends are busy around here during the summer. Just follow the tourists, you'll probably see everything. Turn right out the door, walk up the block, turn right again, then walk a few blocks, and you'll come to Old Town, across from Hallwell Park. There's lotsa little shops, a few art galleries. And in the park you can see the big rock the town was named after."

Gavin thanked her and they left the diner holding hands like the newlywed couple they were supposed to be. The morning was cool with a gray fog shrouding the sunlight, but that would burn off soon and the August heat would settle in. It was an attractive and clean old town. They followed the directions given by the hostess and ended up on a street with old-fashioned Victorian-style streetlamps spaced out along the edge of the red-brick sidewalk. The shops were open and busy with browsing tourists. Across the street, jutting up from the ground in the park, they could see the enormous rock after which the town had been named.

"What exactly do you suppose we're looking for?" Karen asked.

"It seems pretty unlikely that we'll find any, um . . . werewolves window-shopping on the street." Gavin found it just as difficult to say the word *werewolf* out loud as it had been to say the word *vampire* during their first job for Burgess.

"You think they do all their shopping at night?" Karen said.

"They probably shop online."

"Hm. I wonder what kinds of things werewolves would shop for."

"Lots of grooming equipment, I'd think."

"Yeah. They probably go through a lot of combs and brushes. I wonder if they use hair product."

They were whistling past the graveyard, and they both knew it—making jokes about something they hoped never to encounter.

They wandered through an art gallery, an antique shop, then into a bookstore called Shelfspace. A fat gray and white cat slept in the window surrounded by books. They slowly made their way toward the back, passing a wall of Martin Burgess's novels. Karen picked up a couple of mystery novels, then they made their way back to the front and she placed the books on the counter at the register, along with her credit card.

The cashier was a slender, effeminate man in a short-sleeved mauve shirt and black slacks, with a friendly manner and ready smile. He wore a badge on his shirt that read, "I'M CECIL—HOW CAN I HELP YOU?" As he began to ring up Karen's purchase, he said, "Are you visiting Big Rock?"

"Yes," Karen said, smiling. "Tourists."

Sliding an arm around Karen's waist, Gavin added, "We're on our honeymoon."

Cecil immediately forgot about the transaction and put down the book he'd just scanned. His mouth dropped open with a gasp and he clapped his hands together. "Congratu-*lations*! That's *won*derful! Where are you from?"

Karen said, "Los Angeles," and Gavin said, "San Francisco," at the same instant.

Cecil's smile faltered a little as his eyes moved back and forth between them.

"Well, *I'm* from Los Angeles and *he's* from San Francisco," Karen said.

Gavin took the opportunity to say, "We're considering moving here."

"To Big Rock?" the cashier said. His smile returned in force. "Well, we'd certainly love to have you."

"Is it a good place to start a family?" Gavin said.

"Well, I'm not a parent, but we have a lot of families here. It's a very family-oriented town."

"What's the crime rate like?" Gavin said.

"Crime?" He put a hand on his hip, cocked his head to one side and thought a moment. "It's not bad. I'm not saying it's *perfect*, but I think the town has done a good job of keeping things safe."

"What about animals?" Karen said.

Cecil's slender eyebrows, carefully plucked, rose as he turned to her. "Animals?"

She said, "I heard something about animal attacks. Know anything about that?"

The eyebrows slowly lowered and huddled together in a frown. He spoke more quietly and slowly than before. "Animal attacks? What kind of animal attacks?"

Karen shrugged. "I don't know, actually. That's why I'm asking."

Gavin picked it up from there. "Someone at the motel said something about some animal attacks in the area, but they weren't specific. Have you heard about that?"

Cecil's long, skinny arms slowly folded together across his narrow chest as he chewed on the inside of his cheek. "Really? Animal attacks, huh? What motel?"

"We're staying at the Beachcomber," Karen said. "They said people have been hurt in recent months. Some badly. By animals. Is that true?"

Still frowning, Cecil shook his head and said, "Well, I can't say that I've heard about any animal attacks." He dropped his arms at his sides, then continued ringing up Karen's books. Before handing her credit card back, he took a quick look at it, one brow arched. "I'm pretty good at paying attention, and I haven't seen anything in the news, nothing in the papers." He handed her the receipt to sign, then put the books in a small paper bag with handles. "If they were staying at the motel, they must not live around here. Maybe they were referring to another town, or something." He slipped a receipt in the bag, handed it to Karen and smiled. "I hope you enjoy your honeymoon here."

They thanked him, said good-bye, and headed out of the store.

Cecil snatched up a pen and a scrap of paper and quickly wrote down the name on the credit card: Karen Moffett.

"Ida," he said, lifting a hand to beckon a coworker. "Could you handle the register for a second?"

"Sure," Ida said. She came over and stepped behind the counter.

With the scrap of paper in one hand, Cecil removed a cell phone from his pocket as he went to the back of the store. He stepped into a small, cluttered office and closed the door, flipped the phone open, hit a button, and put it to his ear. He listened to the ringing and frowned down at the name on the paper. When a voice answered, he said quietly, "Hi, this is Cecil. Over at Shelfspace. Um, look . . . Something just happened here and I thought I should tell somebody. . . ."

Jeremiah stood before Sheriff Taggart at the top of the stairs that led down to the basement in the house that had belonged to car salesman Marvin Cooper.

"*Who* said this?" Taggart said, cocking his head, right eye squinting.

"Cecil. He's the manager at the bookstore in Old Town, Shelfspace. He says they just left the store."

"And they were asking about animal attacks?" Taggart said, his voice dropping as he frowned.

Jeremiah nodded. "Honeymooners staying at the Beachcomber."

"And he called . . . why, again?"

Jeremiah shrugged. "Something about their questions bothered him. He said they sounded more determined than curious, that they asked the questions too quickly."

Taggart nodded slowly, thought a moment, his frown deepening. "I want you to look into this for me yourself, Jeremiah. Go to the Beachcomber, toss their room. If you want, I'll call ahead and let the hotel know you're coming. See what you can find out about them. Then call me and fill me in."

"Of course. Right away." Jeremiah turned and walked away without hesitation.

Just outside the store, Gavin leaned toward Karen's ear. "Did you notice that?"

"I did. He was *not* comfortable with our questions." She took a cigarette from her purse and lit up.

"And he made a point of taking a closer look at your credit card. I'd bet good money he memorized your name. Maybe wrote it down after we left."

"So he could pass it on to someone? Who?"

They walked aimlessly on the sidewalk as they talked. Gavin kept glancing at her cigarette.

"Can I have a drag of that?" he said.

She rolled her eyes, reached into her purse, and produced another cigarette and a lighter. "Here, smoke your own."

Gavin lit up.

"You're a lousy quitter," she said, taking her lighter back.

"I've been called worse."

After a moment, Karen said, "Maybe we're just being . . . hypervigilant."

"Or maybe the topic of animal attacks makes people uncomfortable around here. Maybe we should bring it up with a few more people."

They came to the corner of the block and stood on the edge of the sidewalk, waiting for the light to turn green.

"Let's try that toy store across the street," Karen said. "I love toy stores."

"Okay. Then we should get out of here. This is the tourist-trap section of town. We want to mingle with the residents, the people who know what's going on around here. The best place for talky locals is a neighborhood bar. Maybe we can find one this afternoon."

The light changed and they stepped off the curb and into the street.

A large white pickup truck with a camper shell sped noisily around the corner without slowing. As Karen clutched Gavin's arm and pulled him backward with her, out of the truck's way, she noticed the driver, a round-faced, bearded, middle-aged man with uncombed, uncut dark hair. He looked . . . distracted. Even a little afraid. He was not aiming at them, wasn't even aware of them until the last moment. Other pedestrians around them backed up just as quickly. One of them shouted an obscenity and another said, "That *idiot*!"

"It's a small town," Karen said, "but the drivers are no better than in the city."

They crossed the street and headed for the toy store.

"Shit!" George Purdy shouted when he realized how close he'd come to taking out a group of pedestrians on the way around that last corner. His hands already had been trembling on the wheel, his heart fluttering a little in his chest, because he was so afraid of being recognized by someone, by the wrong person, by *anyone*—and then he'd rounded that corner and there they were, some people in the crosswalk, and he'd nearly screamed.

He hadn't come into town in over two months. He hadn't wanted to come today, but he'd needed supplies. Saturday seemed like a good day. There would be tourists everywhere, bustling activity and busy sidewalks. Daylight would give him a feeling of safety . . . even though he knew he was not safe. Not in Big Rock. Not anymore.

George let up on the gas pedal, took a few deep breaths, and forced himself to calm down. He'd gotten everything he needed and was ready to head back out of town and up to his cabin. He would feel better once he was out of Big Rock again. Passing the town limits would not erase his fear, but he would feel a little better.

He kept glancing at the speedometer to make sure he stayed at or a little below the limit. That had been his problem earlier—he'd gotten distracted by his fearful thoughts, had allowed his foot to get too heavy on the pedal, and had nearly hit those people in the intersection. He had to be more careful. If he were pulled over for a traffic violation . . . Well, he'd be finished if that happened, and he knew it.

He braked for a stop sign at a four-way stop. To his left, a sheriff's cruiser pulled up to the intersection and stopped a moment later. George looked at it peripherally, without turning his face to it. He recognized the deputy at the wheel in dark glasses—Phil Merrick, a widower in his thirties with a couple of kids. He remembered the torn body of Merrick's wife in the morgue after her car accident a couple of years ago.

George froze up for a moment, paralyzed with fear. So much in his life had become uncertain since January, but George *knew* the cops were dangerous, from the phony sheriff on down. That was a certainty.

The deputy turned his head slightly, aimed his dark glasses directly at George. He nodded once, gesturing for George to take his turn and drive through the intersection. George lifted his foot from the brake, pressed it to the gas pedal. The truck moved forward, but in his fear, George had no sense of his own speed. Was he going too fast? Too slow? He drove through the intersection, past the cruiser, eyes front, knuckles pale as he clutched the wheel. He felt himself relax as he put the intersection behind him. But he tensed again when he looked in the side mirror and saw the cruiser turning to follow him.

"Oh, Jesus," George breathed.

Deputy Merrick's black sunglasses seemed to fill the side mirror as the cruiser kept pace with George's truck.

It was impossible to tell who had been turned and who hadn't, but George knew the sheriff's department was a threat. It seemed impossible that his friend Arlin Hurley had been sheriff just seven months ago. George and Hurley had not been terribly close, but they'd had a good working relationship. Hurley and his wife Ella had invited George over for a couple of barbecues, and he'd enjoyed their company. Hurley had been a good guy, a good sheriff, and George had trusted him. George's job as deputy coroner seemed eons in the past, a life led by another person he'd heard about secondhand from someone else. It no longer seemed to have been *his* life. But it had not been long ago that it all had unraveled.

Things had gone bad in January with that smelly, naked

corpse that had come into the morgue on a stormy night, its left eye missing from its socket. It was a rapist who had attacked a local woman whose car had broken down beside the road. The woman had killed him during the struggle, had driven a dirty old corkscrew she'd found on the ground straight into his left eye. The rapist was dead, there'd been no doubt about that. And yet it had gotten up and walked out. George hadn't *seen* it walk out, but it soon became clear that it had, and after that, things had gone downhill fast. The animal attacks . . . the mangled, torn corpses . . . and then the arrival of that strange, badly scarred man who claimed to be a werewolf hunter, Daniel Fargo. The stranger was hunting werewolves in general, but one man in particular—the dead man who had walked out of George's morgue. The idea that Big Rock had become infested with werewolves was one thing coming from the odd stranger with his scarred face, but when Hurley had become convinced, George began to worry. Hurley had been a reasonable, calm, clear-thinking man, the kind of guy George had listened to, taken seriously. So when *he* started saying there were werewolves in town, George had listened. Closely.

Now Hurley was dead. A *lot* of people were dead. Hurley and several of his deputies had died in an explosion and fire that had taken place in an old abandoned house. That was the official story, anyway. According to the sheriff's department, the house was being investigated for possible drug activity. A meth lab had been set up in there, and while the deputies were investigating, the whole thing had blown sky-high. Although he wasn't sure exactly what had happened, George did not believe *that* story for a moment. There had indeed been an explosion in the old Laramie house on Perryman Road, but George did not believe there had been a meth lab in there. He believed it had been a setup to hide what *really* happened.

He wasn't sure what that was and he had not waited around to find out. Nor had he waited to see what would happen after the deaths of Hurley and all those deputies, after the abrupt disappearance of Daniel Fargo. He'd simply walked away from his life.

When his father died in 2005, he'd left George the family cabin in the mountains above Big Rock. It was secluded and spacious, but run-down. In February, George had poured a large chunk of his savings into quickly building up the cabin, locking it down, and stocking it with food and weapons. Shortly before his death, Hurley had mentioned that, according to Fargo, the old myth of silver bullets effectively dispatching werewolves was true. So George had gone to coin shops in all the surrounding towns and gathered up silver coins and bullion, purchased the proper tools and equipment, and melted the silver down. Then he'd inserted bits of silver into the tips of hollow-point bullets for his .45 automatic and 30.06 rifle, which he kept loaded and ready. He'd been holed up in his cabin ever since, sleeping most of the day and being vigilant at night, starting at the slightest sound, wondering if they would ever find him up there.

It had not been only the deaths of Hurley and all those deputies back in January that had sent George running. It had been the new sheriff, a man who apparently had come from nowhere to take over for Hurley, calling himself the "interim sheriff" until the next election rolled around. He was a tall, slender man with a black patch over his left eye, and George had seen him before. His name was Irving Taggart, and George remembered the sight of him laid out on the table in the morgue with his left eye missing, hairy and bearded, unbathed and stinking, and quite dead. If all the animal attacks and deaths that had taken place in Big Rock back in January weren't reason enough to get the hell out, George decided that having a dead man as sheriff certainly was, and he'd wasted no time in packing up and leaving. He only wished he could go farther away, but he had nowhere to go.

Deputy Merrick's face seemed so stern beneath those big black sunglasses. Unable to see his eyes, George couldn't shake the fear that they were locked on *him*. His heart drummed in his chest and his palms were slick against the steering wheel.

Then Merrick turned right onto another street and disappeared.

George heaved a sigh, his body deflating with relief. He picked up speed for a bit, until he drove past the Seventh-day Adventist church on Crozier Street. The church's parking lot was full, and others parked on the curb as churchgoers made their way into the church, some crossing the street and forcing George to slow. An old green station wagon coming in the opposite direction took advantage of George's decreased speed and turned left in front of him to pull into the church's parking lot.

George told himself he would be back in the cabin again soon, and that made him feel a little better. He never felt safe anymore, but he felt much safer up there locked in his fortress than he felt here in the streets of Big Rock, a town that was no longer peaceful and serene.

# CHAPTER SEVEN

## Church

When the white pickup truck slowed, Bob took advantage of it and turned left into the church parking lot. He eased the car into a slot.

"Stop that, Michael!" Rochelle snapped in the backseat. Bob glanced in the rearview mirror and saw his brother-in-law Mike chewing on a fingernail. Mike sat by the window, with Rochelle beside him and Grandma next to her. Bob's eleven-year-old nephew Peter sat in the rear of the old station wagon. Rochelle slapped Mike's hand away from his mouth. "He won't stop, Mom. What's that stuff you put on fingers to keep kids from biting their nails?"

"Just clear nail polish," Mom said distractedly. "Bob, couldn't you find a space closer to the church so I don't have to walk so far?"

Bob was about to kill the engine, but stopped. "You want me to move?"

Mom rolled her eyes. "What did I just *say*, Bob?"

Sighing, he pulled out of the spot and found one closer.

"I ought to put some of that stuff on your fingers, Mike," Rochelle said. "It'd serve you right, wearing nail polish like a girl. Nail biting is something nervous *children* do."

"Nervous adults do it, too," Mike muttered. He muttered a lot, almost as if he didn't want to be heard. He was a short, bullet-shaped accountant with a bald pate, a fringe of short-cropped brown hair that was starting to gray, and a trimmed beard.

"Nervous, who's *nervous*?" Rochelle said. She'd inherited Mom's shrill voice and manner of speaking, but she had Dad's long face and height—she stood a full six inches taller than Mike. Her blonde hair was long, but she usually kept it pinned up, as it was now. She'd never lost the weight she'd gained while carrying Peter, but still had a figure in spite of her thickened waist. It was just broader than it used to be. "What have *you* got to be nervous about, Michael?"

Grandma said, "He's probably nervous about losing what little hair he's got left."

Bob looked at Peter in the rear of the car. The boy sat with his arms wrapped around his knees, staring out the window, lost in thought. He looked like his father—pudgy, same round, flat face, same dark hair and sad brown eyes.

"Well, what are we *waiting* for?" Mom said, opening her door.

"Peter," Rochelle said. "Get the macaroni salad and go on ahead of us. Go through the multipurpose room into the kitchen and put the salad in the refrigerator."

They piled out of the car. Mom always insisted that they all drive to church together—"Like a *family*," she often said—so it had become tradition for Rochelle, Mike, and Peter to come to the house for breakfast on Sabbath morning before the six of them piled into the station wagon to drive across town.

Bob helped Grandma out of the backseat, then walked slowly between her and Mom to the church. He felt warm and itchy in his charcoal suit from the Men's Wearhouse in Eureka. It was one of two, the other navy blue.

Rochelle complained about the poor state of the parking lot's pavement, Grandma complained about her swollen ankles, and Mom complained about the fact that they were complaining so much on the Sabbath. Bob and Mike walked silently with them up the front steps and into the church while Peter went ahead with his arms wrapped around the big foil-covered bowl of macaroni salad Rochelle had made for the potluck lunch after the church service.

They stopped in the foyer so Mom and Grandma could chat with their old-lady friends and discuss their aches and pains. Bob, Mike, and Peter stood silently as organ music whined reverently from the sanctuary.

Bob spotted Pastor Edson on his way into the sanctuary, smiling and greeting people as he passed. He was a tall man in his midsixties, shaped rather like a bowling pin—wide from the middle on down—with a large head made even larger by a thick shock of wavy silver hair. He had a booming, friendly voice that carried through the foyer as he spoke to members of the congregation. When he saw Bob, Pastor Edson changed his course and headed toward him, his friendly face darkening as he approached.

The pastor leaned close, and his lowered voice lost its friendliness, took on a tone fit for addressing an underling. "Look, Bob, Mrs. Stockton mentioned to me earlier that one of the stalls in the ladies' room had no toilet paper. It caused her some *inconvenience*, if you know what I mean. Now, I've spoken to you about this before. You *have* to make sure the restrooms have paper." He cocked his head and added sarcastically, "Is that too much to ask, Bob?"

"I'm sorry, Pastor," Bob said, nodding. "I'll do better."

"Just make sure it doesn't happen again." Pastor Edson turned to Bob's mother, smiled, and said, "Good morning, Arlene." He turned his smile to Grandma. "Marion, good to see you this morning." He walked away and disappeared through the sanctuary's open double doors.

"Hello, Sheriff!" Rochelle said.

Bob turned to see his sister approaching Sheriff Taggart as he entered the church with his usual group of deputies and friends.

"You look nice today, Rochelle," the sheriff said, smiling.

Rochelle turned to one of the men with the sheriff and her posture changed subtly. Bob watched his sister drop ten years off her age as her eyes brightened and she put on her best smile. "Deputy Cross," she said, her voice dropping in pitch and taking on an uncharacteristic shyness.

Mike had wandered away to chat with a friend and didn't see the change in his wife. Bob frowned, surprised and puzzled to see Rochelle suddenly become so warm and girlish. She stepped closer to Deputy Cross, and they spoke in hushed tones. She had mentioned several weeks ago that the sheriff and his deputies had started coming into the small restaurant where Rochelle was manager, some for breakfast, others for lunch. Bob knew that Sam's Family Diner had become a sort of hangout for the deputies, but he didn't know Rochelle had become so friendly with them—or at least with Deputy Cross.

Bob's attention did not linger on his sister, though. The sheriff's group included Vanessa Peterman, who stopped just inside the church entrance and looked around the foyer. She wore a simple green and white suit, but on her body, even the most modest and understated attire became sexy. She stepped over to another member of the sheriff's group and whispered something to him. Bob kept his eyes on Vanessa while trying not to openly gawk at her like some kind of breathless horndog—but it wasn't easy.

One Sabbath about three months ago, Sheriff Taggart, his companion, and a group of his deputies and friends showed up at church for the first time, and they'd been coming regularly ever since. There were about a dozen of them all together, and they came each week in two groups, then sat together during the service. They attended the potluck lunches after church, the Wednesday-night prayer meetings, and became involved in church activities as if they'd always been regular members. While cleaning the church during the week, Bob often overheard Pastor Edson on the phone or chatting with people in his study, and from his casual eavesdropping, he'd learned that the sheriff had been raised an Adventist, had decided to start attending church again, and had talked some deputies and friends into accompanying him.

"I'm very pleased to have them," Pastor Edson had told his secretary one afternoon while Bob was emptying the waste cans. "Having the sheriff and his deputies in our congregation looks good to the community. It's a plus for us."

However it looked to the community, Bob was just happy that the sheriff had brought Vanessa Peterman with him. He'd never spoken to her and had no plans to; his normal social awkwardness no doubt would be intensely magnified if he were to try to strike up a conversation with her. But he enjoyed watching her, being near her, catching an occasional whiff of her musky perfume as she walked by. He looked forward to it each week.

Bob and his family made their way into the sanctuary and seated themselves in a pew. They went through all the motions—praying, singing hymns, passing the offering plate, listening to the two little girls who sang a duet for special music. Finally, Pastor Edson began his sermon.

"'And lo, the angel of the Lord came upon them,'" he read from the Bible, "'and the glory of the Lord shone round about them. . . .'" Then his voice boomed through the sanctuary as he read, "'*And they were sore afraid.*'" He looked out over the congregation a moment, letting the words sink in. "When angels appear in scripture, people get scared. They drop to their knees and hide their eyes in fear. These are not the angels we see on Hallmark cards. These are not the angels we see on Christmas trees. They are messengers of the Lord, and they are *scary*!"

Bob only half heard Pastor Edson's voice. He was pleased that his family had chosen to seat themselves in

a location that just happened to give him a good view of
Vanessa in a pew across the aisle, with the sheriff and the
others. He watched her during the entire service, thinking about what it would be like to touch her hair . . . wondering how her skin tasted . . . imagining her without those
clothes. . . .

It was a sin, of course—Rochelle knew that and did not
deny it. She was painfully aware of her weakness. But that
awareness did not stop her.

"Angels are not cute," Pastor Edson said, "because the
Lord God is not cute. God is a force to be reckoned with,
the creator of all things, the beginning and the end, and
when he sends someone a message, it's delivered by a being of his creation that will *get their attention!*"

As Pastor Edson preached his sermon, she looked at
her son and husband beside her in the pew, both of them
staring off at nothing in particular, occupied with their
own thoughts. They had no clue that they saw only one
side of her, the side she thought of as Good Rochelle.
The only people who ever saw Bad Rochelle were the
men with whom she was bad. Those men knew a very
different Rochelle than her family, different even than
the Rochelle her husband saw in the privacy of their bedroom. The Rochelle Mike knew in their bedroom was still
Good Rochelle—occasionally playful, willing to please
him but not interested in anything *too* passionate or un-
conventional, though that seldom happened between
them now. And it had been that way for years. She knew
she could not show her bad side to anyone with whom
she had a close relationship, certainly not to someone she
lived with, like her husband of thirteen years. Bad
Rochelle had always been with her, even when she was a
little girl, and she showed no signs of going away.

She remembered the vibrator her mother massaged her
neck with when Rochelle was a little girl. At the age of

ten, Rochelle had been sitting on the couch after school one day, watching cartoons on TV. Dad was at work, Mom was in the kitchen, Bob was in his bedroom. Mom had left the vibrator on the couch, plugged into the wall socket. Rochelle picked it up, turned it on, massaged her neck awhile the way Mom did. Then she'd dropped it in her lap, and the resulting sensation made her mouth drop open and her eyes widen, as if she were screaming, but without a sound. That night, Mom's vibrator disappeared. Mom never found it again.

Rochelle had developed quite a fixation on that vibrator, which she'd kept hidden away in a dresser drawer into which she'd built a false bottom. Her relationship with the vibrator had led to boys early on—none at the Seventh-day Adventist school she'd attended in nearby Fortuna, but boys from the local public school, all of whom she'd managed to see secretly, away from home, and without her family's knowledge. Good Rochelle and Bad Rochelle remained entirely separate. Bad Rochelle was just as bad as Good Rochelle was good. By the time she married Mike, Rochelle had become expert at hiding what she thought of as "the naughty me," and Mike had no inkling of his wife's other side. She spent most of her time as Good Rochelle, but now and then, Bad Rochelle pushed at the walls of her cell, deep inside, and demanded to be let out to take in some air.

"Artists have shown us angels that are pleasing to the eye," Pastor Edson went on. "But the Bible shows us angels that make strong men tremble and drop to the ground, angels that grip hearts with fear."

As Rochelle sat in church and watched Deputy Harry Cross—he was dark and handsome and so sexily aloof—she thought of the few minutes he and Bad Rochelle had spent together in Cross's cruiser. They'd only made out like a couple of hormone-addled teenagers, nothing more. But she looked forward to doing more with him. Much

more. That very night, in fact. She pressed her thighs together hard as her thoughts became more vivid, and she
felt herself becoming moist.

She was startled out of her reverie by the shrill chirping
of a cell phone. A sign outside the sanctuary asked that
everyone turn off their cell phones and other gadgets before entering, but someone had ignored it.

Seated in the same pew with Deputy Cross, Sheriff
Taggart leaned forward and put a cell phone to his ear.
Rochelle supposed that being the sheriff was a good excuse
for ignoring the sign outside the sanctuary. She watched
as Sheriff Taggart stood, scooted out of the pew, and left
the sanctuary.

"All right," Taggart said quietly into the cell phone as he
stood in the empty foyer. "Go."

"I'm in their motel room," Jeremiah said. "I've found
no identification here, but according to their reservation,
their names are Gavin and Karen Keoph. Their reserva-
tions were made by Cornelius Incorporated in Los Angeles, which has also paid their bill."

"Cornelius Incorporated," Taggart repeated under his
breath, making a mental note to look into it.

Jeremiah said, "Under the bed were two suitcases con-
taining two Uzis and a lot of ammunition."

Taggart's eyebrows huddled above the bridge of his nose.
He whispered, "Uzis? Ammunition?"

"The ammunition is silver."

Taggart's eye narrowed and his chin jutted. "*Silver*," he
said in a breath. He was silent for a long moment. Finally,
he whispered through his teeth, "Fargo. He's got something to do with this. Whoever they are, they're connected to Daniel Fargo. That son of a bitch is hounding
me from the goddamned grave."

"What would you like me to do?" Jeremiah said.

"Well, I sure as hell don't want you to leave them there.

Take the Uzis and the ammo. Then go into Old Town. To the bookstore. Talk to that little pillow biter who called earlier—what's his name again?"

"Cecil Canby."

"Find out which way they went when they left. Then question any other friendlies we have down there in Old Town. See if you can trace the steps of these two and find them. And when you do, don't let them out of your sight."

"All right."

"I don't know what I'd do without you, Jeremiah," Taggart said with a slight smile. "You sure you don't miss your old job?"

Jeremiah's chuckle sounded like twigs snapping. "Working for you is far more enjoyable than staring into people's mouths all day, Sheriff."

"Glad to hear it. Let me know when you find those two."

Bob had been surreptitiously eyeing Vanessa all through the potluck lunch, but she finally caught him in the act as he was finishing his meal. Long banquet tables had been set up in the multipurpose room, and Vanessa sat two tables over from Bob next to Sheriff Taggart. The moment she looked up and caught Bob watching her, Taggart looked up and caught him, too. With an icy splash of embarrassment in his chest and heat on his neck and face, Bob quickly looked down at his plate. It took almost a full minute to muster the courage to look up again. Vanessa and Taggart were leaning close, the sheriff talking into her ear, Vanessa smirking. They were both looking at him. Bob looked down at his white paper plate again.

There was still some food left on his plate, but he was full. Before anyone else left a table, Bob stood, took his plate, napkin, and plastic knife and fork to a nearby garbage can and dumped them. He took a stick of Juicy Fruit from his pocket, unwrapped it, popped it into his mouth, then went into the kitchen to begin to clean up. The elderly church ladies who always gravitated to the kitchen when they finally finished eating and talking were always very impressed by the fact that Bob usually had most of the kitchen cleaned up before they got there. It came naturally to him. He was accustomed to cleaning up after everyone at home and cleaning and working around the church, so tidying up the kitchen after potluck lunch seemed only an extension of his part-time job, although he did not get paid for anything he did on the Sabbath.

As soon as he stepped into the kitchen, he came to an abrupt stop. He was met by a warm, pungent smell. His alarm came before he identified the odor, but that followed an instant later. Gas. His eyes went to the gas stove. He did not see the familiar ring of blue pearl-like flames glowing beneath any of the black burners, but he noticed one of the knobs on the front was turned. Someone had not quite turned off the gas. He quickly went to the stove and turned the knob. Most likely one of the old ladies had warmed something on the stove top, then had neglected to turn the knob all the way off. It hadn't happened long ago, because the smell had not gone beyond the kitchen. He went to the window over the sink and slid it open to air out the room.

He washed some empty bowls and casserole dishes, serving spoons and pie cutters. Some of the food remained, and he put the containers in the large stainless-steel industrial refrigerator. All the containers were labeled with tape to identify the owners, who would pick them up on their way out.

Bob stood in the chill that radiated from the refrigerator, the large open door concealing him from the serving window that looked out on the crowded multipurpose room, and arranged shelf space for a couple of large bowls. He turned to get more unfinished food and ran straight into someone standing directly behind him. He inhaled a heady muskiness as he stepped back.

It was Vanessa. She smiled at him, her right arm up, hand resting on the open refrigerator door.

Bob had never stood this close to her, never close enough to smell her perfume so strongly, to see the small mole on the left side of her neck, to see the texture of her cascading auburn hair and the tiny creases in her full lips. He realized his mouth hung open and he snapped it shut.

"You've been watching me," she said, her voice low and husky, just above a whisper. "You don't think I've noticed, but I have. You've been watching me a lot. Haven't you?"

"I—I—I . . . I-yuh . . ."

She smiled and tipped her head forward a bit, looked up at him through thick eyelashes. "You must like what you see, otherwise you wouldn't keep staring so much, would you?" she said. "Bob."

He blinked when she said his name.

"I looked you up in the church directory. Bob Berens." She narrowed one eye and cocked her head. "I think I prefer *Robert*. You're too mature for *Bob*. I hope you don't mind if I call you Robert. Do you? Robert?"

He opened his mouth again, but his throat closed. His gum almost fell out. He shut his mouth and shook his head back and forth slowly.

"So," she said. "*Do* you like what you see, Robert? You certainly watch me enough."

He could not think of a response, and even if he could, he knew he'd be unable to utter it.

"I haven't been able to tell exactly," she said curiously, touching the tip of her forefinger thoughtfully to her bottom lip. "What do you enjoy watching the most, Robert? Huh? What part of . . . me?"

He simply stared at her as his face burned.

Her smile broadened. "That's sweet, you're blushing.

You're too old to blush, Robert. I think you've been spending too much time in this church. I hear you clean it. Is that right?"

A single nod.

"We need to get together someplace other than"—her eyes rolled around to take in their surroundings—"*here*. You're on Belmont Avenue."

He blinked again.

"Your address is in the directory, too." Without taking her eyes from his, she lowered her right arm from the refrigerator door and reached down. Bob gasped when she ran her thumbnail up the zipper of his pants, pressing as she did so, and the vibration against his cock made him grow immediately hard. "I'll be seeing you, Robert," she said. Then she turned and left the kitchen.

He stood there for a long time, the refrigerated air cold on the hot skin at the back of his neck, lips parted, eyes wide. He forgot to breathe for a long time, then finally sucked in a breath with a loud gasp. He felt as if someone had just hit him in the back of the head with a shovel.

*Did that just happen?* he thought.

He knew it did. He could still feel the staticky purr of her thumbnail against his zipper, against his erection. Bob closed the refrigerator and left the kitchen by the back door. He hurried down the corridor to the restroom, went to the back stall, closed and locked it, then dropped his pants and sat on the toilet. He'd masturbated in the church restroom before—always with feelings of deep and disturbing guilt—but never to such a powerful, explosive orgasm.

# CHAPTER EIGHT

*Shadows and Schemes*

The second time Karen saw him on Saturday afternoon, the tall, gaunt, bald man was wandering through the crowd at the Pine County Fairgrounds, which became the Big Rock Flea Market every Saturday and Sunday, except for the week in June when the Pine County Fair was held. It wasn't very busy this weekend. Earlier, someone had told Karen and Gavin that normally there were twice as many people at the flea market, but the crowds had been steadily shrinking in the last few months. It had been a talkative elderly man with a hearing aid.

"Yeah, this place just ain't as busy as it usually is," he'd said. He'd frowned then, thought a moment, and added, "Come to think of it, the streets ain't as busy during the week, either. Hmph. It's almost as if folks just ain't goin' out as much as they used to."

A thin crowd of shoppers wandered over the grounds, walking between rows of booths selling everything from electronics and antiques to pet hermit crabs, dog-eared paperbacks, and secondhand clothes. The smells of popcorn and hot dogs and cigarette smoke blended into a strange aroma that hovered in the hot summer air. A low murmur of chattering voices was punctuated by the occasional shouts of children, and country and western music played from a nearby booth selling stereo equipment.

"I think we're being shadowed," Karen said casually as she and Gavin paused at a table covered with DVDs for sale at discount prices.

"Oh?" Gavin picked up a copy of *Pan's Labyrinth* and examined the text on the back of the case as if he were interested. "Where?"

"Behind us. Right now. About seven o'clock. Tall, skinny, completely bald. Gray sport coat over a pale blue shirt. I saw him earlier when we went into the bar. He was standing across the street. Then I saw him again in the shopping mall. He was in about the same position back then, too. Behind us. Following us, but not looking at us. Like he's doing now. I thought maybe it was a coincidence. This *is* a small town. But I don't think that anymore."

Gavin put his arm around Karen's shoulders and steered her into a U-turn away from the DVD table, past a booth selling clocks, then away from the merchants and into the crowd. He leaned his head close to hers as if to say something to her, his eyes darting around until they found the man she'd described. "Well, it's easy enough to see if it's a coincidence," he said as he directed her toward the parking lot. "It's way past lunchtime, and I'm starving. And I've got a headache from the beer I drank in the bar. Let's go find a place to eat."

As they walked to the parking lot, Gavin took his keys from his pocket. He clumsily and intentionally dropped them, walked on a couple of steps, then turned back and bent down to pick them up. As he did so, his eyes quickly sought out the bald man and found him for a fraction of a second. He grabbed the keys, then they walked on.

"He's making every effort not to look like it," Gavin said quietly. "But he seems to be coming this way." As they approached the Escalade, Gavin thumbed the button on his keychain and the doors unlocked. "While I'm driving, you try to track him to his car, see what he's driving."

Once inside the Escalade, Gavin started the engine. Karen adjusted the side-view mirror so she could keep an eye on the rear of the vehicle. Gavin let the engine idle for a bit.

"See him?" he said.

"Yep. He's a couple rows back, getting into a silver car. Looks like a BMW."

The tires crunched over gravel as Gavin backed out of the parking space. He drove to the lot's exit, checked for traffic, then pulled out and turned left. As he drove away from the fairgrounds, Gavin tossed a backward glance out the side window and saw the BMW slowly making its way out of the parking lot.

"What sounds good for a late lunch?" Gavin said. "Chinese? Italian? Deli sandwiches? A burger?"

With her eyes on the side mirror, Karen said, "See if you can find a place with a salad bar."

Gavin drove through town, looking for a restaurant. "See him?"

"Oh, yeah, he's back there. But he's keeping his distance."

At an intersection, Gavin stopped for a red light.

"He's coming up close," Karen said as she grabbed her purse from the floor. She removed a notebook and pen. As the BMW drew nearer, her eyes moved back and forth between the license plate in the mirror and the notebook as she wrote.

"Can you read it backwards?" Gavin said.

"Yep. Got it."

The light turned green and Gavin drove ahead for another block. He spotted a place called the Blind Dog Bar & Grill. A sign in front read LUNCH BUFFET AND SALAD BAR! He pulled into the small paved lot beside the gray building.

"He just turned down a side street," Karen said.

"He won't go far, I'm sure." He parked the SUV.

They got out, walked along the sidewalk to the front entrance of the restaurant, and went inside.

Coming in from the bright sunlight, the Blind Dog Bar & Grill seemed very dark inside, and it took a moment for their eyes to adjust. The bar was to their left, the restaurant to their right. They were directed to a booth by a hostess, and given ice water and menus by a waitress. A large moose head was mounted on one of the walls. The moose wore enormous red sunglasses and a white cap that bore the slogan I ♥ BIG ROCK on the front. Karen ordered unlimited trips to the salad bar, Gavin a mushroom swiss burger with a side order of fried zucchini, and both asked for coffee.

"Give me the plate number," Gavin said.

Karen removed the notebook from her purse, tore out the page, and handed it to him. As she got up and headed for the salad bar, Gavin took his cell phone from his pocket and placed a call to Burning Lizard Security and Investigations, his company in San Francisco.

"Dudley," he said when a man answered. "Gavin. I need you to run a plate number ASAP."

"Let's have it," Dudley said.

Gavin gave him the number. "I'm on my cell. Call me as soon as you've got something."

There were no windows, so as they waited for their lunch, Gavin got up once and went to the front entrance, looked out the glass door, and spotted the silver BMW parked at the curb across the street and up the block. The side windows were tinted and he could not see the driver. He returned to the table and took his seat. They chatted quietly about nothing in particular as they waited for their orders, each of them looking around and taking in their surroundings.

As their lunch arrived, Gavin's cell phone vibrated in his pocket.

"The car belongs to a Dr. Jeremiah Goodman of Big Rock, California," Dudley said.

Gavin took a pen from his shirt pocket and wrote down the name just below the plate number. "Doctor?"

"He's a dentist in Big Rock," Dudley said.

"A dentist?"

"Yep. Here's his home address."

Gavin wrote down Goodman's address as Dudley recited it.

"You want the address of his practice, too?"

"Sure, gimme." Gavin wrote that down, too. "Anything about this guy stand out? Anything at all?"

"Nope, nothing."

"Thanks, Dud." As he put his cell phone back in his pocket, he said to Karen, "We're being shadowed by a dentist."

"Maybe he wants to make sure we floss after our meal."

"He won't go anywhere. He'll wait for us. Let's enjoy our lunch and let him wait. Then I want to take him on a little trip and see what he does."

In the house that was once owned by used-car salesman Marvin Cooper, Sheriff Irving Taggart gathered in the family room with Vanessa Peterman and several of his deputies. Taggart and some of the others sipped from cold bottles of Heineken, some had soft drinks, while Vanessa nursed a tall glass of ice tea. Some of them sat on the half-dozen chairs and two couches, while the rest stood around as they chatted. Golden Saturday-afternoon sunlight brightened the spacious room through the large windows and French doors. Taggart stood at one of the windows, a dark figure backlit by the sunlight, one hand holding his beer, the other on his hip, elbow jutting.

"Are we going to have to *keep* going to church every Saturday?" Vanessa said, a curl of annoyance in her voice. "Those sermons are torture. A few years ago, an old boyfriend dragged me to a two-hour lecture on the relationship between amino acids and neurotransmitters, and I nearly slashed my wrists. But it was *still* better than those goddamned sermons."

Taggart smirked. "You're not there for the sermons."

"Then why *are* we there, pray tell?" she said. "You told us it was important, but you've never really said *why*."

He dropped his hand from his hip and walked away from the window, perched himself on the armrest of one of the couches. He sipped his beer, then took a deep breath and let it out slowly.

"We're establishing a base," he said. "We're steadily getting a foothold in this community, and ultimately the county. Pine County is the smallest in California and gets very little attention. It's a perfect place for us—a small population, mostly rural. We're taking it piece by piece. We have the sheriff's department. That's given us a conduit to the entire county. In seven months, we've managed to grow some roots here in Big Rock. We have road crews monitoring most of the traffic in and out of town and all around the county. We have several businesses around town, some of them prominent. Some we've taken over completely, others we've infiltrated. We have people in the phone company, particularly linemen who can control communication for us if necessary. We have people in the hospital, some doctors, a good deal of nurses and technicians, a couple in administration, and we're growing there. We're growing everywhere. As we discussed some months ago, we've had to curtail our . . . *needs* a little. No more random raping. Spreading the virus too widely so soon would be counterproductive. On top of that, we now have this latest development to contend with—reproduction. Cynthia was . . . raped . . . by one of us. The result was the First Born. We don't know why yet, we don't understand it. But we're adjusting to it. Now when we fuck outsiders, we risk spreading the virus *and* reproducing. So we're being careful for now, until we're more settled, more established."

Taggart took another swig of his beer, then stood and slowly walked around the room.

"The Seventh-day Adventist church does a good deal of work in the community," he said. "It gives us access to the businesses owned and run by its members, and it has an academy in the area. We've been settling in there the last few months, making friends, getting familiar with everyone. Becoming accepted. You've been getting to know the people at the church, picking out the weakest links. As I told you on the way back from church today, it's now time to close in on those targets. Fuck them, turn them. I'll be having a meeting with Pastor Edson tomorrow morning in his office. I'll introduce myself to him. *Really* introduce myself. Let him know who's in charge now."

"Why the Seventh-day Adventist church?" Vanessa said. "Why not the Baptists, or the Methodists, or Catholics, or *any* church?"

Taggart smiled slightly. "My momma was an Adventist, and that's how she raised me. I went to Sabbath school and church every Saturday as a boy, went to an Adventist school until the seventh grade. They've got schools all over the fuckin' place, you know. Biggest Protestant school system in the world. I *know* Adventists. I know what they believe, how they think. They don't eat meat or smoke or drink— not even caffeine. They don't wear jewelry or dance. They're not supposed to go to movies or read novels or watch TV on the Sabbath. *But* . . . when nobody's looking, they fuck like bunny rabbits. And their state of mind makes them useful to us."

"State of mind?" Vanessa said.

"Religion in general is a kind of brainwashing," Taggart said. "But Adventists take it further. They not only believe in God and Jesus, they also believe the prophecies of a little-educated Victorian-era woman named Ellen G. White to be divinely inspired. In the last twenty years, it's been proven she plagiarized her writings from other writers of her time, that some of her prophecies came from gossip and rumor, and that she behaved *very* differently than she preached. That caused a schism in the church. But to the most faithful, it didn't alter their belief in her. Adventists claim their doctrine is based purely on the Bible, but the fact is, it's based entirely on White's goofy *interpretation* of the Bible, and her writings. They *can't* admit the truth about her, because if they did, their church would collapse. But it's more than that. They believe in her *so* hard that no amount of proof or truth can sway them. Her writings are infallible, her interpretation of the Bible absolute. They don't worship her . . . but they might as well. They call her Sister White and talk about her like she glowed in the dark and crapped daisies. So, you see, they already believe in something *other* than God. They believe totally and completely . . . in a *person*. And an unremarkable person, at that. We can use that weakness to our advantage. If they can be persuaded to believe so completely in someone so obviously flawed and corrupt, then they can be persuaded to believe in anything. When I'm done with Pastor Edson, he'll believe in *me*. And through him . . . we'll have *them*. We'll make the Adventist church in Big Rock a strong base. We can work through it to reach other parts of the community, the whole county, and beyond. We'll make it our own. And that will start right away, with your relationships with some of the members. Use their gullibility and intellectual weakness. Use it well."

Taggart grinned as he lifted his beer in a toast. "To the Seventh-day Adventists!"

While Taggart spoke to the group in the family room downstairs, Ella Hurley sat in a small anteroom reading a book called *Wolves* by Seymour Simon. She had read the book before, but was going through it a second time, more slowly than the first, absorbing the information, thinking about it, studying the photos of wolves in the wild. It was not the only book she'd read about wolves in recent months. Ella was learning—not only about wolves, but about herself, about what she had become.

From the Bible to Jack London, from the Brothers Grimm to Stephen King, from Lon Chaney, Jr. to Jack Nicholson, wolves have been depicted in literature and film as bloodthirsty monsters who regularly prey on humans. Centuries of fear and ignorance have led most people to believe things about wolves that are the exact opposite of the truth. Wolves shun humans, fear them—someone walking in a forest populated by wolves has a better chance of being struck by lightning or being killed in a collision with a running deer than of being attacked by a wolf. They possess a sensitivity that is evident in their deep affection for their lifelong mates and for their offspring, and in the fierce loyalty they hold for their packs. They are intelligent and sensitive, not the monsters myth and misconception have made them out to be.

And yet, Ella found herself surrounded by exactly that—monsters. But she was determined not to be like them. She knew she could rise above what they had become, and what they wanted her to be. She could do that by tapping into the new side of her, into the true nature of what she had become. Those around her were monsters because they allowed their humanity to rule their lupine nature. Humanity was the source of that monstrousness, not their lupine side. If she could do the exact opposite, she was certain she could be different than the others. Better.

Since being raped in her own home in January, her life as she'd known it had ended. That same night, her husband Arlin, sheriff of Pine County, had been killed in the meth-lab explosion at the old Laramie house with a group of his deputies while investigating the house for drug activity. Of course, there had been no such investigation, no meth lab. They had been slaughtered, eaten, and their remains burned in the explosion that had been set up by their killers—by the very people with whom Ella now lived. While Arlin was being killed, Ella had been spirited away to the sheriff's department and kept in her husband's office for the night. She had only a vague, dreamlike memory of that—she'd been in and out of consciousness after being beaten by her rapist. While she was in a daze, Irving Taggart and members of his pack had been busy taking over the department, swiftly dispensing with anyone who did not submit to them and turning those who did. Ella remembered the sounds she'd heard outside Arlin's office during her periods of foggy consciousness—the gargling screams of the dying, the grunts and gasps and fevered cries of those being infected by force so they would turn, as she had been. Arlin's office had always been such a familiar, comfortable, and safe place, but that night it had become part of the landscape of a nightmare. The nightmare had not ended, even after she was brought to this house the next day. She had been there ever since.

She looked different now. Taggart had insisted she change her hair color. If anyone she'd known in her former life saw her, he did not want her to be recognized as the widow of the former sheriff. The strawberry blonde hair she'd once had was now a deep, dark brown, but that was not the only change. The lines around her eyes and mouth were gone, as were the faint creases in the skin around her throat. At forty-seven, she'd looked good for her age, but now she appeared even younger, with smoother skin, brighter eyes. It was part of the change, the result of being turned. She felt better, too—stronger, lighter, more energetic.

She needed less sleep, her mind was clearer than ever, and her sight and hearing had become acutely improved. But her emotional health did not match her new physical condition. She thought of Arlin every day, saw him whenever she slept, in dreams so vivid and clear that she often awoke with his voice in her ears, his scent in her nostrils. When she woke, she always expected to find him next to her. But of course, she did not. She found someone else there, someone for whom she feigned attraction and devotion, while loathing him with every fiber of her being. She hated them all, but none with the force and passion with which she hated him. Every smile she showed him hid her desire to end his life. Every touch, every kiss, every carefully modulated sigh was a lie, a performance, a way to buy time while she plotted and planned. The man with whom she slept now, while yearning for Arlin and silently mourning his loss inside, was the very man who had killed her husband: Irving Taggart.

Ella had plans. She was afraid even to *think* about them, but she had plans. Taggart was the alpha male, the head of this particular pack. Ella quickly learned that this gave him a hold on his pack that frightened her. It was a mysterious, invisible hold, a sort of mental connection that bound them to him. She was not sure how deep this mental connection went. Did it mean he could read her thoughts? Did he know of her plans? She was not sure, and that worried her.

A muffled cry came from beyond the closed door that led into the next room. Ella looked up from her book, waited a moment, and when the cry came again, she set the book aside and stood.

Ella had been given the job of caring for Cynthia Newell, the mother of the First Born. Essentially, it was her task to keep the girl quiet until it was time for the inevitable. But Ella had been making the best of her time with Cynthia.

She opened the door and went into the room. The bed was empty, the covers thrown back, and Cynthia was pacing. Wearing a baggy white T-shirt and a pair of blue panties, she was hunched forward slightly, wringing her hands. Ella approached her and gently placed a hand against her back.

"What's wrong, honey?" Ella whispered.

"Another dream," Cynthia said tremulously. "I dreamed of my baby." She stopped pacing and turned to Ella with wide, glimmering eyes. "Why won't they let me see her? It's been so long. It's been—" She frowned as her eyes darted around searchingly. "How long has it been? What day is it?"

"It's Saturday. You've been here for . . . a few months." They let the girl go outside only occasionally, but only for short, supervised walks in the large, fenced-off backyard. They kept her drugged and disoriented. They gave her TV and music and movies and books to occupy her, but she could seldom concentrate enough to enjoy them. They fed her well, but she looked too thin in spite of that, because she had no appetite. But her comfort was only temporary, until it was time for her to meet her fate—a fate Ella dreaded, and from which she hoped she could save the young woman. It was a fate from which she hoped she could save many.

"Why won't they let me see my baby?" Cynthia asked.

*Because it's not a baby anymore*, Ella thought. "I've told you. They don't want you to have any influence over her. *They* want to be the only influence over your child."

"Why? What are they going to do to her?"

Ella put a hand to Cynthia's pale cheek. "We've talked about this."

Cynthia's voice took on a whining quality. "But you haven't *told* me anything."

"I told you, Cynthia. Your baby is no longer a baby.

Not anymore. And she's not . . . Well, Cynthia, honey, she's not human. Not really. She's a monster."

Cynthia's face screwed up and tears rolled down her cheeks. "Luh-like m-me?"

"It's not your fault, honey. This was *done* to you, like it was done to me. It was done to us by these people, these *things*."

"But why can't I *see* my baby? What are they *doing* to her? Why won't you *tell* me?"

"Because, as I said, it's dangerous for you to know too much."

"I know, I *know*, but I don't care." She became more agitated, pounding the air with her fists as she spoke. "*Tell* me. I want you to *tell* me, goddammit! There's something you're *keeping* from me and I want you to *stop* it!"

Ella stepped in front of Cynthia, put her hands on the girl's forearms, and backed her to the bed. She pushed gently until Cynthia sat on the edge of the mattress. Ella paced slowly in front of her, choosing her words.

"Sheriff Taggart has . . . a plan," she said. "He wants you to have no influence over your daughter. *He* wants to be the only one with any influence over her. He's keeping her to himself, allowing only a select few to see her and speak with her."

When Ella said no more for several seconds, Cynthia said, "What is this *plan*?"

Ella stopped walking and faced her. "I'm not sure when, but at some point, he's going to call a meeting to introduce her to everyone. All of the others. They've heard about her, but they haven't seen her. He wants her debut to be a big deal. And his plan is for you . . . to be there. To make sure he wipes out any possible connection between you and your daughter . . . to make sure she has no possible lingering feelings for you . . ." She bowed her head a moment, took a deep breath, then looked Cynthia in the eyes and said, "He's going to feed you to her."

Cynthia's eyes widened and softened with pain. Her voice was thick when she said, "She'd . . . she would . . . I mean, she would actually . . ."

"You have to stop thinking of her as your child, Cynthia. She's a monster. Even if that weren't his plan . . . his intention . . . if she were here right now, she'd probably do that, anyway. On her own."

As Cynthia thought about that, her eyes wandered from Ella and slowly narrowed. Her jaw set and her lips took on a slight, angry sneer.

"Then she really *is* a monster," she whispered.

Ella hunkered down in front of Cynthia and got serious. "I've asked you this before, but I'm going to ask you again. I'm like you—I don't like what they've done to me, to my life. I hate them. I want to hurt them. They've ruined your life and taken your baby, and you hate them, too—don't you?"

The fear and uncertainty in Cynthia's face faded a little. Her chin jutted and her jaws flexed as she nodded. "Yes. I hate them."

"I have plans to hurt them. I'm not going to tell you what they are, because it's best if you don't know too much. So you'll have to trust me. When the time comes, you're going to have to help me. You'll have to do as I say, when I say it." She lowered her voice to an intense whisper. *"Will you do that?"*

Cynthia's expression became angrier, more determined. "Yes. Yes, I'll do that. Whenever you want, whatever you want."

"Good. Good. Until then, Cynthia, let's do some more of the exercises we've been doing. Why don't you lie back on the bed."

Once Cynthia was stretched out, Ella sat on the edge

of the bed and gently put a palm flat against Cynthia's stomach. She began to rub her hand in slow circles.

"Close your eyes," Ella said. "Relax, and listen to me very carefully." She spoke in a low, soothing tone and kept rubbing Cynthia's abdomen. "There is something in you, Cynthia, that wasn't there before. They put it there, thinking it would make you like them. But they have abused this thing. Debased it. This thing in you is noble. It is loyal and peaceful and pure. Find it, Cynthia. Find it within yourself, like the last time we did this. Find it and embrace it. Let it fill you. They are wrong, Cynthia. It will not make you like them. It will make you better than them, but only if you let it fill you. Let go of what you always have been and become this instead. Learn to surrender to it."

She continued to talk to Cynthia in this soft, gentle way as she rubbed the young woman's abdomen. Ella had done it with Cynthia before, several times. At first, she'd had no idea if it would work and wasn't even quite sure of what she was doing. She made it up as she went along, acting intuitively, doing and saying what *felt* right. It had worked for her, and she hoped it would work for Cynthia, too. Ella was certain it was the only thing that would save them.

After entering their destination into the onboard navigation system, Gavin took a right out of the Blind Dog Bar & Grill's parking lot. He passed the BMW parked at the curb on the left.

"Is he following us?" he said.

Karen looked in the mirror. "He's started the car. Now he's pulling out. Yep, looks like he's making a U-turn." She took a cigarette from her purse and lit it.

"Good."

The navigation system's narcotized female voice told

him to take the next left. He followed the monotone directions out of town and up a hill.

Karen reached into her purse just as Gavin said, "Can I have a drag off that—?"

"Here," she said, handing him a cigarette and the lighter.

In their Saturday wanderings in Big Rock, Karen and Gavin had chatted with several people—at the flea market, in town, and at a bar called the Domino—and the topic of the animal attacks had come up more than once. Sometimes, they hadn't even had to raise it—some of the residents they spoke with brought it up first. But very little had been said. Karen and Gavin had tried to drag information about the attacks out of the locals, but they'd seemed reluctant to discuss them in any detail.

The voice of the navigation system finally directed Gavin into Harmony Estates, an attractive, high-end neighborhood of gated driveways, sprawling yards, and large, attractive houses situated a distance off the road and surrounded by dense trees and foliage.

The voice told him to turn right. Once on Melody Lane, Gavin slowed down. A moment before the voice said, "You have reached your destination," he pulled over to the curb in front of 13774 Melody, stopped, shifted to park, and looked in the side-view mirror.

They sat there a moment and smoked silently.

Finally, Karen laughed. "What's he doing?"

In the mirror, Gavin saw the BMW turn slowly onto Melody. "He's wondering why we're parked in front of his house." The BMW came to a stop. "And now, he's probably feeling rather annoyed." Suddenly, the silver car shot forward and sped by them, then took the first right turn. As soon as it was out of sight, Gavin put the SUV in gear, made a quick U-turn, and increased his speed as he headed back the way they had come.

"Where are we going now?" Karen said.

"Back to the motel. Maybe we can pack up and get out before they search our room, if they haven't already."

"Any guesses as to who *they* are?"

"People who don't like the fact that we're here. We'll have to find another place to stay."

"And then?"

"Good question. By now, chances are they know who we are, and they've probably got some idea as to why where here. And I don't imagine they're too happy about it."

Karen said, "Whoever *they* are."

# CHAPTER NINE

*Sabbath's End/Saturday Night*

"Why don't *you* ever get to pick what you watch on TV?" Royce said.

Bob sighed, holding the phone to his ear with one hand as he clumsily tried to make a peanut butter-and-jelly sandwich with the other. Earlier, he'd cooked vegetarian chicken patties and broccoli for Mom and Grandma, but he had not been in the mood for that. Instead, he'd wanted a PB-and-J sandwich on sourdough bread with a cold glass of milk.

"They won't let me," Bob said.

"Won't *let* you? Jesus Christ, *you* do all the housework, all the yardwork, all the cooking, all the driving. My God, you even *bathe* your fucking *mother*! What has *letting* you got to do with it? You're a middle-aged man, for crying out loud! When are you going to stand up and tell them you live there, too?"

Another sigh from Bob. "Yeah, but that's easier said than done. It doesn't matter, anyway. The sun isn't down yet, so the TV is off."

"Oh, yeah. Don't want the TV on in case Jesus drops by for a surprise Sabbath visit."

Bob laughed.

"That would be just like Jesus to drop by without calling first," Royce said. "Have you ever noticed that Adventists like to do that? Especially on the Sabbath. They love to drop in unannounced to see if they can catch you sinning."

"Look, do you want to have lunch tomorrow, or what?" Bob said.

"Lunch? Yeah, sure. At Winkie's?"

"Where else?" Winkie's was the small diner on the edge of town where they always met. "When?"

"I'll be up late tonight working. Not before one."

"Sure, one o'clock's fine." Bob thought of his encounter with Vanessa in the church kitchen. "I've gotta tell you what happened to me at church today. You won't believe it."

"At church? What'd you do, have a vision during the potluck lunch? Did they serve oysters and vinegar?" He chuckled.

"No, no. It's a *lot* better than that. It involves a gorgeous woman."

Bob heard someone at the door as he finished making his sandwich, cradling the phone against his shoulder. The front door opened onto the hallway that passed the kitchen and dining room on the way to the living room in the rear of the house. You had to be in the kitchen and dining room to hear it open—the sound never quite made it all the way back to the living room. The door slammed shut and he heard Rochelle sigh as she started down the hall. She stopped at the doorway and leaned into the kitchen.

"You're on the phone *again*?" she said with a sneer. "I swear, you're like a teenage girl. You're *always* on the phone." She headed for the living room.

"I should go," Bob said. "My sister's here."

"What's she doing there?" Royce said. "Shouldn't she be at home sucking all the spinal fluid and testosterone out of her husband and son?"

Bob laughed, then said good night to Royce. He put his sandwich on a small plate, poured a tall glass of milk, and took them to the living room.

Mom and Grandma and Rochelle talked loudly to be heard above the radio's high volume. The Christian station was on, as usual, and a group was singing about the glories of worship. Bob hated the music, but he didn't want to go into his bedroom. It was too early, and he didn't feel like locking himself up in there yet. He sat down on the couch and took a magazine from the stack on the end table. He thumbed through it as he ate his sandwich. The sun would be down officially in about fifteen minutes, and he would be able to turn off the radio and switch on the television. Bob found it amusing that Adventists always knew exactly when sunset occurred on Friday and Saturday nights. They used to check the newspaper for the times at the end of each week, and now they got the information online.

"Where's Mike and Peter?" Mom said.

Rochelle's face screwed up for a moment and she waved a hand dismissively as she flopped into the love seat. "Oh, they're lying around at home. As usual."

"What are you doing out?"

"I just wanted to get out of the house on my own."

"This late?" Grandma said.

"Late?" Rochelle said. "It's not even dark yet. I thought after the Sabbath was over, I'd hit the mall and just window-shop, maybe pick up a new pair of shoes for work."

Bob tuned them out and focused on the magazine, a recent issue of *Time*. The room and his family faded away as he immersed himself in an article about the rise in identity theft. After awhile, he realized Grandma was shouting. Then he realized she was shouting at *him*. His head jerked up and he looked over at her seated in her favorite chair.

"Didn't you hear me?" Grandma shouted.

"What?" Bob said.

"I *said*, is that a magazine you should be reading on the Sabbath?"

"It's *Time*."

"*Time* is *not* Sabbath reading," Grandma said. She lifted her hand and pointed a knobby forefinger at him. "You have six days to do whatever you want, and all God asks is that you give one day to him, just *one day*. And you can't do that, can you? You can't give the Lord twenty-four hours out of your whole week!"

Bob sighed, closed the magazine, and tossed it back on the stack. "The sun's gonna be down in just a few minutes."

"Then you can just give the Lord a few more minutes of your precious time," Grandma said.

"Why do you even bother going to church, Bob?" Rochelle said. "You don't practice your faith. You can't wait for the Sabbath to end, you seem to sleep through the sermon, you never read your Bible, and you hang around with that awful Royce Garver. I mean, he might as well be a *Satanist* with the kind of work he does."

"Royce is not a Satanist," Bob muttered.

"What are you doing out here, anyway?" Rochelle said. "Shouldn't you be in your bedroom masturbating?" She laughed as if she'd just said the funniest thing ever heard.

Bob felt his face grow hot as he ate his sandwich and stared at his plate.

Rochelle said, "Mom, remember that time I caught Bob sitting on the edge of his bed masturbating?"

It had happened over twenty years ago, and Rochelle would never let him forget about it.

"I remember," Mom said, her voice darkening with disapproval. "I hope you don't *still* do that, Bob. You know what Sister White said about solitary vice."

"Of *course* he still does it, Mom," Rochelle said. "I mean, he doesn't do anything *else*. He doesn't date or have a girlfriend. He doesn't even have a social life." She turned to Bob, frowning. "Have you *ever* had a girlfriend? I can't remember you ever going out with one."

"He had a little friend years ago," Mom said. "That funny-looking little girl. What was her name? Gloria? Glinda?"

Eyes down, Bob stopped chewing a bite of his sandwich long enough to mutter, "Gladys." His back stiffened and his shoulders hunched forward, making him appear to curl in on himself a bit. The sandwich was sticking in his esophagus in a hard lump. His chest felt swollen and tight, his stomach twisted into a knot, and although he was unaware of it, his right foot began to jitter so that his knee bounced up and down. He hated being the center of attention, but Mom, Grandma, and Rochelle seemed to enjoy his embarrassment when they talked about him as if he weren't even there. He was sure they talked about him when he wasn't around to hear it, too. That was probably worse.

"Yes, that's right," Mom said. "Gladys. She was always hanging around you."

"Did she ever let you lift up her dress, Bob?" Rochelle asked snidely.

"Stop that," Mom said. "I don't like that kind of talk. Your brother doesn't need a girl. He's got Grandma and me. We're all he needs." She looked across the room at Bob. "Now if only you'd get a *job*."

"Why should he get a job?" Rochelle said. "He's got everything he needs right here. Food, a bed, a computer for pornography. You oughtta kick him *out*. Then he'd *have* to get a job. He couldn't afford to be worthless if he really had to *earn* a living."

"He'll get a job someday," Grandma said. "If he ever grows up enough."

Bob felt a tremor move through his body. The sandwich in his right hand wobbled as his arm trembled.

"*Someday?*" Rochelle said. "He's *thirty-eight*! Dad wouldn't have put up with this if he'd lived."

Mom flinched at the mention of her late husband. "A lot of things would be different if your dad hadn't died."

Breathing harder now, Bob stared at the wobbling sandwich in his hands as they talked.

"Bob would be different," Mom went on. "With the influence of a father, maybe he wouldn't be so . . . so . . . oh, so withdrawn and childlike and unable to—"

Bob suddenly lifted his head and shouted, "I'm in the room!" His eyes widened with shock at his own outburst.

The three women turned to him with slack jaws. They stared at him, frozen in disbelief.

Bob's voice lowered to a rasp and his entire face trembled as he said through clenched teeth, "Quit . . . talking about me . . . like I'm not . . . *here*."

Grandma's eyes narrowed and her chin jutted. "Who do you think you *are*, young man? Raising your voice to your mother like that. And on the *Sabbath*!"

"What do you expect?" Rochelle said with a chuckle as she stood from the love seat. "I'm gonna go. Sun's almost down. I'll hit the mall and wander a little."

Still shaking, Bob stood and took his unfinished sandwich and glass of milk back into the kitchen.

"You gonna go into your room now?" Rochelle said, laughing as he left the living room. "Go pout and play with yourself?"

"He'd better go get on his knees and ask Jesus for forgiveness," Grandma grumbled. "Talking to adults that way. And on the Sabbath."

Bob tossed the sandwich into the garbage, poured the remaining milk into the sink. Then he threw the plate and glass into the basin. He threw them harder than he'd intended—they both shattered.

"What was *that*?" Mom shouted from the living room.

Bob quickly tried to gather up the pieces and throw

them away before she came in, but he nicked his left hand on a jagged shard.

"Are you breaking my dishes?" she said angrily as she came into the kitchen. "What did you do?"

He pressed a paper towel to the small cut on his hand.

"Cut yourself," Mom sad. "Serves you *right*. Throwing dishes around. Go to your room. I think you need a *nap*."

Rochelle came in and saw the blood on his hand. "Didn't hurt your whacking hand, did you?" Then she laughed again.

Bob turned and went to his room. He was surprised by the force with which he slammed the door. Normally, he made no sounds as he moved through the house, wanting to draw as little attention as possible to himself. It was not uncommon for him to feel anger and frustration, but he'd never let it out before—not as he had tonight. He paced in his room as blood trickled from the cut on his left hand.

He sat down at his computer but could not get comfortable or hold still. As he surfed the Internet absently, his foot rhythmically kicked the leg of his desk. The light in the room faded as the last of the sun disappeared outside, and before he knew it, Bob was sitting in the dark. He felt taut, like a guitar string about to snap. His foot continued to kick and the cut on his hand kept bleeding.

Outside his room, the religious music suddenly stopped. He could hear Mom and Grandma talking to each other, Mom's voice loud and shrill, Grandma's voice lower, bitter. The television came on and he could hear the laughter of a studio audience. Their voices yammered on, audible over the television.

They scraped at him, those voices. They were like needles being shoved into his ears, stabbing his brain.

*You're a middle-aged man, for crying out loud!* Royce had said. And he was right.

"Middle-aged," Bob muttered as he sat in the dark. "Middle . . . aged."

Another sound rose in the room—crunching, rumbling. He realized he was grinding his teeth. He stood so suddenly, he knocked the chair over. Paced some more. Both fists clenching. He didn't even feel the sting of the cut on his hand.

The voices continued outside the room. Shrill . . . bitter.

Bob felt as if he were about to explode and spatter all over his walls. He had to get out of the house. He stormed out of the room, down the hall, through the kitchen. He grabbed the keys off the counter and headed for the door.

Mom suddenly stepped in front of him and he stumbled to a halt. Frowning at him, she said in her loud, shrill voice, "Where are *you* going?"

"Out."

"*Out?* You don't have anywhere to go."

"Well, I'm *going* there just the same."

"I don't like your tone," she said as he stepped around her and left the kitchen. "Did you hear me?" she shouted, turning to follow him.

Bob stopped, spun around, and faced her, jaw set, face hot with anger this time, not shame. "I heard you. And by the way. Dad did not *die*. He *killed himself*!"

She flinched as if he'd slapped her.

He stalked outside, pulled the door shut hard. The keys jangled at his side as he went to the car, got in, started it, and backed out of the driveway. The car stopped and idled in front of the house for awhile. Mom was right, he had nowhere to go. Royce, his only friend, would be busy with work. For a moment, that made him feel even worse. But he slammed his foot down on the pedal, and the car shot forward as he decided that simply driving without a destination would be better than staying in that miserable house.

Karen and Gavin had cleared out their room at the Beachcomber and quickly learned that their options for lodging

in Big Rock were rather limited. They ended up at a bed-
and-breakfast close enough to the beach to hear the surf
from their window. It was an old postcard-perfect Victorian
with a beautifully tended yard. The owner was a woman in
her fifties named Tilly Blaine. She lived there with her
shuffling, mumbling husband Gus, a bald man with an
enormous belly and a sour expression, who favored dark,
high-waisted pants with suspenders and slightly discolored
white "wife beater" undershirts. Tilly was like a figure from
a Norman Rockwell painting—plump and rosy cheeked, always smiling, with a pleasant, musical voice. That changed
whenever Gus came into view. Then Tilly became impatient, loud, and sometimes even foulmouthed. The first
time Karen and Gavin witnessed the behavior was while
Tilly was showing them through the house. Gus shuffled
out of an upstairs bedroom and stared at them, slowly
smacking his lips.

"This is my husband, Gus," Tilly said, her smile remaining in spite of her sudden apparent discomfort.

"Whozis?" Gus said, tucking his thumbs under his
suspenders.

"Go back in the bedroom, Gus," Tilly said, her voice
suddenly stern through her sweet smile. "We have guests."

"Guests?" Gus said, squinting at them. "Who's coming?"

Tilly's smile crumbled as she rolled her eyes. "*These* are
our guests."

"Oh. They gonna stay?"

"*Yes*, they're staying, Gus, they're *guests*, and this is a
bed-and-*breakfast*. What do you *think* they're doing, looking to *buy* the place?"

Gus frowned and looked puzzled. "They . . . they
wanna *buy* the place?"

"Goddammit, Gus, why do you never *listen* to me, I *told*
you—" She stopped abruptly, pushed her husband back
into the bedroom, and went in with him. She smiled at

Karen and Gavin and said, "Just a moment," then closed the door. Inside, she shouted at Gus while Karen and Gavin looked at each other smirkingly.

"Maybe we should find another place," Karen whispered.

"We already looked around. There doesn't seem to be a big selection," Gavin said.

"Okay. We'll stay here tonight, then try to find someplace else in the morning."

That evening, Tilly had served them dinner of sliced franks in gummy macaroni and cheese, undercooked Brussels sprouts, and biscuits that were as hard as plaster. They sat down to the meal and picked at it a little, but the inedible state of the food was made worse by having to watch Gus eat, something he did noisily and messily, with his mouth open half the time. They apologized for not eating more, said they just weren't hungry, and went to their room.

Karen went online with her laptop and checked the local papers for stories about animal attacks. There were only a couple, and they were very small, reducing the attacks to very minor, negligible occurrences.

While Gavin stood by the window as the sun set, Karen sat on the bed and called Burgess on her cell phone. Once she had him on the line, she turned on the speaker.

Burgess told them he had left Esalen early and was at his home in Los Angeles. "I'll be here from now on, with my cell phone either in my hand or by my side, waiting to hear from you. So, what's going on?"

"We've been followed all day by a dentist," Gavin said.

"A *dentist*. Sounds kinky."

Gavin told him the whole story.

"So you've blown your cover," Burgess said.

"Let's face it," Karen said. "It wasn't *that* much of a cover. But yes, it's blown. We're out in the open now."

"Our room was searched while we were out playing

footsie with the dentist," Gavin said. "The suitcases holding the Uzis and the ammunition were taken. Whoever they are, they know we're armed—or *were* armed—and having seen the silver bullets, they probably have a good idea of what we're looking for."

Burgess was silent for awhile, then, "Talk to anyone?"

"A few locals," Karen said. She told him about their reluctance to discuss the animal attacks and about the scant press coverage of the attacks, which seemed to be more numerous than reflected in the local papers.

"So people know it's going on," Burgess said. "Would you characterize the reaction of those you spoke with as fearful?"

Karen looked at Gavin, who thought a moment. "Maybe," he said. "Certainly cautious."

"Hmm. Any thoughts?"

"I think they *do* seem to be a bit afraid," Karen said. "But I don't know if they're afraid of whatever it is that's attacking people, or of reprisals if they talk."

"Good observation," Burgess said. "That's why I pay you the big bucks. What's your next move?"

"We're going to visit the local hospital," Karen said. "The victims of those animal attacks have to go *somewhere* for treatment. Someone there may have some interesting details, maybe a theory."

"I told you I'd send in the troops if necessary," Burgess said. "I'm making arrangements now to do just that. I think the fact that you have only your handguns is reason enough to give you backup. This is a little . . . stickier than I'd anticipated."

"Where do we meet them?" Gavin said.

"Your backup? Oh, don't worry about that. You'll know when they arrive."

Outside their room, Tilly's voice rose as she shouted, "Goddammit, Gus, zip up your *pants*! How many times do you have to be *told*?"

"That sounds pleasant," Burgess said. "You wouldn't happen to be visiting my parents, would you?"

"That was our hostess having a word with her husband," Karen said. "We're at a bed-and-breakfast."

"Sounds lovely," Burgess said. "I've gotta run. As always, call anytime for any reason."

Karen put the phone aside, and she and Gavin talked about what to do next.

"I don't know about you," Karen said, "but I'm not too eager to hang around here and listen to the honeymooners out there."

"Let's drive over to the hospital. Maybe there's someone in the ER who will talk to us about the local wildlife."

At his Laurel Canyon home in Los Angeles, Martin Burgess made a phone call after talking to Karen and Gavin. He held his cell phone to his ear and waited through the purring sounds that signified the phone at the other end was ringing. He had little doubt the man he was calling would be home. Either he would be playing some extremely violent video game online, or he would be scrolling slowly through Web sites or message boards that focused on UFOs, alien abductions, government cover-ups, and the secret cabal of the megarich, bloodline-sharing elitists who *really* ran everything from behind the scenes.

The purring stopped and a rather high, pinched voice said, "Yeah?"

"Lloyd? It's Martin Burgess."

"Mr. Burgess—hey, fuck, great to hear from you, man. How you fuckin' doin'?"

The voice sounded almost like that of a preadolescent boy, but Burgess knew better.

"I'm good, Lloyd, good. How about you?"

"Oh, the usual. Tryin' to stay outta fuckin' trouble and keep to myself. I was on the computer just now. Hey, you checked the *Illuminati News* Web site lately?"

"No, I haven't."

"You should. Coupla good stories on there the last day or so."

Burgess imagined Lloyd Canwright at the other end of the line: thirty-four years old, five feet eight, his dark hair so severely buzzed that his scalp was clearly visible, his face flat and square with a scar that puckered his left cheek from the outer corner of his eye down into his trimmed beard.

"I'd like to talk about those stories," Burgess said, "but at the moment, I'm calling about something else."

"Sure, Mr. Burgess. What can I do for ya?"

He'd first heard of Lloyd from Harvey Altman, the most trusted member of what Burgess thought of as his "club." Harvey had met Lloyd, and shortly thereafter Lloyd's friends, online some years ago. At that time, Lloyd and all his friends—conspiracy theorists and enthusiasts of the bizarre—were in prison. Harvey found that they were surprisingly intelligent men who knew their stuff. The men had met each other online through their common interests, and when they found that they all had one very significant thing in common—incarceration—they stayed in touch. Although he was extremely well-read and better informed in his strange pursuits than anyone Burgess had ever met, Harvey claimed that he'd learned a lot from Lloyd and his friends. In the years since meeting Harvey, Lloyd and several of his friends had been released from prison. Burgess sometimes sponsored get-togethers for his sources. He paid to have all of them flown to a central location, where he put them up in a hotel, met with them for a weekend, and showed them a good time. Like Harvey, most of them were rather introverted and socially awkward, and Burgess found entertaining them to be personally rewarding. A little over a year earlier, he had held such a gathering, and he'd told Harvey to include Lloyd and his friends—at least, those currently not serving time.

"Well, Lloyd, I told you recently that I might need you and the guys sometime soon," Burgess said. "It's looking like that time could be now. This weekend. I'm going to have a jet pick all of you up in the next, say, ten hours or so. That jet will take you to a little town in northern California."

"No shit? Really? Fuck, man, that sounds great."

"Yes. Can you call the others and let them know? I mean tonight? Right now?"

"Sure can, Mr. Burgess. I'll do that right away. And I know they'll drop what they're doing." A smile opened up in Lloyd's voice. "We're all big fuckin' fans of yours, y'know."

"I'm going to make a couple of quick phone calls, make the final arrangements, and then I'll call you back with the details. Will you be around?"

"Hell, I got nowheres to be. 'Specially if I know you're gonna call."

"One thing, Lloyd. This job I'm sending you on . . . Well, I want to make sure you and the guys don't have any misconceptions."

"Misconceptions? About what?"

"About what you'll be doing."

"You gonna tell me what that'll be?"

"Of course. When I call you back, I'll tell you the whole story. But I want to be sure you and the others understand up front that there are a couple of catches."

"Catches, huh?"

"Yes. It's not exactly legal, for one thing. And it's dangerous. Actually, in doing this, you may be risking life and limb."

"Oh? Well . . . are we gonna get a chance to kick some ass and knock some shit around?"

"More than you might think."

"We gonna be armed?"

"To the teeth."

Lloyd laughed again. "Then, Mr. Burgess, dangerous ain't the catch. That's the fuckin' *attraction*."

When they finished talking, Burgess put the cell phone on the desk, imagining Lloyd and his friends rushing to Karen and Gavin's aid in Big Rock . . . a bunch of badass ex-cons who'd spent a good deal of time behind bars in some hard-core prisons, lifting weights and building up their badly-tattooed muscles . . . ex-cons who wanted very much to stay on the outside, but who would give their left nuts for an excuse to pack some serious heat and kick some serious ass.

Smirking, Burgess muttered to himself, "Goddamned werewolves better put on their game faces."

Bad Rochelle was gasping. With her black-stockinged legs hiked over his shoulders, she closed her fists on Deputy Harry Cross's thick hair as he pressed his mouth hard to the opening in her black crotchless panties and made loud slurping sounds. She released a high, breathy laugh as she tipped her head back and closed her eyes.

"Oh, God, Harry, that's good, so good," she said huskily. She panted for awhile as she clutched his hair, then clenched her teeth and growled, "Suck on my clit. Suck it hard."

Cross lifted his head and Rochelle looked down, saw his face smirking up at her through the little canyon between her breasts.

"You're an animal," he said with a chuckle.

"You bet I am. And I want you to fuck me like an animal. You hear me, Harry?" She pulled on his hair. "Come up here and put it in me. *Fuck* me."

Her black and red half bra had been tossed aside on the bed, and her clothes were scattered over the floor with the deputy's. She kept her lingerie in her closet tucked away in a garment bag that had a lock on it. Mike had never noticed it, so he'd never asked about it. Typical of him. When she'd left the house, she'd told Mike she was going to drop by and see her mother, then do a little shopping. The only reason she'd stopped by her mother's house was so that her story would hold up. It had made her feel deliciously dirty to sit there in her mother's living room talking about her brother masturbating while she wore crotchless panties, a tiny half bra, garters on the black stockings beneath her plain-Jane slacks. The slacks were her Good Rochelle disguise. It had been Bad Rochelle who had left the house that evening, moist with anticipation, eager to meet Harry as they'd planned. It had been Bad Rochelle who'd visited her mother in disguise so that the story she'd told Mike would hold up, Bad Rochelle who had reached down between her legs and pressed her fingers hard to her crotch as she drove to this little motel just outside the town's northern border.

Harry slid her legs off his shoulders and crawled up her body with a lascivious grin, his erection bobbing between his legs. As he settled between her thighs, she reached down and put the head of his cock to her opening, then slapped her hands on his ass and dug her fingernails in.

"Now fuck me, Harry" she said. "*Hard.*"

A squeal escaped her broad smile as he pushed into her and began to thrust hard and fast. He squeezed her left breast as he made low, animal sounds in his chest. Rochelle closed her eyes and drank in the sensation. She lifted her hips off the bed and met his thrusts, clawed at him with her nails, muttered obscenities as they moved together, enjoyed uttering the filthy words and phrases like an adolescent girl talking dirty to herself while no one was around. After awhile, they rolled over so she was on top of him, and she rode him like a mechanical bull. In the back of her mind, she knew she was being loud and that people in the rooms on each side could probably hear her, and she didn't care, hoped they could, hoped they enjoyed it. Then they changed position again so he was on top of her, which was how she liked it, her legs high in the air while he pounded into her. She reached down and roughly fingered her clitoris hard, uninhibited, thinking about how exciting it would be if the people in the other rooms could *see* them, if they were watching them fuck, getting excited and breathing hard and masturbating as Harry slammed into her and her fingers moved at a blur between her lips.

He growled—she loved it, he was actually *growling* as he panted, like a rutting animal—and she laughed loudly. He pushed himself up on his arms, locked his elbows, and glared down at her. The corners of his mouth pulled downward in a brutal sneer as his chin jutted and something silver glimmered and flashed in his eyes—

*Tears?* she thought. *Are those tears, is he actually* crying *while he's* fucking *me?*

—and then she lost her focus on his face as the soles of her feet began to burn as if they were one fire, a sign that she was about to come. She babbled and shouted and clutched at him as she went off inside and lost his face in the violence of the internal explosions that made her body disintegrate into nothingness, leaving only her pounding, vibrating pussy as it flashed blindingly inside her head like a star going nova.

He growled again, louder this time, and she felt his hand on her, pawing at her, even hurting her a little as the explosion cleared. But even as the nova died, another flared more intensely, and she cried out harshly, her voice catching in her throat and breaking through in sharp, staccato sounds. He swelled inside her as he pounded harder, and her hands flailed through the air, fingers stiff and splayed as that nova grew to fill the universe and swallow up everything.

As he came inside her, Harry roared like a bear and slammed into her so hard that her body rocked and jerked on the bed and her teeth clacked together as her breasts slapped violently up and down, and it seemed that he kept swelling, kept coming, kept slamming, and as that last universe-engulfing nova began to recede and fade, she felt as if she were about to fly apart like an abused doll.

Soon, the only sounds in the room were their gasps for breath. She felt sweat trickle over her body, found his skin wet with it when she touched him, her arms and legs weak and trembling, her breasts aching slightly from the fierce jostling they'd received. He lay limp on top of her for awhile, then started to move.

"No, wait," she said, hoarse and breathless. Her voice dissolved into a whisper as she said, "Don't take your cock out yet. I want it inside me as long as it's hard. Just keep it there. Filling me. Yeah. I like that." She closed her eyes and let herself float on the buzz that remained from her orgasm. "Yeah ... filling me ... filling my cunt ... filling me with ... with ..."

But she let the word hang in the air as she wallowed in the humming, cushiony aftermath, too drained to give any thought to exactly what it was he'd just filled her with ... blindly ignorant of what he'd just put inside her ... with no inkling of what had just been done to her.

# CHAPTER TEN

*Convergence: ER*

Bob sat on the hood of the old station wagon, slowly chewed a stick of Juicy Fruit that was growing stale and sour in his mouth, and stared out through the night at the ocean. A cool breeze brushed against his face and whispered through the trees along the edge of Beachview Road. Before him, the ground sloped down to the vast expanse of flat, sandy beach below. The ocean murmured to the shore, its voice rising and falling at regular intervals.

He hadn't been to this spot in years. He used to come a lot, to do exactly what he was doing that night—to sit and stare and think, to be alone when he couldn't tolerate being in the house with his family for another moment. He'd last been there—*how* long ago? At the time, he'd actually had a job driving a van for a medical-supply store. He'd been looking for an apartment, planning to move from his mother's house and finally get out on his own and start his life—*finally*. Fifteen years ago, at least. Then Grandma had gotten sick and had decided she could no longer live alone. She had no one but her widowed daughter-in-law to turn to, and Mom had decided to take her in. But she'd told Bob he couldn't leave, not with Grandma moving in. She would need help, she couldn't handle the old woman by herself. He *had* to stay, he was *obligated*. They were *family*. They'd been throwing the words *obligated* and *family* at him his whole life, telling him how useless he was, how hopeless his future was, how nothing awaited him but disappointment and defeat and a lonely old age that would only end in death. . . . Why get his hopes up? What was one more obligation to his family?

After Grandma moved in, Bob's responsibilities had become overwhelming. He'd had to do everything for both of them, had to answer their every beck and call. They'd eaten up his time and begun interfering with his job. He'd got to work later and later, and his boss began to complain. But Mom and Grandma had complained louder. He'd ended up losing the job. The day he was fired, he'd heard a loud sound in his head that rang with finality: the thunderous slamming of an enormous door. He'd been in the house ever since. They had been his life.

When Bob was ten, his dad had driven his car at high speed into a concrete abutment. There had been no reason for it. Witnesses said he hadn't lost control, traffic was light, there had been no pedestrians in the way, no animals in the road. He'd simply sped directly into the abutment in an explosion of crushed metal and shattered glass that had sent him shooting like a missile through the windshield and headfirst into the concrete. He hadn't been wearing a seat belt. Dad had *always* worn a seat belt, and he'd insisted everyone else in the family do the same. He hadn't been insistent about many things—in fact, the man had hardly spoken in the ten years Bob had known him—but he'd insisted on that. He'd left no note, but it was obvious to everyone that his death had been intentionally self-inflicted. Obvious to everyone but Mom and Grandma. A cat had probably run in front of the car, Mom had said. Maybe a wasp had flown in through the window, Grandma had said. But Bob knew better. The man had simply had enough and had seen no other options available to him. Bob had understood that in an abstract way back then, at the age of ten, but now it was as clear to him as the moon in the sky that night.

He stared up at the moon for a long time, then lowered his gaze to its rippling, undulating reflection on the surface of the constantly moving water below. Fog was starting to move in, but it hadn't gotten thick yet. He knew he had to get out somehow. No cancer could possibly eat at his insides as viciously as the misery caused by living with Mom and Grandma. The constant humiliation and denigration, the shouting, the judgmental finger-pointing, the self-righteous condemnation, and the baths—sweet, holy Jesus Christ on the *cross*, his mother's hot, steamy *baths*. It was all killing him as surely as if he'd been drinking a small dose of lethal poison each day.

The more he thought about it, the more claustrophobic and enclosed he felt. Even there, looking out at the endless ocean under the endless stars, he felt strangulated, trapped, encased like a mummy in a sarcophagus. He hopped off the hood of the station wagon, paced in front of the car for awhile, the ground crunching under his feet. Then he stopped, stared down at the ground, took a deep breath. Suddenly, he felt very tired. Exhausted. He wanted to go to bed.

Bob got back in the car and started the engine, flicked on the lights. He turned the radio on and caught the voice of a San Francisco talk-show host snapping with annoyance at a caller. Bob made a U-turn and headed back the way he had come.

On his way to his old meditation spot, he'd passed the Sand Dollar Coffee Shop, and next to it, the Lighthouse Motel, both aged establishments that were showing their years. The motel was a little U-shaped arrangement of rooms with the office to the right of them. It looked battered by time and weather, the paint peeling and the roof shabby. The courtyard in the middle had not been kept up in ages. Beachview Road had been widened twice over the years, and the little motel now stood on its very edge. A porch light glowed beside the door of each room, and a sodium-vapor light cast a sickly glow over the courtyard. The coffee shop next door was in even worse shape. Bob was surprised it was still open for business.

As Bob drove by, observing the low speed limit on Beachview, movement caught his eye and he turned to the left to look at the motel. Two figures were leaving one of the rooms. In an instant, Bob took in the two dark figures, then did a double take. At first, he wasn't sure why, but on the second look, his eyes were pulled directly to the figure on the left. Both were backlit, and he could see no details, but the figure on the left grabbed his attention. The shape, height, the gait and movements—they were very familiar. And then he'd driven by and they were gone.

Frowning, he checked for traffic in both directions, then went into another U-turn. He drove back to the motel and stopped on the opposite side of the road.

The two figures stood by an SUV now. The one he'd recognized was female, and in a heartbeat, he knew it was his sister. But what was she doing at the Lighthouse Motel? And who was her companion?

The male figure opened the door of the SUV. The light inside came on and spilled out the door onto the two of them. It took Bob a moment, but he soon realized that the man was Deputy Cross, the object of Rochelle's girlish attention at church that day. It didn't take a PhD to figure out why Rochelle was with Cross and what they'd been doing there, but as if to make it even easier, Rochelle and Cross embraced in the splash of light, kissed for a long time, then separated.

Bob's hands gripped the steering wheel so hard, his arms trembled and his knuckles ached. The hot anger he'd felt earlier when he'd left the house began to rise in his throat again like bad food on its way back up.

Rochelle was so self-righteous, always telling Bob how sinful he was, what a lousy Christian he was, how he was going to burn in the lake of fire in the end. She went to church every Sabbath, prayer meeting on Wednesdays, she participated in all the church activities and made Mike and Peter do the same, sent Peter to an Adventist school, wouldn't let him watch much of anything on TV, strictly controlled what he read and wore and did with his spare time—

*And here she is screwing a cop in a sleazy little motel while her husband thinks she's shopping for shoes*, Bob thought as he watched Cross get into his SUV and Rochelle get into her silver Jetta.

Rochelle and Cross started their vehicles. Bob turned off his lights, but let the car idle. He was in the dark and knew they wouldn't see him on their way out. He waited as they backed away from their motel room and pulled out onto Beachview, first Rochelle's Volkswagen, then Cross's SUV. He looked into his side-view mirror and watched their tail-lights fade, then disappear around a curve.

Bob waited a long moment, his body stiff with anger, then he pulled yet another U-turn and drove in the same direction they'd gone. A short distance beyond the motel, the road curved blindly to the right around a dark stand of trees. Still angry, both hands still clenched on the steering wheel, Bob did not decrease his pressure on the gas pedal as he rounded the curve.

The figure appeared as a blur in the headlight beams: arms flailing, open mouth a black hole in the face, long hair flying around her head, her back apparently hunched like Quasimodo's. Bob only vaguely heard the woman's screams through his open window as the lights washed her skin a chalky white.

The thud of the car hitting her body went through Bob's bones, into his bowels. He cried out as he hit the brakes and threw the station wagon into a swerving skid.

When the car finally stopped, he sat there, jaw slack, and listened to the engine idle. It was the only sound in the night.

A woman's voice cried, "Help me! I have to get away! It's coming! Jesus Christ, it's gonna find me!"

*She's not dead*, Bob thought with enormous relief. His throat was dry when he gulped. He shifted the car into park, opened the door, and got out, feeling heavy with fear and dread.

Penny Anderson did not feel well. She hadn't been feeling herself for awhile, and she knew why: she was pregnant. But she had not yet told Gretchen, who would go through the roof when she found out. She figured she still had some time. It had been only three months. As overweight as she was, the condition was not at all apparent. But as she lay on her bed with a near-empty package of Oreos beside her, she began to wonder if she had as much time as she'd thought. Tendrils of pain had been cutting through her abdomen for the last half hour, and it was only getting worse.

Gretchen was in the living room with one of her tricks. Penny could hear the phony moans and cries of a porn movie playing loudly on the television while Gretchen and her trick—a pudgy, homely guy in his thirties, with a mullet and several tattoos—fooled around on the couch.

She swung her legs over the edge of the bed and sat up, turned on the clock radio on her nightstand. Tinny rap music thumped from the cheap speaker, but it helped cover the sounds of the porn movie in the living room. More pain erupted inside her and she bent forward, hugged herself, and groaned. She wore a baggy yellow T-shirt with a faded picture of Heath Ledger's Joker on the front and a pair of black shorts. Quite unexpectedly, she vomited on the floor between her bare feet.

"Oh, no," she said as she reached for a tissue on the

nightstand. She wiped her mouth and stood, avoiding the mess on the floor. Gretchen would be pissed. Not only was she pregnant, but she'd puked on the floor. She cautiously opened her bedroom door a crack and cocked her ear to listen. Down the hall, Gretchen was laughing girlishly while the man moaned. Penny hurried the few steps down the hall to the bathroom, being as quiet as possible, and got a washcloth from the shelf. She wet it at the faucet, then turned to go back to her room and clean up the mess she'd made.

Pain hit her like a fist plunging into her abdomen. She doubled over and cried out, staggered, lost her footing, and fell against the wall before sliding to the floor.

Gretchen's laughter stopped.

"Penny?" she called, her voice sharp, irritated.

Penny quickly tried to get up, but the pain came again, worse this time, and her cry was louder, jagged and agonized. She fell to the floor again.

"Goddammit, Penny, what the fuck're you *doing*?" Gretchen's footsteps thumped rapidly through the living room, coming closer.

On hands and knees, Penny looked over her shoulder and saw Gretchen standing at the other end of the hall, naked, hands on her hips, eyes glaring.

"It's nothin'," Penny said. "Never mind." She tried again to get up, clutching the wet washcloth, but was knocked back to the floor by the pain, the breath shoved from her lungs.

"Penny? What the hell's the *matter* with you?"

Penny sat up to respond, but more pain made her curl up, and she vomited again.

"Oh, Jesus, are you sick, honey?" Gretchen said as she approached her daughter, bending forward, reaching out a hand. Her tone changed suddenly, became softer, more concerned.

"I—I—I'm . . . I'm . . . I'm . . ." Penny finally climbed

to her feet, panting. She leaned back against the wall, hands on her stomach. Before she could continue speaking, the pain hit again. She felt something wet dribbling down her legs. It spattered to the floor.

Gretchen looked down at the clear fluid. "Oh, God, what's wrong?"

Teeth clenched, Penny said, "I'm pregnant."

Gretchen's head jerked backward as she gasped. "Preg . . . How *long*?"

Before Penny could answer, pain made her scream and collapse to her knees.

"What the hell's goin' on?" the man in the living room shouted.

"Come help me!" Gretchen cried.

"Help you *what*, goddammit?"

"Help me get my little girl to the hospital!"

Somewhere beneath all the pain, Penny was touched by her mother's sudden and extremely rare concern. She wished she felt better so she could enjoy it, but she was buried beneath another wave of pain.

Abe leaned against the counter next to the coffeemaker in the small lounge, a cup of coffee in one hand and his cell phone to his ear in the other.

"I'm worried about Illy," Claire said.

"Why? What's wrong?"

"I don't know. She says she's fine, but she's distracted and seems unhappy about something. She's been talking to herself more than usual. All day today, she's been talking to herself, and when she does, she sounds . . . well, almost *afraid*. Then a couple of hours ago, we were watching the local news on TV, and she—Oh, by the way, they said something about Seth. Anyway, for some reason, that really upset Illy. I mentioned that he was your coworker, and she became agitated and started talking to herself frantically. She kept using that one word—*moroi*?

Over and over. She even started *shaking*. She went out back to the cottage. I got all the ingredients for smoothies today, and I just took one out to her. But she didn't want it. One of those strawberry smoothies she loves so much? She didn't *want* it. And she was still talking to herself. When I went out there, she was getting out all of those things, um . . . What do you call them? Those things she has on the wall in the cottage?"

"Talismans?"

"Yes, that's it. She was putting them in her front window."

Frowning, Abe shook his head slowly. "Something's upset her."

"Well, hearing about Seth seemed to do it."

"What did they say about Seth, anyway?"

She sighed. "They said the police had determined that he'd been murdered and they're searching for his killer. They said it was—this was how they put it—'a break-in gone wrong.' "

Abe's eyes widened as he turned and put his coffee down on the counter hard. "A break-in gone wrong?" he said loudly. "That was no goddamned *break-in*!"

"It didn't sound like it, not the way you described it."

"A burglar would've just shot him or stabbed him or knocked him over the head with something and then run." A frown darkened Abe's eyes and he lowered his voice. "Seth was . . . he was torn apart. It looked like— Last night I woke up and couldn't go back to sleep, and I realized parts of him looked . . . well, it looked like he'd been *eaten*."

"Eaten? By *what*?"

Abe merely shook his head. He picked up his coffee again and took a sip, then chewed on his lower lip for a long moment.

"Why would they say it was a break-in?" Claire asked.

He shrugged. "Doesn't make any sense."

"And what would *eat* him? Could an animal have gotten into the house and eaten at his body before you got there?"

*An animal*, Abe thought. It had been bothering him all day—that Seth's remains had looked as if he'd been partially eaten. He kept thinking about the animal attacks, wondering if there was some connection between them and the state of Seth's remains.

"I don't know," Abe said. "But that was *not* a break-in gone wrong."

Winona came into the lounge a little timidly, as usual. Her timidity was deceptive. Abe had seen her shout down a burly, menacing drunk in the waiting room once.

"Excuse me, Dr. Dinescu," she said.

"Just a second," Abe said into the phone. He pulled the phone a few inches away from his head and said, "What is it, Winona?"

"There are two people to see you." She frowned as she said it, as if the situation puzzled her.

"Patients?"

"No, they say they're, uh—" She cleared her throat, then lowered her voice a little. "Private investigators."

He frowned. "Private *investigators*?"

"That's what they say," Winona said.

On the phone, Claire's tinny voice said, "What's going on?"

He put the phone to his ear and said, "I have to go, honey. Somebody wants to see me."

"Private investigators want to see you?" she said.

"I'll tell you all about it later. Hugo should be here any minute. He's late already. I'll be home soon." He said good-bye, then closed the phone and dropped it into his pocket. As he started out of the lounge, he said, "Did they say what they want, Winona?"

"Only that they want to talk to you about animal attacks."

Abe stopped in the doorway and turned to her, his eyebrows rising. "Animal attacks?" he whispered.

"That's what they told me."

As he headed for the waiting room, Abe thought, *This should be interesting.*

Karen and Gavin stood at the reception window and waited. They looked around once again at the empty waiting room. Mounted high on one wall, a television played a cooking show for no one.

"Maybe it's too early for the drunken brawls," Karen said.

"Maybe they don't *have* drunken brawls here in Big Rock," Gavin said.

"Yeah, right. What *else* is there to do in this burg?"

The receptionist appeared at the window again. "He's coming out right now," she said with a smile.

To the left of the window, one of the double doors opened and a doctor in a white coat and dark pants walked out. He was in his late thirties, tall and fit, short dark hair, a handsome face with strong features. His smile was weak, overpowered by the slight frown that conveyed his puzzlement.

"Hello," he said. He offered his hand and shook with Gavin. "I'm Dr. Dinescu. Winona says you wanted to, uh, talk to me about . . . animal attacks?"

"That's right," Gavin said. He introduced himself and Karen.

"You're private investigators?" the doctor asked.

"That's right," Karen said. "We've been hired to look into the rash of animal attacks around here. We thought maybe you'd be able to tell us something about them."

Dr. Dinescu's frown deepened a little. "Why me?"

"Only because you're a doctor in the ER," Gavin said. "We thought maybe you've seen some of the victims firsthand."

"Ah, I see. Well, as a matter of fact, I had one in here just last night. A little boy."

"What kind of animal attacked him?" Gavin said.

"I don't know. Neither did the boy. He didn't get a good look at it." He told them the details of the attack—how the smelly, upright animal had tried to pull the boy through the opening in the fence.

"It was *upright*?" Karen said.

"Yes."

"Are there any zoos or animal parks around here?" Gavin asked.

"There's a small zoo—if it can be called that—in the park in Eureka, but the animals are pretty harmless. Nothing predatory or dangerous. It's pretty tiny."

Karen and Gavin exchanged a look. "Have you treated others for similar attacks?"

The doctor nodded. "A couple. And there have been others I haven't treated."

"Any idea how many?"

He shook his head. "I suppose I could find out, but not right now."

"What do *you* think it is?" Karen asked. "Any theories?"

Dr. Dinescu took a moment to think about his response. "I've been thinking about it a lot lately. I don't have any theories, but . . . it bothers me."

"Why's that?"

"It's been going on for awhile. I'm new to the area. My wife and I moved here from southern California only three months ago, and as soon as I started working here, I began hearing about these animal attacks. I didn't think much of it at first, but after treating one myself and hearing about more from other doctors, I began to wonder what kind of animal was doing it. No one has been able to describe the—" He stopped talking for a moment, and his eyes wandered off as he became thoughtful, moving his jaw back and forth slowly.

"Something wrong?" Gavin asked.

"Well . . . I just remembered something. When I first started here, I heard there was a woman who *did* describe the animal that attacked her." He turned to them again, his eyes moving back and forth between them. He said nothing more.

"And?" Karen said.

"Well, she, uh . . ." His face relaxed and he chuckled quietly. "She wasn't my patient. Maybe it's irrelevant, because apparently she had some . . . problems. I was told she was committed to Ward 18 after she showed up here in the ER."

"Ward 18?" Gavin said.

"The psychiatric ward. She was . . . I guess she was experiencing some kind of breakdown that happened to coincide with the attack."

"You said she described the animal," Gavin said. "What did she say? Do you know?"

The doctor's smile faded, his frown returned, and his eyes wandered away once again. "I can't believe I forgot about this," he muttered, as if to himself. Turning to them, he said, "It was the week I got here. I was preoccupied with settling in and I just . . . I guess I didn't pay much attention to it at the time."

"To what?" Karen said. "What did she say attacked her?"

"It was a, um . . . She said she was attacked by a tall, hairy, fanged . . . uh, man."

"A *man*?" Gavin said.

"Yes. But very hairy. With fangs. And silver eyes."

"But she was committed?" Karen said.

"She was . . . Yes, she was admitted to the psychiatric ward."

"Is she still there?" Karen said.

His face grew darker. "Look, this is all confidential information, and I can't—"

"We're not asking you to *identify* her," Gavin said.

"I have no idea if she's still in the hospital. I seriously doubt it. That was months ago."

"Let me get this straight," Karen said. "The boy you treated last night said the animal that attacked him stood *upright*. Correct?"

Dr. Dinescu nodded. "That's right."

"And this woman who was admitted to the psychiatric ward months ago. She said she was attacked by a tall, hairy, fanged *man*? With silver eyes?"

The doctor thought about that a moment, seemed disturbed by it. "Yes, that's what I was told. I made no effort to confirm it, so I have no idea how accurate it is."

"And several others have come in here to be treated for animal attacks?" Karen said.

"Yes."

Gavin smiled. "You may be new to the area, Dr. Dinescu, but you've been here longer than we have. Do you know if anything is being *done* about this?"

Dr. Dinescu slowly turned his head back and forth, lost in thought again for a moment. "That's what's so strange. It doesn't show up in the papers or on the news. But it's going on. Pretty regularly. It's almost as if it's being . . . *ignored*."

Another look between Karen and Gavin, then Gavin removed a business card from his back pocket and a pen from his shirt pocket, and wrote on the back of the card.

"This is my cell-phone number, Dr. Dinescu," he said as he handed the card over. "I'd like you to call if anything comes to mind, or if anyone else comes in here after being attacked by an animal. Will you do that?"

The doctor took the card hesitantly. "Confidentiality is a very touchy—"

"I don't want you to tell me anything the law prohibits you from telling me, Doctor, but Karen and I were hired to look into this, and it would be very helpful to talk to someone who's actually been attacked. You say no one is doing anything about it. *We* would like to do something about it."

"All right. You'll be staying in the area?"

"For awhile, yes. Is there a number where we can reach you if—?"

The entrance door opened and a tall, fleshy, middle-aged man stumbled in. He was out of breath and looked pale and frightened. What appeared to be blood spattered his pale blue shirt. His wide eyes went directly to Dr. Dinescu, and he took a moment to catch his breath before speaking.

"I need help!" he said breathlessly. "There's a woman in my car! She's been—I—I—I—She's been hit. By a car. *My* car. *I hit her in my car!*" he shouted, near tears. "She just ran out—I didn't see—She wasn't there and then all of a sudden—Please, you've gotta get her in here!"

Dr. Dinescu seemed to forget Karen and Gavin in an instant as he went to work.

# CHAPTER ELEVEN

## Delivery

Bob had to keep telling himself, *Slow down, slow down*, as he sped up the hill to the hospital. He was in a hurry to get there but did not want to have a wreck on the way, or worse, to hit another pedestrian.

The woman he'd hit was slumped in the seat beside him. She was older than he'd originally thought, and the hunch on her back was actually a backpack. Her clothes were filthy, her hair stringy and matted, and she didn't smell too clean. He guessed she was a homeless person. Since getting in the car, she'd been babbling on and on about something she thought was pursuing her, some kind of monster. Along with being homeless, Bob suspected she was also crazy.

"You saved me," she said, her voice hoarse. She held her left leg with both hands and rocked back and forth in pain, but she looked at him with a forced smile, eyes wide. "You saved me from it. It was comin' after me. I could hear it behind me, breathin' and growlin'. I only got a little glimpse at it and I saw its eyes. They was silver. *Silver!* And it had real big fangs. And it was gonna eat me, I just *know* it. It was real tall and hairy and it smelled *bad*, and it came after me, and I ran so hard and so far, and then"—that forced, wide-eyed smile again—"you came along and saved me!"

"I didn't do a very good job of saving you," Bob said tremulously. "Is your leg hurt?"

"Oh, yeah, it hurts real bad, but that's okay, 'cause you saved me from bein' eaten by that thing!"

Bob pulled into the ER parking lot and stopped the car as close to the entrance as he could get. His heart thundered in his chest, he was short of breath, and his palms were wet with perspiration. "You stay here," he said. "I'll get help. Don't move. Don't get out and walk. Okay?"

"Sure, sure, whatever."

Bob groaned as he got out of the car, worried about what was to come. Would he have to deal with the police? Could he be arrested for this? Then it hit him: Mom and Grandma would find out about it and they would *never* let up. He rolled his eyes, dreading their criticism and accusations, as he hurried to the ER entrance. He pushed through the glass door and stumbled over the threshold, almost falling. A white-coated doctor with a man and woman in the waiting room turned to him suddenly, and Bob cried, "I need help!"

Penny released a long, gurgling groan as she bent forward in the car, arms hugging her abdomen.

"Hang on, honey, we'll be there soon," Gretchen said.

Her trick, the mullet with the tattoos, had thrown his pants on and rushed out of the trailer as soon as he'd seen Penny in pain on the floor. "Whatever's wrong with her," he'd said, "you're on your own. I'm outta here." For a second, Gretchen had started to shout at him because he hadn't paid her, but then she'd given up and returned her attention to Penny.

The pain subsided somewhat, and Penny stopped groaning. Her breaths were heavy and loud.

"How you doing, hon?" Gretchen said. She sounded afraid.

"I . . . don't know," Penny said between breaths.

"We're starting up the hill now. We'll be there real soon, so just hang on."

Penny moved her arms away from her abdomen, placed her hands on the seat, and locked her elbows. She clutched at the seat, rigid arms trembling, as another wave of pain tore through her.

As Karen and Gavin left the ER and headed for their SUV, the pedestrian who'd been struck by a car was being wheeled toward the ER on a gurney by Dr. Dinescu and a skinny, baby-faced male nurse the doctor called Ted. The patient wore a neck stabilizer and was moving her arms agitatedly on the gurney. The driver of the car followed a few feet behind, nervous and fidgety, uncertain and cautious.

"Silver eyes!" the patient croaked. "It really had *silver eyes* and it was gonna *eat* me!"

Karen and Gavin came to an abrupt halt and turned to face each other a moment, before looking behind them at the gurney on its way inside.

"It was a monster!" the woman cried. "Jesus help me, it was a monster! He saved me! That man who hit me with his car, he *saved* me!"

Gavin hurried over to the driver and touched his arm, saying, "Excuse me."

The man jerked as he spun around, startled. The gurney was taken inside the ER through a set of double doors that bypassed the waiting room.

Gavin smiled. "Hi. Are you okay?"

"Okay? Uh . . . Well, I'm a little, um . . . upset."

"Sure, I can imagine. Must've scared the hell out of you. What happened?"

As they talked, Karen walked over and joined them.

"Well, I was driving home after . . . Well, I'd just kind of gone out for a ride, you know? To get out of the house."

"Sure."

"I rounded this corner and the next thing I knew, she was just . . . *there*. And then my car hit her." He clenched his eyes shut for a moment. "That sound. It was awful."

"I'm no doctor, but it looks like she's probably going to be okay," Gavin said.

"Gosh, I hope so," the man muttered, staring anxiously in the direction the gurney had been taken. He turned to Gavin suddenly. "Do you think the police will show up?"

"The ER will report it to the police. That's routine, nothing to worry about. An officer will show up and ask you for a statement, and all you have to do is tell him exactly what happened."

The man's face grew even more pale as his eyes became wider.

"I don't think you have anything to worry about," Gavin said. He offered his hand and shook with the man, whose palm was moist. "By the way, I'm Gavin Keoph. This is Karen Moffett."

"Bob Berens. I *hope* I don't have anything to worry about. I mean, it was an *accident*, she just *appeared*."

"I understand," Gavin said, trying to sound reassuring. The man seemed almost on the verge of tears. "You did the right thing in bringing her here so quickly. Don't worry, Bob, everything will be fine."

Karen stepped forward. "She was saying something just now, something about a monster. Do you know what she was talking about?"

"Oh, yeah. Well, she's homeless, I think, and she might be a little . . . um, you know, not in her right mind. She said some kind of monster was chasing her just before she ran in front of my car. Something hairy with fangs and silver eyes."

"She said 'silver eyes'?" Gavin said.

"Yeah, several times. It was all she could talk about all the way here."

"Did she say anything else about this monster?" Karen said.

"Uh, well . . . She said she could smell it. That it smelled bad. And, um"—he cleared his throat—"she said this thing was going to eat her. I don't know if she's on drugs, or what. But I figured she was hallucinating."

Gavin turned to Karen and said quietly, "I think we should try to talk to her."

Karen nodded. "Let's go back in."

Turning to Bob with a smile, Gavin said, "Why don't you go park your car and then come inside where—"

Headlights swept over them as a car rushed into the lot. The three of them turned as a small, battered, red pickup truck sped toward them. The driver slammed on the brakes at the last moment and the tires squealed on the pavement, but the car did not stop in time. Its bumper slammed into a back corner of Bob's station wagon with a crunch of metal.

"Oh, no!" Bob shouted, putting a hand on each side of his head, elbows sticking out. He groaned and said, "My mom's gonna kill me."

The driver side door opened and a woman scrambled out of the cab. She was in her early thirties with mussed blonde hair that looked like she'd just gotten out of bed. She wore a gray T-shirt with the logo of a local bowling alley on the front, a pair of white shorts, and flip-flops on her feet. As she ran around the rear of the pickup to the passenger side, she said, "Help me! My little girl's havin' a baby and she needs help right away! She's in labor!"

Bob's hands remained on his head, elbows in the air, eyes wide beneath a frowning brow, the corners of his mouth pulled back in a look of shock. As if he hadn't heard the woman, he said again, "My mother's gonna *kill* me!"

"Somebody get a wheelchair or something!" the woman shouted.

As she spoke, Karen rushed into the ER while Gavin hurried to the woman's side. Bob did not move.

A moment later, Karen came out with Ted, who pushed a wheelchair to the open door on the passenger side of the pickup. Gavin helped the morbidly obese pregnant girl out of the cab and into the wheelchair. She screamed in pain as the male nurse wheeled her into the ER with the mother hurrying alongside the chair.

"How am I gonna move my car *now*?" Bob said, his arms dropping to his sides as he stared at the pickup truck with its nose planted firmly in the rear of his station wagon.

"I'll go inside and get her keys," Gavin said. "We can move them both together, then we'll go inside." He turned to Karen. "Go on in and see if you can manage to talk to her about that, uh, monster."

Karen nodded once, turned, and went inside with Gavin.

"I don't understand," the receptionist said, eyes narrowing slightly. "You want to talk to the *patient*?"

Karen read the receptionist's name tag, then smiled pleasantly. "I understand if she's not available at the moment, Winona, but it's very important that I have a word with her as soon as she is. It's regarding the conversation we had with Dr. Dinescu. My partner and I came to discuss the outbreak of animal attacks in this area."

Winona nodded knowingly. "Oh, yes. There've been quite a few."

"I think the woman in there—the one who was hit by the car—might know something. I think she was being attacked by an animal when she was hit."

"Reeeeaaally?" Winona said, frowning. "Well, I can see how she's doing. Maybe she can have a visitor now." She stood. "Be right back."

Sighing, Karen seated herself in the chair before receptionist's window and waited. There was a sudden commotion back beyond the window, and a voice screamed in pain, while another shouted, "Help her, for God's sake, *do* something, *help* her!" She sat there and listened to the racket for a few minutes, until Winona finally returned.

"She's in a booth right now and Dr. Dinescu is preoccupied with another patient," she said. "He said a visitor might help calm her down, so why don't you come on back. But please, don't do or say anything to upset her, because she's kind of agitated as it is."

Another painful wail rose from the back, followed by a woman shouting, "You don't have *time* for that, goddammit!"

"Come to the door," Winona said, then she disappeared.

Karen went to the door to the left of the window and Winona let her in. As she walked through the door, another scream tore through the ER.

"What's going on?" Karen said, nearly whispering.

"A young woman in labor," Winona said. "They may not have time to get her to maternity."

Winona led her through a short hall, then into one end of the emergency room and to the first in a row of curtained-off booths. To the right, the room opened up into a larger, brightly lit area. Beyond the short counter to the far right, behind which an officious-looking woman sat, frantic activity caught Karen's eye, and she saw Bob standing nearby, eyes bulging in his pale, slack-jawed face as he stood frozen in place, clearly afraid and uncertain. But she didn't have time to stop and look—Winona pulled the thin, pale green curtain aside and led her into the booth.

"Hannah?" Winona said. "I have someone who'd like to see you. Is that okay?"

The woman on the table said, "A visitor? Really? I don't mind. I'd *like* a visitor." Her voice was hoarse and weak. She still wore her dirty clothes and had the stabilizing collar around her neck. Her backpack was slumped on a small plastic chair.

Winona gave Karen a quick smile as she left.

Karen went to Hannah's side and smiled down at her. "My name is Karen Moffett."

"Hi, Karen. The doctor says I'm gonna have to have X-rays. I'm just waitin' for 'em to come and get me."

The screams continued beyond the curtain.

"Sounds like somebody's really hurtin' out there," Hannah said. "Guess I'm pretty lucky."

"The man who hit you—"

"Oh, he was a nice man. He saved me, y'know. I mean, I know he hit me with his car, an' all, only 'cause I ran right in front of him scared outta my life, but really, he *saved* me."

It was obvious that Hannah was rather simpleminded. She looked to be in her midforties, but her voice and manner of speaking were childlike. Her narrow face was weathered and lined, eyes deep set. Strands of gray ran through her long, filthy, brown hair.

"What did he save you from, Hannah?" Karen said.

"The thing that was chasin' me."

"And . . . what was that?"

"Some kinda monster. A big thing. Hairy. And it had big fangs, and *silver eyes*. See, there's a little coffee shop on Beachview, the Sand Dollar. Right next to the Lighthouse Motel. It's just a dinky little place, real old and run-down. Sometimes I go there 'bout closin' time. The owner, he's a real nice guy named Zeke. Sometimes if I show up, he'll give me a free meal. Whatever's left over from the day, y'know? So I was on my way there, walkin' through—"

The screams beyond the curtain got worse.

Dr. Dinescu snapped, "Goddammit, Ted, get her to maternity before—"

"I said you don't have *time* for that!" the girl's mother shouted. "That baby's coming *now*, damn you, and you'd better—"

"Okay, Ted, get over here," the doctor said.

Hannah stopped talking a moment and listened to the commotion. "Sounds like somebody's 'bout to have a baby, huh?" she whispered.

Karen nodded.

"Anyways, uh . . . What was I sayin'? Oh, I know. I was walkin' through the patch of woods beside Beachview, down by the beach, when I hear somethin'. Whatever it is, it's movin' along with me in the dark. Scared the hell outta me, y'know? I got this flashlight, see. I don't use it often 'cause I don't like to run down the batteries, but I took it outta my pack and turned it on, looked around to see what was makin' that noise."

The curtain was pulled aside and Gavin joined Karen in the booth.

"Hannah, this is my friend Gavin," Karen said.

Hannah smiled. "Hi, Gavin. Did you come to visit me, too?"

Gavin tossed an uncertain glance at Karen, then smiled down at Hannah and said, "Sure."

Karen said, "Hannah was telling me about the, uh, thing that was trying to attack her when she ran in front of Bob's car." When Gavin nodded, Karen turned to Hannah again and said, "Go on."

"Well, with my flashlight, I got a look at it," Hannah continued. "Not a *great* look, but it was good enough. It was a big hairy thing. Scary as all get-out. A big snout with long fangs. And silver eyes. *Silver eyes!* And I could *smell* it. A stinky animal smell, like at the circus, or somethin', y'know what I mean? It growled and came after me and I ran for my life. When that man hit me—"

Voices raised beyond the curtain.

"What do you mean *three months*?" Dr. Dinescu shouted.

"That's what she says," the mother replied.

"Well, that's *impossible*!"

"It's coming!" another voice shouted.

There was a bustle of movement as the girl continued to scream in pain.

"Hope everything's okay out there," Hannah said. "Anyways, that man hit me and saved my life. If he hadn't, that thing woulda got me, I just know it. It was gonna eat me."

"Push, push!" Dr. Dinescu said.

"It's coming, everything's fine, honey," the mother said in breathless reassurance.

Hannah said, "I don't know what that thing was, but it sure weren't no regular animal. It was standin' up, like a person. I never seen nothin' like it before."

More calls of, "Push! Push!" came from beyond the curtain.

"How tall was it?" Gavin asked.

"Taller'n me, I know that. I couldn't tell you 'zactly how tall, though." She winced and released a sharp breath.

"Are you in pain, Hannah?" Karen said.

"My leg's hurtin'. My leg and hip. I feel okay otherwise, though, you don't gotta worry 'bout me." She gave Karen a lopsided smile.

"As soon as they're finished out there," Karen said, nodding toward the curtain, "I'm sure Dr. Dinescu will take good care of you."

"Is it breathing?" the pregnant girl's mother asked worriedly. "Is it okay? Is it a boy or girl?"

An indecipherable blur of voices and words followed and rapidly grew louder. Then, another scream filled the emergency room. It was a man screaming in pain and fear and it came again and again, quickly followed by the screams of a woman, and then another woman. Something clattered to the floor as footsteps scrambled.

"Oh, Jesus!" Dr. Dinescu screamed.

Karen and Gavin quickly turned, tossed the curtain aside, and left the booth. Each of them gasped loudly. They were not prepared for what they found on the other side.

# CHAPTER TWELVE

*Night Visitor*

While Bob and Gretchen were driving their passengers to the emergency room, George Purdy was in his cabin cooking a stew on his woodstove. He was listening to a call-in talk show on a San Francisco radio station. The topic of discussion was the war on terror. The host was a very funny, sharply intelligent gay man engaged in a heated argument with an extreme right-wing caller who was very angry. George went to the stove and lifted the lid on the pot. As he stirred the stew, a noise made him jerk, made his back stiffen. He heard it even above the voices on the radio. He put the lid back on the pot, hurried across the room, and killed the radio. He cocked his head and listened carefully.

It had been a solid thump right outside the front of the cabin. He stood motionless and listened.

It came again, more distinct this time—movement just outside the door.

George's veins flowed with ice water, and gooseflesh spread over his shoulders and back as he stared at the door. Getting ahold of himself, he took three quick steps and snatched up the .45 automatic that was always on the small table near the door. The gun was loaded with silver-tipped rounds. As he held the cold grip in his hand

and stared at the door, he hoped Arlin Hurley had been right about silver being effective against the creatures that had taken over Big Rock.

A tentative knock at the door made George's breath catch in his throat like a fish bone.

*Nobody knows I'm here*, he thought.

He opened his mouth to ask, *Who is it?* but he had no voice. His mouth was suddenly dry. He tried to stir up some spit and swallow, but it turned into a loud, dry gulp.

The knock came again, harder this time. Then came a cautious voice.

"George? Are you in there?"

It was a woman.

He moved close to the door and put his eye to the peephole. The face on the other side, distorted by the tiny lens, was unfamiliar at first. She was pretty, with long, dark brown hair, smooth skin, full lips. The longer he looked at her, the more familiar she became. He'd seen her before . . . *somewhere* . . . but he could not put his finger on where, on who she was.

"George, it's me," she said. "Ella."

*Ella?* he thought, frowning. *Do I know an Ella?*

It came to him in an eye-widening rush—Ella Hurley! But she looked different. Younger, prettier than usual. She appeared to have shed ten years from her age, and her hair color was different. But it was *Ella!*

"Ella?" he said loudly, surprised.

"Let me in, George. We need to talk."

He instinctively reached out to unlock all the locks he had on the door, but jerked his hand back as if he'd been burned. What did she want? How did she find him? Most of all, he had to wonder if she was *safe*.

"What, uh . . . What do you want, Ella?" he asked, moving very close to the door until his cheek lightly touched the wood.

"I want to talk to you, George. It's important."

"Talk to me . . . about what?" He could not keep his fear from creeping into his voice.

"I'm not going to hurt you, George. I promise."

He gulped again. "How did you find me?"

"I couldn't find you anywhere else, so I thought you might have come here. You brought us up here once. Arlin and me. Remember?"

He had brought them up to the cabin a few summers ago. He'd shown them around, and they'd had a picnic lunch in the yard.

George scrubbed a hand down his face and took a deep breath as his stomach wound into tight knots. "Look, Ella, I'm just . . . I don't know what to . . ." His hand clutched the grip of the .45 tightly. "Where have you been? What happened to you after Arlin . . . after he was . . ." He cleared his throat, stood up straight, steeled himself. When he spoke again, his voice was firm, resolute. "Where have you *been*, Ella?"

"I'll tell you everything, George, I promise. Just let me in. I'm not going to hurt you. I'm on your side."

A long silence stretched out between them in which George did not move, just stared at the door.

"I'm here for Arlin," Ella said. "I want to make them pay for what they did to him, George."

It was so good to hear her voice—a voice with which he associated fond memories, a pleasant, friendly voice that reminded him of a time when his life was safe and mundane, when he could relax and read a good book by John D. MacDonald or Mickey Spillane and all would be right with the world. That time seemed so long ago.

*But she can say anything she wants*, he thought. *That doesn't mean she's telling the truth.*

"They turned me," she said finally, her voice breaking slightly, as if she were holding back strong emotions. "But I'm not like them, George. I'm not. I swear. I want to get them. I want to make them *pay*." She said the last six words through clenched teeth. "They turned me, but I haven't hurt anyone. I've already fed for tonight, George. A deer. Not a person. I won't do that, I refuse. Because I'm not like them. You're safe. I'm not even hungry."

His eyes stung with tears as he struggled with his decision.

"I'm on the *inside*, George! I want to take them down from the *inside*. And I need your help."

He reached out and unlocked the three dead bolts he'd installed on the door, then removed the thick plank of wood that stretched across it. He tossed the piece of wood aside and opened the door.

Ella rushed in through the doorway, and for a moment—a brief, terrifying moment—George thought she was pouncing on him. During that instant, his lungs emptied of air as he expected her to close her mouth on his throat.

Instead, she fell against him, threw her arms around him, and began to cry against his shoulder. He wrapped an arm around her and closed the door with the other, quickly throwing the locks. He put both arms around her and held her close, so happy to see her—someone familiar, someone from his past, from a time when he had friends and life was safe and orderly. A lump rose in his throat, and his chest suddenly burned with emotion.

"What's happened, Ella?" he whispered. "What the hell is going *on* out there? Hardly a day goes by that I don't wonder if I've gone insane, if I've locked myself in this cabin up here in the woods because of some paranoid delusion that's filled my head, some kind of mental illness."

"You're not crazy, George," she said. "But I understand how you feel, believe me." She pulled away and looked up into his face, her hands still holding his shoulders tightly. "I've been living with *them* since January."

"So you're, uh . . . You're . . . You're a . . ." He couldn't bring himself to say it and finally shut his mouth and quit trying.

"A werewolf," she said, dropping her arms to her sides. A smile flitted across her mouth. "I know. It sounds crazy, doesn't it? Saying it seems . . . I don't know. Insane. But yes, that's what I am. It's sexually transmitted, and I was raped in our house. The night Arlin was killed. Ever since then, I've been in a big house where a bunch of them are staying. It's out on Edgerly Drive, a narrow little road that branches off of Perryman and goes down by the beach. I've been . . . I'm . . . with Taggart now."

"The new sheriff?"

"Yes."

George slowly nodded. "Yeah, I remember him from the slab in the morgue, back when he was a corpse. Or when I *thought* he was a corpse."

"They're not corpses, George. They're working hard. They've put down roots in Big Rock, and they plan to spread. I want to stop them, but I need help."

George took her hand and led her into the cabin. "Come in, sit down. Can I get you anything? I've got some real good coffee here. It's hot."

"That would be nice. Just black is fine."

He got her the coffee, then they sat down on the couch.

"Roots?" he said. "What kind of roots?"

She sipped from the thick ceramic mug. "Well, obviously, they have the sheriff's station. They have road workers guarding the town, monitoring who comes in and out. Linemen to cut communications if necessary. They've taken over several businesses in town, but they've got their eyes on two particular things they want that will allow them to spread out of Big Rock and into the surrounding area: Sisters of Mercy Hospital and the Seventh-day Adventist church."

"The Adventist church?" he said, frowning.

"Taggart was raised an Adventist and he knows them, knows their beliefs. He wants to use the church as a base, take over the businesses owned by its members, and use the church's outreach programs to get into surrounding communities."

"You know, they don't eat meat, the Adventists," George said. Then he chuckled nervously. "They're not gonna be too crazy about your diet."

She smiled wearily at the joke, sipped the coffee, then said, "Taggart wants to do the same with the hospital. It serves more than just Big Rock. It would be valuable to them if they could take it over. They've already got people in there, but they're moving slowly and cautiously to avoid being discovered by the wrong people—people who might be able to stop them. The hospital made me think of you."

George nodded. "Okay. What do you want me to do?"

"I'm not sure. I assumed you would know people who work there."

"Sure. Several people. A few I know very well."

She took a few more swallows of water. "Somehow, George—I don't know how, but *somehow*—you've got to tell them."

His eyebrows rose. "That werewolves are trying to take over the hospital?" He chuckled humorlessly. "A story like that is liable to *land* me in the hospital—in a locked room in Ward 18."

"They have to know. They have to be told that they're in danger, that some of the people they're working with are not what they seem to be."

"The whole *town* is in danger!"

"Now, yes. That danger will spread a lot farther if we don't do something to stop them."

George thought about that and slowly nodded. "Yes. The hospital would be a strategic target. It would give them access to people from all over the area. From there, they could spread to other towns."

"There must be someone you know there, someone you trust, who will listen to you and believe you. Can't you think of *anyone*?"

George rubbed the back of his neck as he thought, then finally nodded. "There is one person who might listen. Hugo. He's very intelligent, a freethinker, a man with an open mind. And we've known each other for half a dozen years."

"Who is he?"

"A doctor. He works in the emergency room. Dr. Hugo Rodriguez."

"Can you call him?"

"Right *now*?"

"We can't afford to wait around, George. They've had months to plan and work and get organized."

"Why have you waited this long to come to me?"

She sighed heavily and set her coffee on an end table. "I've tried to find you before. It wasn't easy to get away tonight. I'm supposed to be feeding. I did that as quickly as I could and came straight here. They have me under close scrutiny most of the time. I'm supposed to be taking care of this young woman. She's . . . a mother. The mother of the First Born."

"First Born?"

"They're reproducing, George. This woman, her name is Cynthia. She was raped by one of them. Not only did that turn her, but she became pregnant."

"With . . . one of *them*?" George's horror was evident on his face.

"Yes. A three-month gestation, and the thing that was born . . . It's partially human, and partially . . . not." She frowned and her entire face darkened, became fearful. "It's not like someone who has been turned. It's different, much stronger. I saw it only once. A girl. A beautiful girl, really. She has a . . . I don't know . . . an air about her that's . . . frightening. It's almost as if she knows what I'm

thinking. Her eyes are . . . incredibly sharp and percep-
tive. The rest of us . . . Our eyes only turn silver when we
transform. Hers are silver all the time. So far, there's
been only one. But if there's one, there are bound to be
others."

"Why is this happening?"

"None of them know. They don't understand it. Taggart's explanation is that we are evolving, that this is a
sign we are destined to be dominant."

Deeply disturbed by everything she'd said, George
stood and went to his desk, picked up his cell phone. He
turned to Ella. "What should I say to Hugo?"

"Just arrange a time to talk to him. Right away. I'd join
you, but I just can't, I couldn't possibly explain such a
long absence. Tell him everything I've told you. Do your
best to convince him."

George opened the cell phone, thought for a moment
about what he would say, took a moment to remember
Hugo's number, and then punched it in. Hugo's wife
answered.

"Hello, Stella," George said. He identified himself. "Is
Hugo in?"

"No, George, Hugo's gone to work."

"Oh, okay. So he'll be at the hospital?"

"He should be, yes. Unless there's something he's not
telling me." She laughed. "He turns his cell phone off at
work, so you might want to call the hospital."

"Thanks. That's what I'll do." After ending the conversation, he punched in the hospital's number. He asked the
switchboard operator if he could speak to Dr. Hugo Rodriguez in the emergency room. As he waited to be connected, he paced in front of the couch. Ella sat there
watching him pensively. She nervously jittered one foot,
making her knee bob. The aroma of the stew cooking on
the stove grew richer, warming the cabin.

"Emergency room," a woman's voice said. She sounded

shaky, frightened. There was some kind of racket in the background.

"Could I speak to Dr. Rodriguez, please?" George said.

"Dr. Rodriguez isn't—Dr. Rod—" Horrible screams rose in the background and the woman on the line gasped, then said, "Oh, my God."

George stopped pacing and frowned. "What's wrong?" he said, alarm in his voice.

"I don't know, we've—There's something—"

More screams, a chorus of them, came piercingly over the line. Chaos was exploding in the ER like a bomb.

Away from the phone, the woman on the other end of the line cried, "Oh, God, what's happening? *What's happening?*"

Someone a good distance away screamed, "Jesus, help him! *Help him!*"

The sounds stopped abruptly and were followed by a long, dead silence. The connection had been severed.

George turned to Ella to find a look of dread on her face.

"What happened?" she said.

"I don't know. That was the ER. There was a lot of noise and screaming, and the woman on the phone screamed, and then I was cut off."

Ella slumped back on the couch, as if weak with fear. "Oh, God," she whispered. "What have they done?"

George closed the phone and put it in his pocket. "What should I do?"

Ella stood. "You need to go there. See what's happening. Try to find your friend. Maybe there's something you can do."

"And maybe I'll end up dead."

She gently placed a hand on his arm. "George, someone needs to do something . . . and you're all I've got. I don't know who else to turn to. You can either lock yourself up in this cabin and live in fear, or you can try to do something about this. Yes, it's dangerous. But so is staying here. They'll find you eventually. When they do . . . well, you'll wish you weren't here when they arrive. I promise you that."

He nodded slowly and muttered, "Might as well go out fighting."

"Don't talk that way. You may be able to do more than you think." She moved forward and hugged him again. "I have to go, George. I can't stay away any longer, or they'll want to know why."

"Will you check in with me again?"

They quickly exchanged cell-phone numbers.

"I'll do my best," she said. "If I can't call you . . . well, do your best to call me. Okay?"

He led her to the door and unlocked it. "Take care of yourself."

"You, too. And get down to the hospital right away."

"I will."

After she was gone, George took the stew off the stove, then paced rapidly for awhile. *I'm wasting time*, he thought. He grabbed his keys off the desk and headed out of the cabin.

# CHAPTER THIRTEEN

*Loose*

The wet sound of blood spattering over the tile floor was, for a brief moment, the only sound in the brightly lit emergency room. That brief moment seemed to stretch into an ugly eternity.

Karen and Gavin froze and stared, and a few feet away from them, Bob did the same. They took in the nightmarish tableau while the silent moment extended as if time had been frozen.

Ted lay on the floor, his legs spread wide. Something small had attached itself to his crotch, and the blood was coming from there. It was a baby, its body smeared with blood and fluids. But it did not look . . . quite right. Aside from the surreal fact that its mouth was latched onto Ted's crotch, something was very wrong with it physically. Its face was distorted, elongated into what appeared to be a long, narrow snout. It had clamped that snout firmly onto Ted's crotch and was turning its head back and forth viciously, clenching its jaws, its body thrashing and jerking as it tried to bite harder and harder. Ted's dark brown pants were rapidly darkening with blood. His mouth was a yawning hole, and his wide eyes stared down at the thing as he lay stiff and motionless for that brief moment, which stretched on and on. All eyes in the room were on him, mouths gaping, bodies frozen. Everyone stood and stared in shocked disbelief at what they were seeing.

The silence was shattered by Ted's scream. At first, it was an inarticulate, ululating wail, and that collapsed into a gurgle, followed by a ragged, screamed plea.

*"Get it off me get it off me Jesus Christ get it off me!"*

Standing beside her obese daughter lying on a table, the blonde woman in the gray T-shirt screamed, "Jesus, help him! *Help him!*"

Then others—the girl who had just given birth and two female nurses—began to scream.

"What's going on out there?" Hannah shouted in her curtained-off booth, her voice shaky and tense with fear.

Dr. Dinescu and Gavin moved at the same time. Both lunged toward Ted and reached for the small, bloody figure between his legs. Dr. Dinescu's right foot slid in a slick puddle of blood, and it took him a moment of flailing to keep from falling. Meanwhile, Gavin grabbed hold of the infant's squirming torso with both hands and struggled to pull it away. Ted only screamed louder, writhing on the floor, legs kicking, arms flapping. The creature would not release its hold on Ted's crotch, and when Gavin tried to pull it away, he only made the man's pain worse. The creature was firmly fastened to Ted. Gavin was shocked by the strength of the monstrous infant's slippery little body. Dr. Dinescu bent down to help.

The creature released Ted, jerked its head around sharply with a small, pinched growl, and closed its fanged snout on Dr. Dinescu's left wrist. The doctor screamed in pain and tried to pull away, but the creature only buried its fangs deeper in his flesh.

Gavin's mouth dropped open and his heart skipped a beat when he saw the flash of fangs in the infant's snout. They were like curved, glistening needles surrounded by thin, black lips.

The instant Ted was released, he kicked his legs and crawled backward away from the creature as fast as he could, still screaming in pain.

The blonde woman continued to scream as she stared in horror at the thing that was now clamped to Dr. Dinescu's wrist. She threw both arms around her daughter and pulled her close, as if for life. Her daughter returned the embrace and screamed shrilly, "Mommy! Mommy! Mommy!"

One of the two female nurses ran screaming from the room, her body swaying, arms outstretched before her.

Bob gawked at the scene with an expression of breathless shock, and a few feet away from him, Karen did the same.

Dr. Dinescu fell backward with the creature still clamped onto his wrist. He swung his arm through the air, trying to dislodge it.

"What's happening?" Hannah cried behind the curtain. "What is it? What's going on?"

Gavin reached under his sport coat and removed his Glock from its shoulder holster, swung it around and held it with both hands. He tried to get a bead on the creature, but Dr. Dinescu staggered and flailed and made it impossible.

As if suddenly remembering she was armed, Karen drew her 9-millimeter and, like Gavin, tried to take aim at the thing on the doctor's wrist. She could not.

There were too many people gathered around for wild shots to be safe, and neither of them wanted to hit an onlooker. The creature never stopped moving. It's body continued to thrash as it made muffled growling sounds.

When Hannah shouted again, her voice was wet with tears. "Somebody tell me what's goin' on, pleee-heeeze! I'm *scared*!"

Crying out in pain and fear, Dr. Dinescu flew backward and fell onto a small table set up just outside one of the curtained booths. Objects flew in all directions in a clatter as the metal table crashed to the floor, spilling its contents. The creature made a vicious gurgling sound as it clung to the doctor's wrist.

"Slam it against the floor!" Gavin shouted.

Lying on his back, Dr. Dinescu raised his left arm high, then brought it down as hard as he could. The creature was bashed against the floor with a wet smacking sound, and spatters of its viscous, bloody coating splashed out over the floor on contact. It did not let go and continued to squirm and jerk. The doctor repeated the action once, twice, and a third time.

On the last swing, the creature's head struck the floor with a loud crack. It dropped from the doctor's wrist and rolled over the blood-spattered floor, landing on its back, its snout open wide to reveal its fangs, a pink tongue wriggling inside the mouth as it rolled. It finally came to rest on its back.

Karen and Gavin both moved forward, aiming their weapons carefully, ready to fire.

It was still for less than the length of a heartbeat. It flipped over onto its stomach as Gavin fired. The gunshot exploded inside the room but missed its intended target, and the bullet pierced the tile where the thing had been only an instant before. The creature crawled at a shocking speed over the floor, heading directly for Karen and Gavin. It growled as it raced between them, then disappeared under a bed in one of the open booths.

The emergency room resembled a small battlefield. Ted, who had crawled backward until he was against a wall, had managed to lift himself into a half-sitting position, legs still spread. He had left a trail of blood smeared over the floor. He sobbed and groaned in pain, his face as white as chalk as he gawked down at the torn crotch of his blood-soaked pants, arms and legs quaking.

"Tell me!" Hannah screamed. "What's *haaappeniiing*?"

Dr. Dinescu struggled to his feet, blood dripping from his torn wrist. Eyes squinting and lips pulled back over his teeth in a mask of pain, his attention was focused on Ted.

"He's in shock," the doctor said, nodding at Ted. "Irene, he needs help. We've got to—"

"Everyone out of this room," Gavin said firmly as he eyed the bed under which the creature had crawled, his gun aimed in that direction. Karen stood beside him, her gun pointing in the same direction.

Dr. Dinescu turned to him. "Ted needs—"

"Get him out of here and *then* help him," Gavin said. He turned to Dr. Dinescu, then looked at the others, who stood with slack jaws and bulging eyes, staring beyond him at the space into which the creature had disappeared. "I'm serious, get out of here! *All* of you!"

Bob started to move stiffly toward the door.

The thing shot out from under the bed. It growled as it moved across the floor and left a bloody trail. It went straight for Bob's left leg and closed its jaws. Its fangs pierced the leg of Bob's pants and barely missed his calf. With a shrill, terrified scream, Bob began to hop around on his right foot while kicking his left leg, his arms straight and spinning circles in the air in an effort to maintain his balance.

*"Oh Jesus Christ God it's got me help somebody help Jesus oh Lord help me—"* Bob screamed, the words tumbling from his mouth in one long, rapid stream that finally crumbled into terrified babbling.

Karen and Gavin tried to hold their guns on the creature, but Bob kept kicking his leg. They both knew that if they fired, they had a better chance of hitting Bob than the thing attached to his pants. Karen stepped toward him and kicked the creature hard with her right foot. When her foot connected, the thing yelped as it tumbled through the air with a torn bit of Bob's pant leg in its mouth.

With the little monster off of his leg, Bob fell forward and landed facedown on the floor.

The creature arced through the air, hit the floor with a splat, and rolled and slid under the curtain that surrounded Hannah's booth.

"Oh, no!" Karen cried.

The creature made an ugly growling noise as sounds of movement came from the other side of the curtain.

Karen and Gavin started toward the booth, but before they could reach it, Hannah's throaty, jagged scream of pain and fear tore through the room. At the same time, the sound of tearing cloth ripped through the air. With chittering clicking sounds, a few buttons scattered over the tile from under the curtain.

The two investigators struggled with the curtain, trying to pull it aside and get into the booth. Like actors in a silent-era slapstick comedy, they fumbled and fought with the curtain as Hannah's screams went on and on. Other sounds came from inside the booth, as well—wet smacking sounds and small, breathy grunts. Frustrated, Gavin finally grabbed the curtain and pulled with all his strength as Hannah's screams ended with a harsh retching. The hooks that held the curtain in the track on the ceiling pinged and snapped as the curtain partially fell away, just enough to reveal Hannah on the table in the booth.

Hannah still lay on her back, but now the small creature hunkered on her chest like some kind of demon. Its little hands clutched her filthy, blood-stained shirt, the sharp claws at the tip of each chubby finger piercing the material. The shirt had been torn open over her abdomen. The creature had ripped her open with its teeth. There was blood on Hannah, the table, and the small thing on top of her. When the curtain fell aside, it lifted its head and glared at Karen and Gavin with shiny silver eyes, its snout chewing hungrily on the rope of intestine it had pulled from Hannah's open abdomen.

Karen made a sickened sound in her throat as she and Gavin leveled their weapons at the creature.

Its bloody mouth opened wide and it growled at them, then sprang from Hannah's chest. The creature became a blur as it lunged through the air directly for Karen and Gavin, its little arms outstretched, sharp claws ready to tear, wet meat-flecked fangs ready to bite.

With guns raised, Karen and Gavin each fired once as they instinctively stepped apart to avoid letting the creature slam into them. It sailed past them and smacked to the floor.

Karen spun around first, just in time to see the monstrous infant, on all fours, scuttle through the same door through which she had come and into the short hall. Karen's mind jumped ahead and imagined the creature getting into the waiting room, and then either into the rest of the hospital or outside the hospital, where it could go *anywhere*.

"Stop it, quick, before it gets out!" she shouted as Gavin turned and ran after the creature. Karen followed him through the short hall.

It's body jerking back and forth, it crawled past the closed door that led into the waiting room and passed into the small office behind the reception window. The office was empty. Apparently Winona had fled.

*The window*, Karen thought. *It's open.*

As the creature climbed up on Winona's empty chair, on which lay the abandoned telephone receiver, Gavin fired his weapon again. In such small quarters, the gunshot seemed even louder than before. Gavin missed his target.

The creature hopped from the chair to the desk and moved toward the window.

Karen frantically shouted, "Don't let it get out that—"

It went through the window.

A woman screamed in the waiting room, "It's in here! Somebody! Oh, God! It's in here, in here!"

They quickly backtracked to the door and went into the waiting room. Winona stood in a far corner, her palms pressed to her cheeks below terrified eyes. She pointed a finger at the open door that led to the corridor outside. As she pointed, her mouth opened and closed, but nothing came out.

A bloody trail led through that door and into the corridor.

Gavin went out the door first, followed by Karen. Their jogging footsteps slapped the tiles as they followed the trail to the left. Up ahead, the trail rounded a corner to the right and disappeared down another corridor.

From beyond that corner, a woman screamed. Half a heartbeat later, a man shouted, "What the *fuck*?"

They rounded the corner and saw that the red trail was fading as the creature moved along. Up ahead and on the left, a woman stood against the wall clutching her purse to her chest, her face registering shock and fear. Across the corridor from her, a man stood just inside a doorway, his back pressed hard against the open door as he gawked at something on the other side.

Karen and Gavin approached the open door and looked through it. It led to the stairwell, and the man was staring slack-jawed at the stairs.

"Shit," Gavin muttered.

The man's eyes widened when he saw their guns. He looked from one gun to the other, then at Gavin, and said, "Whuh-what *was* that?"

They ignored his question and hurried up the stairs.

Bob staggered into the waiting room and headed for the glass door that led outside. He had no particular destination in mind—he wasn't even thinking specifically of going to his car out in the parking lot. All he knew was that he *had* to get out of the emergency room, out of the hospital, outside where there was plenty of air to breathe and space in which to move.

The floor seemed to tilt beneath his feet, first in one direction, then in the other. He couldn't quite walk in a straight line, and he kept swaying from side to side and moving his arms to keep his balance. He reached out to push the door open, then fell against it heavily.

He could still hear Ted crying out in pain and the women sobbing loudly in the back. As he went out the door, the sounds faded.

The night had cooled somewhat since he'd been outside last, and it felt good against his skin. He felt clammy as he made his way from the ER door to the parking lot, still walking unsteadily.

On his way out, Bob passed a brown-skinned, black-haired man going in. The man looked deep in thought and walked with confidence and authority as he went into the ER.

The lot was quiet and there was no activity, no one else out there other than Bob. Tall lights stood at regular distances around the edges of the lot. A mist was beginning to move in, curling around those lights like thin ghosts.

Bob could not arrange his thinking into clear, coherent thoughts. It was as if his brain were babbling inside his head, gibbering nonsense like some kind of crazy person.

He kept seeing that . . . *thing*—

*Impossible*, he thought vaguely. *That thing is impossible, it can't exist, it can't, can't, can't . . .*

—kept seeing the baby it had been, then suddenly, the creature it became, with a fanged snout that jutted from the small, round face, the eyes suddenly silver and animal-like—

*. . . that couldn't have happened, I couldn't have seen that, things like that don't happen, it's impossible, I couldn't have seen that.*

—kept seeing it clamping onto Ted's crotch, onto Dr. Dinescu's wrist—

*Did I see that? Really? Did I really see that, or is something wrong with me? Am I losing my mind? Am I mentally ill? Am I having some kind of breakdown?*

—wriggling across the floor with impossible speed, chewing noisily and sloppily on Hannah's intestine. He tried to make the images stop, but he had no control over them. They infected his mind like some kind of virus, seized him like a fever as he staggered through the parking lot.

He was halfway to his car when his stomach seemed to explode. He began vomiting a moment before he bent forward, the contents of his stomach spewing in an arc before splashing onto the pavement.

Bob stood in place for a long moment, bent at the waist. He swayed back and forth a little as he waited to see if more was going to come up. When it did not, he moved on, staggering around the puddle of vomit. But even as he walked, his head began to feel like a balloon filled with helium. It seemed to lightly lift off of his neck and rise higher and higher in the air above his body.

He was unconscious before he fell to the pavement and was unaware of the fact that he had fainted.

There was no one else in the parking lot. The night was silent except for the sound of a cricket chirping sharply and the almost-inaudible patterings of moths throwing themselves against the glass covers of the parking lot's tall lights.

After awhile, a faint sound rose somewhere in the distance. It grew for a moment, then faded, and stopped. It could have been a train sounding off somewhere, or a horn. Or a howl.

# CHAPTER FOURTEEN

*Aftermath*

Abe sat in a chair while Irene cleaned, disinfected, and dressed the wound on his wrist. It wasn't as bad as he'd first thought; it had bled so much that at first he'd worried he might lose his hand. He had not spoken a word since Karen and Gavin had pursued that hideous little creature out of the ER.

Before going to work on Abe's wrist, Irene had pulled the curtain around the booth where Hannah lay dead with her abdomen open, her intestines dangling over her side and onto the table.

Everyone was still rocked by what had happened, and no one was behaving normally. Irene's hands and arms shook as she tended to Abe's wound. Winona kept humming—a tuneless, almost monotonous sound that went on and on—as she nervously tried to go about her work. Maggie sat at the desk and occasionally burst into laughter for no apparent reason. She tried to fight it but could not hold it back, and bursts of it came out of her again and again. Gretchen and Penny were in a booth quietly comforting each other, too shocked to deal with anyone else. Ted was in a booth as well, being cared for by Hugo and a nurse named Carly, whom he had brought in from outside the ER.

Hugo had arrived only minutes ago, shortly after Karen and Gavin had left the ER. He'd walked in with no expression on his face, ready to go to work. Suddenly, he'd stopped, and his mouth had dropped open as he looked around in disbelief at the blood on the floor and at Abe's bleeding wrist.

"Jesus Christ, what the—" Hugo had said breathily. Then he'd seen Ted on the floor, back against the wall, sitting in a silent, frozen state of white-faced shock, his crotch a bloody mess.

Hugo had gone to work immediately. He'd run out for just a moment and had come back with Carly, then he'd gotten Ted into a booth.

"Have they come back yet?" Abe said. His voice was dry and hoarse.

"Who?" Irene said.

"Those two private investigators."

"They were private investigators?"

"Yes, they wanted to talk about . . . Oh, never mind. Have they come back?"

"Not yet. They ran after that thing." As she dressed his wound, her eyes kept glancing at Abe's face. Her expression was tense, lips parted. Finally, she said, "Dr. Dinescu, what . . . what *was* that thing? I mean, I—I—I know what it *seemed* to be. A buh-baby. That girl's baby. I mean"—a small, nervous laugh erupted from her—"I helped deliver it, I saw it come out of her. But it wasn't. A baby, I mean. That thing wasn't really a *baby* . . . was it?"

Abe sighed. "Irene, if I told you I had any inkling of what just happened here, I'd be lying. I think the best thing to do is to take care of everyone's injuries first. Finish with that dressing and I'll look in on Penny and her mother." He looked up at her. "Has anyone called . . . anyone?"

"Winona said she was going to call the police. What are you going to tell them when they get here?"

"We will all tell them exactly what happened. That's the only thing we *can* do." With his right hand, he removed his cell phone from his pocket and called home. When Claire answered, he said, "Honey, I'm going to be late. Something, uh . . . Something has come up."

"What is it?" Claire said. "You sound upset. What's wrong?"

Karen and Gavin came in suddenly, both out of breath and looking stressed.

"Look, honey, I'll explain when I get home," Abe said. "Don't worry, everything's fine. I'll see you later. Love you." As he closed the phone and put it in his pocket, Irene finished his dressing. He stood and approached the investigators. He did not know what to say, so he waited for them to speak.

"This hospital has to be locked down," Gavin said. "Now. If that thing gets out, we'll *never* find it."

"What thing?" Hugo said as he came out from behind the booth's curtain. As he approached them, he asked Abe firmly, "What *happened* in here? Who are these people? What's going on?"

Abe introduced Karen and Gavin, then gave Hugo a brief, but accurate, description of what had just happened in the room. As Abe spoke, a frown gradually deepened on Hugo's forehead. When Abe was done, Hugo stared at him for a long time, examining his face, then he slowly turned to Karen and Gavin.

Gavin nodded and said, "That's what happened. Karen and I chased that thing out of here, through the waiting room, and into the hospital. It went upstairs and we lost it. Like I said, this hospital needs to be locked down immediately so that whatever that thing was, it won't be able to—"

"Hospitals aren't *locked down*," Hugo said, his eyes darting back and forth between the investigators and Abe. "They remain open. And even if that weren't the case, no one in this room has the authority to close this one." He chuckled coldly, with no smile, and took one step back away from them. "Now, I don't know what the hell you people have been up to in here, but the idea that an infant, a *newborn* infant, popped out of the womb and went on some kind rampage is absolutely—"

Gavin moved forward, grabbed Hugo's lapel with his left hand, clenched his right into a fist and pulled it back as if to strike. "So help me God," he said quietly, "if you tell me this didn't happen, I will knock your teeth right down your fucking throat. Look around. You see all this blood? You think *we* did this? You think somebody in this room did all this and then we sat around and came up with a story about a killer baby to cover it up? Huh? Is that what you think? Tell me. Go ahead, *tell* me that's what you think, and you'll be laid out on this floor faster than cat hair on velvet." He released Hugo's shirt, pushed him away, and relaxed his fist. "We don't have time to stand here and argue with you, or convince you, or *deal* with you. Either help, or get out of the fucking way."

Hugo's eyes were enormous and his face trembled with rage, but he said nothing. He turned to Abe as if to see how he was reacting to Gavin's outburst.

Abe said, "He's right, Hugo."

Karen stepped toward Abe and said, "Who do we talk to about locking this place up? We have to do it *now*."

"Maybe we should wait till the police get here," Abe said.

As their faces fell, Karen and Gavin turned to each other.

Abe frowned. "Is something wrong?"

"Just a second," Gavin said, taking Karen's elbow and steering her away from them.

Hugo moved close to Abe until their noses almost touched. "Ted's going to need surgery. How are we going to explain his injuries?"

Abe pointed at Hannah's booth and said, "The same

way we're going to explain the eviscerated dead woman behind that curtain."

Hugo's jaw dropped again. "There's a—?"

"I don't pretend to know what that thing was, Hugo, but it definitely was *not* in anyone's imagination. You weren't here, you didn't see it. It's loose in this hospital right now, somewhere, and it's dangerous." He lifted his left hand and put a rigid forefinger in Hugo's face. "If you get in the way of handling this problem, Hugo, I swear I will devote my *life* to getting your ass kicked out of this hospital."

Abe turned away and headed for Penny's booth. He could hear both her and her mother crying quietly behind the curtain. Before going into the booth, he looked over his shoulder. Hugo had his cell phone to his ear, his head bent forward. He began to talk quietly into the phone while his eyes darted around the room, as if with caution.

Abe pulled the curtain aside and went into the booth.

As everyone in the emergency room tried to recover from what had just happened, George drove his pickup into the ER parking lot.

He was a nervous wreck. Since he'd left his cabin, he had been vacillating between his fear of being pulled over for speeding and his eagerness to see what was happening at the hospital. Whatever was going on, he would help if he could—but he was afraid.

Fear was not new to George Purdy, of course. He'd been living in fear ever since he'd fled Big Rock and moved into his cabin. But that was the fear that accompanied an escape from danger. In this case, he was walking right back into it, and that amped up his fear so much that his stomach had ached with anxiety as he'd driven through town. Now it felt as if his insides were on fire.

He slammed his foot onto the brake pedal and brought the pickup to a jerking halt as the headlights splashed onto a man who was stretched out on the pavement. The man was slowly lifting himself up on hands and knees and looking around as if confused. He turned to George, squinting in the headlights.

George backed up a little, pulled into a parking slot, and killed the engine. He got out and went to the man, who was up on his knees now.

"Are you okay?" George asked. He reached out and helped the man to his feet.

"Uh, yeah, I . . . I think so," the man said, his voice weak. He looked pale and frightened and quite unwell. He looked around as he took a deep breath. "I think I, uh . . . I think I fainted on the way to my car."

"You gonna be all right?" George said.

"I . . . think so. I'm . . . well, I'm not exactly sure."

"Well, I don't think you should be driving. I'm going inside. Why don't you come with me?"

The man looked back at the ER entrance and a wave of fear passed over his pale face. "Uh . . . I don't know if I want to, um . . . I don't know if . . ." His voice weakened as he spoke until it fell silent, even though his lips kept moving for a moment, as if he thought he were still talking.

George tried to take his mind off of whatever was disturbing him by introducing himself. "I'm George Purdy, by the way."

The man looked at him and his mouth twitched into a weary approximation of a smile. "Bob Berens," he said with a nod.

"I used to work in this hospital. I was the deputy coroner. What happened in there, anyway?"

Bob turned his head back and forth slowly and said, "You wouldn't believe me if I told you."

"Try me."

Karen and Gavin walked away from Dr. Dinescu, huddled close at the other end of the room, and whispered so they would not be overheard.

"Big Rock doesn't have a police department," Gavin said. "Just the county sheriff's department."

"Where Irving Taggart is boss," Karen said.

"That's right. A man who came out of nowhere and suddenly replaced the dead sheriff. Now, *somebody* knows we're in town, and they don't like it."

Karen nodded. "And if that somebody is connected to Taggart, we could be . . . a late-night snack."

"Exactly. We do *not* want to deal with local law enforcement. Not until we know who and what we're dealing *with*."

"Which means we'd better haul ass."

They turned around in time to see Dr. Dinescu disappear behind a curtain. Dr. Rodriguez stood several feet away talking urgently on his cell phone in hushed tones. They hurried over to the curtain.

"Dr. Dinescu," Karen said. "We need to talk."

The doctor reappeared in a moment.

"We have to go," Gavin said.

"Go?" the doctor said, surprised and dismayed. "You're *going*? *Now*?"

"We have to," Gavin said. "Something's come up and we have no choice."

Dr. Dinescu said, "B-but what do *I* do?"

"Tell the police exactly what happened," Karen said, "and call whoever you need to call to get this hospital locked down as soon as possible. That's the most important thing. It may already be too late."

Gavin took a business card from his coat pocket and handed it to the doctor. "My cell-phone number. Call me in a couple of hours and let me know what's going on. Don't worry about waking me. Call. We need to talk some more."

"Talk?" the doctor said, taking the card. "But if you leave, that, that *thing* is going to—"

"There's nothing we can do here, Doctor," Karen said.

"You're the one who works in the hospital. You know the ins and outs, who to talk to about this. *You* need to get this done."

Dr. Dinescu said nothing, just stared at Gavin with a frown, a slack jaw, and a hint of dread in his eyes, as if he were being told to do something he did not want to do.

"Call me," Gavin said again.

They turned and hurried out, going through the waiting room. On their way out, they passed a tall, disheveled, bearded man on his way in. As they went out the door, taking long, rapid steps, a voice said, "What's it like in there?"

Karen and Gavin stopped and turned to the right, toward the voice.

Bob sat on a concrete bench just outside the door. His hands were pressed to the bench at his sides, elbows locked and arms stiff. He was bent forward slightly and looked drained of energy.

"You don't look well, Bob," Karen said.

"I've felt better, I guess." He reached up, scrubbed a hand down over his face, then looked at his palm. "I'm still a little clammy."

"You gonna be okay?" Gavin said.

"I think so."

"What did you see in there?" Karen said. "We were behind the curtain with Hannah during some of it."

He looked a little woozy for a moment. "That girl . . . Her baby came before they could move her. It came out. And it looked like a baby. At first. But then it . . . Something happened to its . . . It changed. Then all of a sudden, it was on Ted and he was screaming."

"Look," Gavin said, "we're in a hurry, we've gotta go. But I want to hear everything you saw. The police are coming. You should go inside and wait for them, and tell them everything you saw, too. And then will you do me a favor?"

"What's that?"

Gavin stepped closer, produced another business card, and handed it to Bob. "Call me. That's my cell phone. As soon as you're done here, no matter what time it is, call me. We need to talk. Will you do that for me, Bob?"

He frowned slightly as he took the card. "Sure. Yeah, okay."

"Good. Thanks. Talk to you later tonight." Gavin took Karen's elbow and said, "We've gotta go."

They hurried to the SUV.

George stopped in the waiting room a moment to stare down at the smear of blood on the floor, then went through the door to the left of the reception window. He walked into the back without hesitation, as if he still worked in the hospital. He was tense as he walked through the short hall, not knowing what he would find.

First, he saw a dark-haired doctor he did not recognize standing in one of the booths, the curtain pulled back. On the table before the doctor was a woman lying on her back, her shirt and abdomen torn open, her intestines exposed and hanging out on the table. The doctor, whose left wrist was bandaged, looked down at her with an expression of great distress. After a moment, he turned to George, who quickly turned to the right and moved on past the booth.

George looked at the blood on the floor and thought, *Jesus, this was bad.* Then he saw Hugo standing in the room, just finishing a conversation on his cell phone. He pocketed the phone, glanced at George, then did a double take. He frowned as he turned slowly to face George, looking at him as if he weren't sure who he was.

"George?" Hugo said.

George went to him and said, "Hugo, what the hell happened here?"

Hugo moved toward him hesitantly. "George, where . . .

where have you been? You disappeared, you just vanished from your job and your house."

George nodded. "Yes, that's right, I vanished. Because there's something going on in this—" He stopped to look around, then moved closer to Hugo and lowered his voice. "There's something going on in this town, Hugo, something bad. That's why I left." He laughed once. "Actually, I didn't leave—I *fled*."

Hugo continued to frown, but it took on a darker look as he tilted his head to one side. "What are you talking about? You fled from what?"

George looked around again, his eyes stopping on the blood that was all over the floor. "What *happened* here, Hugo?"

"I'm not sure yet, but I'm going to find out. Now tell me, George, I'm very interested. What were you running from?"

George wet his lips, took in a steadying breath, and let it out slowly. "Look, Hugo, I know this is going to sound . . . well, it's going to sound crazy. But just hear me out. Do you remember Arlin Hurley? The sheriff?"

Hugo shrugged. "I remember him. I didn't know him."

"I did. Arlin was a good guy—honest, honorable, and a very sane man. I mean that. He wasn't the type to believe in crazy things or to act on unreliable information. In fact, he was just the opposite. While I was still deputy coroner, before Arlin was killed, a body came into the morgue. It was a man who'd been killed by the woman he was raping. She'd stabbed him in the left eye. Took his eyeball right out of his socket; it was gone. That guy was dead, Hugo. You know me, you know I'm a pro. He was *dead*." He lowered his voice even more. "Well, he got up and walked out." He waited for that to sink in.

Hugo slowly lifted his arms and folded them across his chest. His facial expression remained the same, although his eyes narrowed slightly.

"That man, the corpse on the slab, the guy with one eye, is now"—George dropped his voice to a mere breath—"the new sheriff. Irving Taggart. *That's* the guy who was stretched out dead in the morgue."

Still no reaction. Hugo's eyes narrowed only a fraction more.

George realized his body was rigid with tension. He laughed, hoping it didn't sound too forced, and tried to relax.

"Look, Hugo, like I said, this sounds crazy, I know, but I'm not done yet. That dead guy who walked out of the morgue brought something to this town. Arlin knew about it. A man named Fargo knew it, too. Daniel Fargo. In fact, he came here *looking* for it. He knew about it already."

Hugo's right eyebrow rose. "Knew about what?"

George closed his eyes a moment and thought, *Should I say this? Knowing how it's going to sound?*

Hugo said, "George?"

George opened his eyes, thought, *I can't believe I'm about to say this,* and whispered, "Werewolves." He braced himself for Hugo's reaction, expecting utter disbelief, a loud guffaw, something to suggest that he was crazy.

Hugo did not move, and his facial expression did not change. He continued to stare into George's eyes. Finally, he reached out and put a hand on George's right shoulder.

"You haven't been taking very good care of yourself, have you, George?" he said quietly. "You look . . . pale. Tired. You've gained some weight. How long has it been since you've had a decent haircut?"

"I know, Hugo, I know. You think I'm crazy. But please, just listen. You know me, you know I'm not a nut, that I don't buy into just any old crazy thing that—"

Behind George came the sound of footsteps, people entering the room. He stopped talking for a moment and glanced over his shoulder. When he saw the uniforms, he looked again, and his blood chilled.

Three deputies walked into the room and looked around.

George turned to Hugo, who looked beyond him and smiled at the deputies. He glanced at George again, and suddenly George saw something in Hugo's eyes he had not noticed a moment earlier: an icy coldness.

# CHAPTER FIFTEEN

*Preparing for the Worst*

Later that night, Bob drove home, still confused about what had happened back at the hospital—not only the horrifying creature that had wreaked havoc in the emergency room, but the behavior of Dr. Rodriguez and the deputies who had shown up. Bob was amazed that their reactions to everything had not been stronger. The doctor and the deputies hadn't seemed all that surprised to hear that a newborn infant had sprouted fangs and attacked people in the room, killing one by ripping her open and gnawing on her intestines. They hadn't seemed all that concerned that the creature in question was running loose somewhere in the hospital. Once they were done questioning him, the deputies had assured him that everything would be handled, and they'd told him to go on home.

On his way out of the ER, Bob had passed Sheriff Taggart on his way in. The sheriff had nodded at him and said, "Hello, Bob," as they passed.

Thinking of the sheriff on his way home brought Vanessa to mind. He remembered his encounter with her in the church kitchen, went over it all again in his mind, every wonderful detail.

As he had so many times before, Bob wished he were

more at ease in social situations, more comfortable inter-acting with people. It seemed he'd spent nearly his entire life interacting mostly with his family and other Seventh-day Adventists. He was uncomfortable enough in *those* situations. When he found himself in a situation that in-volved something other than his family or their religion, it was as if his brain seized up and his entire body became rigid and clumsy, as if his tongue doubled in size. His self-image had never been a good one. Being told all your life that you were worthless by your family and an unre-pentant sinner by your church did not exactly foster a lot of self-confidence or self-esteem. But being told those things was the norm for him, and when he stepped out of that arena into a casual social situation, he seemed unable to do anything other than prove all those things correct.

He remembered Vanessa's perfume, the touch of her hand, the electricity that had shot through him when she'd run her thumb up the zipper of his pants over his erection. In spite of his exhaustion, in spite of the horrible experi-ence he'd been through that night, the very thought of Vanessa and what she had done made him hard as he drove.

He turned onto Belmont Avenue, slowed as he ap-proached his house. He pulled into the driveway. The house was dark except for the light glowing over the porch. It was one of those antibug lights and gave off a sickly yellow glow, turning the entire porch the color of urine. He looked at his watch; it was just after midnight. He was surprised Mom and Grandma weren't still up. They tended to stay up late at night on the weekends. He never understood why they bothered to go to bed early during the week. Neither had anywhere they needed to be in the morning.

The garage was closed, as usual. It was so full of junk, there was no room for the car. Bob parked, killed the en-gine, got out, and went slowly along the walk to the porch. His legs still felt weak and his stomach remained queasy.

He wondered why he hadn't gone insane. After what he'd seen, why wasn't he gibbering like a lunatic? Apparently, the mind had a great capacity to adapt.

At the door, he found the house key and slipped it into the lock.

"I've been waiting a long time," a woman said behind him.

Still on edge, Bob gasped as he spun around. The keys dropped to his feet with a jangle, and he swayed with his sudden movement, nearly losing his footing. He craned his head forward and squinted out at the dark front yard.

A figure stood in the dark just beyond the reach of the yellow glow.

"Who's there?" Bob said.

The figure stepped into the light. Vanessa smiled up at Bob as she stood there in a short, low-cut dress in summery earth tones, a dress that showed off her smooth, bare legs and exposed plenty of deep cleavage.

"Hello, Bob."

"Oh, uh . . . huh—hi. Vanessa."

"Where've you been? I've been waiting around for you to get back."

"How long have you been here?"

"Hours. I knocked on the door earlier tonight, looking for you. Your mother said you were out. Where have you been?" She tipped her head forward and gave him a look that was sultry and suggestive as she came slowly toward him. "Did you have a hot date, Bob? Do I have some competition?"

"A hot, a—a—a hot *date*?" He laughed, but it came out as a weak, broken sound. "No, I wasn't, I didn't, uh, no, I didn't have a date. I just, um, I went for a ride. That's all. And I ended up, uh . . . Well, it's a long story, and you probably wouldn't believe it, anyway, so never mind."

She kept coming forward, stepping off the lawn onto the concrete walkway. "It's late . . . but it's not *too* late, you know." She stepped up onto the first step of the porch. "No need to turn in yet." The second step. "Unless you'd rather go inside and go to bed . . . all by yourself."

Bob stepped back as Vanessa joined him on the porch. She stood directly in front of him, so close their bodies nearly touched.

"What do you say you and I go someplace where we can . . . get to know each other better," she said in a throaty whisper.

Bob's heart felt as if it were going to shatter through his rib cage at any second. His mouth became dry and his penis became hard. "Go—go someplace? Where?"

She slipped a finger into his shirt between two of the buttons and tickled his bare chest with her fingernail. "Oh, we can find someplace. That won't be a problem."

"Well, I—I guess we could—"

A sudden rattling sound behind him made Bob jump and spin around as the front door was pulled open. His mother stood there in her robe and squinted out at him.

"What're you doing out here?" she said, her voice harsh, as if she were angry about something. When she saw Vanessa, she blinked several times before saying, "Are *you* still here?"

Bob felt the heat of a raging blush rise in his face as he quickly stepped away from Vanessa before his mother could see how close they'd been standing. "Uh, Mom, just go back, uh, look, I'll—"

"I was just visiting with your son, Mrs. Berens," Vanessa said pleasantly, flashing a bright smile.

"In the middle of the night?" Mom said.

Vanessa shrugged, still smiling. "I was out late tonight, and I happened to be in the area, so I drove by just as Bob was getting home."

Mom turned to Bob and frowned. "Why are you getting home so late? Where have you *been*?"

Bob rolled his eyes as he said, "Mom, I wish you'd

just—" He stopped abruptly when he heard a plaintive whine in his voice. It was not a whine he wanted Vanessa to hear.

"Why don't we get together some other time, Bob?" Vanessa said.

"Uh, sure, sure." He turned to his mother. "Mom, go inside and I'll be with you in just a second."

"I can't believe it," Mom said as she backed away from the door. "Standing on the porch with friends at all hours of the night . . ."

Bob pulled the door closed, then turned to Vanessa. "Really? I mean, you want to get together?"

"That's what I said, isn't it?"

"Well . . . when?"

"What are you doing tomorrow night?"

"Uh . . . nothing."

"Good. I'll come by around sunset and pick you up. We'll go do something fun. Or maybe we'll just go someplace and get to know each other, like I said."

She smiled, then placed a hand to his cheek, leaned forward, and kissed him on the mouth, briefly but tenderly. With a slight, secretive smile and a suggestive, heavy-lidded look in her eyes, she turned and went down the porch steps, then disappeared into the dark.

Inside the house, Bob tried to avoid his mother, but failed.

"Where have you *been*?" she demanded again, stepping in front of him on his way to his bedroom. She frowned as she looked him up and down in the glow of the hallway light. "You look awful. Are you sick?"

"I'm fine, Mom. Just let me go to bed."

"Do you have a fever?" she said as she lifted a hand and pressed it to his forehead.

"No, I don't have a fever, I'm just—"

"Your pants are torn," she said, looking down at his pant leg. "What did you do to your pants?"

He took a deep breath and blew it out, puffing his cheeks. "Look, Mom, I'm tired. I'm going to bed. I'll see you in the morning." He stepped around her and continued on to his room.

"Fine, then, *be* that way!" she shouted after him. "All I'm doing is showing a little motherly concern. You don't have to bite my head off!"

On his way to his room, Bob came face to face with Sister White. This particular dusty-gray picture showed the Seventh-day Adventist prophet in her declining years. Taken in 1899 while Sister White, then in her seventies, was in Australia, it showed her seated, body turned to her left, head turned to look into the camera, silvered hair pulled back severely, as always. She seemed to be looking *into* Bob instead of simply *at* him, her knowing eyes disapproving of his unclean thoughts about Vanessa. He tore his eyes away from the disturbingly mesmerizing picture and went down the hall.

Once in his room, Bob closed the door, locked it, and leaned back against it heavily. When he closed his eyes, he saw that thing . . . its snout shooting out of its round face . . . its fangs sinking into that man's crotch . . . the horrible little sounds it made as it darted around at impossible speeds. . . .

As he was wondering if he would be able to sleep that night, Bob remembered Gavin Keoph and his beautiful friend Karen. Gavin had made him promise to call, no matter what the hour. He took the business card out of his pocket and put it on the desk.

Bob took off his clothes, put on a T-shirt, and sat down at his desk in his boxers. He picked up the phone, looked at the number on the card, and punched it in.

After leaving the hospital that night, Karen and Gavin ate a late dinner in a seaside restaurant, a meal over which they said very little, as if both were afraid to speak. Without saying so, each one knew they both were thinking the same thing—that this assignment for Burgess was not as harmless as the last two, which had turned out to be nothing. This assignment was turning out to be more like the first.

They smoked on the way back to the bed-and-breakfast.

"We should look for another place in the morning," Karen said. "I think it's a good idea not to stay in one place too long."

Gavin nodded. "True."

When Karen spoke again, her face was turned slightly to the right, toward the window, and her voice was just loud enough to be audible. "I . . . don't know . . . if I can stay here . . . much longer."

Gavin waited for her to continue. When she didn't, he said, "You want to leave, Karen? Seriously, if you do, just say so. It's only money. Neither one of us will be broke without Burgess's fee for this job."

After awhile, she said, "Our first job for Burgess wasn't that long ago, but it seems . . . ages. Looking back on the person I was before that job . . . it's like looking back on my childhood. Distant memories. Back then, I was a person who had solid ideas of what was real and what wasn't. I knew things like ghosts and goblins and . . . vampires . . . didn't exist. Since that job, I've spent my life walking on eggshells, wondering what else was going to pop around the corner and say 'boo' . . . wondering just how deeply in the dark I've been all my life. Now this. Tonight. That . . . *thing* in the emergency room." She turned her head and looked at him.

Gavin felt a pang in his chest when he saw her face in the glow of the dash lights. She looked at him with a blend of sadness and fear, and somewhere in the mix was a slight look of accusation. It was almost like the look in the eyes of a loving pet after being unexpectedly struck by its trusted master.

"You said it was just a fluke," she said, nearly whispering.

Gavin's shoulders slumped heavily as he watched the road. "Yes, I did. And at the time, I meant it. I honestly thought what happened in Los Angeles . . . That it was . . . just some kind of freak occurrence."

"Then what was that thing in the emergency room?"

He slowly turned his head back and forth. "I don't know, Karen. I'm sorry, I don't know."

As she went on, she became more confident. Her voice grew a little louder, and she hit her words with a bit more emphasis. "It had a snout. You saw that, didn't you? A snout. Like dog, or a *wolf*. Bob said it looked perfectly normal at first, that it was a newborn baby, just like any other. And then it *changed*, he said."

He nodded. "I know. I know." He knew she was just letting off steam, that she had to vent somehow. They'd both witnessed a horrible thing that night, something impossible and nightmarish and deeply upsetting, but he knew that Karen had good reason to be more sensitive to this situation than he. So he let her go on.

Now she almost sounded angry. "And why are we here, Gavin? To look for *werewolves*. Gee, do you think a newborn baby that suddenly has a snout with fangs and likes to eat the intestines out of people might somehow be *related*?"

When she didn't continue, Gavin said, "I'm not arguing with you, Karen. Like I said, if you want to go, we can. Just say so."

Once again, she turned to the right and stared out the window silently.

Gavin kept driving, waiting for her to continue. As he turned onto the road that led to their bed-and-breakfast, Karen finally spoke.

"I don't want this to be called off just because of *me*, for one thing," she said. "If you can take it . . . I guess I can, too."

He knew more was coming. He pulled into the drive-way, killed the engine, and turned to Karen. "But . . . ? I know there's a *but* coming."

"Well, for another thing . . ." She turned to him. "We're among the few people who know about this. If we don't do something about it, who will? And if something isn't done . . . how much worse is this going to get? How fast and how far will it spread, if nobody tries to stop it?"

Gavin nodded in agreement, then said, "Let's go inside and call Burgess."

They let themselves in with the key Tilly had given them. Tilly and Gus were in bed. On the way to their room, they could hear Gus's snores behind the closed door. He sounded like an old, untended boiler that was about to blow.

Gavin called Burgess, put him on speaker, and they told him everything that had happened. When they were done, Burgess waited awhile before speaking, and when he did, he did not joke, and his usual smart-ass tone was gone.

"Wow," he said. "This is some serious shit, isn't it?"

"*Very* serious," Karen said. "One person is dead, an-other has been severely injured. He's probably in surgery by now, and he may never be the same again. Yes, Martin, this is *very* serious, and from this point on, I'd appreciate it if you'd stop treating this as if it's some kind of romp. You seem to take a great deal of pleasure in all this weird stuff. I know it's your livelihood and all, but in our case, it's our *lives*. Right now, I am a fraction of an inch from walking away from this. Whether or not I do will depend on how seriously you proceed from here."

Gavin spoke up and said, "We don't know exactly what this is yet, Martin, but it's *something*. And it looks an aw-ful lot like it might be the, um . . . werewolves you sent us here to find. Somebody knows we're here and they don't seem to like it. I think there may be a connection between them and Pine County's mysterious sheriff. When we left the hospital, deputies were on their way. Even if what cover we had wasn't blown before, it is by now. I suspect they are very anxious to find us right about now."

No one said anything for a long moment.

"The troops are on their way, I promise," Burgess said finally. "They'll be there tomorrow."

"When, tomorrow?" Karen said.

"I'm not sure exactly. I'm doing my best. I'm not the Pentagon. But they *will* be there. I promise."

"Who are they?" Gavin said.

"Oh . . . some friends of mine."

"Some friends?" Karen said in disbelief. "You're sending some *friends*? Who? Stephen King? Dean Koontz? What're they gonna do, come tell the werewolves a *scary story*?"

"Trust me," Burgess said.

After talking to Burgess, they agreed they needed to get some sleep. It had been a long, draining day. They prepared for bed. Karen pulled the covers back and got in first. Gavin sat on the edge of the bed for a moment and fiddled with his cell phone.

"What are you doing?" Karen said.

"I'm resetting my ringtone. Dr. Dinescu and Bob will be calling sometime tonight, I hope. If the ringtone is new and unfamiliar, it'll jar me out of my sleep faster." He finished and put the phone beside the lamp on the nightstand, then turned out the light. He noticed that the light in the partially open closet was on.

"I left the closet light on for you," Karen said quietly, turning on her side with her back to him.

Gavin got under the covers and said, "Thank you."

# CHAPTER SIXTEEN

*Calls in the Night*

"Aah-*oooooo*, werewolves of London," Warren Zevon sang on Gavin's cell phone. "Aah-*oooooo*!" The song rang out in the darkness of their room and they stirred in bed.

As Gavin sat up and groped for the phone, Karen rolled over and muttered sleepily, "Is that supposed to be some kind of a joke?"

Gavin answered the phone and Bob identified himself. Sitting up on the edge of the bed, Gavin rubbed his eyes in the dark and tried to clear his head.

"Hi, Bob. I'm glad you called. Where are you now?"

"I'm home."

"What happened at the hospital?"

"I talked to the deputies and tried to tell them everything I saw, but they didn't seem that interested. They were more interested in shutting up Dr. Dinescu and talking to Dr. Rodriguez."

"Who?"

"One of the doctors in the emergency room. Hispanic, a little pudgy."

Gavin remembered the doctor who had gotten on his nerves so fast, the one he'd threatened to punch, while still thrumming with adrenaline.

"But Dr. Rodriguez wasn't there when it happened," Gavin said.

"Yeah, I know. That's what was so weird. I talked to them awhile, they took my name and number and said I could go. As I was leaving, the sheriff arrived."

"The sheriff? You know him?"

"Not well, but yeah. He goes to my church."

"Which church?"

"Seventh-day Adventist."

"Did you talk to him at the hospital?"

"No. He said hi, but we didn't talk. There was another guy there. I met him outside. He helped me up on his way in, after I passed out in the parking lot. He was a nice guy. George Purdy, that was his name. Said he used to be the deputy coroner there. Anyway, he wanted to know what had happened in the hospital. I didn't want to tell him because I was afraid he'd think I was crazy, but I told him. He didn't seem all that surprised, but he sure did look scared. I mean, for a second, I thought he was going to start crying, or something. After that, he went in ahead of me, just as you and your friend were coming out."

Gavin remembered the tall, disheveled man they'd passed on their way out of the ER and assumed that was the man to whom Bob referred.

"Then, when I was in the waiting room talking to one of the deputies," Bob continued, "George came running out from the back. He looked scared again, real upset. It looked like he was on his way out, but then a couple of the deputies stopped him at the door. They took him into the back again, but he didn't seem too happy about it. I got the feeling that . . . Well, I don't know." He seemed hesitant to say what was on his mind.

"You got the feeling that what?"

"That there was something going on there that I wasn't

seeing. Like there was something happening just below the surface. Does that make sense?"

"It makes perfect sense, Bob. And it's very helpful. Thank you."

"Can I ask you a question?"

"Sure."

After pausing for a moment, Bob said, "Are you and your friend some kind of cops?"

"We're private investigators."

"What are you looking for?"

"Long story. I can't really discuss it, because it's privileged information."

"Okay. What about . . . that thing? In the emergency room? What was that?"

"What do *you* think it was?"

Bob released a single cold laugh, like a cough. "Something really scary that's messed me up. I mean, I keep wondering if I really *saw* it."

"You really saw it. And we don't know what it was, either. But we're working on it."

After finishing the conversation, Gavin stretched out in bed again. It was warm, and he pulled only a corner of the sheet up to partially cover him.

"Who was that?" Karen said, her words muffled as she spoke into the pillow.

"I'll tell you in the morning. Go back to sleep."

A moment later, she was snoring softly.

Gavin was just beginning to drift off when Warren Zevon startled him a second time. He sat up on the edge of the bed again and grabbed the phone. "Hello?"

It was Dr. Dinescu, and he sounded very agitated.

"Something very strange is going on here," the doctor said, "and if you know what it is, I wish you'd tell me."

"I'm not sure what you're talking about, Doctor."

"I tried to do as you said. I tried to have the hospital

locked down. I tried to *do* something about that creature running loose in the hospital. But they wouldn't let me."

"*Who* wouldn't let you?"

Dr. Dinescu spoke rapidly and loudly. He was clearly upset. "The deputies! They acted like—like—I don't know, like it was no big deal. Like it was nothing out of the ordinary. Like they knew exactly what was going on and they had it all under control. They wouldn't answer any of my questions. Hell, they wouldn't let me finish a *sentence*. And then when the sheriff arrived, he practically kicked me out. He told me to go home and go to bed. When I pressed it, when I tried to convey the *urgency* of the situation, he said if I didn't calm down and leave, he'd arrest me for—I don't remember what he said—unruly behavior or disturbing the peace, or some damned thing."

Gavin listened as Dr. Dinescu paused and caught his breath. Finally, Gavin asked, "Doctor, do you know a man named George Purdy?"

"Yes, that's *another* thing. George Purdy. No, I don't know the man, but he showed up in the ER after you left. Do *you* know him?"

"I don't, no."

"Apparently, he came to see Hugo. Dr. Rodriguez, the doctor you almost punched."

"Yes, I recall. What happened while he was there in the emergency room with you?"

Dr. Dinescu calmed down a little, and his voice took on a puzzled tone. "Hugo said he used to be the deputy coroner, before I got here. Anyway, he seemed very concerned about something when he showed up. I didn't hear everything he said to Hugo, but I got the distinct impression that this George showed up at the hospital *expecting* something to be wrong. Maybe I misread him, but it certainly seemed that way. And he seemed . . . scared. Especially after the deputies arrived. Then he got *very* nervous.

And the deputies seemed extremely interested in *him*. It almost seemed as if he were trying to get away from them. He rushed out while I was talking to a couple of the deputies about locking down the hospital, but then he came back with two other deputies. In fact . . ." He fell silent, as if in thought. "Now that I think about it, it seemed as if those deputies were escorting him."

"Escorting him? What do you mean?"

"Almost as if they were taking him into custody. But I was so preoccupied at the time—I was getting very frustrated with the deputies, and with Hugo, who seemed just as eager as the sheriff that I leave—that I really didn't pay very close attention. I can only give you my impressions, and those are somewhat vague."

"Tell me, Dr. Dinescu, what do you make of all this?"

"I don't know *what* the hell is going on, but I'm not happy about it. I called the hospital administrator at home tonight, as late as it was. But he's out of town. I called Mrs. Padaczeck, the nursing supervisor, but I'm new here, so she was more interested in talking to Hugo. I'm going to raise hell about this, believe me. God knows what that thing did after it got out of the ER. I've called Hugo twice, but he didn't answer and he hasn't returned my messages."

"Are you at home now?"

"Yes."

"Do me a favor. Keep me up-to-date on all this, will you?"

"Yes, I'll do that."

"Call me if anything related to this comes up, or if you remember anything, or hear something—anything at all."

"All right."

"Thank you, Doctor. I appreciate your help."

After wrapping up the conversation with Dr. Dinescu,

Gavin sighed and rubbed a palm up and down his face rapidly. Then he called Dudley at home. When he answered, Dudley sounded only half awake.

"Sorry to wake you," Gavin said. "I need you to look into a name for me."

"A name? Right now?"

"I'm sorry, Dud, but it's important. At least, it might be, and right now we need all the help we can get. The name is George Purdy. I'm not sure of the exact spelling of the last name, but I know he was deputy coroner here in Pine County. Not sure when, but I suspect it was fairly recent. Get me anything you can find about him. Will you do that?"

Dudley yawned. "Yep. I'll get on it."

After hanging up, Gavin put down the phone and stretched out in bed again. He stared up at the ceiling in the dim light from the closet, half expecting Warren Zevon to start singing a third time.

Ten minutes later, he was asleep again.

Sitting at the dining-room table, Abe put the phone down and lowered his face into his palms.

In the living room, music and voices came from the television. Claire was watching an old movie with Illy, who had been unable to sleep and had come back into the house just before Abe had gotten home. They were watching something old and in Technicolor with singing and dancing. The sounds seemed distant to Abe, who was lost in his disturbing thoughts.

Something was not right. Something bad was going on. First, Seth's brutal, savage death. Then the unthinkable, the *impossible*—a baby he delivered suddenly had changed before his eyes into something that was not human, and it had created a bloodbath in the ER. His mind, as if under its own power and without his help, kept trying to connect the two events: Seth's bloody remains in the upstairs hall of his house and that hideous little creature that had dug its fangs into Abe's wrist.

He had not felt like himself since leaving the hospital. After nearly being chased out of the ER by Sheriff Taggart and Hugo, Abe had driven home in a numb state, as if he were filled with novocaine, unable to feel the steering wheel in his hands. Claire and Illy had noticed the dressing on his wrist as soon as he'd walked in, and he'd dismissed their concerns with a distracted response about *just a little injury at work*. Fortunately, they did not notice the blood on his shirt or pants as he went through the dark living room. He went straight to the bedroom and undressed, stuffed his shirt and pants into the hamper, and put on jeans and a T-shirt.

He had shared none of it with Claire yet, and wasn't sure he wanted to. Although he kept telling himself not to panic, he could not stop thinking that perhaps he should send Claire and Illy out of town, away from Big Rock, away from whatever it was that had happened and was still happening at the hospital. He could not imagine what was behind that thing in the ER that night or behind the bizarre behavior of the sheriff and Hugo, nor could he imagine what was behind Seth's awful death or the sheriff's bizarre behavior at the scene. But was it possible that they were *not* somehow connected? That seemed unlikely.

A hand came to rest on Abe's shoulder, and he shouted out in fright as he nearly jolted to his feet.

Illy jerked back, startled by his reaction.

"Sorry," he said tremulously as he tried to relax and settle back into the chair, tried to behave as if nothing were wrong.

It was too late. Illy's heavy-lidded eyes, surrounded by scores of small creases, narrowed as she watched him.

"It is something bad, yes?" she said quietly.

"What, Illy?"

"That bandage. The fear in your eyes. They are for something bad, yes? Something bad that is happening. Something with your friend's death? Something with the hospital?"

Abe took in a deep breath. Before he could let it out, Illy added something.

"Something with the animal attacks?"

He froze a moment before exhaling.

Illy nodded slowly as a frown grew over her narrowed eyes. "Yes. I thought so. It is the *moroi*. The evil spirits that come as animals. They rend the flesh. They drink the blood. They are here in this place by the sea. Yes?"

He wanted so very much to smile and chuckle and say that no, of course it wasn't the *moroi*, of course it was not evil spirits in the form of ravenous animals. But an image of that monstrous infant flashed in his mind, and he saw its canine snout and fangs, its silver eyes. He could not reassure Illy . . . or himself.

George opened his eyes slowly. His head hurt, and when he slowly lifted his stiff arm and touched his fingertips to his forehead, he felt warm, sticky blood. He lay on a hard, cold floor. The memory of how he'd gotten there and the beating he'd received on the way came back to him in a rush. He slowly, painfully got up, seated himself on the uncushioned bench against the wall, and looked around.

He was in a small cell with two concrete walls and two walls made up of bars. Behind him and to the right was concrete. In front of him, the bars looked out on a corridor; to his left was another cell, and beyond that another cell, both empty. His memory of being brought there was sketchy, blurry. He was sure he was in the Big Rock Sheriff's Department.

As his head slowly cleared, his fear set in. It was a fear colder than the floor of his cell, harder than the bars that blocked his escape.

They were busy for now. They had that bloody mess in the emergency room to clean up, witnesses to deal with, a story to contain.

But they would get to him sooner or later. They would deal with their problem, then come for him. They would look in through the bars at him, then open the door and come into his cell.

He stretched his aching body out on the bench and tried to get comfortable. It was impossible. He lay there for what seemed a long time, staring up at the ceiling.

Footsteps sounded from somewhere outside the cell. They sounded tentative at first, then came faster, growing closer. Keys jangled softly.

George made a small wimpering sound in his throat. One of them was coming for him.

"George." The whispered voice was female and was quickly followed by a metallic rattling sound.

He sat up and saw Ella unlocking the door of his cell. He quickly got to his feet as she came in.

"Oh, God, it's good to see you," he said.

She put the keys on the bench and began to unbutton her blouse. "They're preoccupied right now, but we don't have much time."

"Much ti—Ella, what are you doing?"

Taking the blouse off, she said, "Listen to me, George. Your options are pretty limited. They're going to kill you and eat you. Not necessarily in that order. They're cruel. Sadistic. Sometimes they like to start eating their prey before its dead, just to hear the prey scream and beg. Are you listening to me?" She wore no bra and her bare breasts swayed with her movements as she kicked off her shoes.

George stood there wearing the facial expression of a man who had just received an electrical shock. "Luh-listening? Yes, yes, I'm lis—What're you—"

"I need help, George. I can't take them down alone.

I'm just one person. I have the advantage of being like them, but I need your help." She pulled off her jeans.

"*My* help? What can I—"

"In your present condition, you can't do much. But we can change that."

"Change . . . Change . . ."

"You can face them and be eaten. Probably alive. You'll die screaming while they bite into your flesh and tear it away. They'll—"

"Stop it! What, what're you—"

"Or we can fuck. Right now. But we have to do it *now* if you're going to turn in time to be of any help to me. Even now it might be too late. It varies with each individual. We'll just have to hope it works fast in you."

"You want—I mean, we're—You want to—"

She stepped forward, naked and beautiful, and clutched at his belt, jerking it hard to unfasten the buckle.

"Quit babbling. We have to do it *now*, George. Are you with me?"

"I—I—I—"

"Are you *with* me?"

He thought of what she'd just said: *You can face them and be eaten. Probably alive. You'll die screaming while they bite into your flesh and tear it away.*

He thought, *What choice do I have?*

The cell floor was hard and cold and uncomfortable. But they weren't interested in romance.

# CHAPTER SEVENTEEN

*Handling the Problem*

Sheriff Irving Taggart stood at the end of a long corridor on the third floor of Sisters of Mercy Hospital with two of his deputies, Jeremiah, Dr. Rodriguez, and Gregg Dunfy, chief of hospital security. He struggled to conceal his excitement. He kept his face stony, his mouth in a straight line. It simply wouldn't look good for the sheriff to be *happy* about the fact that a small, vicious creature that already had killed one person and injured two others was running loose in the hospital. But he was.

There was another one like the First Born. It had not been a fluke. It had happened again, and would continue to happen. This supported Taggart's suspicion that they were evolving, improving, becoming something more than they already were—something that would be dominant, if it wasn't already.

He'd gotten the whole story from Dr. Rodriguez and knew that the infant's mother—some fat teenager who apparently had engaged in sex with a member of his pack—was being kept in the hospital for observation. The bloodbath that had taken place in the emergency room a few hours ago was under control. His deputies had secured the scene and were doing everything possible to keep the story from getting out. Dr. Rodriguez had been instrumental in the proper handling of the situation. His phone call had alerted Taggart to the problem immediately, and the doctor had been working with them for the last few hours to find the infant. They behaved as if they did not know each other, as if they did not share a secret.

"The last sighting we know of was on this floor," Dunfy said. His hair was mussed and he looked rumpled after being dragged out of bed by Dr. Rodriguez and the nursing supervisor, Mrs. Padaczeck. The doctor had not been satisfied with the security officer on duty. He'd insisted to Mrs. Padaczeck that the head of the department be involved, and he had called Dunfy himself.

"A nurse in the south wing reported to one of my men that something small had raced by her and knocked over a small table," said Dunfy. He turned to Dr. Rodriguez and squinted slightly, his upper lip curling with confusion. "*What* kind of animal did you say this was?"

"I didn't say," Dr. Rodriguez said. "We, uh . . . aren't sure. It came in through the open door of the ER earlier tonight and attacked a couple of people just before I came on duty."

"It *attacked* people?" Dunfy said. "Was anyone hurt?"

Dr. Rodriguez cleared his throat. "There were injuries, yes."

Dunfy frowned. "And *they* don't know what kind of animal it was? The people it attacked, I mean?"

Clearly annoyed by Dunfy's questions, Dr. Rodriguez said, "It was a chaotic situation and apparently the, um, animal was very fast."

Taggart turned to Dunfy. "I think we've got this under control now, Mr. Dunfy," he said. "My deputies and I will corner the animal on this floor and get rid of it. I appreciate your help, but I think you can go home now and go back to bed. Sorry to have bothered you at such a late hour."

Dunfy said, "Oh, I don't mind being here and—"

"That's good of you, Dunfy," Taggart said, raising his voice slightly to overwhelm Dunfy's words. He put a hand on the security chief's shoulder and squeezed firmly. "But really. We've got things under control." He was a few inches taller than Dunfy and looked down at him, his good eye narrowing slightly. He squeezed Dunfy's shoulder again. "Really. Go home now."

After Dunfy was gone, Taggart turned to Jeremiah and said quietly, "What's taking them so long?"

Jeremiah stood beside the sheriff, tall and slender, his hands joined behind his back. He tipped his head toward Taggart and said quietly, "I just spoke with Carmen a moment ago. She said they were on their way."

Taggart frowned impatiently, but nodded once. He turned to Dr. Rodriguez. "Are we going to have any problems with anyone from here on?"

Keeping his voice low, the doctor shrugged and said, "Well, obviously there are patients and nurses everywhere—this *is* a hospital. No one in authority will get in your way, but I'm sure any witnesses will have questions."

Taggart said, "I'll worry about that." To Jeremiah and the two deputies, he said, "Keep track of who sees what. Get names whenever possible. We'll have some cleaning up to do once this is over."

"What about George?" Dr. Rodriguez whispered.

Taggart said, "Who?"

"George Purdy, the man I told your deputies about. He could be . . . troublesome. To say the least."

"Oh, him. Don't worry. He won't be any trouble. He's under lock and key for now, and he'll be taken care of later." They stood in silence for a moment, then Taggart sighed and said to no one in particular, "Goddammit, what's taking them so long?"

Jeremiah removed his cell phone from his pocket and

punched a button with a long, bony forefinger. He spoke briefly and quietly, then slipped the phone back in his pocket as he turned to Taggart and said, "They're coming."

At fifty-three, Wilma Radnitch had been a registered nurse for twenty-eight years, and normally she was very good at her job. But this was not one of her better nights in any respect, and she had difficulty concentrating on the work.

"You feeling okay, Wilma?" Ana asked. Ana was a certified nursing assistant in her twenties who had started on the floor only a month ago.

"Just tired," Wilma lied as she prepared a heparin injection for a patient. "I'm fine, Ana, thanks."

With a slight frown, Ana said, "You look . . . I don't know, like you might be angry. You're sure everything's all right?"

Wilma's face tended to appear angry whenever she was in deep thought or bothered by something, a trait she hated. She made an effort to relax her features, then smiled. "Really, I'm fine." She placed the syringe on a small tray the size of a paperback book and headed down the corridor.

But she was not fine. The day before, she had learned that her husband Brandon, a pharmacist, was having an affair with a twenty-something cashier in his pharmacy, some tart named Debi. With an *i*. Just thinking about the name made Wilma's stomach burn. It had been going on for almost two months. When she'd confronted Brandon about it, he'd said he had no intention of ending the relationship.

"I don't love her," he'd said calmly, as if he were discussing the weather. "It's not at all emotional, it's just sex. You haven't been interested in sex in years, so why should you care?"

*Not interested in sex in years?* she thought as she approached Mrs. Dorcy's room. *I've always been interested in sex, but he lost interest in* me. She thought of all the times she'd tried to stir him, tried to instigate sex, and had either been ignored or told he didn't feel like it.

When he'd told her she hadn't been interested in sex and shouldn't care about his relationship with Debi, first Wilma had wanted to slug him. Then she'd wanted to pick up something heavy and bludgeon him with it. She was devastated, and his refusal to discuss it any further made her feel worse. Their thirtieth wedding anniversary would be in February. She wondered if they'd still be together to celebrate it. She worried about how their son and daughter would react to all of this. If possible, she wanted to keep them from ever finding out.

By the time she got to Mrs. Dorcy's room, her face had regained its dark expression. She broke it with a slight smile as she pushed through the door.

Mrs. Dorcy, a woman of sixty who'd just had a total hip replacement, was asleep, and the room was dark. Wilma left the door open, and light from the corridor fell into the room as she went to Mrs. Dorcy's bedside. She reached up and turned on the light above the bed.

There was a small sound in the room. It came from beyond the curtain that was drawn between Mrs. Dorcy's bed and the second bed in the room, which was occupied by a morbidly obese sixty-nine-year-old widow named Mrs. Woodlawn, who'd had knee surgery. Wilma stopped and listened to the sound a moment, then decided it was Mrs. Woodlawn smacking her lips in her sleep.

"Mrs. Dorcy," Wilma said gently, touching the woman's arm. "Mrs. Dorcy, it's time for your heparin shot."

Mrs. Dorcy stirred as Wilma pulled down the covers and moved the hospital gown out of her way. It was not necessary for the patient to be fully awake for the shallow injection into the subcutaneous tissue of the abdomen.

Mrs. Dorcy opened her eyes slightly and muttered, "Mmm . . . Blood-clot shot?"

"That's right," Wilma said.

Mrs. Dorcy drifted back to sleep almost immediately.

Wilma's smile did not last long. Her teeth were soon beginning to clench as she imagined plunging the needle she held into Debi's eyes. Then, even better, into Brandon's eyes.

As Wilma went about her task, she realized she could still hear that quiet smacking sound beyond the curtain. Was Mrs. Woodlawn *still* smacking her lips? She administered the injection, replaced Mrs. Dorcy's gown, tucked the covers back up, and turned off the light.

As Wilma started to leave, a wet, guttural sound came from the other end of the room. Wilma stopped and listened, frowning. She heard it again. It was like someone trying to make a noise through a constricted throat. She went around the edge of the curtain that fell between the two beds. In the bad light, it took a moment to understand what she was seeing.

Something—her first thought was that it was a monkey—was hunkered atop the hill of Mrs. Woodlawn's enormous belly. The pale blanket and sheet seemed darker than they were supposed to be.

Wilma's heart began to pound. She still could not quite make out what she was seeing—dark shapes, no detail in the bad light—but whatever it was, it was wrong. She reached up and swept the curtain back. The light from the open door splashed over Mrs. Woodlawn's bed.

There was blood everywhere, and the blanket and sheet had been shoved to the foot of the bed. Mrs. Woodlawn's great belly had been torn open. The little creature on top of her lifted its head. Its silver eyes fell on Wilma as the lips of its bloody snout peeled back over red, meat-flecked fangs, and it growled.

Wilma's scream cut through the silent room like a piercing alarm as she swept her arms up defensively. The tray and syringe sailed through the air as she threw herself backward away from the thing. She was so horrified by the growling creature that her brain seemed to become momentarily disconnected from her body. Her feet stumbled clumsily over each other, and she fell backward. She was still screaming when she hit the floor.

Her arms stretched outward as she rolled over and tried to do two things at once—get to her feet and move toward the door, away from that thing on Mrs. Woodlawn. She screamed again and again as she rose and fell, rose and fell, in her clamber to get out of the room.

"What's happening?" Mrs. Dorcy cried, her voice hoarse with sleep. "What's going on? What's *happening*?"

Suddenly, Ana was in the open doorway, hands clutching the frame. She stared down at Wilma in horror.

"What is it, what is it?" Ana cried, frightened by Wilma's screams and obvious terror.

There was a commotion of footsteps in the corridor.

The thing on Mrs. Woodlawn made another sound, like the harsh gurgling of a clogged drain, amplified.

Ana's wide eyes lifted and she looked beyond Wilma, across the room. Her mouth opened wider and her eyes became impossibly large as she froze for a moment, gawking. Then she backed away from the doorway and screamed.

More footsteps joined the others outside the room. The new ones were moving fast, running, slapping the tiles. A man's voice snapped, "Out of the way, out of the way!"

Ana looked to her right, then stepped aside and out of sight, leaving the doorway empty again. Wilma struggled to her feet and threw herself at the safety of that doorway and the corridor beyond, arms outstretched, mouth open even though her screams had stopped.

Just as she reached it, the bright light of the doorway was darkened by a figure. Wilma collided with it as the figure's hands came up and gripped her upper arms, steadied her as it led her out of the room and to her right. Wilma gasped for breath as if she'd come up from deep water.

The man holding her wore a uniform. His left eye was covered by a black patch. His right eye was looking intensely at something behind Wilma. She recognized the sheriff. Still gasping for breath, Wilma pulled away from him, turned around, and backed up a step, until she was standing beside him.

In the room, Mrs. Dorcy called, "What's going on? Somebody! What's happening?"

Wilma heard it, then—that horrible creature making its awful, throaty growling sound—and her blood chilled.

"What's in here?" Mrs. Dorcy shouted. *"There's something in here!"*

A small crowd was gathered in the corridor just beyond the open door of the hospital room. A couple of sheriff's deputies stood with nurses, and in front of them stood a doctor Wilma recognized, Dr. Hugo Rodriguez. Standing in front of Dr. Rodriguez were two women—a somewhat pear-shaped, middle-aged woman with short, graying brown hair, and a lovely blonde woman in her twenties. Between them stood a girl in her middle to late teens.

The girl was tall and fit, her body neither skinny nor fat, but substantial, voluptuous, healthy. Hair the color of rich, dark honey cascaded past her shoulders. Her skin was creamy and unblemished, smooth and taut with youth. She wore a long black satin robe. It was belted at the waist, with a shadow of cleavage showing in the V formed by the lapels. Her shapely feet were bare, her toenails painted red. She looked like she had left the house quickly, with no time to throw on clothes. But it was her eyes to which Wilma's gaze kept returning. At first, she thought the girl's eyes were a very pale blue, but when she turned her head just slightly and her eyes caught the glow of the overhead lights, Wilma gasped. They were silver.

More guttural, gurgling sounds came from the creature inside the room.

"I can see your shadows!" Mrs. Dorcy cried. "You're standing just outside the door! Somebody come in here. Please! Somebody *come in here*! I'm scared!"

Looking at the teenage girl standing in the corridor, Wilma momentarily forgot her terror, and her breathing steadied. She was mesmerized as her gaze locked on the girl, whose expression was peaceful, serene. She was the most beautiful girl Wilma had ever seen.

"In there," the sheriff said quietly, nodding toward the open door.

The girl looked at the older woman at her side, who nodded once. As she stepped forward, her right leg appeared through the opening of the belted robe, pale and shapely. She turned to her right and went into the room.

The creature in the room continued making its menacing sounds.

"No!" Wilma cried, reaching out, moving to stop the girl.

The sheriff clutched her arm and held her back.

"Don't let her go in there!" Wilma said breathlessly. "That thing, that *thing* is in there! That thing will—She'll be—"

The creature fell silent.

When no sounds of distress came from the open room, Wilma said nothing more and watched the open door. She held her breath, tense, waiting for a scream, a crash, something that would indicate the creature in the room had attacked that young woman. But she heard nothing.

No one moved. Everyone watched the door. Not even their breathing could be heard.

Wilma had no idea how much time had passed. It

seemed an eternity as she waited for the screams, as she waited for that little blood-soaked monster to come shooting out of the door, snapping its fanged jaws.

Finally, the girl came out of the room. She held something in her arms. When Wilma saw what it was, she gasped with shock, and her shoulders slumped as the tension drained out of her.

The girl held a small infant in her arms. It was tiny, as if it was only hours old. Its body and face were smeared with blood, but it appeared unharmed. It had no snout, no fangs. Its chubby little arms and legs twitched and gently kicked as it gazed up at the girl's face. It made a little spitting sound as the girl turned her back on Wilma and began to walk down the corridor.

The two women who had flanked the girl now turned and went with her. The deputies and Dr. Rodriguez and the other nurses stepped aside to let them pass, their heads turning as they watched them go. As if under a spell, everyone stood perfectly still and watched as the three women went down the corridor.

The spell was broken abruptly when Dr. Rodriguez stepped forward and went into the room, his footsteps clacking on the tile floor. Wilma heard Mrs. Dorcy say something, her voice lilting upward at the end in a question. She heard Dr. Rodriguez respond abruptly, followed by more of his footsteps. After a brief silence, she heard the hiss of the curtain dividing the two beds being pulled along its track, more footsteps, then silence.

Wilma thought of Mrs. Woodlawn, her large belly torn open, blood all over her and the bed.

*Did I imagine that?* she wondered. *Have I had some kind of neurological event? Am I having a breakdown?*

A moment later, Dr. Rodriguez's footsteps sounded again and grew louder as he came out of the room. He turned to her.

"I want the patient in Bed A moved to another room

immediately," he said. To the other nurses, he said, "This room is off-limits to everyone as of now, including staff." To the sheriff, he gave a single, silent nod. "It's all yours, Sheriff," he whispered.

The sheriff said quietly to his deputies, "We've got work to do."

The deputies separated, and one of them approached Wilma. He smiled and said pleasantly, "Excuse me, but what's your name?"

# CHAPTER EIGHTEEN

*Eavesdropping*

*Bob finds himself bathing his mother again, as he has so many times in the past. The shower hisses and the bathroom is murky with steam, even hotter and more smotheringly humid than usual. Bob squats beside the bathtub fully clothed, but his clothes are damp from all the steam, and they cling to his body heavily. Through the unceasing hiss of the shower, he can hear music. Its source is indefinable. It is religious music, of course—dirgelike and repressively reverent. He can't quite follow the song, but catches bits of the lyric occasionally. Words like* death *and* blood *and* bleed *and* pierced *and* holy ghost *occasionally rise up out of the mournful wail and become clear, but most of it is nothing more than an endless, painful sound that will not stop.*

*As the music plays and beads of perspiration break out stingingly on Bob's face, he squats there washing his mother. A wet, soapy washcloth covers his right hand like a mitten and he runs it up and down her thick, heavy thighs. Her flabby, ghost white legs are spotted with varicose veins—spindly, jagged formations that look like delicate purple spiders clinging tightly to her skin.*

*Bob's eyes fall on the inverted triangle of thin, mostly gray hair. The flesh is puffy, lumpy, and the lips hang wearily from the crease in the center. He begins to wash it. Rubs it with the washcloth. Works up a lather.*

*"Make sure you get that good and clean,"* his mother says, *her voice harsh, commanding, and unnecessarily loud.*

*He slowly moves the washcloth up and down in that crease. Up and down, up and down . . .*

*She makes a sound in her throat. It is guttural, as if she's trying to swallow a sound, to keep it from getting out.*

*. . . up and down, up and down . . .*

*"Use your* fingers,*" she snaps, her voice tense. "Can't you do anything* right?*"*

*He can't take his eyes off of it—smeared with white, soapy lather, the hanging lips jiggling with each movement—as he pulls his hand away and drops the washcloth. It hits the floor of the tub with a heavy, wet slap. He slides his fingers into the crease, between the lips, over the lather.*

*. . . up and down, up and down . . .*

*She breathes faster, her breaths becoming heavier. Occasionally, there is a high, tense, trembling sound behind one of the breaths.*

*Bob is conscious of the tightness in his crotch, the ache of his growing erection pressing against the wet material of his pants. Soon, he feels the heat of fluid surfacing at the end of his penis.*

*As if driven by some exterior force over which he has no control, he finds himself focusing two fingers on the slippery nub nestled in the top of the crease. He moves his fingertips over it in a steady circular motion.*

*The sounds behind her breaths become more frequent and louder as her body begins to tremble and twitch.*

*Bob slowly tilts his head back to look up at his mother's face, breathing through his open mouth. But the naked, trembling woman standing before him in the tub is not his mother.*

*Ellen G. White's head is tilted down at him. Her wide, round eyes glare condemnation at him as her fat lips peel back a bit, her dark hair pulled back severely into a bun behind her head, the part in the center razor straight. Her frantic, passionate breaths hiss between her clenched teeth and puff her cheeks with each exhalation. Her teeth separate, and the glis-*

*tening tip of her tongue appears between them to slide slowly over her bottom lip. The high, ecstatic sounds in her throat deepen and become a growl. Her head jerks once, and suddenly the lower half of her face juts violently outward. Her mouth becomes a canine snout, and its black lips pull back over sharp fangs as she reaches for him and bends down abruptly with a deadly growl—*

Bob jerked awake with a strangled cry and sat up in his bed, legs tangled in the sheet, fingertips digging into the mattress. He sat there—back stiff, chest rising and falling with each heaving breath—for a long time, trying to rid his mind of the images that had been so vivid in his sleep.

Daylight oozed into the room around the edges of the drawn window shades. There were quiet sounds elsewhere in the house, the sounds of Mom and Grandma stirring in their bedrooms. The clock read 8:27.

Bob flopped back on the bed. It was too early to get up. He wanted to sleep longer, but his attempts to get comfortable and drift off again failed. Each time he closed his eyes, he found himself looking up at Sister White, her round, ugly face taut with passion as he fondled her genitals. The image made him squirm and wince.

He got up, put on his robe, and peered cautiously into the hall. When he saw neither Mom nor Grandma, he went to the bathroom and took a shower, dried his hair, brushed his teeth. He returned to his room and dressed. By then, it was 9:53.

Bob looked forward to his lunch with Royce, but it was hours away. He had the rest of the morning to kill, and he did not want to do it in the house. He knew his mother would bludgeon him with questions about last night over breakfast, each one louder than the last, and she would not rest until she got some answers. If he did not answer her immediately, Grandma would accuse him of disrespect and tell him how severely God disapproved of his attitude and behavior. And Bob, of course, would be expected to make breakfast, as always. And as always, it would not be good enough for Grandma, who would complain endlessly about how bad his cooking was and how much better her cooking was, while never getting up to cook anything herself.

He felt like a child, a little boy who did not want to leave the safe haven of his bedroom. Bob sat on the edge of his bed, put his elbows on his knees, and rested his head in his hands. Over and over, in a whispered voice, he reminded himself, "I'm thirty-eight years old. . . . I'm thirty-eight years old. . . ."

He closed his eyes, and instead of seeing a naked, panting, monstrous image of Sister White from his nightmare, he saw the bloody, fanged little creature that had brutally snapped its jaws shut on that man's crotch in the emergency room the night before. He groaned as he scrubbed his face with both hands.

*Did I dream that, too?* he wondered, but only for a moment. He knew it had not been a dream. It had happened, all of it. And the terror he'd felt while he'd watched in horror in the ER returned to him there in his room. A chill passed over him.

Along with the sickening events at the hospital, he remembered seeing his sister leaving the Lighthouse Motel with Deputy Cross. For a moment, he tensed with anger at her hypocrisy, but he closed his eyes and made himself relax.

There was no way he could tell Mom and Grandma about what had happened at the hospital last night. They would tell him he was crazy, laugh with derision, tell him he'd been watching too much television, or something. But he could raise holy hell in the family by telling them about Rochelle's little secret. He just didn't feel like listening to all the shouting that would follow, not so early in the day.

He looked at his pants draped over the back of the

chair at his computer desk. The left pant leg was still torn, vivid evidence of the creature that had tried to bite his leg last night. That would be the first thing Mom would ask him about when he left his room. She would remember seeing the torn pants last night, and she would want to know how it had happened. She forgot nothing.

Bob had to get out of the house. He had nowhere to go until lunch, but simply driving without a destination would be preferable to staying in the house. He wasn't hungry, he wasn't in the mood to cook, and he most *definitely* was not in the mood for Mom's questions or Grandma's criticism. He grabbed his wallet, steeled himself to face them, and left the room.

They were seated at the kitchen table drinking hot herbal tea.

"It's about time you came out of your lair," Grandma said. "I'm hungry."

"I won't be cooking breakfast," Bob said distractedly as he looked around for the keys. He grabbed them off the counter and headed out of the kitchen.

"Where are *you* going?" Mom snapped.

His back to them, Bob set his jaw and resolved to keep walking as he said, "Out." As he went out the front door and pulled it closed behind him, he heard Mom shouting at him, but could not make out her words. He quickened his pace, went to the car, got in, and started the engine. He increased his speed as he drove away from the house.

He drove around aimlessly for more than half an hour, then went to the drive-up window of a Jack in the Box and got an order of French-toast sticks and a cup of coffee. He hadn't had his first cup of coffee until the age of twenty-four, and he wasn't crazy about the taste, but sometimes it was just the thing he needed in the morning. He couldn't imagine God damning him to the lake of fire over coffee.

He drove to the beach, parked, and killed more time

there watching the surf and listening to the radio as he ate his French-toast sticks and drank his coffee. It occurred to him that he could go to the church and do some cleaning up. He almost never went on Sundays, but that was okay, he could make an exception. The church would be empty and quiet, a tremendous relief from his house.

He finished his sweet, meager breakfast and drank the last of his coffee, then started his car and headed for the church.

Karen was in the bathroom connected to their room when Warren Zevon began to sing again. Gavin finished buttoning his shirt in front of the mirror, then picked up the phone on the nightstand. It was Dudley.

"Sorry it took me so long to get back to you," Dudley said, "but I've been up since you called digging for information. I've been on the computer, and this morning, I talked to a couple of people in Big Rock. Your man George Purdy *was* deputy coroner in Pine County. According to my information, he walked away from his job in late January."

"Walked away?" Gavin said.

"Just up and walked away. Didn't tell anybody he was leaving or where he was going. The house he lived in is currently up for sale. George Purdy is not living in it."

"Where did he go?"

"I don't know for sure, but I haven't come to you empty-handed. He owns a cabin in the mountains above Big Rock. George withdrew a hefty chunk of his savings in February and made purchases that seem to suggest he was doing a little household renovation."

"You think he's living in the cabin?"

"Like I said, I don't know for sure. But all the available arrows seem to be pointing in that direction."

"Where's the cabin? Exactly, I mean?"

"I've already e-mailed you directions and a map."

"Thank you. That might be a big help. Anything else?"

"One thing. I also e-mailed you George's cell-phone number."

Gavin sighed. "Why didn't you say that in the *first* place?"

"And make it easy on you?"

After finishing with Dudley, Gavin grabbed his laptop and checked his e-mail. He punched George's number into his cell phone. It rang several times, but there was no answer. He decided to try again later.

It was already quite warm when Bob arrived at the Seventh-day Adventist church on Crozier Street. He did not turn left into the parking lot. Instead, he parked at the curb in front of the small strip mall across the street. The church parking lot was empty. Pastor Edson always parked his blue Ford Focus behind the church, just outside the door of his study, but he never showed up at the church on a Sunday unless a particular function had been scheduled, so Bob expected to be alone.

He used his key to let himself in through the front entrance. Inside, the church was cool and silent. Bob decided to occupy himself with work. He checked the front restrooms for toilet paper, then went to the utility closets for replacement rolls. When he was done there, he headed for the smaller restrooms in the rear of the church.

He stopped abruptly in the main corridor when he thought he heard a sound. Still shaken by the events of the night before and by the awful nightmare he could not get out of his mind, he was certain at first that he was imagining it. But as he listened, he heard what sounded like voices coming from the rear of the church.

Frowning, Bob proceeded more slowly. The sounds became more distinct, and he realized they were voices—two of them alternating back and forth. As he turned left down the corridor that ran behind the sanctuary, he recognized one of the voices as Pastor Edson's. The other one sounded kind of familiar, but he could not yet place it.

Just before reaching the side entrance at the end of the corridor, he turned right down the corridor that ran along the side of the multipurpose room. Yes, one of the voices definitely belonged to Pastor Edson. Up ahead, he saw that the door of Pastor Edson's study was cracked open about six inches. The voices came from beyond that door. As Bob slowly, silently drew nearer to the study door, Pastor Edson said something in a sharp, angry voice. Bob stepped up to the door without a sound, not wanting to be heard. As he peered through the opening, the other voice said quietly, "Calm down, just calm down."

Pastor Edson stood behind his desk leaning forward, hands flat against the desktop. He looked upset. A tall figure stood across the desk from the pastor, its back to Bob.

Bob's eyes widened when he saw who it was: Sheriff Taggart in his uniform and hat.

"Just listen to what I'm saying," the sheriff said. "I don't mean that you have to give up control of your church. All I'm saying is that—"

"Who do you think you *are*?" Pastor Edson spat through clenched teeth. Bob had never seen him angry before—not *this* angry, anyway. His fleshy face was mottled with red and his round cheeks trembled slightly.

"That's what I'm trying to tell you," Sheriff Taggart said. "Yesterday, your sermon was about angels, right? About how frightening they are in the Bible, how they're messengers of God and they mean business."

"What has *that* got to do with anything?"

"In Hebrews, we read, 'Be not forgetful to entertain strangers: for thereby some have entertained angels unawares.' "

Pastor Edson stood up straight. His chest swelled as he sucked in a breath; then he let it out sharply in frustration. "You're quoting the Bible to *me*? How is that verse relevant?"

The sheriff took off his hat and put it on the desk, then waited a moment before saying, "Well, you never know when you're going to find yourself talking to a scary messenger of God."

"Are you implying that—"

Something happened to Sheriff Taggart then. It happened so suddenly that Bob slapped a hand over his mouth to keep his shocked gasp from being heard.

The sheriff's shoulders broadened, his torso and thighs thickened, ripping his shirt and pants, all accompanied by the sound of crackling bones. His skin became dark—it took Bob a moment to realize that the darkness was rapidly growing hair. The sheriff released an animal-like growl as he moved around the end of the desk toward Pastor Edson. When he did this, Bob got a clear view of his face. It had a hairy snout with a black nose at the end and black lips peeled back over vicious fangs. The only reason Bob's whimpered reaction was not heard was that it was drowned out by Sheriff Taggart's growl.

Images from the emergency room the night before flashed in Bob's mind. He saw that hideous infant-creature with the small fangs in its little snout—a snout very much like the sheriff's.

Pastor Edson stumbled backward and fell heavily into his chair with a high, shrill cry of fear. He stared up at the creature Sheriff Taggart had become with his mouth hanging open, his arms draped limply over the armrests of the chair. The angry redness in his face disappeared and he became very pale. Pushing with his feet, he rolled the wheeled chair backward until it bumped the bookshelf behind him.

The sheriff closed in on Pastor Edson, arms held out slightly at his sides. His hands—now with long slender fingers that ended in sharp claws—curled slightly, and he lifted one, palm out, to the pastor. He growled again, louder this time, more menacingly.

Pastor Edson scrambled out of his chair and dropped to his knees. Words tumbled out of him in a long, gibbering plea.

*"Please don't hurt me Jesus oh God forgive me I am sore afraid dear Lord protect me cast your light upon me oh Lord oh Jesus oh—"*

The creature that towered over Pastor Edson made another sound—not a growl, but a *roar*—that filled the room.

The pastor screamed like a woman and fell forward behind the desk, still on his knees, arms outstretched, screaming and crying and babbling hysterically.

The creature became silent. Slowly, it reached out its right hand and seemed to place it gently on Pastor Edson's head behind the desk.

Bob's entire body was quaking and his knees felt as if they were about to collapse. He moved backward away from the door of the study, then turned and jogged unsteadily down the corridor, his feet silent on the carpet. He was so frightened, that he could not breathe until he passed through the front door and got out of the church. Then he gasped loudly for breath.

He did not hear his own quiet sounds of terror as he ran to the car.

# CHAPTER NINETEEN

*Royce*

Royce Garver woke slowly late on Sunday morning. He lay in bed for awhile, dozing, then got up, put on a robe and slippers, and shuffled out of his bedroom. He'd set the coffeemaker before going to bed, and now followed the dark aroma to the kitchen, where he poured a cup and dropped a slice of bread in the toaster.

He was a couple of inches under six feet, a little soft from a sedentary lifestyle. His sandy hair had grown shaggy, and he'd gone without shaving long enough to develop a beard on his round face. He'd stolen his white terry-cloth robe from a hotel in San Francisco years ago, and it needed washing.

He had been working hard and had neglected housework. Dirty dishes were stacked in the sink, the garbage can was about to overflow and was starting to smell, and the floor needed mopping. A half-empty bottle of whiskey stood on the cluttered counter. He had worked late the night before, painting in his small studio in the early hours of the morning, and Jack Daniels had provided some inspiration in those last few hours. Six weeks ago, his girlfriend Lauren had moved out after living with him for almost ten months. She didn't like his habits—any of them—and particularly disliked the fact that his paintings were scattered all over the house. It was his work, his living. Did she expect him to hide them? He missed her sometimes, usually when he was horny, but he did not miss her frequent complaining about nearly everything he did.

When the toast popped up, he spread a little peanut butter on it. Feeling groggy and thick tongued, he took his toast and coffee to the bar between the kitchen and the small dining room, perched on a stool, and turned on the little television he kept there. CNN came on and the blonde, luscious-lipped newsreader talked about the latest politician to be embroiled in a sex scandal.

Royce sipped his coffee and muttered, "And now the sex news, with our news slut."

Beyond the short, tiled bar, several of his paintings were scattered around the dining room. The canvases leaned against walls, against chairs, lay on the table, all sporting colorful monsters and bloodshed—a vampire baring its fangs, a snarling werewolf, the decaying face of a zombie, some kind of reptilian creature, a wide-eyed psychopath with a knife in one hand and a severed head in another, and others.

As he went from channel to channel, looking for something interesting, he remembered that he had agreed to meet Bob at the diner for lunch at one. That left him less than an hour to wake up, dress, and drive over to the diner. He took a bite of his toast, found an old Abbott and Costello movie, and rested his chin in his hand to watch sleepy eyed as the boys ran from Boris Karloff. His head bobbed as he chewed.

He had known Bob since they were six years old. He loved the guy, but he got so frustrated with him. Royce had put his Seventh-day Adventist upbringing behind him after the horrible treatment he'd received from the church and his family in response to his work. There was no love lost between Royce and Adventism—or, as he called it, the Seventh-day Adventist cult. But the church still had a ring through Bob's nose, and his mother and grandmother led him around by it gleefully. Bob's life was dominated by guilt, shame, self-hatred, and fear, all of which had been drummed into him by his Adventist upbringing, from which he had never escaped. While Royce had rebelled against all that, Bob had been cowed by it, hobbled and whipped into submission. Royce tried to stir some of that rebellion in him. Sometimes he saw sparks of it in Bob, but the flame was never quite ignited. Royce tried to reason with him, and sometimes it seemed he was getting somewhere. But before long, Bob's fear fell like a shadow over his face and reason was smothered in the lack of light.

It had been a long time since Royce had gone anywhere near the Berens household. Bob's mother and grandmother and sister were so hateful in their Adventist arrogance, they could anger him almost to the point of violence. Bob was their whipping boy and they seemed to take pleasure in beating him down until he could barely function anymore. The last time Royce had been there, Bob's mom had shouted that he was a bad influence on her boy, while Grandma had called for the wrath of God to come down on his head. That had been six years ago, and he had not gone back since. If he'd still believed in a God, Royce would have prayed for both of those miserable women to get crotch rot and die. But he had given up God the way he had given up Santa Claus, the Easter Bunny, and faith in America's allegedly two-party system of government.

He finished his toast and washed the last bite down with a gulp of coffee. His coffee was cooling off, so he got up to freshen it. He was halfway across the kitchen when he heard a car approaching rapidly outside. Tires squealed against pavement and a heavy, crunching thunk sounded directly in front of his house.

"What the hell," he said as he put his cup down on the counter and peered out the window over the sink.

Bob's station wagon was parked half on his driveway and half on his lawn. His mailbox lay on the grass like a corpse, its wooden post bent and splintered near the middle with dirt still clinging to its base. Bob sat at the wheel with his mouth open, the engine idling. For a moment, Royce wondered if his friend, who had never tasted alcohol, was drunk. Pulling his robe together in front and tightening the belt, Royce hurried out of the kitchen, into the small foyer, and out the front door.

"It's a good thing my car was in the garage!" he shouted as he approached the idling station wagon. Bob's window was rolled down and Royce leaned toward it, both hands on the door. "If it had been in the driveway, you'd be lying on your hood right now, and we'd have a real—" He got a good look at Bob's face and lost his joking tone. "What's wrong?"

Looking close to tears, Bob killed the engine and clumsily struggled to open the door. He repeated a word several times, but his voice was so hoarse and breathy that Royce could not understand what he was saying.

"What?" Royce said, stepping back so Bob could open the door. "Wait a second, calm down, what're you saying, I can't—"

"I said *werewolves*!" Bob shouted.

Royce started to smile as he blurted a nervous laugh, but Bob was not joking.

*Oh, my God*, Royce thought, *he's snapped. Those two miserable Adventist cunts have pushed him over the edge.*

Bob pushed him out of the way and hurried to the open front door. Royce quickly followed him. Inside the house, Royce closed the door as Bob paced in the foyer. Then Bob went to the door and locked it.

"What is *wrong* with you?" Royce said with real concern.

Bob put his hands on the sides of his head and walked into the kitchen. Royce followed.

"The sheriff," Bob said breathlessly. "I saw him. He changed. Into a—a—a . . . It was a—a werewolf. A *werewolf*."

Royce began to get very concerned. Bob was not joking, and he did not seem to be in the grip of some kind of breakdown. He was simply very scared.

"Calm down, Bob. Really. Stop for a second and just calm down, take some deep breaths." Royce turned to the counter, snatched a glass from the cupboard, and poured some whiskey into it. "Here, drink some of this."

Bob kept pacing. "It happened right in front of me. And if the sheriff is—is—is . . . Then what . . . what about Vanessa and all his other—" Bob stopped and closed his eyes. "Oh, God, it was just like the buh-baby last night, that horrible baby, it was—"

"What baby are you—? Look, Bob, I don't know what you're talking about. *Here*," he said firmly. "Take a couple swallows of this."

Barely glancing at the drink, Bob took the glass and swallowed some whiskey. He burst into a fit of gagging coughs and handed the drink back to Royce.

"That's *awful*," he said. "How do can *drink* this stuff?"

"Take a few more swallows and you'll see."

Royce took Bob to the bar, seated him on a stool, and slowly began to extract from him everything that had happened to him recently.


"It seems the only thing we've really accomplished on this trip is moving from room to room," Karen said as they entered their new room at the Rocking R Motel. She put her bag on the bed and Gavin set his down in front of the dresser.

Warren Zevon began to sing about werewolves again, this time from Gavin's pocket. He took the phone out and answered.

As Gavin listened to the caller, Karen lit a cigarette and looked around the room. The Rocking R was a little run-down place just outside of Big Rock. It looked like it had been built sometime in the early fifties and had last been cared for well and cleaned regularly sometime in the early seventies.

"Wait, slow down," Gavin said, "I can't understand what you're—"

Karen turned to him. A frown darkened his face as he listened and he gave her a look that let her know something was up.

"You're saying the *sheriff* was—"

She could hear the pinched sound of the voice on the phone as it interrupted Gavin and kept talking.

"Hold it a second, Bob," Gavin said. "Where are you? Right now, where are you calling from?" He looked at Karen and made a writing gesture with his free hand.

She quickly took a pad and pen from her purse and placed them on the dresser.

Gavin bent over slightly and wrote as he listened. Then he dropped the pen and stood. "Listen, Bob, I want you to stay right there, okay? Don't leave. We're going to come over right now. You can tell me the rest when we get there, okay?"

A moment later, Gavin pocketed his phone. He grabbed Karen's cigarette, took a drag, then stabbed it into the ashtray on the dresser until it was dead.

"What's going on?" Karen said.

Gavin tore the page from the notebook and took his keys from his pocket. "That was Bob, our friend from last night. He just watched as Sheriff Irving Taggart turned into a monster and terrorized the pastor of Bob's church. He's a wreck. Let's go."

They left the room, got into the SUV, and fastened their seat belts. Gavin started the engine, then handed her the notebook page and said, "Enter that address for me." As Karen entered the address into the navigational system, Gavin pulled out of the motel parking lot and headed back to Big Rock. "If the sheriff and his friends know that Bob has seen what he says he's seen, then Bob won't be long for this world."

"What was the sheriff doing with Bob's pastor?"

"Bob told me last night that Taggart is a member of his church. Seventh-day Adventist. I'm just guessing, but it kind of looks like Taggart wants to use the church somehow, and he's using the pastor to do that."

"Then Bob could be in danger right now."

"Yes." Gavin removed the cell phone from his pocket and handed it to Karen. "Call the number Bob just called from. Tell him everything we know so far, everything. Then find out if he's had sex recently with anyone who might be connected to Taggart in some way."

Karen frowned as she thought about Bob. "You think that's likely?"

"Is what likely?"

"That he's had sex with . . . well, anyone?"

Gavin chuckled. "Just to be safe."

Karen called the number. While she talked with Bob, Gavin drove into Big Rock. Karen had difficulty getting Bob to quiet down and listen to her at first, but he finally calmed and she talked at length.

It was a hot day, and humidity was setting in. The air conditioner gave them relief from the heat.

"What does sex have to do with anything?" Bob said on the phone.

"I just told you," Karen replied. "This is a sexually transmitted virus. If you've had sex with anyone who might be connected to the sheriff somehow, you might have contracted that virus. Do you understand?"

Bob became very quiet. Finally, he whispered, "Vanessa."

"Who's Vanessa?"

"Uh . . . nobody."

"She's *somebody*, Bob, or you wouldn't have mentioned her. If we're going to help you, we need you to be honest with us."

"She's someone from my church. A . . . a friend of . . ."

"A friend of the sheriff's?"

"Yes."

"And have you had sex with her?"

He sighed, a sound that contained both relief and frustration. "No, I haven't. But she's been, um . . . trying."

"Trying? To seduce you, you mean?"

"Yes. But I . . . know better now."

"Good. When you were at the church this morning, did the sheriff—"

"Oh, shit," Gavin said, suddenly slowing down the SUV.

Karen turned him. He was scowling at the rearview mirror. She looked out the window at the side-view mirror and saw the right side of a sheriff's-department cruiser behind them, the bar of lights across its roof pulsing.

"Oh, shit," Karen said.

"Excuse me?" Bob said.

"Look, Bob, I'll have to call you back. If I don't, then we should be showing up soon. And if we don't . . . Well, you need to find something made of silver that can be used as a weapon, like I told you."

"You mean you might not come?" Bob said, a note of panic in his voice.

"We're being pulled over by a deputy, Bob," she said.

Bob's words were spoken in a breath. "Oh no."

"We'll do our best to get there, but we've got other things to worry about right now. Remember what I told you. Talk to you later."

Karen closed the phone as Gavin pulled the SUV over to the shoulder and slowed to a stop.

"What do we do?" Karen said quietly, trying to keep her fear and tension out of her voice.

Gavin said, "Call Burgess. Right now. Leave the line

open, tell him to listen. That way if we're . . . If the worst happens, he'll know about it."

Karen made the call. Burgess answered after one ring.

"We've been pulled over by a deputy," she said quietly. "I'm going to leave the phone on. Listen closely. This . . . may not end well." She placed the phone on the center console between the seats.

The cruiser's door opened and out stepped a tubby deputy whose uniform was a bit too snug. He slowly made his way forward to the SUV as Gavin rolled down his window.

The deputy peered in through the window, looking the interior over closely before saying a word. Karen read the name on his badge: Deputy Maurice Eckhart.

"The speed limit through here is forty-five," he said. "You were doing fifty-seven, did you know that?"

Gavin smiled and said pleasantly, "Sorry, I was in a hurry and I guess I just wasn't paying attention." He produced his wallet and opened it.

"License and registration," Eckhart said.

Gavin handed over the license, got the registration from the glove compartment, and passed that through the window, too.

Eckhart's eyes narrowed as they went back and forth between the license and Gavin's face. "Gavin . . . How's that pronounced?"

"*Kee*-off."

"Gavin Keoph, huh?" More looking back and forth as a frown set in. "Gavin . . . Keoph." He looked beyond Gavin at Karen. "And who might you be?"

Gavin said, "This is my—"

"I wasn't talking to you," Eckhart said abruptly. "Your name, ma'am?"

"Karen Moffett. Well, Karen Moffett-Keoph, now." She smiled. "We're on our honeymoon."

Eckhart nodded slowly as a smirk turned up one corner

of his mouth. "On your honeymoon, huh? I see." He stood up straight, arched his back a little, and for a moment the buttons of his shirt looked ready to pop. "Gavin Keoph and Karen Moffett, huh?" he said as the smirk became a smile. "On your honeymoon here in Big Rock. Well, how about that. Tell you what. Why don't you two just sit tight here for a second while I call this in?" He gave them a nod, then headed back to his cruiser.

"This is bad," Gavin whispered, watching Eckhart in the rearview mirror.

Karen snatched up the phone. "He says he's calling this in," she said. She looked over her shoulder and saw Eckhart getting into his cruiser. "I think it's pretty clear he knows who we are. He's calling someone—probably the sheriff—for further instructions."

"I'll have people in Big Rock this afternoon," Burgess said.

"Do that." She watched Eckhart through his windshield as he held the radio microphone to his mouth and talked, his eyes on Gavin's license.

"Leave the line open," Burgess said.

Karen placed the phone back on the console.

"We can make a run for it," Gavin said.

"Where would we go?" Karen said. "He'll follow us and it'll only be minutes before he's got backup." She thought a moment, watching Eckhart. "Of course, we can always shoot the son of a bitch."

Gavin thought about that a moment. "So far, everything we've got is mostly speculation. You want to shoot a law-enforcement officer and take the chance that we're wrong?"

Eckhart got out of his cruiser and started toward them again.

"Here he comes," Gavin said.

"Fuck speculation," Karen muttered. "If he goes for his gun, I'm going for mine, and he's going down."

At the window, Eckhart smiled and said, "I'm gonna have to ask you both to get out of the vehicle. And ma'am, if you'd come around to this side of the vehicle, I'd appreciate it."

For just a moment, Karen was unable to inhale. She remembered her experience in Los Angeles with the vampires—the beating and torture and rape—and it turned her lungs to ice.

Gavin glanced at her and whispered, "Let's go."

They got out of the SUV. As Karen walked around the front to the other side, she felt the weight of her 9-millimeter under her light jacket. She wondered if she would have it much longer.

# CHAPTER TWENTY

## Lupa

"We have a bit of a mess, and we need to decide how to clean it up," Taggart said. He sat at a desk in the room he was using as an office in the house that once had belonged to Marvin Cooper. It was a large old scuffed-up desk of pale wood. He'd cleared the cluttered mess off the top, and now it held only a telephone, a lamp, and the notebook that was open in front of Jeremiah, who sat opposite him.

"There aren't that many alternatives," Jeremiah said. "We have people who have seen things that could be . . . problematic. We can either turn them or kill them. That about covers our options."

Taggart sat back in his chair and folded his arms across his chest. "We don't want to do anything that would cause *more* problems. I have no problem with killing them, of course, as long as we can cover it up easily enough. Turning them is an option, but we've got our hands full right now. We don't necessarily want to add new ones to the pack unless we absolutely have to at the moment."

"What about"—Jeremiah consulted his notebook—"Dr. Abel Dinescu?"

"Who?"

"I believe Dr. Rodriguez mentioned him to you. He

was the doctor on duty in the emergency room when the infant was born."

"Oh, yeah, that's right. What about him?"

"He's been making phone calls. He's been trying to reach the hospital administrator, who's on vacation, and he's been calling other doctors, as well. He's also called the department a few times wanting to do know what the sheriff intends to do about what happened last night. He's telling people some kind of mutant infant was born that killed a patient and injured two other people, himself included."

Taggart frowned. "Is anyone believing him?"

"I don't know."

"He's a troublemaker." He cracked his knuckles as he gave it some thought. "If he's calling around, then he's told his family. I don't want to take any chances with him. Send a couple of deputies to his house. Kill the whole family. Make it look like Dinescu did it. Like he snapped, or something, I don't care, as long as it's done."

"You want this done tonight?"

"No, I want it done *today*. Right away."

"I thought the cover of night might be helpful in—"

"They're sheriff's deputies," Taggart said with a shrug. "Nothing to hide. We're the good guys, remember?" He grinned. "Just make sure the deputies mention to neighbors that they came to the house answering a domestic-violence call. In fact, send Olbermann. He's good with people."

Making a note in his notebook, Jeremiah said, "We should deal with each problem individually like this. I have a list of all the other names here."

"How's our new baby boy, by the way?"

Jeremiah smiled. "Doing very well. Dr. Rodriguez says he's quite healthy. He's upstairs right now. Carmen is caring for him."

Taggart smiled and nodded. "Good, that's good." He leaned forward, joined his hands on the desktop. "My conversation with Pastor Edson went very well this morning. I think he's properly . . . submissive." He smiled and added, "To be honest, I scared the piss out of him."

Jeremiah chuckled.

"I'm serious. He wet himself like a little boy. I calmed him down and convinced him I mean him no harm as long as he . . . goes along. He'll do anything I ask now. He thinks I'm a messenger of God. Just like Ellen White, their crazy prophet. Except, what took Ellen years of copying other writers and lying about visions from God to accomplish, I was able to do in a few minutes."

"What did you tell him to do?"

"Wait for instructions. Now that we have a good place to meet, I want to get everyone together in the church this evening. It's time we had that meeting I've been talking about. Everyone you can pull together. The entire pack, if we can manage it. Get the word out and tell everyone that it's important. I'll give them all a little mental nudge, too. That'll let them know this gathering is not optional. Tell them they're finally going to get to meet the First Born." He smiled. "She'll finally be able to have her debut. Make sure Cynthia is there, too—awake and alert."

As Taggart spoke, Jeremiah wrote in his notebook.

"What time?" Jeremiah said.

"Whenever you can get the biggest number together. Just let me know as soon as you've got it nailed down. And let Beth know right away. She did some shopping the other day, bought some nice clothes for our girl. Beth will need to make sure she's dressed for her debut. We want her to look nice."

"Will do."

Taggart stood. "I'm going down to the basement. If anything comes up, just come get me." He smiled. "But, uh . . . knock first, okay? I want to spend some quality time with her."

He left the office, went down the hall to the stairs, then went down to the basement door. He knocked gently. "It's me," he said.

A female voice from the other side said, "Come in."

He opened the door, stepped through it, then stood there and silently looked at her for a moment, drank her in with his one good eye.

"Hello," he said, his voice low, deep in his throat. All he had to do was look at her to feel heat between his legs.

She was sitting up at one end of the couch, her legs stretched out over the cushions, a hardcover book open on her bare thighs. The glow of sunlight coming in through one of the three small rectangular windows high on the western wall behind her shimmered in her long, deep-golden hair, creating a soft halo around her head. She had been given clothes, but she preferred to be naked. Her trip to the hospital the night before had been her first expedition out of the house to mingle with humans. Before that, she had gone out only to feed. It had been the first time she'd put on clothes, as well, and she had agreed only to wear the loose-fitting satin robe.

Normally Taggart had an endless supply of confidence. That had been the case before he was turned. Back then, nothing and no one had made him flinch, and he'd been able to handle himself in any situation. Now, bolstered by the knowledge that he was much more than he'd been before, much more than most of the people around him at any given time, he often felt invincible, and sometimes had to remind himself that he was not—no, not quite. But when he looked at her, all of that confidence and strength seemed to crumble. The steel he liked to think he had in his bones melted into a bubbling liquid. Something about her reached inside him and squeezed his internal organs—and she was only four months old. Four months . . . in which she had absorbed everything around her, especially the language and all its nuances, both spoken and written. Her eyes and ears missed nothing, and once observed, nothing left her memory.

"Am I interrupting anything?" he said quietly, taking a couple of tentative steps toward her.

She smiled. "You're not interrupting anything." She closed the book on her lap.

Her voice sounded the way satin felt against flesh. Nothing about her was haughty or arrogant or in any way unpleasant. Her appearance was that of a beautiful teenage girl, no pretensions or affectations, a face that exuded innocence. But her eyes—those startlingly pale-silver eyes—held behind their mesmerizing beauty a paralyzing authority. He had taken her several times over the last couple of weeks, once she'd finally matured, had rutted with her passionately, noisily, hard. And yet she possessed something, projected something he could not yet define, something that he suspected might be entirely new under the sun. Something about her made him . . . cautious. He jutted his chin a little and tried to assert himself, returning her smile.

"What are you reading?" he said, moving closer.

She picked up the book, looked at the cover. "Oh, some book I found on the shelf over there. *Gone with the Wind* by, uh—"

"Margaret Mitchell."

Her eyes widened a little. "Yes. Have you read it?"

"No, but I saw the movie," he said as he went to the couch and dropped to one knee beside her.

"It's very good. I just started it this morning, but I think it has real—"

He bent forward, took the book from her, and dropped it onto the floor. Her sentence remained suspended in midair as she watched him. He pressed his nose into the triangular patch of honey-gold hair between her legs and inhaled deeply. Breathing in her scent was like sucking fire into his lungs. It made him hard instantly, of course, but caused other changes in his body just as fast, changes he'd grown accustomed to controlling, but which slipped from his grasp when he smelled her. He felt the sting and tingle of rapid hair growth on his skin, the stirring under his fingernails of the long curved claws that were on the verge of jutting from his fingertips. A pressure began to build in his gums in anticipation of the changes in his teeth. Soon his body would shift noisily beneath his flesh as his muscles transformed, a part of the transformation that had been painful in the beginning, but had since become exhilarating.

She pulled the strap of his eyepatch over his head and tossed the patch aside, revealing his empty eye socket. She placed a hand on his head, slid her fingers into his hair, and closed them into a fist. With the authority of a dominatrix and the playfulness of a child, she pulled his head back so his face was looking up at hers. Her lush breasts rose with a deep breath and slowly fell as she smiled slightly, lips pulling back to show the tips of her fangs.

When he spoke her name, his voice was different—thicker, deeper, with the sound of something not quite human. "Lupa."

He had named her after the she-wolf that had nursed Romulus and Remus—the infants who would become the founders of Rome—and kept them safe from harm on the Palatine Hill after they'd escaped their deaths, ordered by Amulius, the king. Taggart had chosen the name because, as he'd looked into her beautiful silver eyes when she was only an infant, he could see her nurturing a newborn species—something that was more than human, more than wolf, and even more than the werewolf that combined them both.

Lupa pulled his face to hers. Their writhing tongues met before their lips, then their fangs clicked together thickly. Taggart's hands went to work removing his shirt as he kicked off his shoes. She slid one hand over his bare back, which was rapidly becoming thick with hair. He slid a hand over the hair growing fast on her breast and squeezed, rubbed a thumb back and forth over her hard, dark nipple.

As they both grew hairier, his body popped and crackled with the changes taking place within it, while hers changed smoothly and quietly. He pulled her down onto the floor and their bodies writhed over one another as hands groped and clawed. Each inhalation was a gasp, each exhalation a throaty growl.

Taggart turned her over roughly so that she was facedown on the floor. He reached under her and pulled hard until her ass was in the air. Using his knee to shove her legs apart, he clutched the cheeks of her ass, squeezing them hard. Then he plunged into her.

Their growls and pants filled the room and grew louder as Taggart pounded into her repeatedly, his rhythm picking up speed. The room took on their gamey, carnal scent as she writhed beneath him and dug savagely at the floor with her hands, claws tearing through the carpet.

Four knocks sounded at the door.

"Sheriff?" a voice said.

The voice was ignored at first as they continued rutting. Lupa reached up and gripped the front of the couch with both hands, her claws piercing the cushions.

More knocks, then, "Sheriff, I'm sorry to interrupt, but it's important." It was Jeremiah. He knocked again.

Taggart stopped thrusting and pulled away from Lupa. His growl went from passionate to annoyed as he turned and looked at the door. He stood, and as he went to the door, much of the hair on his body disappeared. His erection remained as he reached out and pulled the door open.

Jeremiah did not express even the slightest surprise or discomfort. He looked Taggart in the eye and said, "Eckhart called in. He's pulled over Gavin Keoph and Karen Moffett. The two you asked me to follow yesterday. The ones with the Uzis and the silver bullets. He's waiting to know what you want to do."

Taggart reached up and passed a hand over his face. A shaggy beard that nearly reached to his eyes covered the lower half of his face, and his chin jutted, two fangs curving upward from his lower jaw. He made a grumbling, growling sound. As he diverted his thoughts away from Lupa and to the situation at hand, the hair on Taggart's body became thinner. His fangs disappeared.

"I want to know who they work for," he muttered. "Fargo is behind this somehow, I just know it. I want to know *how*."

"What should I do?" Jeremiah said.

"Get Eckhart some backup right away," Taggart said. "Tell him to bring them in and put them in the lockup for now."

"Anything else?"

"Yes. I don't want to be interrupted again until I'm done in here. Is that understood?"

Jeremiah nodded. "It is."

Taggart slammed the door and turned around.

Lupa was sitting up now, facing him, her back to the front of the couch. Her hairy legs were spread wide and bent, knees up, a hand between them, fondling her genitals. Her tongue slid back and forth over her lower lip.

Taggart growled harshly as he hurried toward her to continue what they had begun.

# CHAPTER TWENTY-ONE

*The Moroi*

Sunday was Abe's day off, but no matter how hard he tried, he could not relax and enjoy it. He tried to occupy his mind by working on a bat house he was building for the backyard. He hoped it would attract some bats, which would then eat up the annoying insects that made sitting on the back deck on warm summer evenings such an irritating experience.

He had slept little the night before, and what little sleep he'd gotten had been shattered by nightmares in which the vicious little creature in the emergency room clamped its fanged snout on *his* crotch. He had jerked awake with a sharp cry at one point, and Claire had sat up beside him. As they lay in the dark together, he'd told her everything that had happened in the ER. At first, she'd thought he was describing his nightmare to her. When he told her it had actually happened earlier that night, she became concerned, at first for his stability. But he convinced her by removing the bandage from his wrist and showing her the bite. When she asked him what he made of it all, he'd said, "I don't know. But Illy is starting to sound a lot less superstitious."

Over breakfast, Illy had said little, but she had given

him several looks. Her eyes seemed to be saying, *You know I'm right, Abel. You* know *it.*

He kept thinking of that look in her eyes as he worked on the bat house, of her many crazy superstitions and old-world beliefs. Being a doctor, a man of science, Abe took pride in his ability to reason. But all reason collapsed in the face of the creature that had attacked him in the ER. As much as he hated to admit it to himself, that experience was leading him to wonder just how "crazy" Illy's superstitions were, and how "old-world" her beliefs.

He knew in his gut that something was very wrong in Big Rock, and after their behavior last night, he knew that the sheriff's deputies somehow were connected to it, perhaps the entire sheriff's department. He could not shake the fear that he and his family were in danger. But because he could not point to a specific source of that danger and give it a name he understood, he kept *trying* to shake it.

A splinter of wood dug painfully into his thumb, and he cursed as he shook his hand up and down. He gave up on the bat house for the time being and went inside. Illy was seated at the dining-room table reading the paper. He could hear the sound of the vacuum cleaner running in another part of the house. He got a pair of tweezers and sat down at the table across from Illy to remove his splinter. A large, pale green Roseville vase—one of Claire's prized possessions—stood between them holding a bouquet of flowers from Claire's garden in the backyard.

"This place is cursed," Illy said quietly without looking up from the newspaper.

"What place?" Abe said. He slid the vase of flowers aside so he could look directly at her.

"This place. This town. They have come here. The *moroi.* They have come and they will take root. Like thornbushes, like poison ivy. Already they spread. Animal attacks nobody cares about. Mauling, biting, hurting. People care, but they are *afraid*. And they *should* be." She lifted her eyes from the paper and looked at him. "You have not told me what happened last night, but I know."

When she didn't continue right away, he said, "You know what, Illy?"

"I know it was bad. I see fear in your eyes—last night, today. What happen to your wrist? Why the bandage?"

"Well, I was . . . uh . . . bitten."

Her tired old eyes widened as she crumpled the paper in her knobby hands and looked at him with horror. "*Bitten*? By the *moroi*?"

"I honestly don't know *what* it was, Illy, but—"

"It was the *moroi*! And you know it. You *know* it!"

The doorbell rang. Abe listened as the vacuum cleaner continued to operate. The bell rang again, and this time, the vacuum cleaner fell silent. That meant Claire had the door. He turned his attention back to Illy.

"Illy, the *moroi* is a myth that—"

"No myth!" Illy insisted, weakly hitting the table with a fist. "Call it what you like. It exists, it is evil, and it has come *here*."

Abe heard voices in the living room and wondered who had come to the door.

"You keep resisting it," Illy said in a whisper as she leaned toward him. "You cling to your science, your medicine— but *before* science and medicine, there was good and evil. They have always been, *always*, and they will always be. And the evil that has come to—"

Illy was interrupted by Claire's voice.

"Abe?"

He turned to her standing in the archway. She looked worried.

"There are deputies at the door," she said, frowning.

Abe suddenly felt as if someone had thrown a sheet that had been soaked in ice-cold water over him. His first clear thought was of the gun he kept in his nightstand drawer, the .357 Magnum he kept for emergencies but had never needed. He thought of it now and had the strong sense that, for the first time, he needed it.

When he looked at Illy, he could tell she had seen it in his face—his sudden fear. He realized it was an irrational fear, the specific source of which he could not yet pinpoint. But part of that source was the deputies he'd dealt with the night before, perhaps all the deputies, perhaps the sheriff himself.

"Abe?" Claire said. "What's wrong? Is there something I should know? Something you haven't told me?"

He found himself unable to speak or move for a moment. He was frozen by his fear, bound and gagged by it.

"They're waiting," Claire said.

Abe heard movement in the living room. He forced himself to stand, tried to make himself walk forward into the living room with Claire. But he kept thinking about that gun. Claire turned and went ahead of him, and he followed her—but only for a few steps. Then he turned and headed down the hall to the bedroom.

"Where are you going?" Claire said, annoyed.

"I'll be right there," he said over his shoulder. "Just give me a second."

He hurried into the bedroom, opened the drawer, and removed the gun. He kept it loaded, but he checked the cylinder just in case.

Claire's scream cut through the house.

His body suddenly numb, Abe dashed out of the bedroom and down the hall, the gun in his right hand. As he passed by the dining room, he vaguely noticed that Illy was no longer at the table, where the open newspaper had been abandoned. He made the left turn into the living room so sharply, he almost fell over, then jerked to an abrupt stop, his jaw slack.

Two deputies stood in the living room, neither of whom he recognized—neither had been in the ER the night before. The deputy on the left was a lanky blond man, the one on the right shorter and stockier, with dark hair cropped short. The dark-haired deputy had his left arm wrapped around Claire's neck from behind and was holding her tightly. Claire's eyes were round with fear and confusion, and her mouth opened and closed silently several times.

When the deputies saw the gun in Abe's hand, they instinctively reached for their own sidearms.

Abe didn't think first. He acted immediately, wasting no time. He quickly leveled his gun at the blond deputy and fired.

A small hole appeared in the deputy's chest and he fell backward, landing hard on the floor. Dark blood began to spread quickly on his khaki shirt.

The dark-haired deputy was clearly caught off guard. His shock registered in his face. As he clutched his gun with his right hand, his grip on Claire loosened and she took advantage of it. She threw herself away from him and came toward Abe with her arms outstretched.

As the deputy pulled his gun from his holster and raised it, Abe turned his own gun on him and fired. A chunk of the left side of the deputy's face and head exploded in a spray of red, and he dropped to the floor with an awful, sickening, groaning sound. He writhed and twitched there, struggling to get back to his feet but unable to control his limbs.

Startled by the luck of his unpracticed aim, Abe grabbed Claire's arm with his left hand and pulled her away from the fallen deputies. He dragged her stumblingly back to the archway that led into the dining room.

"Where'd Illy go?" he said. He almost didn't recognize his own voice, which was high, breathy, and hoarse.

"I—I—I . . . I—I—I . . ." Claire could not get the words

out. Her eyes darted around the dining room as if it were unfamiliar to her. Obviously, she was having difficulty processing everything that had just happened.

"Come on, come on," Abe muttered as he led Claire into the dining room.

"What happened?" she said. "What just *happened*? My God, they were at the door, and the next thing I knew—"

"Do you know where Illy went?"

Claire looked around, her head moving in jerky spurts. "I—I don't know, she was just here." She looked at the sliding glass door, which stood half open, then turned to Abe and said, "She must have gone back out to—" She looked past Abe and whatever she saw made her scream.

Abe spun around just in time for the blond deputy to grab his right wrist and twist with one hand while closing his other hand on Abe's throat. Abe's voice was reduced to a gagging, gurgling sound. A large spot of dark blood had spread over the front of the deputy's shirt.

The deputy wrenched Abe's wrist hard, trying to make him drop the gun. Instead, Abe tightened his grip on the .357, which was pointed at the deputy's abdomen. At the same time, he squeezed the trigger once, twice, a third time.

The deputy's body jerked in response to each gunshot, but his grip on Abe's wrist and throat did not weaken. Instead, his lips pulled back and he growled as his teeth sharpened before Abe's eyes. Dark blond hair grew rapidly on his face, neck, and hands. His eyes went from blue to a shimmering silver. Abe felt sharp, piercing pains in his throat and wrist as the deputy's fingers sprouted curved, deadly claws. The lower half of the deputy's face extended into a tapering snout. Abe's mind flashed on the snout of the small creature in the ER, on its menacing fangs.

As his body changed with thick, sickening sounds, the deputy's uniform ripped to reveal more hair underneath.

He was changing completely, transforming into something else in front of Abe.

As the deputy squeezed tighter and tighter, Abe's face felt on fire and his vision blurred. His tongue seemed to be double its normal size. He feared he would black out soon, and he was afraid for Claire and Illy.

His bleary eyes caught a quick movement behind the deputy. He got a glimpse of the pale green Roseville vase as Claire lifted it into the air, saw the flowers sail into the air and burst apart, like something in a fireworks display. She brought the vase down hard and it shattered against the back of the deputy's head with an explosion of sound as water splashed in all directions.

The deputy—who was no longer a deputy, but now a vicious, hairy creature in a torn khaki uniform—flinched at the impact of the vase and growled angrily, spraying spittle all over Abe's face. It loosened its grip on his wrist and throat and turned its head toward the attack from the rear.

Abe swam through the fuzziness that filled his mind, through his blurry vision and the pain he felt, and took advantage of the weak moment. He swung his knee up with all his might and it slammed into the creature's crotch.

As the creature grunted in pain, it let go of his wrist and swung its left arm back hard. Its hand collided with Claire and she yelped like a kicked puppy as the impact knocked her over.

It swung its left arm forward again and its claws ripped across Abe's face, knocking him backward. He hit the floor hard and felt the warm blood on his cheek almost instantly, followed by the burn of broken flesh. But he was free of the thing's clutches, and he tore his focus from his own pain and put it on acting as quickly as he could.

The creature seemed to take a moment to get its bearings after the blow to the head. In that moment, Abe scrambled to his feet. The dining room tilted and spun around him for a couple of seconds. Then he realized his right hand was empty.

He'd dropped his gun.

Abe unconsciously made a little whining sound as he looked around his feet for his weapon. He turned around and spotted the gun on the floor a few feet away. He reached out his hand and was about to step forward and bend down to get it when the creature behind him roared furiously. It slammed into the back of him, and together they flew forward as it embraced Abe's chest from behind, pinning his arms firmly to his sides, his roar so loud in Abe's right ear that it made his head hurt.

Fangs sank into Abe's shoulder and the creature's jaws closed tightly. Agonizing pain radiated from each puncture point, and Abe cried out as he struggled under the creature's weight, lifting his head.

Through the red heat of his pain, Abe saw two feet in front of him. They wore stubby dark brown shoes and had thick, puffy ankles that grew into fat calves encased in flesh-colored support hose.

In her ragged old voice, Illy screamed something in Romanian, something that ended with the drawn out word, *"Moooorrrrrooooiiii!"*

The creature's growl shot up into a high squeal, a harsh, painful sound that dragged on as it began to writhe and jerk on top of Abe. A moment later, its hold on Abe's upper body loosened and it fell to the right.

His teeth clenched against the pain, Abe dragged himself over the floor and away from the suddenly weak creature. He grabbed the edge of one of the dining chairs, pulled himself to his feet, and turned around. He looked down at the thing on the floor.

It lay on its side, arching its back as it convulsed, making wet, strangled sounds of distress. It rapidly changed again and again, its coating of hair coming and going, its snout melting away, then reappearing. As it transformed back and forth, its flesh split open in places all over its face and neck and hands, and on the spaces visible through the tears in its clothes. Each splitting of the skin became an ugly, red, dribbling sore. As it screamed in anguish, it rolled over onto its stomach.

Abe saw the crucifix handle of Illy's dagger sticking out between the creature's shoulder blades. The eight-inch blade had been buried to the hilt in the thing's back.

He turned to Illy and saw something in her face he had never seen before. Anger burned in her eyes, and somehow it took ten years from her appearance. Her hands were curled into loose fists at her sides as she glared down at the creature that was suffering on the floor.

Fluids coming from the open sores began to gather on the floor around the thrashing, wailing creature. It kicked its legs, flailed its arms. Then, within seconds, its movements slowed. Its sounds became weaker but more desperate. Finally, the creature fell still.

"Get the dagger," Illy said, a little winded, her voice hoarse.

Abe bent down and removed the dagger from the creature's back. He held it before him and looked at the blade. Through the streaks of blood, the intricate silver inlay glimmered.

"I have always said it has great power," Illy said. "It is—"

Claire's scream rose shrilly in the living room. An instant later, it collapsed in a horrible wet bubbling sound, as if she were gargling with mouthwash.

Abe turned and ran into the living room. He could not believe what he was seeing. The deputy whose face and head had been shattered by a bullet was on his knees beside Claire, who was stretched out on the floor. The deputy's face was pressed against her throat. Her legs kicked and her arms twitched as she continued to make a voiceless gurgling sound. Abe could see that the deputy's hands were covered with dark hair.

He rushed forward, lifting the dagger high in both hands. He brought it down hard and sank the blade into the deputy's back.

Almost instantly, the deputy rolled away from Claire with a high growl. His face was hairy, with a half-developed snout. When Abe had last seen the deputy only minutes ago, a large segment of the left side of his face and head had been gone, torn away by the bullet. It looked different now. It was still bloody, but much of the missing segment had returned.

With the knife in its back, the deputy-creature tried to get to its feet, but fell forward helplessly. It began to go through the same agonizing convulsions and to open up in the same ugly sores as the thing in the dining room.

Abe ignored the creature on the floor, as well as his own pain, and went to Claire's side. Someone in the room was sobbing and babbling incoherently. As Abe scooped Claire up in his arms, he realized the sobbing and babbling was coming from his own mouth.

Claire's throat was gone. It had been torn away, revealing the broken trachea and wirelike tendons beneath the skin. Blood puddled in the cavity that had replaced her lovely throat, and sputtered up out of her mouth. Her body jerked repeatedly in his arms. Her wide eyes locked with Abe's as her lips trembled and she tried to speak. All that came out was more gurgling, more blood. She lifted a hand to touch his face, but did not quite make it. The hand dropped away as her eyes seemed to look through Abe and beyond him.

Abe shouted her name again and again as he held her limp body to him tightly and rocked back and forth on his knees. He sobbed until his chest ached. The wound on his shoulder throbbed painfully. He hugged Claire to him as his sobs weakened.

"More may come," Illy said, standing beside him. She placed a hand on his shoulder and he could feel it trembling. "We should not stay here."

He forced himself to process her words, to think about them. He knew she was right. But he did not want to let go of Claire.

# CHAPTER TWENTY-TWO

*Convergence: Jail*

Abe drove the Navigator with no destination in mind. He heard a low thrum in his ears, but it was not coming from an exterior source. It was the sound of his own pain and fear droning inside his head. Adrenaline coursed through his body, but at the same time, he felt drained of energy, so impossibly weak that it was difficult to keep his arms up and his hands on the wheel.

He could not take his mind off of Claire. He kept seeing the insides of her throat brutally exposed beneath torn flesh . . . hearing her last horrible sounds . . . watching the life evaporate from her lovely eyes. The pain created by these thoughts was not located in one particular part of his body. It radiated from his gut and spread from the soles of his feet to the crown of his skull.

Illy's dagger with its crucifix handle lay in the center console, its silver-inlaid blade still glistening with wet blood.

He looked over at Illy and saw that she was hunched forward as far as her seat belt would allow, as if in pain.

"You okay, Illy?" he said, his voice rough and dry.

She gave him a familiar gesture—a short, dismissive wave, as if to say, *Don't mind me.*

Abe headed south out of Big Rock. Just beyond the

town's border, he came to a road-construction crew in orange smocks and hard hats. One diamond-shaped sign read SLOW, and another read PREPARE TO STOP. In spite of the trucks and the crew, he could see no actual roadwork being done.

"Oh, no," he groaned as one of the men stepped into the road with a red stop sign and held up his hand, palm out. Abe slowed to a stop.

The man with the stop sign stared at the Navigator. It looked to Abe as if his eyes were on the license plate. Still holding up the stop sign, the man took a radio from his belt, held it in front of his mouth, and pushed the button on the side with his thumb.

Something about this disturbed Abe, but it wasn't quite able to penetrate that low humming sound in his head.

"I hope this doesn't take long," Abe said. He turned to Illy. "It's strange that on a Sunday there's—Illy!"

She had removed her seat belt and slumped forward, her head against the glove compartment. Abe unfastened his belt, leaned over, and eased her upright until she was resting against the back of the seat. Her knobby fingers clutched at her chest and her mouth hung open.

"No, Illy, no," he said, surprised by the flat, lifeless sound of his voice, as if his pain and dread had sucked all the emotion from it.

Illy made a dry, raspy sound in her throat as she slumped further into the seat. Her hands dropped heavily from her chest and fell into her lap.

"No, not both of you, not both of you, please, God, not that," Abe babbled as he quickly got out of the SUV. He ran around to the other side, opened the door, and pulled Illy out. He clumsily stretched her out on the pavement beside the Navigator and began to perform CPR. He did not hear his own voice uttering pleas to God as he worked on her.

The sun beat down on the hot pavement. There wasn't

even the hint of a breeze in the air. A set of footsteps crunched over the shoulder toward Abe, closely followed by another.

"She sick?" a man said.

As he pumped Illy's sternum with both hands, Abe tossed a very brief glance up at the man in the orange smock. "Dying," he said abruptly, then bent forward to perform mouth-to-mouth.

Abe was so desperate to revive his grandmother, so immersed in what he was doing, that he did not hear the man's muttered comment about calling the police.

Karen and Gavin were led in handcuffs to their cell in the rear of the station. Inside the cell, Deputy Eckhart removed their cuffs, closed the door, and walked away without a word.

Karen turned to the right and looked at the man on the other side of the bars. He sat on the bench in his cell, leaning forward with his elbows on his thighs, joined hands hanging between his knees. She was badly frightened, but as usual, she pushed that deep down inside her and instead smiled at the other prisoner.

"So, what are you in for?" she said.

The man looked at her cautiously, uncertainly. He had a bloody scrape on his forehead. Finally, he smiled slightly and said, "I guess they don't like me." He stood and came to the bars. "George Purdy."

Karen flinched and turned to Gavin, who quickly came to her side.

"Well, well," Gavin said, reaching out and shaking George's hand. He introduced himself and Karen. "We've been talking about you. Your name has come up more than once in the last several hours."

"My name?" George said suspiciously. "Has come up?"

"We're private investigators," Gavin said. "We've come to Big Rock to . . . Well, we, uh—"

"Among other things," Karen said, "we're here to look into the disappearance of Daniel Fargo."

George's eyes widened.

"You were a friend of Arlin Hurley's, right?" Gavin said. "The former sheriff?"

A look of amazement followed by great relief passed over George's face, relaxing his features. "My God, you knew Arlin?"

"No, we didn't know him, but we know of him. And we know of *you*. We have a lot of questions to ask you."

George's shaggy beard opened in a broad smile. "And I've got a few things to tell you, too."

When it became clear to Abe that Illy was irretrievably gone, he finally stopped working on her. He was on all fours beside Illy, his head sagging, sweat dribbling down the sides of his face. It occurred to him that fifty years ago, back when a doctor never went anywhere without his bag, he might have had something on hand that could have saved her. But doctors didn't carry bags anymore.

*Such is progress,* he thought.

He had no idea how long he'd worked on her. His sense of time had become warped. He suddenly realized he couldn't remember what day of the week it was; he only knew it was the day he lost his family.

Footsteps crunched toward him again. He looked up, expecting to see one of the hard-hatted men in orange. Instead, a deputy stood over him. Three of the road workers stood behind him. It was one of the frustratingly casual deputies from last night's bloodshed in the ER. Abe groped through the fog in his mind and found his name: Deputy Cross.

"Hello again, Dr. Dinescu," the deputy said with a smile.

In too much emotional pain to feel anymore dread, Abe got to his feet, brushed grit from his pants, and faced the deputy.

"I suppose you want to see my license and registration," Abe said, stepping over Illy and leaning into the open door of the SUV. He reached across the seat and wrapped his fingers around the handle of the dagger.

"No, that's not really necessary," Deputy cross said. "I know who you are. In fact, I'm kind of surprised to see you out here."

"Well, I'm going to give this to you, anyway," Abe said as he spun around. He threw himself recklessly at the deputy and buried the knife to the hilt in the lower part of his flat abdomen, then dragged the knife upward. The blade cut through flesh, muscle, and khaki shirt until it hit bone.

Cross laughed as the three road workers pounced on Abe and pulled him away from the deputy. Smiling down at the knife jutting from his body, Cross said, "For a doctor, you sure are—" The smile vanished as he groaned. "What the *fuck*!" he shouted, his voice suddenly high and shrill. He screamed as he stumbled backward, pawing at the knife. He jerked it out of his abdomen and threw it to the pavement with a clatter, as if that would help—but it did not. His screams grew louder as he collapsed to the ground and began to kick and convulse.

"You son of a bitch!" one of the three road workers—the biggest of the three—barked at Abe.

The last thing Abe saw for awhile was the man's thick-fingered fist suddenly engulfing his field of vision.

As he drove his Chrysler Crossfire coupé, Royce kept glancing to his right at Bob, hoping to see signs of improvement in his friend. But Bob still looked terrified, a nervous wreck, near tears. The route from Royce's house to Bob's required him to drive by the Seventh-day Adventist church. As they passed it, Bob's eyes locked onto the pointy building surrounded by its empty parking lot, and his entire body stiffened.

Royce said, "Tell me again why I'm taking you back to your house and opening myself to abuse from the wonderful women in your life?"

"Weapons."

"Weapons," Royce repeated.

"My dad's cane."

"Yes, you mentioned that. Why his cane? Are you having trouble walking?"

"Because it's *silver*!" Bob snapped impatiently.

"Look, Bob, you've been telling me things in fragments since you got off the phone with that detective. Can you run it all by me in one piece?"

As he spoke, Bob nervously rubbed his hands up and down on his thighs. "Silver. We need silver. Real silver. Karen said that the werewolves have some kind of bad reaction to silver."

"You mean . . . like in the movies? Silver bullets?"

Bob nodded jerkily. "I know how it sounds, but *yes*. My dad hurt his knee when I was a kid. Had to have surgery. Grandma gave him an old cane to use while he was recovering. It's an old thing that used to belong to her grandfather, or something. It had a silver handle in the shape of Anubis."

"Anubis? The Egyptian god with the jackal head?"

"Yes, the handle is in the shape of the jackal head."

"You mean to tell me your grandmother allowed something in the shape of an Egyptian god into the house?"

"She doesn't approve of that, but she says it has sentimental value. Anyway, the handle is silver." Mostly to himself, he muttered, "I don't remember where it is. . . . Haven't seen it in years . . . Somewhere in the house . . ."

"But what about me? Don't I get a weapon? Or am I shit outta luck?"

"Don't worry, we'll find something for you. I've got an idea."

Frowning, Royce considered his words carefully before speaking. "Look, Bob, I know something awful has happened, that's obvious. But . . . do you hear what you're saying? You're talking about . . . well, about werewolves and silver bullets and—"

Bob suddenly turned to him angrily and shouted, "I know you think I'm some kind of pathetic geek, Royce, you always have, but don't give me any crap about this! I don't care if you think it's weird or funny, or if you think it's a side effect of my lifelong religious brainwashing! I don't even care if you don't *believe* me! Just *humor* me for now, okay? You'll probably find out I'm right soon enough. And when you do, I promise not to say I told you so."

Royce had never seen Bob behave with such fervor and was taken aback. In a way, it was encouraging—there was a passionate person in that quiet, shy, frightened body after all. It was clear that Bob had seen something horrible. Bob had been seriously damaged by his Seventh-day Adventist upbringing, but other than those pounded into him by his family, the church, and that long-dead drunken plagiarist Ellen G. White, he was not prone to delusions or fantasies. Whatever it was that had so upset Bob was beginning to have the same effect on Royce.

He stopped at the curb in front of Bob's house and killed the engine.

"You go ahead," Royce said. "I'll wait here."

"No, you have to come with me. I'm going to need help finding that cane. I'm not sure where it is."

"Can't your mother help you?"

Bob turned to him and, for a moment, the fear and anxiety left his face and he looked as if Royce had just told a bad joke. "Be serious. She's not going to help me. With two of us looking, we'll find it faster. But first, I want to make a weapon for you."

They got out of the car and Bob jogged across the lawn to the front door. Royce followed slowly. He was in no hurry to go in the house, where he knew he would not be welcomed by Bob's mother or grandmother.

Bob went inside and left the door standing open behind him. Seconds after he went in, Royce heard Arlene Berens's shrill, unpleasant voice.

"Where have you been?" she shouted. "Where did you go so fast this morning? You've been gone all day! You haven't gotten a single thing done!"

*Here we go*, Royce thought as he walked through the door and quietly closed it behind him. He followed Bob through the doorway to the right and into the combination kitchen and dining room.

Religious music played on the radio. Bob's mother and grandmother sat at the table with books open before each of them: a Bible in front of each, accompanied by what Royce recognized as the Sabbath-school lesson. He rolled his eyes behind closed lids. It seemed to him that Seventh-day Adventists were incapable of reading their Bibles unless they were guided by some kind of Adventist literature that would put the proper Ellen G. White spin on the scriptures. Grandma appeared to be quite engrossed in her Sabbath-school lesson and sat hunched over the books, her head tilted back so she could peer through her bifocals.

"I'd like to know what was so important that you had to rush out of here this morning," Bob's mother demanded. "You didn't even fix breakfast for—" Then she saw Royce. Her mouth slowly closed as she set her jaw and narrowed her eyes. "What is *he* doing here?" she asked.

Grandma looked up from her reading then. When she saw Royce, her wrinkled face quickly became more creased by a disapproving frown.

"Well," Grandma said, dragging the word out venomously. "Still being a bad influence on our boy?"

"What is he *doing* here, Robert?" Mom said again, her voice getting louder with each word.

Both women sounded as defensive and offended as if Royce had walked into the room, uttered obscene insults at them, whipped out his penis, and urinated on the floor. Royce was relieved when Bob started talking right away, taking the pressure off of him.

"Mom, where's your sterling-silver serving tray?" Bob said as he began to look through the cupboards beneath the counter.

"My sterling-silver—What do you want with *that*?" she said, confused and angry at the same time.

"I can't explain now, Mom, I just need it."

"You don't need my sterling-silver serv—"

He stood, spun around, and snapped at her, "I *do* need it! Now where is it?"

Royce flinched, surprised to hear Bob speak to his mother so harshly. It was the first time in all the years he and Bob had known each other.

"Don't you shout at your mother like that!" Grandma shouted, slapping a hand to the tabletop.

Bob continued to search the cupboards, and in the third one he found it. He pulled the tray out, stood, and handed it to Royce.

The tray was heavy, and Royce grabbed it with both hands.

Turning to his mother again, Bob said, "Now, where's that cane Dad used after his knee surgery?" Bob said. "The one with the silver handle?"

"Cane?" she said.

"The cane, yes, the cane." Impatient and under pressure, Bob spoke rapidly and abruptly. "Where *is* it?"

Mom shook her head. "I don't know. But what do you want with that cane?"

"I need it, that's all. Would it be in your bedroom?"

"Why do *you* need it?" Grandma said. "What for? You're not going to *sell* it, are you? I gave that cane to your father when—"

"I just need it!" Bob said firmly, raising his voice but not quite shouting.

Proceeding cautiously, Mom said, "Well, it might be in the bedroom, but I—"

"Never mind for now," Bob said with a distracted wave. "We'll find it when we're done with the tray." Frowning, he turned to Royce. "Come with me."

Bob led him across the front hall into the laundry room, opened a narrow closet, and removed a broom. It was an old-fashioned straw broom with a wooden handle.

"What're you doing with that tray?" Mom shouted.

"We've got all the tools we need out in the garage," Bob said to Royce, opening the door to the garage. "And Dad's old grinding wheel."

"Grinding wheel?" Mom said. "*Grinding* wheel? What are you *doing*?" She tried to follow them out to the garage, but Bob turned around in the doorway, put a hand on each of her shoulders, and began to walk her backward through the laundry room.

"Mom, listen to me, please," he said, his voice low and tremulous but urgent. "I don't have time to explain now, okay? I just can't. You have to trust me, okay? Just leave me alone for now, let me do what I have to do, and I'll explain later."

"You'll explain *what* later?" she barked, scowling.

Bob stopped walking and just stood there with his hands on her shoulders. His sigh had a slight groan behind it. "Just trust me and I'll—"

"That's my *good silver tray*!" she shouted. "I have a right to know what you're going to *do* with it!"

Bob's voice dropped nearly to a whisper as he said, "Are you trying to do to me what you did to Dad? Huh? Is that what you want me to do? Drive my car into a concrete wall and kill myself, like he did? Because if that's what you want, Mom, just keep this up. Otherwise, leave me alone and let me do what I have to do."

Mom's upper lip curled and her eyes narrowed. She pointed beyond Bob at Royce, who stood just beyond the doorway in the garage. "He makes you hateful," she growled. "God is *not in him.*"

Bob's arms dropped to his sides. "Mom, I don't think you know *where* God is." He turned away, stepped down into the garage, and closed the door. To Royce, he said, "Let's get to work."

Karen and Gavin had been listening attentively to George, occasionally asking a question, fascinated by what he had been telling them. The three of them stood close to the bars and spoke very quietly.

"So Hurley's widow is one of *them*?" Karen asked quietly.

Nodding, George said, "Yes, but she hates them, and she wants to stop them. That's why she came to me last night. Here."

"She was here in your cell?" Gavin said.

"She told me what they were planning to do to me," George said. "Probably the same thing they intend to do to both of you." A sardonic smile pushed his round cheeks up and narrowed his sparkling eyes. "We're dinner."

"Dinner?" Karen said. She had to swallow hard and take a breath to keep her fear from breaking out on her face.

George nodded. "She said they were planning to eat me, and they'd probably do it while I'm still alive. And I know she's right. I didn't have much choice. I could face that or help her, and the best way to help her was to become like her."

Frowning, Gavin said, "You mean . . . the two of you . . ."

George nodded again. "She's hoping it happens fast in me. If I'm like them, at least I'll stand a fighting chance against them. And as it turns out, she's going to need me sooner than we thought. A little over an hour ago, she told me they're planning a meeting tonight in the church. They'll be together under one roof."

"She told you?" Karen said. "You mean she was here again?"

"No. She called me." He removed a small, slender, black cell phone from his pocket. "When she came last night, she left this with me." He shrugged. "I mean, why not, right? They've already taken my phone, and they figure I'm still phoneless. She wanted to be able to stay in touch. She'll be back later. She promised. I'm just waiting for her to show up. She's going to let me out of here and we're going to hit the church." He smiled again. "Wanna come?"

The sound of the door opening startled all of them. George quickly stuffed the phone back into his pocket. They stepped away from the bars so they wouldn't look like they'd been talking.

Two deputies came down the corridor, each holding the arm of the slumped man between them. The man's head drooped as his half-dragged feet tried to keep up with the deputies. One of them opened the last cell in the row of three. Its far wall was cinder blocks rather than bars. The deputies took the man inside, dropped him heavily on the bench, then left the cell, locked the door, and disappeared back up the corridor and around the corner without even glancing at them. The door down the corridor closed heavily.

Karen went to the bars of the man's cell, getting a good look at him. "Dr. Dinescu," she said.

The doctor slumped against the wall. He slowly lifted his head to reveal the purple swelling around his half-closed left eye. Blood dribbled from a swollen cut on his lower lip. His shoulders and chest rose and fell with his breathing, and his mouth hung open.

"Dr. Dinescu, it's Karen Moffett," she said urgently. "We met last night, in the emergency room."

His head dropped down again, chin resting on his chest.

"Jesus, he was *there*," George said. "In the ER. He seemed really angry about something. I think he was pissed at the deputies, judging by the way he talked to them."

"Looks like they showed him how they felt about that," Gavin said, frowning through the bars at the doctor. He turned and went to George. "Can I use your phone?"

"Sure." George took the phone from his pocket and handed it between the bars. Gavin took the phone, opened it, then closed his eyes for a long moment.

"What's wrong?" Karen said.

"I'm trying to remember Burgess's phone number." Karen recited the ten digits and Gavin punched them in. He waited a few moments with the phone to his ear, then said, "It's Gavin. We're in trouble and we need help. Now listen up."

# CHAPTER TWENTY-THREE

*Domestic Problems*

After nearly four hours of searching for the cane, Bob was exhausted. It was not in his mother's bedroom and it was not in the walk-in closet in the hall. He and Royce had spent most of their time searching the garage, where they already had spent forty minutes working with the sterling-silver serving tray and the broom.

Using a hacksaw, Bob had cut a six-inch spearhead from the tray, edged it on his dad's old grinding wheel until it was very sharp, then drilled two holes in the center of the tang in line with the tip. Royce had cut a three-foot segment from the broom handle. Then they'd fastened the silver head to the broom handle with a couple of bolts and nuts. The result was too short to be a spear. It looked more like a Zulu's assegai.

It was hot and stuffy out there, and the two of them had been soaked with sweat in no time as they worked. Then, after searching the master bedroom and the hall closet, they'd gone back out there for more stifling heat to continue hunting for the cane.

Mom and Grandma had been shouting the entire time. Mom was trying to slice cucumbers at the kitchen counter and was angry because not only were Bob and Royce creating a mess with their search, they were distracting her from her task. Grandma was upset because she wanted to know what Bob intended to do with the cane she had given her son.

When they came out of the garage and into the laundry room, Bob and Royce were dripping with sweat, their wet hair flat against their heads.

"Well, that was fun," Royce said.

Bob turned to him and said, with genuine regret, "I'm sorry for putting you through this, Royce, but I don't have anyone else."

Royce smiled wearily and nodded once. "I know you don't. That's why I'm here."

Bob suddenly wanted to hug his friend—his *only* friend. Mom and Grandma had been terribly abusive toward Royce for four hours, yet Royce had held his tongue. Bob knew how difficult that was for him to do. Royce had spent those hours diligently searching for the cane without a word of complaint, without a single joke about werewolves. Bob knew that couldn't have been easy, either—he was well aware of how crazy he'd been sounding that day. He'd known Royce all his life, but he'd never felt such an overwhelming rush of love and affection for him as he did at that moment.

Bob reached over and squeezed Royce's shoulder. "I appreciate that. You don't know how much."

"I suppose you've messed up the garage now, too, huh?" Mom said from the kitchen counter, where she continued to slice cucumbers. "Like you've messed up the whole house?"

Bob sighed as he led Royce out of the laundry room and into the hall. "Mom, the garage was *already* a mess." He raised his voice a little and became more irritated when he added, "And since *I'm* the one who cleans the house, I don't know what *you're* worried about!"

From the kitchen, Grandma shouted, "Don't you talk to your mother that way, young man! And you still haven't told me what you want with that cane. I gave that cane to your *father*, not to *you*, and I'm not going to stand by while you—"

Bob said, "Grandma, *shut up*!" He turned to Royce. "The only other place it might be is the attic. I'll get the ladder from the garage."

Suddenly, Grandma was in front of Bob and swinging her right hand through the air. Her palm connected with Bob's left cheek with a loud smack.

Mom cried out sharply in the kitchen and something clattered to the counter.

Bob recovered from the slap, and his eyes grew wide beneath a frown. He moved close to Grandma, his fists clenched at his sides, as he breathed hard through clenched teeth. He thought of every cruel thing the old woman had ever said to him, every self-righteous accusation and finger-pointing condemnation, and sour anger rose in his throat. But it passed rather quickly, like the stinging pain in his cheek. His breathing slowed and his face relaxed. For one quick, white-hot heartbeat, he had been tempted to slap her right back. But he realized that nothing he could do would inflict more damage on her than she'd already inflicted on herself. She was a bitter, hateful old woman who used her religion to justify that bitterness and hate. Other than Mom and himself and that ugly, long-dead woman in the old pictures on the wall, that stern, judgmental, uptight "prophetess" she admired so much—that vinegar-swilling *huckster*, Royce would say—Grandma was alone in the world with no friends, no life, no happiness, and nothing to look forward to but the grave. In that moment, he saw something in her that chilled him to the marrow of his bones. He saw his future.

In that instant, Bob was hit hard by the certainty that

he had to move in with Royce and look for a job, and he had to do it as soon as possible.

"Look at you!" Grandma said, a slight smile appearing at the corner of her wrinkle-stitched lips. "Look at the anger in your eyes! That comes from *Satan*, boy! From hanging around with wicked people!" She turned to Mom as she pointed a finger at Royce. "See? *See?* I told you this satanic troublemaker was a bad influence on our boy. I *told* you!"

"*Now* look what you made me do!" Mom shouted. She stood at the kitchen doorway with blood dribbling down her right wrist from her thumb. "I cut myself!"

Grandma stepped over to Mom and frowned at the thumb. "That's a deep one."

Sounding offended that he had ignored her, Mom said, "Bob! I cut my *thumb*!"

Rob turned to her and said, "Well, you know where the Band-Aids are, Mom. I'm busy." He turned to Royce again. "Let's get the ladder." They went back out to the garage as Mom and Grandma ranted on and on.

Five minutes later, Bob climbed up the ladder they'd positioned under the entrance in the hallway ceiling, which he unlocked with a key and pushed open. Royce followed him up to the attic. It was as hot and stuffy as the garage. Bob tugged on a chain and lit up the bare bulb in a socket on the low, slanted ceiling, then wiped away the sweat dripping from his forehead.

"They drive me crazy sometimes," Bob whispered with a sigh.

"With good reason," Royce said. "But they're Adventists, Bob, which explains everything. Like I've told you hundreds of times, Adventists in Nazi Germany *loved* Hitler and praised him as a man led by God—which isn't surprising given the fact that they think that lying drunk, Ellen White, was having personal conversations with God and his angels over Postum. What do you *expect* from such nutbags? Your mom and grandma are typical. They're *insane*—it's practically a baptismal *requirement* for Adventists. They don't even—" He stopped, closed his eyes, held up his hands palms out, and said, "Ah— ah—ah. Don't get me started." He dropped his arms at his sides and let out a long sigh. "You've *got* to get *out* of here, Bob. Come live with me for awhile until you can find a place of your own."

Bob considered that for a moment. Slowly, as if reluctant to speak the words, he said, "That's sounding more and more appealing."

"Well, you're always welcome. You know that."

As they searched through the clutter of boxes and bags and dusty family relics, Mom and Grandma continued to voice their anger and indignation below. Twenty minutes later, Royce said, "Is this it?"

Bob turned to him, brightened when he saw the cane, and said, "Yep, that's it. Let's go. Back to the garage."

They ran the gauntlet of hysterical shouting from Mom and Grandma and returned to the garage. Bob used the grinding wheel again, this time on the cane's jackal-head handle. He began to grind the snout down to a sharp, deadly point.

He heard a familiar sound and stopped what he was doing to listen. The front door had opened and closed. It sounded like there was a third voice in the house. Bob listened until he heard that third voice again. It was Rochelle.

"My sister's here," Bob said.

Royce rolled his eyes. "Oh, great. The unholy trinity."

In spite of the smothering heat in the garage, Bob was overwhelmed by a sudden chill as something occurred to him that he had been too preoccupied to consider before.

"Oh, no," he whispered. "She was with Deputy Cross. . . ."

Royce frowned, cocked his head. "What? Who? Your sister?"

Still speaking mostly to himself, Bob muttered, "They were at the Lighthouse Motel last night."

Royce's eyes widened. "Your sister and a deputy were at a motel? *Fucking?* What're you talking about?"

Ignoring the question, Bob said, "If the sheriff is one of those things . . . Karen said the whole sheriff's department was . . . Oh, no." He turned to Royce. "It's sexually transmitted. She's got the virus." To Royce, he said, "We've got to get out of here."

Rochelle stumbled across the kitchen and leaned both arms against the dining table, elbows locked. She dropped heavily into a chair, a distressed expression on her face.

"What's wrong with *you*?" Grandma said. She sat at the table eating crackers with a glass of fruit juice.

"I'm sick, Grandma."

Mom stood at the counter, where she'd been slicing celery to go with her sliced cucumbers. She went to Rochelle's side, concerned. "You think it's a flu bug or something?"

"I hope you didn't bring something *contagious* into the house," Grandma grumbled, frowning as she backed away from Rochelle.

"I don't know what it is," Rochelle said, her voice weak. "Mike and Peter were getting on my nerves, so I came over here even though I didn't feel like driving. I just feel . . . Well, I know it's weird because I feel sick, but at the same time, I feel . . . *hungry*."

"Have you eaten?" Mom said.

Rochelle shook her head and chuckled. "Nothing tastes good. It's almost like being pregnant, because it's like—"

"*Are* you pregnant?" Mom said.

"No."

"You're *sure*?"

Annoyed, Rochelle shook her head and said, "No, Mom, no, I just had my period."

Grandma clicked her tongue and made a breathy sound of disgust. "Don't *say* such things out *loud*."

Rochelle ignored her. "It's like I'm . . . *craving* something. But I don't know what it is."

Grandma reached across the table and took Rochelle's hand in hers. "We should pray," she said. She waved Mom over and said, "Come on, join hands." Once their hands were linked, Grandma said, "I just hope God hears our prayer while we've got that satanic *artist* in the house," spitting the word *artist* from her mouth like a lump of phlegm. They closed their eyes and Grandma said, "Our father in heaven, we come to thee humbly, in righteousness, with devotion to your word and the word of your prophets. We ask thee to take this affliction from your daughter Rochelle. Cast it from her body as you cast demons from the possessed. We ask this in Jesus' name, amen."

Rochelle sighed and fidgeted in the chair, then stood and went to the refrigerator. "Maybe if I eat something . . . Maybe if I figure out what it is I *want* . . ." She bent down and examined the contents of the shelves inside the refrigerator. "Nothing looks good, nothing sounds good." She stood, closed the refrigerator.

Mom stepped over to her with a frown and put the palm of her right hand to Rochelle's forehead. "Do you have a fever?"

Rochelle's eyes rolled up to Mom's bandaged thumb and her nostrils flared as she sniffed. She reached up and took Mom's hand in both of hers, an intense expression on her face. "What'd you do to your thumb?" she said quietly, sniffing the bandage.

"Oh, I was cutting cucumbers earlier, and Bob and Royce were making such a racket that I—"

Mom stopped talking and flinched as Rochelle clawed

at the bandage with her fingernails and quickly peeled it off.

"Rochelle, what are you *doing*?"

She removed the bandage, quickly sniffed Mom's thumb, then stuck it in her mouth and closed her lips around it. As she sucked noisily, clutching Mom's hand, her eyes closed with satisfaction, her body relaxed, and she slowly began to grind her hips.

Grandma gasped and Mom tried to pull her hand away, shouting, "Oh, for crying out—what are you *doing*, Rochelle?"

Rochelle clung to her hand and moaned as she sucked on the cut thumb.

Grandma shot to her feet and shouted, "Stop that *right now*, young lady! It's *obscene*!"

Mom finally jerked her hand away. Rochelle's eyes widened as she reached out for the hand with a childlike sound of distress.

"But i-it was s-so *good*," she said.

Horrified, Mom said, "Rochelle, what is *wrong* with you?"

Rochelle smiled slightly beneath her wide eyes. "I'm just . . . hungry."

The moment he was finished with the cane, Bob said, "Okay, let's get—" He looked around frantically. "Where's the broom handle?"

"Oh, shit," Royce said. "I left it in the hallway, leaning against the wall."

"Damn," Bob whispered. "Here." He handed the cane to Royce and said, "Come on, let's go. I'll get it."

As they headed for the door, a scream sounded beyond it.

"Oh, God," Bob whispered as he opened the door. They passed through the laundry room and crossed the hall.

Royce stopped just inside the kitchen, but Bob continued on toward the doorway to the back hall. Mom rushed toward him with a look of horror, her hands up, and stepped in his path.

"Something's wrong with Rochelle!" she shouted.

"Out of the way, Mom," Bob muttered as he stepped around her and went into the hall.

She spun around and went after him, snapping, "I suppose you and your friend are more important than your *sister*? She's *sick*, Robert!" She disappeared through the doorway after him.

Rochelle was lying on the floor on her back, knees drawn up, arms flailing as she screamed.

Grandma stood beside the table gawking down at her, saying, "Oh, Jesus help us! Jesus help us!"

A moment later, Bob returned carrying the silver-tipped broom handle.

"You've got to take her to the hospital, Bob!" Mom shouted, following him into the kitchen.

Bob glanced at Royce, who looked very uncomfortable and worried. Turning to Mom, Bob said, "There's nothing I can do for her, Mom. I have to go."

"Who do you think you are?" Mom shouted at him, her eyes wide. "We're your *family*! She's your *sister*!"

Grandma pointed at Royce and cried, "He's being led astray by that blasphemous deceiver!"

Meanwhile, strange sounds began to come from Rochelle's convulsing body.

"Holy shit!" Royce said, watching Rochelle with growing horror.

On the way out of the kitchen, Bob stopped at Royce's side. He turned to Mom and Grandma, and as he looked at the anger and accusation in their faces, he felt a hot, churning sensation in his stomach. It moved up into his chest, then in his throat. He was only vaguely aware of grinding his teeth together.

Rochelle's screams deepened as wet popping sounds continued to come from her body. Her clothes ripped loudly as her skin became hairy.

"Jesus Christ!" Royce shouted.

Bob smiled at his mother. He clutched the broom handle so tightly that his knuckles became milky. His smile was cold, and its chill was reflected in his eyes. He pointed the broom handle at his sister on the floor and said, "Why don't *you* help her, Mom? Huh? *You* help her! She needs you! Look at her!"

Mom looked down at her daughter and moved toward her, but stopped and jerked backward as Rochelle sprang to her feet. She looked different, now—very, very different.

"What the *fuck*!" Royce shouted as he gawked at her silver eyes and the fanged snout that now made up the lower half of her face.

Grandma screamed as Rochelle pounced on Mom. The fangs closed hard on Mom's throat. As Mom released an awful, gurgling cry, Grandma began to gibber for God's help while she staggered backward and pressed herself against the stove.

Royce shouted in horror as blood sprayed from Mom's throat.

Walking backward, unable to take his eyes from his mother's death, Bob grabbed Royce's elbow and pulled him toward the doorway. Bob's cold smile had not faded.

A moist crunching sound ended Mom's gurgling, and her head snapped back. As the creature that had been Rochelle chewed its way through her neck, Mom's head flopped backward until it smacked against her back, coming to rest between her shoulder blades. The creature knocked her to the floor, straddled her, and began to eat with loud, sloppy sounds. All the while, Grandma's ragged screams kept coming, stopping only so she could take a breath. She stood backed against the stove, arms bent at the elbows, hands waggling on each side of her head as her mouth hung open. As Bob and Royce backed out of the kitchen, Grandma's upper dentures flopped crookedly in her mouth.

"You better pray harder, Grandma," Bob said through that cold smile. Then he shouted, "You better pray *a lot* harder!" He turned and pulled the terrified, babbling Royce out of the kitchen, out the front door, and across the yard to the car.

# CHAPTER TWENTY-FOUR

## Preparations

Standing beside the bed, Ella gently nudged Cynthia's shoulder. The girl stirred but did not wake up. She lay on her right side, her back to Ella, who shook her more firmly.

"Cynthia? Cynthia? You have to wake up now."

Cynthia rolled toward Ella slowly and opened her eyes a little, squinting and blinking. "What? Whassamatter?"

"You have to get up, Cynthia. Quickly."

The girl sat up and came around, swiping a hand roughly over her face. "Is something wrong?"

"It's time. Remember how I've been telling you that when the time came, we would hurt them together, but that you would have to do as I told you?"

"Yes."

"Well, that time has come. Get up and put your clothes on. We have to go get a friend of mine out of jail."

Bob and Royce sat in the cool darkness of the Bottletop, a small bar just a few blocks from Bob's house. They'd been there for what seemed a long time, but Bob knew his sense of time had been distorted since Royce had driven him away from the house with Grandma's screams still sounding in his ears. He was still trembling; he couldn't make his hands or feet stop moving, and he still felt each heartbeat in his throat.

Royce, on the other hand, had calmed down quite a bit with the help of a couple of martinis.

"Want a sip of my martooni?" Royce asked with a smile.

"It smells like paint thinner from here," Bob said. "Besides, one of us has to be able to drive. What time is it?"

"Time for another martooni." Royce grinned happily.

"You know, you can get falling-down drunk if you want, but that doesn't change anything. Those things out there aren't going away."

The grin melted from Royce's face like frost in the sun, and he became very serious. "I'm sorry I doubted you," he said quietly. "This has been . . . Well, seeing what happened back at your house . . ." He took a deep breath, lifted his glass in a toast, and said, *"Nostrovya,"* then took a sip.

"Maybe we should just get out of town," Bob said. "Right away. We can go back to your place and you can pack some stuff."

"What about you? Don't you have stuff?"

"Nothing I need." He thought about it a moment and a heavy feeling of sadness fell over him. "Nothing. I have nothing."

"You want me to pack up and just . . . go? Where?" He finished his drink.

"Away from *here*. You want to end up like my mother?"

Royce frowned, then shuddered. With a sigh, he said, "All right. After one more drink."

"Being drunk is not going to help."

"I'm not drunk. I can hold my liquor pretty well."

"It's *still* not going to help."

Royce waved at the cocktail waitress. "It sure as hell won't hurt."

Karen had been standing at the bars of the cell talking to Dr. Dinescu since he'd been brought in. He'd been unresponsive at first, but once he began to come out of his stupor, he cleared up fast. He remembered Karen and Gavin and George from the night before. He'd told them what had happened to his wife and grandmother.

"Now they're going to kill me," he'd said, his voice heavy with quiet defeat.

"Not so fast," Karen had said. "We've got a plan."

She and Gavin had brought Dr. Dinescu up-to-date. George sat on the bench in his cell looking unwell. He'd said he didn't feel good and suspected it was part of his change.

"So you're . . . like them?" Dr. Dinescu said to George in the next cell over. He sounded suspicious, a little afraid.

"I will be," George said.

"But don't worry, Dr. Dinescu," Karen said. "He's on our side."

"Please, call me Abe."

As Gavin and Abe continued to talk, Karen heard the first sounds. They came from elsewhere in the station, muffled by walls and doors—first a crash, then an alarmed shout. The others did not seem to notice the sounds, but Karen listened for more. And more came.

"Hey," she said. "Something's happening."

The three men looked at her, then listened.

Shouting voices were buried by an animal-like growl that grew into something more like a roar. A great deal of crashing mixed with the growls and the shouting. The shouts quickly became more roars, which then became agonizing wails and yelps.

Still looking unwell, George smiled slightly. "Sounds like Ella's here."

All four of them moved to the doors of their cells and waited as the sounds continued, crescendoed, then began to die out. A door opened and soft, slapping footsteps sounded. Karen, Gavin, George, and Abe looked to their left, down the corridor outside their cells.

Karen saw a woman come around the corner followed by a second, younger woman. She assumed the dark-haired woman in the lead was Ella Hurley. Both of them were naked, their bodies covered with a fine layer of fur. Ella's was a dark, reddish color, the girl's was blonde. They had blood on them, but it did not seem to be their own. A cloth bag hung from Ella's right shoulder on a strap, and with her every move, the bag made a soft jangling sound. In her right hand, she held a ring of keys. She walked with determination and resolve, while the girl behind her tried to keep up and looked a little stunned.

The appearance of the two women—the hair on their bodies, the slight distortion of their facial features, the silver glint in their eyes—reminded Karen that she and Gavin once again were dealing with something far stranger and more dangerous than their usual cases of infidelity, theft, or missing persons. Her immediate reaction to the women was one of fear, but she quickly got that under control and reminded herself that they were all on the same side.

"Boy, it's sure good to see you," George said as Ella went to the door of his cell and unlocked it. "I'm not feeling so good, Ella. Is that . . . to be expected?"

She opened the cell door and stepped aside so he could come out. "Yes," she said, her voice oddly thick. "It's a good sign. It means the change is in progress. We'll need you this evening. Let's go."

"Wait, wait," George said. "Ella, this is Karen Moffett and Gavin Keoph. They're private investigators who've come to look into the disappearance of Daniel Fargo. The man in the next cell over is Dr. Abe Dinescu."

Ella stepped over to the door of the cell and looked at Karen and Gavin with interest. "Daniel Fargo?" she said.

"They want to help us," George said. "You have to let them out. Abe, too."

"We have weapons," Gavin said. "Two handguns."

Ella said, "Guns won't do you any good because—"

"We have silver bullets," Karen added.

Ella's thick eyebrows rose. "Silver bullets?" When she spoke, she smiled slightly and the tips of fangs flashed behind her lips.

Karen tried to smile despite her discomfort and said, "We're loaded for werewolf."

Ella let them out of the cell. She went to Abe's cell and looked him over. "Looks like they worked you over. Can you get around well enough?"

"I'm just bruised up," Abe said. "I'm fine, really. Please. Let me out. I want to help you."

Ella opened his cell and he stepped out.

"This is Cynthia," she said, nodding at the young blonde woman, but offered no further information. Standing before the four of them, Ella reached into the bag that hung from her right shoulder. Something inside it jangled again. She handed each of them a silver knife and fork.

"Flatware from the house Taggart and his crowd have taken over," Ella said. "It's the best I could do, but it's the real thing. Reed & Barton sterling. You'll see how well it works when we go out front. Don't hesitate to use these. The second one of those things gets close enough, pierce its skin with one of these. That'll do it. Let's go."

She turned and led them along the corridor.

The station was a bloodbath. Six bodies lay on the floor, two more across desks. If there were more in the waiting area beyond the long counter, Karen could not see them yet. A few of the bodies were still twitching. All of them wore the tattered remains of uniforms and sported open, running sores.

"I told you the flatware worked," Ella said. "Now let's get your guns."

Taggart met Beth at the top of the basement stairs. He'd been too busy in the last few months to pay much attention to Beth. She was always around, it seemed, and he'd talked to her countless times. But for the first time, he took a good, healthy look at her.

She was tall and willowy with golden hair that fell to her shoulders. Her face looked mischievous, as if she were secretly up to something naughty, and her large blue eyes were beautiful. He smiled as he ran his eyes down her body slowly, then back up again. He decided she was extremely fuckable. But as promising as she looked, he wondered if any woman would ever live up to the experience of rutting with Lupa.

"Is she ready?" he said.

Beth smiled. "Almost. Besides that satin robe, this is the first time she's ever worn clothes. She's trying to adjust."

"Good." He checked his watch. "Jeremiah said they're already gathering at the church, but she's got a little more time." He met her eyes again and she kept smiling as she held his gaze. The tip of her tongue appeared at one corner of her mouth, making the smile even more wicked. Taggart reached out and cupped her braless breast with his hand, squeezed it. His thumb found the nipple through her shirt and felt it harden. She moved a little closer to him.

"You've finally noticed me," she whispered.

He nodded. "Yes, I've noticed you. I'll do something about it later, when I'm not so busy. I have to go get Cynthia."

"She's gone."

Taggart spun around and found Jeremiah standing a few feet away. "What did you say?"

"Cynthia is gone," Jeremiah said. "Her room is empty.

I can't find Ella, either. I've looked all over the house. Both of them are gone."

Taggart's forehead creased above his black patch and his good eye narrowed as his lips pulled back over his teeth. His fists clenched at his sides as he growled, "That *cunt*. Find them, Jeremiah. Put the word out, tell the deputies. Find them. And as soon as they're found, call me. Immediately." He stalked away, his footsteps heavy.

Ella drove the white van with Cynthia in the passenger seat and Karen, Gavin, Abe, and George in back. Ella and Cynthia were naked, but their bodies were covered with hair—not thick at the moment, but clearly visible.

Karen leaned forward and said, "Don't you think the fact that you're not wearing any clothes might draw attention?"

"From whom?" Ella said with a shrug. "At this point, what difference would it make?"

Karen sat back with a nod, thinking, *Can't argue with that.*

"Besides," Ella said, "at night and from any distance, it'll look like we're wearing clothes because of our fur. Don't worry, it won't be a problem." Her tone became serious. "Now. There'll be a lot of them there. Don't let that intimidate you. The one we want is Taggart. He has a . . . Well, it's hard to describe, but he has a hold on them. On all of us. He's the alpha male, he leads the pack. He can transmit—yes, I guess *transmit* is the right word—he can transmit thoughts and feelings to us. He's been nudging the pack all afternoon about this meeting at the church. He wants them all there. He's going to discuss strategy, but more importantly, he's going to introduce everyone to the First Born. She's the other one we want. First Taggart, then Lupa. That's her name. Lupa."

"What does she look like?" Karen asked.

"Like the most beautiful teenage girl you've ever

seen—and she's only four months old. You'll know her when you see her. There's something about her that . . . Well, you'll just know."

"What do we do when we find the sheriff?" Abe asked.

"Kill him," Ella said. "Don't hesitate, don't even think about it. Just stick a fork in him and he'll be done. Once he's dead, the others should be easier to handle. I don't know this for a fact, but I have a feeling that with Taggart dead and his hold on the pack broken, they'll be . . . I don't know, confused, maybe. Uncertain. Vulnerable."

"Is there anything in particular we should know about this girl?" Gavin asked. "About Lupa?"

"I wish I could tell you more," Ella said. "Taggart has kept her under wraps. In fact, lately he's been keeping her pretty close to him, which has been a big relief to me, if you know what I mean. When he's not spending time with her, he's talking about her. He's obsessed with her. He thinks she's the beginning of some kind of new . . . race."

None of them spoke for awhile. Then Cynthia, who had said nothing since they'd met her, turned and looked at them in the backseat. She said, "She's my baby."

Ella tossed a concerned glance at Cynthia.

"I'm her mother," Cynthia said. "I brought her into this world. And if one of you doesn't get to her first . . . I'm gonna take her out of it."

Bob headed back to Royce's house at the wheel of his friend's coupé. The first gray of dusk was beginning to settle over the day's final hour. Shadows lengthened and light slowly faded.

"I wish I had a cigarette," Royce said, his voice a little thick after a few martoonis. He was slumped in the passenger seat. The silver-tipped stick they'd made rested between his legs, the sharp point against the floor. Next to it was the cane with the severely sharpened Anubis-head handle.

"You quit smoking four years ago," Bob said.

"I think this would be the perfect day to take it up again."

"You never should've started in the first place."

"Hey, it was inevitable. I stepped out of that miserable religious cult like Hillary Clinton stepping out of an ugly pantsuit, and suddenly I was ready to see the world. I wanted to taste everything. Including tobacco."

"You *knew* it was bad for you, that it would kill you, and you did it, anyway," Bob said, shaking his head. "The Seventh-day Adventist church isn't all bad, you know. Their health message has been on the money. Now even non-Adventists are adopting it, and we know that—"

"Health message, schmealth schmessage. You *always* bring that up, as if it somehow absolves that brainwashing, Ellen-toadying sect. Remember—meat eating leads to meat beating. *That* was God's big health message to Ellen White." He sat up in the seat, warming to his topic. "You know, *Hitler* didn't eat meat or drink tea or coffee or alcohol. That's one of the reasons the German Adventists *loved* the little fucker so much. He was all healthy and vegetarian and caffeine free. And he threw Jews into ovens! So don't say that just because—" He closed his eyes, sat back in the seat, and raised both hands, palms out. "Ah—ah—ah. Don't get me started."

"And the moral of your little story is . . . ?"

Royce shrugged. "Jews should stay the fuck away from vegetarians." He smiled at Bob, gave him a halfhearted Nazi salute, and said, "*Heil* Ellen!"

Bob suddenly decreased his pressure on the gas pedal. The Seventh-day Adventist church was coming up on the left—and the parking lot was crowded with cars and people.

"What's going on?" he muttered as the coupé slowed even more.

"What?" Royce said. "What's going on where?"

"The church—something's going on at the church."

"On a *Sunday*? I didn't think Adventists went *near* their churches on Sundays. Wouldn't want to be confused for the evil, Pope-loving Sunday-keepers." He looked ahead at the crowded church parking lot and squinted a little. "How about that. Next thing you know, they'll be eating wafers and carrying rosaries."

Bob pulled the car over to the right and stopped at the curb, then killed the engine.

"What're you doing?" Royce said.

"I just want to see what's happening. There's nothing scheduled today, and I don't recognize any of those cars."

"More people are coming in, too," Royce said, nodding toward a car that was pulling into the church parking lot. He rolled down his window and cocked an elbow on the edge.

Another car slowed and turned into the parking lot—a silver Jetta.

"Oh, God," Bob whispered. "That's my sister."

Royce quickly unfastened his seat belt and leaned forward to peer across the street, his eyes suddenly wide. "What? Where? *Where* is your fucking sister? I haven't had enough booze yet to face *her* again."

"It's them," Bob said. "All of them."

"All of who?"

"Look—three sheriff's-department cars. It's *them*! They're all getting together at the church."

"*Who?*" Royce said, a little impatiently.

"The *werewolves*, dummy. The sheriff was there this morning, scaring Pastor Edson to his knees, and now they've taken over the—"

"Well, well, well."

The voice came from the open window on Royce's right and startled both of them so severely that they nearly hit their heads on the ceiling as they jumped and turned to the right. Royce made an involuntary squeak sound.

Vanessa smiled at Bob as she peered into the open window. She was bent at the waist, her hands leaning on the door.

"Who's your friend, Robert?" she said.

Royce turned to Bob, his face pale with fear.

Bob could not speak. He was not sure he could move, as he stared into Vanessa's beautiful eyes. Those eyes had held such promise just the night before. Now they terrified him.

"Who is this, Bob?" Royce breathed quaveringly. He reached down and closed his hand on the broom handle.

"What are you guys doing here, anyway?" she said. "Just . . . watching? That's no fun. You should come inside and join us."

Bob felt as if his body had turned to stone, but he fought it, struggled to move, summoned all his strength, and finally cracked through the rigidity. He reached out and turned the key in the ignition. The engine started.

Royce grabbed the stick and began to bring the deadly silver-tipped end up.

Bob was reaching down to shift into drive and placing his foot on the gas pedal when Vanessa pulled her face away from the window and reached in through it with a low growl.

Royce screamed as Vanessa pulled him through the window like a doll. He clung to the broom handle, which became wedged in the window and snapped in two loudly, dropping to the empty seat. Bob cried out as he saw his friend's feet slip through the opening in a heartbeat.

Vanessa's face appeared in the window again. Out of view, Royce struggled and made strangled sounds of terror. There was hair on her cheeks now, a silver glint in her eyes, and her smile bared fangs.

"Leave now and you leave your friend," she said, her voice deeper, almost masculine. "Come inside with me and maybe I'll let him live."

Bob's heart pounded so hard, it felt as if it were about to explode and shatter his ribs. After a long moment, he turned the key with a trembling hand and killed the engine.

# CHAPTER TWENTY-FIVE

*Sunday-Go-To-Meetin'*

Rochelle made her way through the chattering crowd inside the church. The meeting had not even started yet, and already the church was more crowded than it was for services on a typical Sabbath. She stood in the foyer and looked around. She saw a lot of unfamiliar faces and some she had seen around town. But she did not see the one person she was looking for—Deputy Harry Cross.

She did not feel quite herself. She had a light-headed sensation, as if she were about to separate from her physical body and float away. Everything that had happened in the last few hours seemed to have happened to someone else.

Earlier, Rochelle had been overwhelmed by such an intense feeling of pleasure and satisfaction that it became easy to ignore the fact that she was eating her mother and grandmother. That feeling had gone beyond satisfying a hunger—it had been sexual. In fact, she seemed to remember reaching a mild orgasm at one point while using her teeth to tear the flesh away from Mom's varicose-veined left thigh. Afterward, she had sat slumped against the lower cupboards, her clothes in tatters, legs spread. She'd remained there for some time, her belly full, her mind fuzzy with pleasure as she smacked her lips on the intoxicating taste of blood and flesh and absently fondled her genitals with one hand. After eating, she'd wanted to fuck very, very much. She'd thought of Harry then. From Harry, her thoughts had wandered, blurred, and begun to take on the character of something that was not at all of her own making. It was as if the thoughts of another person were cropping up in her mind—not specific words, but a desire to do something, to go somewhere. An image of the Seventh-day Adventist church came into focus in her mind. Suddenly, she'd wanted to go there. *Like the others*, she'd thought, even though she was not quite sure who those "others" might be. Perhaps she would find Harry there. Then they could fuck again, like last night, fuck hard and fast. She'd taken a shower then, cleaned the blood and bits of tissue from her body, masturbated a little. Then she'd found some of her clothes that she'd left there weeks ago, put them on, and left the house. She hadn't gone through the kitchen, because the floor was covered with blood. She'd left the remains of Mom and Grandma on the kitchen floor the way one might leave behind a discarded orange peel or candy wrapper.

As she walked through the church, it seemed odd to see it crowded with people who were dressed so casually—jeans, T-shirts, shorts, tank tops. She was accustomed to seeing only people who were dressed up and scrubbed clean, with their hair perfectly coiffed. It gave her a strange out-of-place feeling that was almost dreamlike.

Rochelle left the foyer and wandered down the corridor, looking for Harry. She turned left and made her way into the multipurpose room. There were others there, standing around talking, laughing.

Finally, she decided to go into the sanctuary and find a seat. That was why she had come, to sit in a pew and listen to . . . something. She wasn't sure what, or why, but she was supposed to be there, she knew that much. She went back to the front of the church and walked through the open double doors into the sanctuary.

She looked around for Harry but did not see him in there, either. She made her way down the center aisle and ducked into a pew on the left, near the front. She sat on the very end of the pew because she wanted to be able to get up if she saw Harry. She would join him, and maybe they would wander off somewhere together. She was wet, and her vagina seemed to thrum with the need to be filled. Rochelle got horny often enough, but she could not remember the last time she'd been *this* randy, and she'd been feeling that way ever since she'd finished feeding earlier.

More people came in and began to seat themselves in the pews. The light coming in through the tall rectangular windows to the left grew dimmer as night fell. In the front of the sanctuary, three steps led up to the stage. The modest, narrow pulpit of blond wood stood in the center, its microphone jutting up like a rigid penis. Rochelle was accustomed to seeing a large, colorful bouquet of flowers standing directly in front of the pulpit during church services, but there was nothing there now. The baptistery—a large covered tub that was opened and filled for the immersion baptism ceremony—was to the right, with a peaceful woodland scene on the section of wall directly behind it. Behind and to the left of the pulpit was a column of empty pews where the choir would be during a Sabbath service. Behind and to the right of the pulpit stood an American flag. Above and behind the pulpit, suspended from the ceiling, were three pale tan fabric banners, with the image of the cross on each one, the center cross suspended above the other two. To the left of the stage was an organ, to the right a piano.

Rochelle looked over her shoulder, searched the faces of the crowd, looking for Harry. He still had not arrived. There were plenty of other uniformed deputies, though. She wondered where Harry could be.

A commotion in the front left corner of the sanctuary got Rochelle's attention. Just inside the side door that led out into the corridor stood a milling clot of people. Their voices rose in a celebratory tone. Laughter broke out in the group and a few people applauded happily. The side door was open and others were coming in. The group expanded and spilled into the sanctuary, then opened up to let someone through.

A familiar woman entered the sanctuary. There was a thin coating of fur on her face, and she was smiling around small, unfinished fangs. She was flanked by two men. Both her arms were stretched out and she clutched a handful of each man's hair, leading them in by it as she grinned. Those around her cheered.

Rochelle recognized the woman as Vanessa Peterman, a friend of Sheriff Taggart's. When she recognized the two men, she gasped as she rose abruptly to her feet.

The one on the left was Royce Garver. The one on the right was her brother Bob. Suddenly, Rochelle was confused. She didn't know what their presence at this gathering meant or what was about to happen. Jaw slack, she slowly lowered herself back into the pew. She decided to watch and see what happened.

Even as she did that, she was distracted by the hot moisture between her thighs and her gnawing hunger for sex.

For the first time since he was a little boy, Bob found himself on the verge of crying. He fought the urge, gulped repeatedly, tried to ignore the sting of unspent tears in his eyes. He feared not only for himself, but for his friend.

In the sanctuary, they became the center of attention as Vanessa led them through the crowd by the hair, showing them off like a fisherman proudly displaying his catch.

"Look what Vanessa caught!" someone in the crowd said, eliciting some raucous laughter.

Another onlooker joked, "Nobody said anything about a buffet!"

"No, no," Vanessa said, "this isn't dinner. At least not *yet*. This is the floor show. See this one here?"

Bob's scalp burned as she shoved him forward, tightening her hold on the clump of his hair.

"He's been wanting something for months now," she said, "and tonight I'm gonna give it to him. He's been wanting to *fuck* me." She jerked his head around toward her and grinned at him. "Haven't you?"

Bob was repulsed by the auburn hair that grew on her face, by her shiny argentine eyes, by the way her mouth protruded slightly from her face, by the fangs she licked with her glistening tongue. Then, within seconds, all of that went away—the hair, the silver eyes, the fangs. It was gone. The beautiful Vanessa Peterman, who had stirred so much lust in him, smiled and pulled him close, until his face was just a couple of inches from hers.

"Here," she said, pushing Royce toward a man who stood nearby. "Hold him for me."

The man smiled cruelly as he grabbed Royce's shoulders and held him close. Vanessa let go of Royce's hair and put her left hand to the side of Bob's face. She loosened her hold on his hair but did not let go. She pressed her lips to his and sucked his tongue into her mouth so hard that it hurt. Her left hand moved down his body, never losing contact with him, and squeezed his crotch repeatedly, rhythmically, until he felt himself hardening. It was the last thing he wanted and he tried to fight it, but he had never been kissed so fiercely, and she seemed to know precisely how to touch him, where to squeeze, how to squeeze.

A cheer rose up in the crowd as more people turned their attention to Vanessa and Bob.

Vanessa ended the kiss, pulling her face back just a little, smiling. Her hand stopped fondling his crotch and unbuckled his belt, then unfastened his pants and jerked his fly down. She slid her hand beneath the elastic waist of his undershorts and curled her fingers around his erection. He gasped involuntarily.

"You want to put this in me, don't you?" she asked, squeezing his cock hard.

Bob felt a cold, withering sensation in his abdomen. He knew what would happen to him if he did as she said. He remembered what Karen had told him about the virus. The words *sexually transmitted* flashed on and off in his head like a garish neon sign.

Grinning, Vanessa said, "We need to get rid of those clothes."

As if she had given them an order, the crowd moved forward, cheering and laughing, and began to tear at Bob's clothes. His shirt was ripped off, his pants pulled down. Hands roughly jerked his shoes from his feet. Then his feet left the floor as clutching hands lifted him and began to move him toward the front of the sanctuary. He struggled at first, but the hands pinched and clawed and hurt him, so he stopped.

Bob tilted his head back and looked at Royce. Now two people held Royce in place. He was pale with terror, his eyes bulging as he watched Bob being taken away. He didn't even struggle against those holding him. He looked too weak, too afraid.

Naked except for his undershorts and socks, Bob was carried up the steps to the stage. Others disconnected the pulpit's microphone and placed the pulpit on its side on the floor in the center of the stage. They put Bob down on the overturned pulpit as if it were an altar, and hands held him down rigidly. Some of the hands pulled at his undershorts and slid them down his legs, while others groped roughly at his genitals, the laughter growing louder.

The pulpit was cold and hard against Bob's back. His penis and scrotum shriveled and his utter humiliation made him feel small, like a helpless, naked child. An oval of leering, grinning faces hovered above him, some sporting the beginnings of fangs and a few tufts of hair on their faces. Bob felt the sharp scrape of claws from some of the hands touching him.

Those at Bob's feet parted and Vanessa stepped forward. She stood naked, smiling down him, back straight, her firm, round breasts thrust forward. She bent at the waist, leaned one hand on his leg, and reached forward with the other to wrap her fingers around his cock. She squeezed and stroked it as she looked directly into his eyes. In spite of his terror and humiliation and withering helplessness, Bob's penis began to harden.

A chant began in the rowdy crowd. It was scattered at first, but became more unified, then louder and louder.

"Fuck! Fuck! Fuck! Fuck!"

As she enthusiastically stroked his erection, Vanessa's eyebrows rose high above her eyes and her mouth formed an O in an expression of mock surprise. "Sounds like *they* want us to do it as much as *you* do, Bob!"

Bob begged God for help. And just in case he was living his final moments, he begged God for forgiveness, as well.

Rochelle had been standing for a few minutes now, her hands clutching the back of the pew in front of her as she leaned forward and watched what was happening. She was confused and a little afraid and extremely horny. Her eyes moved back and forth between Bob and Royce a few times, then settled on her brother as he was held down, naked and pale, on the overturned pulpit by the chanting crowd.

Something stirred in Rochelle as she watched her naked brother, unable to keep her eyes from lingering on his genitals. She felt shame—but only for a very brief moment. In spite of the spectacle, she could not get her mind off of her own crotch, now sopping wet. She could not divert her attention from her own nagging desire. It was a hunger, a thirst, a need.

Then she saw Vanessa standing up there on the stage, naked under the cross-bearing fabric banners. For just a moment, Rochelle was struck by the oddity of seeing a beautiful woman where she usually saw Pastor Edson preaching, or someone praying or singing a religious song.

As if it were a party, someone began to play the organ loudly. Rochelle looked to the left to see a dumpy, house-wifey woman in her thirties, hair on her cheeks, grinning leeringly as she played the organ with elaborate motions of her arms. It was a tune Rochelle had heard before, but she did not recognize it—something secular and very in-appropriate for a church, whatever it was.

Others in her pew shoved at her as they tried to make their way to the center aisle. She glanced to her left and saw an unfamiliar man in a T-shirt and jeans, with some hair on his face, trying to nudge by her. She felt a low buzzing in the spots where the man touched her. Then she touched him back.

In a heartbeat, they were pawing each other. He squeezed her breast hard, reached around and dug his fingers into her ass as he put his mouth over hers. She clutched his shoulder with one hand and groped at his bulging crotch with the other.

All around them, the chant was joined by growls and gasps and low, throaty moans. One of those growls came from Rochelle as she felt the man's hands move all over her, felt his fangs against her neck, felt him get hard against her. The sound of clothes tearing rose from the crowd like the hissing of beetles.

The next thing Rochelle knew, she and her new friend were in the center aisle with the others. She looked around and saw penises standing erect, saw hairy hands groping pubises that glistened wetly through hair. She felt as if she were caught up in something out of her control, as if she were being helplessly tossed by a powerful wind.

The man was rough with her, and she loved it. She caught glimpses of others around her fucking and grunting, and she loved it. She breathed in the strong combined scent of all the others, and she loved it.

She leaned her bare hips against the edge of a pew, spread her legs, and let the stranger enter her. Their panting growls were lost in the growing peal of savage sounds that filled the church.

Royce's terror was a rope around his neck that grew tighter and tighter, cutting off his breath, making swallowing almost impossible. He felt dizzy with fear, sick with it, crushed under its weight. It became so great that he cast his eyes down, too afraid to look around.

As the hands that held him tightened their grip, Royce felt sharp points piercing his clothes and threatening to break through his flesh. Without moving his head, his eyes turned to the hands holding his arms. They were hairy now, and sharp, curved claws stuck out of the fingertips, digging into him.

The voices all around him became deeper and began to growl. As they grew louder, a rank, gamey smell filled the sanctuary. He heard sounds he recognized, no matter how animalistic the voices—the sounds of sex.

He was pushed forward, then jerked back, nearly knocked over. He could feel the threat of violence in the air, as thick as the odor he could smell. When he finally stirred up the courage to lift his head and look at his surroundings, he saw them fucking all around him. They were violent in their rutting, slobbering as they growled.

Then he saw something that would have made him gasp

if his throat had not felt so constricted. Rochelle was leaning against a pew, naked, her legs spread as a man pounded between her thighs. Both were naked and hairy, and their bodies undulated in the midst of their transformations.

"Royce! *Royce!*"

His eyes widened as he looked to his right, up the center aisle. Several of them stood on the stage up front. Through gaps between their bodies, he saw Bob lying on his back, being held down, naked and pale. Royce glimpsed his friend's face, wide with terror as it searched for him.

"Run!" Bob shouted. "Hear me, Royce? *Run! Get out of here! Now!*"

There was an urgency to Bob's voice, as well as a finality. It made Royce feel that if he did not do as Bob told him, if he did not run *now* and try to get out, however unlikely the possibility seemed, he would never escape. It would be the end for him.

His body exploded with energy. He began to flail his arms and kick his legs, to fight the hands that held him. Claws tore through his clothes and skin as he pulled away, his lips open and pulled back around clenched teeth, tendons in his neck pulled taut.

He was free—for a moment. He could not think clearly enough to do anything but throw himself forward, to keep moving, dodging the others, darting left and right and—

Flames of pain burned his scalp as something closed on his hair and jerked him backward hard, making a reflexive grunt sound in his chest.

Something wet touched his ear and a low growl filled his head as hot, smelly breath blasted against him. He was spun around violently.

Royce's head tipped backward, pulling his mouth open wider and wider, his eyes feeling as if they were about to pop from their sockets. He was so completely paralyzed by his terror that for a long time—*days*, it seemed, long slow summer days—all sound was swallowed up by a throbbing silence and he was able to focus on nothing more than a single quivering drop of saliva that dangled precariously from a narrow, curved fang.

It dripped.

Sound rushed back.

Somewhere far away, Royce heard Bob shouting his name over and over with terror in his voice.

Royce was able to scream once before his life ended.

Thin black lips and deadly fangs swallowed up his field of vision and engulfed the whole world.

# CHAPTER TWENTY-SIX

*A Congregation of Beasts*

Across Crozier Street from the Seventh-day Adventist church, the sandwich shop, cell-phone store, insurance office, and comic-book shop in the small strip mall were closed. Behind the strip mall was a grove of oak trees and brush, and beyond that was Miller Street. A white van was parked at the curb on Miller. Karen and Gavin made their way from the van through the dark patch of trees and brush with George and Abe, all led by Ella and Cynthia.

Karen was tired, but at the same time, adrenaline coursed through her. She was dreading whatever awaited them, but she tried not to show it.

They walked around the strip mall and stood in the parking lot. Across the street, tall sodium-vapor lights illuminated the church parking lot, which was crowded with cars. A few people were making their way into the church.

George was pale and a little winded. He had shuffled along with them wearily and now looked as if he was having difficulty standing.

"I don't feel so good," he said, his voice weak and hoarse.

Ella put a hand on his shoulder. "Hungry, George?"

He turned to her and nodded heavily.

"That's a good sign," she said. "There's food across the street." She turned to the church.

From the corner of her eye, Karen watched Ella in the dark gray night and noticed her nostrils flare as she sniffed the air, saw her head turn this way and that in short, staccato movements as her eyes narrowed. Karen realized that she had been right: at night, she and Cynthia looked like they were wearing jumpsuits of some kind because of their fur.

"There he is," Ella said quietly.

A sheriff's-department cruiser slowed on Crozier and pulled into the church parking lot. It eased through the lot until it found an empty slot, then parked.

"He's probably got her with him," Ella said.

As they watched, the cruiser's lights went off and the driver's door opened. A tall figure got out, walked around to the back of the car, and opened the door on the passenger side. Another figure rose slowly and walked with the first toward the church.

"Okay," Ella said. "He's taking her inside." She turned to them. "There's no point in trying to sneak in. Obviously, they're everywhere over there. I'll take the lead. You follow me in. Gavin, Karen—don't hesitate to use your guns. The rest of you, use your knives and forks."

Ella walked into the street, and the rest of them followed.

Taggart opened a side door and stepped back to let Lupa into the church. She walked cautiously, uncertainly, sniffing the air along the way. She was unaccustomed to being outside the house, and everything was new, unfamiliar, and a possible threat. She wore a simple, cotton, periwinkle blue shift with a low neckline and a skirt that fell just above her knees. She looked delicious, like a voluptuous teenager.

Taggart's eyes darted around the parking lot. He'd

assigned a few deputies to hunt for Ella and Cynthia. When they were found, they were to be brought to the church. He hoped to see the deputies driving in with the two women in custody. He was furious at Ella. He should've known better than to trust that cunt. He thought being turned would change her, that spending so much time with him would condition her. But apparently she was still the widow of the former sheriff, and her aim was to cause trouble. They would find her, though, he was certain of that. She and Cynthia wouldn't get far.

They went into the church and crossed the main corridor to follow the branch that led behind the sanctuary. Taggart could hear the gathering.

"Sounds like they've started without us," he muttered, smirking. The organ's peals rose and fell. It took a moment for Taggart to recognize the song, because he'd never before heard it being played on a church organ. It was "Born to be Wild."

The sounds seemed to alarm Lupa. Her body became tense and her silver eyes darted around cautiously.

"It's okay," Taggart said reassuringly. He took her hand. "This way."

He led her through a door and into a small alcove, then through another door. They went up a few steps and through a passageway behind the baptistery, around a large planter holding shiny, green artificial plants, and out onto the sanctuary stage.

Taggart stopped, still holding Lupa's hand. He saw Vanessa's back as she ground her hips on a man who was naked except for the socks on his feet. The man was stretched out on the overturned pulpit and was being held down by others around them, most of whom had one hand on him while they masturbated with the other and chanted, "Fuck! Fuck! Fuck!"

He turned to his left and looked out over the crowded sanctuary. Clothes, some ripped and tattered, were scattered in all directions. One corner of his mouth curled up into a slight smile.

The sanctuary reeked of them—of their bodies, their fluids. As the church organ bellowed, they writhed and convulsed, growling and grunting and panting. Some were stretched out and entwined on pews, while others were bent over the backs of pews being fucked from behind. They were on the pews, on the floor, on the steps leading up to the sanctuary stage, and all over the stage itself—bodies moving with frantic, savage rhythm.

Taggart's eye was drawn to a rectangular sign above the double doors at the rear of the sanctuary. It read,

THIS DO IN REMEMBRANCE OF ME.
LUKE 22:19

He remembered going to church every Saturday as a boy, led by his mother's hand, having to sit through Sabbath school and then the church service, having to stand while his mother chattered with her friends before and after the services, all of them towering over him like great monoliths. He remembered the accusing tone of the pastor's voice, the scowling, disapproving faces of all the adults around him, the stiffness and discomfort and smothering repression of it all. And he remembered a Bible verse that was carved into the front of the pulpit in the sanctuary of that church. The same verse was displayed on the wall of that church's multipurpose room, as well. The verse was Luke 22:19, a popular verse among Adventists that always brought to his mind the Seventh-day Adventist "communion" ritual, which was done "in remembrance" of Christ.

Part of communion involved eating little pieces of unleavened bread and drinking grape juice from tiny glasses—never wine, of course, because Adventists didn't drink wine and believed that when the Bible described

Jesus drinking wine, it really meant grape juice. The rest of the communion ritual involved the segregation of men and women into two groups in separate rooms, where they ritualistically removed each others' shoes, socks, and stockings and washed each others' feet in shallow pans of water. This practice was known as the "Ordinance of Humility." It symbolized the biblical account, found in the Gospel of John, of Jesus washing his disciples' feet at the Last Supper, and was intended to remind Adventists of the importance of serving one another with humility.

Watching the group ritual taking place before him, Taggart chuckled as he thought how much more honest it was than the Seventh-day Adventist group ritual of foot washing that so floridly reeked of sublimated fetishistic homosexuality. Still chuckling, he turned to Lupa and said, "Stay right here, okay? Don't move. I'll be right back. I just want to greet my friends."

As "Born to be Wild" continued to play on the organ, Taggart made his way down from the stage and carefully stepped around and over the preoccupied figures. As he moved through the crowd, he stopped occasionally to bend over and quietly say something to the thrusting, slurping, panting bodies all around him. He grinned and chuckled as he said, again and again, "This do in remembrance of *me*. . . . This do in remembrance of *me*. . . ."

Among all the wet thrusting and gasping and growling, Taggart came to a splash of dark red. A few more steps later, he saw the part of the torn and bloody remains of a human body surrounded by fragments of torn, soaked clothes. Just beyond that, he found a couple of hairy figures chewing the meat from that body, gnawing it off of bones while they fucked, their fur matted and wet with blood. Around them, a few others ate pieces of the same body as they rutted.

He wound his way back around to the stage, walked up the steps, and went to Lupa's side. Facing the crowd, he raised his arms and shouted at the top of his lungs, "This do in remembrance of *meeee*!" His laughter rang out through the sanctuary as he clapped his hands together hard three times to get their attention.

The organ music hit a sour note and abruptly stopped. The panting and grunting rapidly died down as a lake of silver eyes turned to Taggart. Soon, the church was silent but for the sound of movement as some sat up and some stood, all focusing their attention on the sheriff.

After Bob heard Royce's gargled, strangling scream cut off abruptly, tears finally began to cut hot trails across his temples and into his ears. He felt whatever hope he had left pump out of him in throbbing jets, like blood from a severed artery.

Since then, he had been lost in a bleary miasma that blended the intense pleasure of sex with the most nightmarish horrors he could imagine. As they chanted, "Fuck! Fuck! Fuck!" the faces around him lost their humanity and became hairy, slavering animals. Vanessa climbed on top of him and slid down on the erection he had been unable to defeat. She moved on him, sometimes grinding slowly, other times bucking as if she were riding a mechanical bull. The music added a touch of surrealism to it all; hearing "Born to be Wild" played on the church organ made Bob feel as if he were lost in a sweaty fever dream.

The sensation of being inside Vanessa was intoxicating, even in his terrified, sickened state of mind. But he kept thinking—

*virusvirusvirusvirus*

—of what it would do to him—

*I'll be like them please Jesus no don't let that happen*

—of what he would become because of it—

*like Rochelle I'll be like Rochelle and eat human flesh and blood and*

—and it made his guts twist into knots, even as he was panting and thrusting his hips upward in the throes of passion.

Every now and then, he lifted his head and looked around, hoping against hope that some chance of escape would crop up, some opportunity to get away from them. Even though he knew it was most likely too late to escape the virus that no doubt already infected him, perhaps he could find some way to spare his own life. If nothing else, maybe he could find some way to hurt *them*, to go down fighting, maybe take one or two or three out with him. Each time he lifted his head, there was Vanessa, hovering over him in various stances: hands leaning on his chest as she bent forward, head down, breasts swaying, hair draping each side of her gasping face, flesh smooth and silky; sitting up and grinding on him, one hand clutching her breast, the other fingering her clitoris, auburn hair appearing on her body and covering her quaking breasts; clawed hands buried in her hair, jutting elbows up, head back as she humped, snout open wide. Before long, the beautiful voluptuous woman on top of him had become a ravening animal.

Then Bob heard the voice—"This do in remembrance of *meeee!*"—followed by loud laughter and three sharp hand claps.

Vanessa's movements slowed as she turned to look over her shoulder.

The others surrounding Bob turned their attention from him, stood up straight and stepped away from him, and turned their eyes toward the voice and the clapping hands.

Bob lifted his head, blinked his stinging, teary eyes, and saw Sheriff Taggart standing on the sanctuary stage.

"I hate to interrupt, but I'd like your attention, please," the sheriff said.

The crowd around Bob thinned out, and he turned to the right to look out over the sanctuary. It seemed the sight of all those hideous, fanged creatures staring up at the sheriff should have been shattering to him, should have spread weblike cracks through his mind and sanity. But in a relatively short time, he had gotten past that—and *that* frightened him as much as the monsters that filled the church sanctuary.

"I've called you here for a reason," Sheriff Taggart said. "We have things to discuss, plans to make. But first, before we do anything else, I want to introduce you to someone . . . to the person about whom you've heard so much recently. Just a few months ago, you stood in the front yard of the house on Edgerly Drive and I told you that she had been born, that she was thriving. You cheered. We all felt elated. She was the first of her kind. The First Born. But not the last."

*First Born*, Bob thought vaguely as his eyes passed over the congregation of beasts. He thought briefly of that vicious infant creature in the ER. But the thought melted away when his attention was caught by something in the rear of the sanctuary—one of the double doors opening just a few inches.

"She still thrives," the sheriff went on. "She has grown a lot in the last few months. We don't fully understand her yet, but that's changing. And as we learn more about her, we learn more about ourselves. Everyone, I want you to meet Lupa—the First Born!"

The crowd of upright animals went wild. They howled and growled and jumped up and down.

Bob's eyes remained on the door at the back of the sanctuary.

It opened a little farther. Another of the creatures walked in—female, hairy, apparently halfway between her two physical states. Another one followed behind her, its hair blonde. But behind the two creatures were *people* who wore clothes over their hairless skin and who looked . . . familiar.

Bob blinked his eyes several times.

Karen Moffett and Gavin Keoph . . . Behind them, Dr. Dinescu from the emergency room . . . Behind him, the man Bob had met in the ER parking lot—what was his name? George, that was it.

A surge of relief moved through Bob like adrenaline and he felt his mouth stretch into a smile.

The female werewolf that led them into the sanctuary turned and said something to them over her shoulder. Then she and her hairy companion broke away and moved forward into the congregation while Gavin and George went to one side of the sanctuary and Karen and Dr. Dinescu went to the other.

Karen and Gavin each had a gun in hand.

*I've gotta get up*, Bob thought. *I've gotta do something. They're here to help me—I need to help them.*

He clutched the edges of the pulpit and sat up.


"There he is," Ella said, trying to be heard above the melee. "Cynthia and I will go straight up the center aisle. You should split up and approach from the sides. Don't sneak up—move fast. When he sees Cynthia and me, he's going to know something's up, but he'll be distracted. Take advantage of that when it happens." She turned to Cynthia. "Come on."

As she and Cynthia moved into the raging crowd, Karen and Gavin moved close and put their heads together, their mouths curling in response to the foul smell that was so thick in the air.

"You okay?" Gavin said.

"No. You?"

"Nope. You go that way, I'll go this way."

They looked around, registering surprise that they had not been noticed. Sheriff Taggart continued shouting from the stage, trying to be heard over the growling and grunting from the hairy congregation. They stood in the center aisle and on the pews, all of them moving, jumping, swaying, never still.

"Don't waste any time or take any chances," Gavin said. "Just get a bead on Taggart and shoot, and I'll try to do the same."

Karen nodded. Their eyes met and held, and they saw each other's fear.

Then Karen smiled and shrugged with one shoulder. "Hey," she said, "we're in a church. How bad can it be?"

George said, "I was raised Catholic. You'd be surprised."

Karen turned to Abe. "Come with me."

They split up.

Moving fast, Karen went to the right with Abe by her side. He had a fork in one hand, a knife in the other. She was alert, on guard, ready for the worst, but she was amazed that she and Abe were able to walk up the aisle on the right without being noticed and attacked, or at least pointed out.

The werewolves were focused on Sheriff Taggart and the beautiful young woman who stood beside him. She assumed that was the First Born Ella had told them about, the girl who was born only four months ago.

The sanctuary rang with the sound of their excitement. Sheriff Taggart had difficulty being heard above it.

Karen spotted an empty space at the end of one of the pews near the front. She went to it, stepped up on it as if it were a stepladder, and rose above many of the heads that faced the stage. Others were standing on pews as well, but Karen's position gave her a clear view of the sheriff. There was a narrow canyon of space between heads and shoulders that cut diagonally across the column of pews. Standing at the end of that narrow canyon, as if in the sights of a gun, was Sheriff Taggart on the stage.

She didn't like the distance, but it wouldn't be necessary for her silver bullet to hit his head or a vital organ—as long as it hit him, the damage would be done. Holding it with both hands, Karen lifted the gun, arms straight, and leveled it with the most dense segment of the sheriff's body.

To her left, two of the creatures caught the movement of her arms and turned their heads to her. A heartbeat later, one of them released a piercing howl of alarm, and the other quickly followed suit.

Karen squeezed the trigger of her Taurus 9-millimeter as a hairy, clawed hand closed on her left forearm.

Even in all the racket, the crack of the gunshot stood out.

Another hand grabbed her shoulder. An arm wrapped around her waist and pulled her to the left.

The bullet missed its mark. Sheriff Taggart's smile disappeared as his head jerked toward the sound of the gunshot.

Abe squeezed in past her and swung his right hand up from his waist with as much force as the tight space allowed. Abe buried the fork he held in the abdomen of the creature grabbing at Karen. It lifted its head and screamed.

But others had noticed her by now, and they moved forward.

Abe swung with both the knife and the fork. The utensils pierced flesh, but there were too many of the creatures.

Karen clenched her teeth and began to kick as arms snaked around her and lifted her from the pew. Finally, in spite of her resistance of the urge, she screamed.

Gavin searched for a clear shot at the sheriff as he moved quickly along the far left aisle. He tossed a glance over his shoulder to see how George was doing, but didn't see him. He stopped and turned around.

George had collapsed against the wall between two of the vertical rectangles of glass, clutching his stomach, his head down, body convulsing. His silver knife and fork were on the ground at his feet.

"George!" Gavin said, moving toward him.

George's skin had darkened. As Gavin approached him, he realized that the darkness of George's skin was fur. More of it became visible as his growing body ripped through his clothes.

George's head snapped up and he glared at Gavin with silver eyes, the tip of his tongue moving along the lower lip of his snout. He straightened up, pushed away from the wall, and grabbed the lapels of Gavin's sport coat, pulling him close.

Gavin's heart thundered in his chest as George's foul breath filled his nostrils.

"G-George," Gavin said. "George, it's muh-me. Gavin. Remember whuh-where you are . . . Why you're here."

George's silver eyes narrowed and he cocked his head to one side.

"Them," Gavin said, jerking his head toward the crowd of werewolves. "Remember? *Them*."

George's head turned to the right and looked at the other werewolves. After a moment, he growled and released Gavin's lapels. He turned to face the growling, howling werewolves as they watched Taggart on the stage. George bared his fangs and plunged into the crowd with a roar. He pounced onto a werewolf and buried his fangs into its neck. George's victim began screaming with surprise and pain as it was dragged to the floor.

Gavin turned and headed for the front of the sanctuary again, looking for a good shot at Taggart. He heard a gunshot. He looked at the sheriff, hoping to see him go down. Instead, he saw Taggart's attention shift to the source of the gunshot.

Amidst all the clamor, a louder furor arose on the other side of the sanctuary. One of the creatures cried out in pain. That was followed by a scream—Karen's scream.

"Shit," Gavin said, breaking into a jog toward the stage. He dodged around the werewolves that spilled out of the crowded pews and into the side aisle, and he was still unnoticed as attention was turned from the sheriff to the sounds coming from the other side of the sanctuary. As he neared the corner of the column of pews, Gavin held his Glock in both hands and lifted it in anticipation. He caught glimpses of Taggart through the gaps in the crowd, then rounded the corner of the column of pews toward the stage.

An opportunity opened up before him, and Sheriff Taggart became clearly visible from head to foot. Before that gap closed, Gavin stopped and aimed his gun.

Taggart leaned over and said something to a beautiful girl on the stage. She hurried away from him, ran behind a clump of artificial plants, and disappeared.

Gavin had a clear and open shot at Taggart. In the endless, eternal fraction of an instant during which Gavin squeezed the trigger of his gun, that perfect line of fire was broken.

Suddenly, Bob stepped in front of the sheriff, naked and haggard looking, and he swung a woman around in front of him, holding her hair with one hand and her arm with the other.

"Kill her!" Bob shouted, looking directly at Gavin, a wild, teeth-baring expression on his face. "Kill her, Gavin, *kill her*!"

It was too late to stop. Gavin was already squeezing the trigger when Bob and the woman appeared.

Gavin fired.

The body of the woman in front of Bob jerked violently in response.

Sheriff Taggart spun his head around and looked from the first gunshot on one side of the sanctuary to the second gunshot on the other side. His good eye widened in alarm.

Karen screamed again.

The woman Bob had held up in front of the sheriff released a piercing shriek of pain as she fell forward.

"Fuck *me*!" Gavin shouted as the creatures in the front

of the congregation began to close in on him like piranhas on a bleeding animal in the water. He fired off a succession of shots into the advancing crowd as dark, clawed hands reached out for him, clutching, grabbing.

As he went down, Gavin heard Karen scream a third time. He hoped she would die quickly—he did not want her to suffer.

# CHAPTER TWENTY-SEVEN

*The Delivery of Take-Out*

As they started down the center aisle together, Ella leaned toward Cynthia and said, "That's her—the girl standing behind him and to the right. I'll take him, you take her. When he sees us, he'll know something's up and he'll probably try to protect her. Don't lose her."

Ella reached into the bag and removed two forks. The Reed & Barton table knife had a fine serrated edge, but Ella preferred the deadly tines of the fork. She held one in each fist and used her elbows to push others out of her way as she plowed ahead of Cynthia. She kept her eyes on Taggart, even though she lost sight of him occasionally on her way up. He was shouting at the crowd, getting them worked up. She knew that Karen and Abe and Gavin and George were heading up there along the side aisles, and she hoped they were alert and ready to act.

She and Cynthia were at the halfway point in the crowded center aisle when a gunshot rang out to the right. A pained howl was followed by a scream.

Ella shoved other werewolves out of her way as she neared the front. She glared directly up into Taggart's eye as he looked in the direction of the gunshot.

A lupine shriek of pain cut through the noise.

Several seconds later, another gun fired, this time to the left.

Taggart's head jerked in that direction as real panic moved over his face. He stepped backward, reached out, and took the girl's arm. He turned and leaned toward Lupa and said something to her, then pushed her to the back of the stage and to the right.

Meanwhile, to the left of Taggart, a naked man grabbed Vanessa Peterman and shouted, "Kill her! Kill her, Gavin, *kill her*!" Another gunshot sounded to Ella's left. Vanessa fell to the floor of the stage, then rolled down the steps.

When Taggart turned back to the crowd, his eye fell directly on Ella as she broke through the group. Taggart's eye bulged and his upper lip curled back to reveal fangs.

Clutching the forks in her fists, Ella stopped, bent her knees, then lunged forward, planning to jump over the three steps and land directly on Taggart.

At that moment, several gunshots went off in rapid succession from the left side of the sanctuary.

Ella was in midair, on her way to Taggart, ready to plunge those forks into his body.

As if from nowhere, a growling werewolf slammed into her on the right and tackled her. Her left side hit the floor under her assailant's weight and air gushed out of her lungs. The flatware in her bag jangled out over the floor as the other werewolf closed its snout on Ella's neck.

After Taggart spoke to the beautiful girl with the long, dark, honey gold hair, Cynthia watched her turn, hurry away, and disappear behind a large planter filled with artificial greenery. She did not allow herself time to think about the fact that the girl was her daughter, that she had given birth to her only four months ago, or that had it not been for Ella, she would have been fed to the girl that night like a plump, pink baby rat to a pet snake. Breaking away from

Ella, Cynthia shouldered her way through the crowd as confusion broke out in response to the gunshots.

She leaped up the three steps onto the stage and rushed past Taggart, who was much too distracted to notice her. Cynthia ducked around the plastic plants, went behind the baptistery and through the passageway, hurrying to catch up with the girl. She turned left into the corridor behind the sanctuary just in time to see the girl go through a doorway to the right.

Cynthia hurried after her, stopped outside the door, and peered around the doorjamb into the room. It was a large room with folding chairs and tables against a couple of the walls. Through a rectangular opening in the wall to the far right, she saw a kitchen.

The girl stood at a window across the room, looking out at the night.

Cynthia clenched the fork in her hand and quietly went into the room.

Martin Burgess's eighteen "troops" arrived in two SUVs, which parked in front of the strip mall across the street from the church. They wasted no time. Lloyd Canwright led them across Crozier Street. A car stopped abruptly in the street when its headlights fell on the group of beefy men carrying Uzis and wearing camouflaged tactical vests loaded down with grenades, ammunition magazines, pistols, and knives.

Lloyd wore a whistle on a chain around his neck. Once they were inside and doing what they had come to do, the whistle would be their signal to get out.

They had already agreed to break up into three groups of six. One was to go into the church through the front, another through the rear, and the third was to try to find a side entrance.

Lloyd was still absorbing the last phone conversation he'd had with Mr. Burgess, who had explained exactly what was going on in Big Rock, why they were going in, exactly where they were to go, and what they were supposed to do when they got there. Lloyd had passed this information on to the other men.

They had been slowed down late that afternoon by mechanical problems with the jet Mr. Burgess had sent for them. When they'd landed in Eureka, the two SUVs Mr. Burgess had arranged were waiting for them, each driven by an employee of Mr. Burgess's who knew exactly where they were going.

*Werewolves*, Lloyd thought, as he and the others walked by the long rectangular sign into which was carved the words SEVENTH-DAY ADVENTIST CHURCH. *Who knew there were fuckin' werewolves anywhere? This just proves that I'm right—there's a whooole lotta shit goin' on in this world that we don't know a fuckin' thing about.*

Mr. Burgess had explained that it might be difficult to tell who was a werewolf and who wasn't, if they were in their human form. Lloyd hoped this wasn't the case. He didn't want to shoot the wrong people, but neither did he want to have to pussyfoot around about who to shoot and who not to shoot.

The men split up into their three prearranged groups. Lloyd's group was going in through the front, so he led his five men straight up the steps and through the glass doors in front. As soon as they were in the empty foyer, Lloyd heard the howling and screaming coming from the sanctuary. The crack of a gunshot was soon followed by another, then a succession of shots.

Lloyd and the others exchanged a look as P. J. Galt, a thick-necked, tattooed redneck with a lump of chewing tobacco under his lip, said, "What the fuck is *that*?"

Lloyd went to the big, wooden double doors that stood open across the foyer and looked into the sanctuary. What he saw and smelled made him a little dizzy.

"Holy shit," he said as the other men joined him.

Cyrus Cooper, a tall, broad, muscular black man with a shaved head, who vaguely resembled a human gun safe, said, "Is this them?"

"Oh, yeah," Lloyd said. "Gotta be."

"We take 'em out?" Cyrus said.

"Yeah, take 'em out," he said. Then he smiled and chuckled and muttered to himself. "Take-out."

Lloyd stepped into the sanctuary, leveled his Uzi, and sent a spurt of fire into the backs of the hairy creatures standing at the rear of the crowd. Those hit spun and dropped to the floor, crying out in pain. Others turned to see what was wrong, saw the wounded writhing on the floor and screaming in agony, then saw Lloyd and the men spreading out on either side of him.

"Oooookay!" Lloyd shouted at the top of his lungs. "Who ordered the take-out?"

The sanctuary filled with the sharp, sputtering sound of machine-gun fire as Lloyd and his group began to mow down werewolves.

Still holding the forks in her fists, Ella buried her fangs deep in the arm of her tackler. The creature released its bite on her neck and shrieked in pain. She took advantage of the moment and rolled on top of her assailant, then tore at the werewolf's throat with her fangs.

With her attacker's blood in her mouth, Ella quickly got to her feet. She knew the other werewolf would heal quickly, but that the wound would give her the time she needed. She took a brief second to push from her mind the pain of her bleeding neck wound, then looked up at Taggart on the stage. He was transforming, his muscles bulging to rip through his uniform and reveal his rapidly thickening fur. Beyond him, she saw Cynthia hurrying behind some artificial plants.

From the rear of the sanctuary, the thick, menacing

rattle of a machine gun cut through all the noise. Someone shouted something in the back, but Ella's attention was focused on Taggart.

Taggart's eye—silver now, since he was transforming—was darting around the stage like that of a cornered animal as several machine guns began to fire in the rear of the sanctuary.

Ella sprang toward him again, holding the forks up at each side, ready to drive them into Taggart.

As she shot toward him through the air, the corners of his mouth pulled back over his snout as if in a smile. At the last instant, he swung his right leg up high and hard. His foot landed in Ella's solar plexus. A moment after the kick, he lost his footing and fell backward.

The second time she hit the floor, everything went dark for a moment.

Hunched forward slightly, Cynthia rushed across the room without a sound. She pounced on the girl's back, swung her right arm around hard and drove the fork into her daughter's throat.

An elbow swung back and stabbed into Cynthia's gut hard enough to knock her to the floor.

The girl turned around, the fork jutting from her throat, and looked down at Cynthia. She frowned slightly as she reached up and jerked the fork out, then held it up and looked it over as if she'd never seen one before.

Gasping for breath and hurting from the elbow to the abdomen, Cynthia quickly got to her feet. She expected the girl to drop the floor and start screaming from the pain created by the silver. Instead, she simply continued to examine the fork.

Something wasn't right. Had Ella been mistaken about the flatware? Was it made of something other than silver?

Cynthia shifted the knife from her left hand to her

right and prepared to attack again the creature that was her daughter.

The girl's eyes moved slowly from the fork to Cynthia. She smiled, and her transformation happened smoothly and quickly, with virtually none of the bone-popping, muscle-tearing sounds that usually accompanied it.

*She's different,* Cynthia thought in a rush of panic. *She's not like the others. Silver doesn't hurt her!*

The door to the left of the window burst open. Large, imposing men in camouflaged vests rushed into the room holding compact machine guns.

"Jesus Christ!" one of the men shouted as he looked back and forth between Cynthia and the now-hairy creature in the room with her.

Cynthia remembered how she looked and realized how frightening she must be to the armed men who gawked at her now, horrified. They raised their guns.

"Wait, *no!*" Cynthia shouted.

They opened fire. Three of them turned and sprayed bullets into the creature by the window.

Both werewolves went down.

The distraction of machine-gun fire, combined with all the pained, terrified screams and Abe's rapid, unceasing stabs with the silverware, allowed Karen to break away from the werewolves. As she stumbled out into the side aisle, she grabbed Abe's arm and dragged him with her. His hands glistened with blood and red was splattered all over his shirt.

Chaos was breaking out in the sanctuary as the creatures tried to run screaming from the machine-gun fire.

"That's the backup Burgess said he was going to send," Karen said to Abe, shouting to be heard. "Let's get out of here."

Toward the front of the sanctuary, about fifteen feet from them, was a side entrance. Werewolves were rushing out of it, but it had not yet become bottlenecked. Karen grabbed Abe's arm and they jogged to the door. Once they got through it, they were in the church's main corridor.

Karen's heart hammered in her throat as she said, "God, I hope Gavin's able to get out of there."

Once they saw what Gavin's bullets were capable of doing, the werewolves backed off. Those he had shot lay squirming and kicking in pain on the floor. Then the machine guns began to fire, and this seemed to worry the creatures. They quickly forgot about him.

Apparently, Burgess's troops had arrived.

*"Finally!"* Gavin barked as he looked up at the stage and saw Bob standing there with his mouth hanging open, gawking at a werewolf at the foot of the steps in the final ugly moments of its life.

Just beyond Bob, Taggart struggled to his feet, his uniform in tatters on his hairy body now. As he stood, the sheriff kept his attention on something just in front of the stage. When Gavin followed Taggart's gaze, he saw Ella on the floor. Bleeding and dazed, she tried to get up.

Gavin wanted to get Bob and Ella out of the church before they were killed in all the gunfire, but most importantly, he wanted to kill Taggart.

George had stopped thinking. He followed his sense of smell and taste, and his hunger. He wrestled one werewolf to the floor after another and tore their flesh away, chewing noisily as the wonderful taste of their blood filled his mouth. He did not keep track of the number of werewolves he had attacked, he just kept attacking them, eating chunks of them. Blood matted the fur around his snout, and strips of glistening meat clung to his fangs.

He turned to attack another one—any one, it didn't matter, the blood had him in a frenzy—and instead of a werewolf, he faced a broad-shouldered man with a black machine gun.

"Good night, Gracie!" the man shouted as he sprayed bullets into George's chest and abdomen.

Suddenly, George found himself on the floor. The other werewolves trampled him as pain flowed through his body. He cried out as his skin opened up in wet, burning sores.

In spite of his pain and through the sound of his own agonized, dying shrieks, he was aware of the fact that he was still hungry.

Bob stood on the stage in a state of numb, paralyzed shock. His eyes did not move from Vanessa, who convulsed on the floor at the foot of the stage steps, her body bubbling with open, running sores. Her convulsions gradually slowed. Bob was certain she was dying, but he felt nothing in response to it. He felt nothing at all.

Hell was breaking out in the sanctuary—screams and howls, gunshots, machine-gun fire. But Bob stood frozen, a slight frown creasing his brow. Bullets shattered the windows, a web of dark smoke began to rise from the rear half of the right column of pews, and somewhere in the back of his mind he understood that something was burning, probably one of the pew cushions, perhaps set off by all the gunfire.

A hand grabbed Bob's left arm and shook him hard, startling him from his stupor. It was Gavin.

"Get out of here!" he shouted at Bob. "*Now!* There's a way out over there behind those plants. *Go!*"

Gavin pushed him hard, then moved past him.

Suddenly, Bob became fully aware of the fact that he was naked and standing in a dangerous nightmare. The hairy creatures in the sanctuary that weren't dropping to the floor after being shot were fighting to get to the exits. The smoke rising from the pews was thickening rapidly.

He thought of Royce, and a pain stabbed through his chest. Bob knew Royce would not want him to suffer the same fate.

He turned and dodged around the scattering, growling werewolves toward the planter.

As Bob hurried away, Gavin watched Taggart go down the steps to Ella. He hunkered down beside her as she tried to get up, grabbed the hair on the sides of her head, and pulled her up to face him. Blood glistened on her neck and shoulder. Taggart's snout slowly widened as he pulled Ella closer.

Gavin was less than ten feet away from Taggart, and he covered that distance quickly. He saw Ella's eyes flick toward him, register his presence, then turn back to Taggart. The sheriff had not noticed Gavin at all.

With a convulsive jerk of her head, Ella spat in Taggart's face.

Gavin put the barrel of his gun to the right side of Taggart's head and fired.

The left side of Taggart's head opened up in a spray of brain matter and bits of bone. He released Ella and fell to the floor, turning as he dropped so he landed on his back. His silver eye became wide with fear and confusion as his snout opened and closed like the mouth of a fish out of water.

Gavin quickly lifted Ella to her feet. "Come on, let's get out of here." Supporting her as she limped along beside him, he hurried for the side door that led out into the corridor.

Lloyd hoped the other guys were having as much fun as he. It was deeply satisfying to squeeze the trigger and watch the slobbering, growling monsters go down.

A fire was growing among the pews, sending black smoke up toward the high ceiling. The air was bad enough with the reek of the hairy beasts that filled the sanctuary, but soon the smoke would make it unbreathable and deadly.

Then, in an instant, something changed in the werewolves. The sound level in the sanctuary suddenly dropped for a moment, and their eyes widened. They seemed to forget Lloyd was there as they looked around at each other, up at the high ceiling, down at the floor. Then, as if they'd been set afire, they went crazy.

They no longer seemed to care about his gun. They flailed and thrashed and even began to attack each other wildly, viciously.

Lloyd backed away from them. He coughed as the biting smell of smoke filled his nostrils. He spotted P. J. and Cyrus heading for the open double doors through which they'd come in, and Lloyd decided to do the same. He darted around the manic creatures, stopping a couple of times to fire a few spurts into them, then went to the open doorway. He turned to face the sanctuary again, put the whistle to his mouth, and blew as hard as he could.

The sharp, piercing sound cut through the racket. Lloyd saw his other three guys running toward him. He glanced down at his vest. It seemed a waste to have all the grenades Mr. Burgess had provided and not use them. He took one from his vest.

As the other guys ran past him into the foyer, Lloyd jerked the pin out with his teeth and threw the grenade into the crowd of werewolves that were still standing.

He ran through the foyer shouting, "Let's get the fuck outta here!"

Karen felt a rush of relief when she saw Gavin and Ella come out of the sanctuary.

"We've got to get out," Gavin said. "There's a fire in there."

"You're hurt," Karen said as she put an arm around

Ella's shoulders. After nearly being killed by the creatures in the sanctuary, it no longer made her cringe inside to look at Ella in her hairy, fanged state.

"Bob!" Gavin shouted.

Karen followed Gavin's gaze down the corridor and saw Bob peering around a corner.

"Come on, let's go!" Gavin called to him with a beckoning wave.

Bob rushed naked along the corridor toward them.

"Where's the other one?" Karen said to Ella, referring to Cynthia.

"We don't have time to find her," Gavin said.

Abe said, "What about George?"

A look of pained sadness passed over Gavin's face. "We just don't have time."

"And Burgess's guys?" Karen said.

"I think they can take care of themselves," Gavin said. "Let's go. *Now.*"

The six men in the multipurpose room stood openmouthed and watched as one of the two werewolves they'd just shot quaked and squirmed on the floor. Both were female, but the one that convulsed held a silver table knife in her hand. She made awful, strangling sounds and a thin white foam gathered at the corners of her mouth as her snout wrinkled and trembled. The other one lay near her, perfectly still and apparently dead.

"Jesus H. fuckin' Christ!" Paulie Timpone said. He was a big, beefy Italian originally from New Jersey, who had narrow, cruel eyes that looked incapable of expressing fear. But they expressed it now. "I—I—I thought he was fuckin' *jokin'* when he said *werewolves.*"

"That look like a joke to you, Paulie?" Max said. At sixty, Max Faraday was the oldest of their entire group, with long silver hair and a bushy, silver beard. He looked as if he should be mounted on a big, noisy Harley. "That's some fucked-up shit. But we got 'em. I just wanna make sure there's no more in this room."

Max and Paulie walked over to the window that looked in on the kitchen. They leaned through it and looked behind the counter and over the floor to make sure the kitchen was empty.

Jules Carpenter, a short guy built like a fire hydrant, saw the still creature on the floor move first. He blurted, "Oh, shit!"

She moved fast. Too fast.

Max and Paulie started to turn.

"Look out!" Jules shouted. "She's—"

She was on them before they'd turned all the way around. She slapped her hands over their faces and pushed them back hard.

Brett Chaney lifted his Uzi to shoot at her, but Jules grabbed his arm and pushed the gun aside.

"No, you dumb fuck!" Jules shouted. "You'll shoot *them* if you do that!"

His last few words were swallowed up by the loud, throaty grumble from the werewolf that was on Max and Paulie. She pushed them back hard until they were lying on the narrow counter along the bottom of the rectangular window.

From somewhere in the church, they heard the muffled *whump!* of a grenade going off.

Both of Max's arms were stretched up over his head. As the creature pushed his head farther back, he fired his Uzi wildly and the bullets sprayed all over the kitchen.

Jules and Brett stood with two other men—Ollie Tucker, another large black man, and Buddy Haye, whom everyone called Haye Buddy, whose pale muscles were covered with bad prison tattoos. They didn't move at first, riveted by what they were seeing.

"We *shot* her!" Haye Buddy said. "I thought Lloyd said the fuckin' silver bullets would *work*!"

Max's gun continued to fire in spastic spurts, shattering glass in the kitchen. He and Paulie released keening, strangled wails as they kicked and flailed. The creature pushed their heads back hard, farther and farther over the edge of the counter, bending their necks sharply.

"We should help them!" Brett shouted.

"*You* fuckin' help 'em!" Ollie said. "I ain't goin *near* that motherfuckin' thing!"

"Oh, shit," Haye Buddy said as he tilted his head back and sniffed the air. "You smell gas?"

There was a thick, wet crack and Paulie's body fell limp, neck broken. Max kept shooting and kicking as the creature put both hands on his face and pushed harder.

One second after Max's neck snapped, the gas stove in the kitchen exploded.

After a loud, explosive sound that lasted only an instant, Lupa felt unimaginable heat. It washed over her as she was blown forcefully through the air. The sound was replaced by a throbbing, rushing hiss in her ears. Her body hit something as she flew threw the air—hit it, then broke through it and kept flying.

The world blinked out like a light for a moment.

When she awoke, she was lying on the ground, and she was on fire.

# CHAPTER TWENTY-EIGHT

*Outside*

Corky Lerner and John Teague were stoned, and they were on their way to a party to join other stoned people in a communal effort to get more stoned. They laughed together as Corky drove the black Volkswagen Beetle along Crozier. They'd been laughing for awhile, and neither could remember why, but they kept laughing, tears rolling down their cheeks. Corky drove slower than usual because he was afraid of attracting the attention of a cop. The Seventh-day Adventist church was coming up on the right, and cops often lurked in the two narrow side streets that flanked the church, watching for speeders. The church's lights were on and the parking lot was full.

"Okay, okay, that's enough!" Corky said as he fought to stop laughing. "I gotta drive, here, dude, stop it."

"Stop what?" John said as his laughter calmed.

"Whatever you was doin' that was so fuckin' funny."

"Was *I* being funny? I thought *you* were being funny."

"I don't care who was—"

A sudden flash of light from the side of the church startled Corky. A gout of flames vomited from the building, and Corky cried, "Shit!" as he slammed his foot onto the brake pedal. The Volkswagen jerked to an abrupt stop in the road.

Corky and John gawked at the fire that had appeared from nowhere. The brief explosion of flames retreated, but the side of the building continued to burn. A segment of the fire remained on the parking-lot pavement outside the church. It lay there motionless for a bit. Then it began to move back and forth, rolling over the blacktop. It shot to its feet suddenly and flailed its arms as it staggered.

"Fuck, man, that's a *person*!" John shouted.

"Oh, Jesus, somebody's on fire!" Corky said.

The burning figure dropped to the ground again and rolled frantically. The flames shrank, dimmed, and went out. The figure lay there for a moment, then struggled up onto hands and knees.

"Shuh-should we d-do something?" John said, his voice weak.

"I don't know, maybe we should—Wait a second."

The figure stayed on all fours as it moved slowly away from the church. In the orange glow of the fire, Corky and John saw something extend from the back end of the figure. A tail.

"Hey," John said. "That . . . that's a dog. It's a fuckin' *dog*!"

"But it—it—it . . . It was a *person*," Corky said, confused.

"Well, it's a dog *now*."

The four-legged animal disappeared among the parked cars, then came out the other side. It left the parking lot and limped across the side street, leaving the flickering orange of the fire and the yellowish glow of the parking lot's lights. It disappeared into the darkness.

John said, "Dude . . . We are so fuckin' *wasted*."

"Shit, there's gonna be cops comin'," Corky said.

"Then what're you waitin' for? Get the hell *outta* here!"

Corky faced front and was about to step on the gas when he saw a scattered group of people hurrying across

Crozier. One of them wore what appeared to be some kind of hairy costume, like an ape suit. The group crossed the street to the parking lot of the strip mall.

Corky hit the gas and hoped they were a good distance away before any police showed up.

They stood in the parking lot for awhile, watching the church burn.

Lloyd gathered his men and they counted heads. From the looks of the church, the missing men would not be joining them.

Abe tried to examine Ella's neck wound in the dark as she leaned against one of the SUVs. Her naked body was hairless now. Blood from the bite ran down over her right arm and breast.

Bob stood alone, his own nakedness forgotten, and watched as the growing flames engulfed the church.

A few feet away from Bob, Karen and Gavin leaned against the other SUV. They looked at each other for a long time, weary and splattered with the blood of the werewolves they'd killed. They looked into each other's eyes without speaking. Finally, they turned and watched the fire.

"Hey," Karen said softly with a shrug of one shoulder. "At least I wasn't raped and tortured this time."

Gavin nodded once. "It's important to see the glass as half full."

She sighed and said, "I need a cigarette."

Abe stepped in front of them. "She needs help," he said, nodding toward Ella. "She's losing a lot of blood, and that wound needs to be treated."

Karen stepped toward him and looked closely at his left shoulder. The shirt was soaked with blood around it. "She's not the only one who needs help. Looks like you've lost a lot of blood, too, Abe."

He nodded. "There's a hospital in Eureka. I'm acquainted with a couple of people in the ER. We need to get her there as soon as possible."

Gavin nodded and pushed away from the SUV. "All right, we'll do that. We want to get out of here before the authorities start showing up, anyway." He walked over to Bob and stood silently at his side for a moment. "You want to come with us, Bob?"

He did not respond for a moment. His eyes did not leave the fire as he said in a weak, trembling voice, "Sure. I've got nowhere else to go."

Gavin watched Bob's face for a moment, tinged by the orange glow of the fire across the street. "Bob . . . You're smiling."

Bob's smile grew a little wider as he nodded, his eyes still on the burning church. "Yeah. I'm smiling."

# JOHN EVERSON

**Bram Stoker Award-Winning Author of *Covenant***

They're coming. They are a race of sadistic spirits known as the Curburide, and they are about to arrive in our world, bringing with them horrors beyond imagination. The secret to summoning—and controlling—them has fallen into the hands of a beautiful, sexy and dangerously insane woman.

Ariana has dedicated her life to unleashing the demons in our realm through a series of human sacrifices, erotic rituals of seduction and slaughter. As she crosses the country, getting ever closer to completing her blood-drenched mission, only three figures stand in her way: an unwilling hero who has seen the horrors of the Curburide before, a burgeoning witch…and a spiteful demon with plans of his own.

# SACRIFICE

ISBN 13: 978-0-8439-6019-8